A Shift in Death

Lost Legacies
Book 6

Maddox Grey

GREYMALKIN

Published by Greymalkin Press
www.greymalkinpress.com

Dev/line editing by Proofs by Polly
Copy editing and proofreading by Rachels Top Edits

Cover Design by Seventhstar Art

eBook ISBN: 978-1-963368-00-0
Paperback ISBN: 978-1-963368-01-7

The Lost Legacies Series

A Shift in Darkness*

A Shift in Shadows

A Shift in Fate

A Shift in Fortune

A Shift in Ashes

A Shift in Wings

A Shift in Death

A Shift in Tides

*A Shift in Darkness is available for free download at maddoxgreyauthor.com.

To the Boston art, drag, and burlesque scene who have been low-key inspiring me for years.

And Walter Sickert & the Army of Broken Toys whose song, "The Legend of Squid and Moon" inspired a subplot of this book and filled the kraken-sized hole in Nemain's family of misfits.

Quick Little Note From The Author

I am a strange, strange person, and I've lived a bit of an odd life. I was born and raised in California, but was mostly raised by my Canadian grandmother and was then unofficially adopted by an Irish family in my late teens. You might be wondering why I'm mentioning this, and the reason is that I have a bit of a magpie approach when it comes to the English language.

Sometimes I like the American English spelling... sometimes I'm really attached to that extra "u" and go for the Irish version (yes I'm specifically choosing to say Irish and not UK because I don't want my family to smother me in my sleep).

Bless the soul of my copy-editor because she just sighs heavily at the start of each manuscript and deals with my eccentricities. So if you're an American and looking at a word and thinking it's not spelt right... it is most likely the non-American version of the word.

Okay. We got that out of the way. Let's chat real quick about what to expect in this book. This is a fantasy novel that contains adult content and situations. If it was a movie, it would probably be rated "R" for violence and language. If you want to go into this book completely blind and prefer not to read content warnings, you can skip on ahead, my friend.

If there are certain topics that you need to avoid for the sake of your own mental health, or that you simply don't like, please take a look at the list below for some things you will find in this book.

- There is a brief reference to a character having suicidal thoughts in the past. This takes place in Chapter 11.
- Brief references to emotional and physically abusive relationships.
- Consensual explicit sex scenes (there is no dub-con or non-con)
- Similar to previous books, this one has lots of fantasy violence and gore.

Chapter One

Was there anything better than taking a nap while soaking in the afternoon sunlight? Winters on the Washington coast were rather dreary, and it felt like it'd been weeks since the sun had shone here, but while it was cold outside, our apartment was nice and toasty. I'd decided that I'd more than earned some naptime after finishing a gig this morning.

I stretched, arching my back and letting my claws shoot out of my paws. My golden-brown feline coat practically shimmered beneath the rays of sunlight beaming through the floor-to-ceiling windows. I was absolutely stunning in my feline form, if I did say so myself.

Apparently, Elisa wasn't impressed by my gorgeousness because she had not only decided to interrupt my nap but had been pestering me to shift back to my less amazing, but still very nice, human form for the past ten minutes so we could talk. Technically, I was telepathic, so I *could* speak to her in this form, but I was weak in that department, and Elisa was too. It also required more work than I was willing to put in at the moment.

Because again… *naptime*.

"You're being ridiculous!" Elisa growled. I raised my head, tilting it slightly to the side as I peered at her. It took a lot to annoy the well-composed young vampire, but apparently, I was doing it. Go me.

She narrowed her dark blue eyes and pulled something out of her back pocket before placing it onto the floor directly in front of me. I hissed and batted the cell phone away.

"It's the twenty-first century, Nemain." She planted her hands on her hips. "You spend enough time in the human realm that you need a phone."

I stared at her before slowly blinking and then laying my head back down onto the floor. Maybe she'd go away if I ignored her.

"I know it won't work outside of the human realm, and you'd probably break it or destroy it anyway," Elisa said, and I heard her move to crouch directly in front of me. My tail twitched several times in annoyance. So much for the hope she'd go away. "But while you're here, you can use it. Even if you just leave it in the apartment and check for messages."

That's what the mirror's for. I shoved the thought out, letting my annoyance drip through as well. *Cell phones are for humans.*

"So is sushi!" she snapped. "And you love that! Plus, those dojos you've been visiting lately are also human."

Food and violence, I countered. *That's different. Besides, most of those dojos aren't run by humans.*

"You're setting a bad example for Finn."

I let out a frustrated growl and moved to a more upright position like a sphinx. The concentration required for me to use telepathy had chased away all lingering sleepiness, and now I was fully awake. Goodbye, wonderful nap.

Elisa reached out to where the phone rested and placed it back in front of me. Once again, I batted it away, and an enraged hiss poured out of the vampire girl as she glared at me before reaching out and booping me on the nose.

"You're almost four hundred years old!" She booped me again as I stared at her in stunned silence, unable to move at the pure audacity of her actions. "Act like it!"

Elisa smirked at my shocked expression, but her eyes widened when I twisted to my feet and the muscles around my hindquarters tensed.

Vampires are fast. Shifters are faster.

I pounced, pinning Elisa to the floor as she shrieked while trying to get away, and the offensive piece of human technology went flying further across the hardwood floor. Hopefully it slammed into something and shattered.

HOW DARE YOU BOOP ME!

Elisa fought in vain to get away, but even with her impressive strength, I weighed nearly five hundred pounds in this form, so she stood no chance. Chuffs of amusement rumbled up my throat as I set about punishing her for daring to not only interrupt my nap but freaking smacking me on the nose.

When Bryn walked in five minutes later, I still had Elisa pinned to the ground and was licking her face while she squirmed and screamed about cat drool.

"So," the auburn-haired valkyrie drawled, "I see the conversation about getting Nemain to use the cell phone is going well."

"Help me!" Elisa yelled as she desperately tried to move her face away from my tongue.

"You did this to yourself, babe." Bryn shrugged and plopped down on the couch, adjusting her wings until she found a comfy position. Then she propped her feet up on the coffee table and proceeded to watch us like we were her favorite show. "Besides, this is good practice for how to deal with an enraged shifter."

"You'll pay for this treachery!" Elisa vowed as she glared at her girlfriend. I took advantage of her distraction and swiped my tongue over her cheek all the way up to her hairline,

3

making sure to get a little extra drool there. "UGGGHHHH!" Elisa wailed as Bryn cackled from the couch.

The apartment door opened again, and I raised my head to glance at who was coming in. Magos. My shoulders slumped. He would definitely ruin my fun.

Magos paused, taking in the scene before he slowly closed the door behind him. He was dressed in a well-tailored suit of daemon make. The fit downplayed the broadness of his shoulders and chest, and the dark blue complemented his rich, dark brown skin. His braids were long enough to reach his shoulders now, and he was wearing them loose today instead of pulled back.

"Really, Nemain?" He gave me a disapproving look. "You are almost four hundred years old."

Elisa snickered beneath me, and I smacked her lightly with my paw, keeping the claws contained so I didn't scratch her.

"The cell phone is a good idea." He moved to the kitchen and pulled some mugs out. "Shift back. We have a few things to discuss. I'll make you some coffee."

After giving Elisa one last sloppy kiss, I padded across the living room and down the hallway to my bedroom. Magic rushed through me as I called on the shift, and bones crunched while fur receded until I was back in my human form. It didn't hurt but was mildly uncomfortable and left my skin feeling tingly.

I yanked open drawers as I tried to find some clean clothing. It'd been at least a few weeks since I'd done laundry, and I was running low on everything and was apparently completely out of underwear. An annoyed sigh slipped out of me. Gods, I hated doing laundry.

Finally accepting commando as my only option, I tugged on a pair of stretchy, soft, black pants and a dark grey muscle shirt that read, "Shifters Do It Better." It'd been a gift from Misha, who had also gotten one for Mikhail that read, "Vampires Do It Better." Unlike Elisa, who tried to keep the peace, Misha and Damon were absolutely instigators.

When I returned to the main living area, Elisa stalked towards me and shoved the cell phone into my hand. With one last parting glare, she spun on her heel and walked out, mumbling something about showering for the next hour.

Bryn laughed under her breath as she slid onto the barstool next to me. We looked at Magos expectantly, and he shook his head, a small grin playing across his lips before sliding two mugs in our direction.

"See, things would have gone better for Elisa if she had offered me coffee before launching into her argument." I took a sip and savored the sweet foam layer before the hot liquid broke through. My version of coffee was basically fifty percent sweetened cream with the coffee layer on the bottom. It was absolutely delicious, and Magos always made it perfectly.

I glanced over at Bryn's mug and let out an exaggerated gasp. "Black coffee?! You monster!"

"Too much sugar is bad for you," she lectured.

"You're a valkyrie." I pointed at my chest. "I'm a shifter. Sugar intake is one of the few things we don't have to worry about."

She grunted in response but didn't argue. I rolled my eyes. I supposed it was only a matter of time before she picked up Sigrun's habit of grunting as a form of communication.

"How did the job go?" Magos asked from where he was leaning back against the kitchen counter.

"Fine." I shrugged. "The dragons seem to be settling in well there, but Pele isn't comfortable with establishing a permanent gateway until we're sure there are no devourers left. The ones that took over that realm are crafty sons of bitches and can camouflage extremely well, so it's hard to know what their remaining numbers are."

"Hmm," Magos hummed as he took another sip of coffee. "We might have to find a way to draw them out."

I wrinkled my nose before drinking more of my sugary, caffeinated deliciousness. It'd taken some trial and error, but we'd finally found an uninhabited realm that worked well for the dragons and had helped them move there six months ago. It probably had a name once, but the previous inhabitants had been wiped out by devourers.

The dragons named it Acleonia and had been setting about clearing out the remaining devourer population that had dwindled without a reliable food source.

Ideally, we would have been able to tackle the devourer problem first, but we'd been pressed for time. Hundreds of dragons had come with us when we'd fled their home realm, and we'd had to temporarily house them in the forest outside of Emerald Bay. Over ten thousand had remained in the original dragon realm and fortified themselves in the remaining cities as the devious and powerful devourers of that realm, known as the trakdi, laid a siege against them.

Moving them from one realm full of devourers to another slightly less full of devourers hadn't been anybody's first plan. But beggars couldn't be choosers, and while the devourers in the new realm were crafty and vicious, they weren't nearly as lethal as the trakdi of the dragon's home realm.

It helped that the dragons were more than happy to hunt them down. Like me, they were predators and enjoyed the hunt. The problem was they also had other things that required their attention. They were busy building new cities to provide housing for everyone plus figuring out food to support their large population.

Pele was helping to orchestrate everything and, as a sign of good faith from the Daemon Assembly, had arranged for food, clothing, and anything else the dragons needed to get on their feet in a new realm. The bad history between the dragons and daemons was still there, but at least both sides were working well together and healing from their traumatic past.

However, until the devourer problem was solved, only temporary gateways could be used to get to the realm, which meant either myself or Badb had to open and close them. Pele had enlisted my help in hunting down the devourers, at least in the immediate areas where the dragons were constructing their cities. Being part-devourer myself, I was able to sense their presence and locate them far easier than the dragons, who had to rely on sight and smell.

My stomach rumbled loudly, causing Magos and Bryn to glance at me before looking at each other. Some sort of nonverbal communication happened between them before Bryn got up and started pulling stuff from the fridge. Magos took a seat on the stool she'd just vacated, and I slid him a glance out of the corner of my eye.

"Did you guys just do some sort of psychic rock, paper, scissors for who had to make lunch?" I pursed my lips. "Why wasn't I involved in that?"

"Because we've all agreed that you're banned from cooking," Bryn said smoothly.

"Oh?" I leaned back and crossed my arms. "And when was this decided?"

"When you almost set the kitchen on fire while boiling water for pasta," Magos replied as he fought to keep a smile off his face.

I thought about it. It had taken days for the smell of smoke to get out of the apartment, and if they all wanted to cook for me, who was I to say no?

"Okay, fair enough." I went back to sipping my coffee while Bryn threw together some tuna melts.

We ate our late lunch, Bryn joining us once she'd finished making her sandwich, and relished the peace and quiet of the apartment.

I'd never admit it out loud, but I did actually enjoy the chaos the vampire brats had brought into our lives. I wasn't exactly a nurturing parental type, but Elisa played the role of elder sister well and kept everyone in line. Misha and Damon were both nineteen now and took care of themselves. Between all of us, we shared the responsibility of watching over Isabeau and Finn.

Still, it was nice to get moments of companionable silence, especially when those moments came with a delicious sandwich.

"Where's Mikhail?" Magos asked, peering around me down the hallway to where my bedroom was. "I figured he was resting, but it's not like him not to come out for food."

I shoved the remaining quarter of the tuna sandwich into my mouth. Oh noes. Mouth is full. Can't answer.

Magos' bright, copper-colored eyes focused on me, brimming with suspicion. "I know he left with you this morning for that job. Where is my nephew, Nemain?"

I blinked innocently at him as Bryn laughed softly under her breath. When Magos continued to stare at me, I sighed and hopped off the stool. Then I walked over to the center of the living room, between where we'd grouped together a bunch of couches and the sparring mat, and raised my hand before tugging it down again.

My fingers twitched at my side, but I held them there. I was getting better about opening gateways without directing the magic with my hand. The speed at which I could open them was increasing too, but it was easy for me to slip into old habits, especially when Badb wasn't around to scold me.

Six feet in front of me, the air shimmered before snapping open and revealing a heavily forested area with a crystal clear lake glimmering in the background. I'd dipped my toe into it earlier this morning, and it was way too cold, even for me.

Magos moved to stand behind me, and we waited... and waited...

"Are you sure he's there?" he asked when Mikhail failed to appear.

"Yes." I shifted from foot to foot. My awareness of Mikhail's existence had only become more intense the past few months. It'd started when my magic had begun to wind itself around him more and more, almost like it was flirting. It drove me nuts, but sometimes I was just too tired to pull it back, and it never harmed him, to my dismay.

On top of that, Mikhail had been feeding from me regularly. As a vampire, he needed blood on a regular basis. I told him he could drink mine because it would make him stronger and he needed to build up a tolerance to the side effects anyway, in case we were ever in a situation where he absolutely had to drink from me. Shifter blood was like an aphrodisiac to vampires, which Mikhail had learned the hard way the first time he'd drunk from me and we'd ended up making out against a tree.

But the other reason I allowed him to drink from me was I had been finding myself feeling more and more territorial over him, which wasn't like me. Logically, I knew that while vampires enjoyed sex while feeding, they could easily separate the two. But the idea of Mikhail feeding from anyone else, especially if it were a regular thing with someone else, sent a surge of jealousy and irrational possessiveness through me.

I was pretty sure he suspected this and was trying to get me to admit it, but so far, I had successfully danced around the issue.

Between my magic being weird and the regular blood drinking, I could *feel* Mikhail. His physical presence. His mood. His hunger. I'd never experienced this with anyone before, and it scared the shit out of me.

Things between Mikhail and me had gone from zero to a

hundred, and some days, we dealt with that really well... and some days, we didn't.

I loved Mikhail, and he loved me. We both chose this, but that didn't mean we didn't still drive each other crazy and that I didn't leave him behind in a realm when he pissed me off while screaming, *"Find your own fucking ride home, you bloodsucking asshole!"*

Because I was a godsdamn adult.

Bryn walked up to stand at my other side, sipping a fresh cup of black coffee like the psychopath she was.

"Do we need to send a rescue party or something?" She took a few steps forward until she was leaning through the gateway and looking around. "Isn't this part of Acleonia still crawling with— FUCK!"

Magos and I leapt back when Bryn's golden wings snapped open in alarm as she stumbled back, spilling coffee everywhere and almost tripping over the giant monster head that was rolling through the living room. The sleek scales were deep brown, and the bottom half of the short, powerful beak was missing.

Mist swirled in the air before darting through the gateway and solidifying into a very pissed off vampire. I smirked as I closed the gateway and watched Mikhail snatch the head off the floor by the large ridges that ran down the back, causing more blood and fleshy bits to drip onto the floor. Magos had a pained expression on his face as he looked at the ever-expanding mess, but instead of chiding Mikhail about it, he just grabbed Bryn by the arm and pulled her back.

"Tell me something, shifter... " Mikhail said in a low, threatening voice as he stalked closer to me. It probably said a lot about me that instead of being scared or intimidated, I felt a thrill run up my spine. "When you decided to run off and leave me behind, did you know there was a *second* one of these things?"

He shook the head at me, and my lips curled as specks of blood landed on my cheek. I wiped them off and grinned wickedly. "Yes."

Mikhail stepped closer, his twilight eyes practically glowing. Okay, maybe it had been a bit of a dickish move to leave his ass behind in that realm... especially when I'd known there was a devourer sneaking up behind him. But in my defense, he had been really annoying me and was more than capable of dealing with one measly devourer on his own.

"That's what I thought," he said calmly, some of the anger bleeding out of his face. Alarm slammed into me, and I tried to leap backwards and create more space between us, but I was too slow. Mikhail dropped into a low kick and knocked my feet out from under me. He tried to slam the decapitated head down onto my chest, but I slapped it out of his hands as he straddled my hips.

Bryn's startled, "Oof!" told me where the head had landed.

"What's the matter, vampire?" I snarled. "Are you getting slow in your old age? One devourer too much for you?"

"We were in the middle of a conversation!" He punched me hard in my solar plexus, and I gasped. Despite struggling to breathe, I shoved my hips up and twisted. Mikhail tried to jump to his feet, but I reached out and yanked on his right ankle, causing him to crash to the floor.

"Come on, Bryn," Magos said tiredly. "There's no point in talking to them until they get this out of their system."

"Oh, this won't take long," I growled as I flipped over to sit on Mikhail before hammering a fist into his chest. The bastard vanished in a puff of mist, and my hand slammed into the hardwood floor. "Damn it! Quit doing that!"

"I'm not cleaning this mess up," Magos declared before ushering Bryn out the door and closing it behind them.

My leg snapped out, and I caught Mikhail in the stomach as he materialized in front of me. He snatched my foot and twisted, but I went with it, pushing myself off the ground and kicking out with my free foot as I rotated in the air.

"Fuck!" he swore as my kick connected with his head and we both fell to the floor. I spun to land on the balls of my feet, my fingertips pressing into the floor as I flipped my long braid back over my shoulder. Unlike me, Mikhail had landed on his ass. "Have I ever told you how annoying your feline reflexes are?"

"You might have mentioned it once or twice." I cocked my head to the side. "Although, you've also mentioned how much you appreciate my flexibility, which also comes from my shifter side. You can't have one without the other, love."

We both rose to our feet. Mikhail wiped away the blood leaking from his busted lip as heat flared in his eyes. "You've cost me a lot of blood today. I think I'm going to need a top up before the party tonight."

I gave him a feral grin. "Come and get it."

Chapter Two

I DARTED towards the brick wall and grabbed my favorite bo staff before whirling back around to face Mikhail as he stalked towards me. Then he vanished in an instant and reappeared by the weapons wall, grabbing his own staff. Magos had a very firm "no bladed weapons" rule while sparring in the apartment because he was tired of cleaning up the blood, and given the mess Mikhail had already made by throwing that decapitated head in here, I didn't want to annoy him further.

Mikhail twirled his bo staff as he watched me circle him on the mat. His black hair fell around his face in a dark wave, brushing the tops of his shoulders. He was watching me like I was prey and he was going to enjoy every aspect of this hunt because he knew it would end with his fangs in my flesh.

Heat unfurled in my core as my lips quirked into a smirk, which I knew drove him insane. "You gonna earn your meal, or what?"

I barely managed to get my staff up in time to block his strike, and even then, I felt the impact of the blow reverberate down my arms. Mikhail grinned at me over our crossed staffs, barely an inch away from my face. If I'd been half a second slower, he would have broken my jaw with that strike and probably knocked me out. Mikhail played for keeps while sparring, which was fine because I was the same. Unfortunately for me, the days when I'd been faster than him were of a bygone era.

He was getting stronger and quicker, probably because of his regular intake of my blood. It meant there might come a time when I'd be too slow to block his strikes, but I didn't care because it meant he would be that much harder for someone else to kill. I still had nightmares at least once a week of him beaten and bloody on the sands of an arena with an executioner stalking towards his kneeling frame.

Crystal-blue flames surged out of me, dancing along my arms before wrapping around Mikhail, as if we could protect him from everything. Pressure expanded inside my chest, and for a moment, thinking became difficult as my magic threatened to suffocate me. As if it sensed my distress, my magic retreated as quickly as it had leapt out.

"You good?" Mikhail pushed his staff against mine before taking a few steps back. He scanned me up and down with a concerned expression.

"I'm fine." I snapped my staff out, aiming for his left side. He instantly moved to block it, and I adjusted my aim so that I struck his knuckles, eliciting a pained hiss from him. "Don't go soft on me now, vampire."

Less than five minutes later, I was struggling to breathe after Mikhail swept my feet out from under me again and slammed his staff down onto my chest.

"Still worried about me going soft?" he taunted as he straddled my hips, dropping his staff next to where mine had rolled out of my fingers after I'd hit the ground.

"Hitting me when I was already down," I wheezed, "was a dick move."

"Pretty sure that's one of your favorite moves."

"True." I chuckled as my breathing finally evened out.

Mikhail traced his thumb along my jawline before brushing it over my bottom lip. The echoes of pain from our sparring match instantly vanished as an entirely different tension ran through my body. He pushed a little harder with his thumb, and I parted my lips, letting my tongue out to swirl around it.

A low groan tumbled out of his throat, and I arched my hips up, grinding into him. He pulled his thumb away as I raised myself up, and he met me halfway, his mouth crashing against mine. One hand cupped the back of my neck as the other slipped beneath the waistband of my pants.

"Fuck," he ground out as he found me hot and wet. I buried my fingers in his hair as I kissed him like it'd been months since we'd seen each other and not a few hours. He thrust two fingers inside me as his thumb pushed down on my clit.

I was so keyed up that I instantly climaxed, and Mikhail chuckled darkly as my body trembled around his fingers. "If you hadn't left me behind in that damn realm, we could have been doing this all day."

"Noted," I breathed out. "I'll keep that in mind for next time."

"No next time," he growled. "You're not leaving me behind again. In fact, I think you need some punishment to remember that."

"Mikhail!" I started, but my words instantly died when he started pumping his fingers in and out while simultaneously playing with my clit. My thighs shivered as pleasure started to build in my core once more, and I bit my lip, refusing to let the moan caught in my throat come out. Mikhail was cocky enough; he didn't need to know just how easily he could play my body.

Just as I was about to explode, Mikhail ripped his hand away.

"What the fuck!" I snarled.

"Oh, sorry." He grinned down at me. "Were you not done?"

"You motherfu—"

I yelped as Mikhail moved back and flipped me onto all fours. He didn't give me a second to recover before yanking my pants down and thrusting into me.

My enraged scream turned into one of pleasure as Mikhail gripped my hips and fucked me hard and fast. We fucked the way we fought—no holding back. His fingers dug in harder, and my body clenched around him, eliciting a low groan.

I could feel his hunger rising with every thrust, and it only drove me more wild. Heat and need built in my core. More. I needed more. Spreading my legs a little wider and arching my back, I screamed as Mikhail took advantage of the new angle and thrust even deeper.

"Fuck!" I moaned as I clenched around his hard cock. "Yes, Mikhail! Right fucking there!"

Trembles raced through my body, making my legs quiver. My mind was so gone, it took me a few minutes to realize that every time I was on the verge of coming, Mikhail was adjusting his pace just enough to deny me. The third time he did it, a torrent of threats tumbled from my lips, and the bastard laughed.

He reached down and wrapped a hand around my throat, pulling me up so my back was against his chest as his other hand snaked down my stomach before trailing down to stop just short of my clit. I growled, but it quickly changed to a whimper when he grazed my neck with his fangs.

"If you ever pull the shit you pulled this morning, I'm going to borrow those enchanted ropes from Pele and tie you to the bed. Then I'm going to bring you to the edge of pleasure over and over again, denying you each and every time."

His hand left my throat to pull back on my braid, baring more of my neck to him at the same moment his fingers brushed lightly over my clit. My pussy tightened around his cock, and I let out quick, panted breaths as I tried to push back against him, but he just wrenched my head further back, stilling my movements.

"You understand me, Nemain?" When I didn't answer, he nipped at my neck, and I writhed as much as I could in his grip. "Say yes, and I'll give you what you're aching for."

Two fingers swirled over my clit again, and my resolve broke.

"Yes," I half screamed, half moaned. "Fucking yes!"

"Thought you'd see it my way."

I felt Mikhail smile against my skin before his fangs sank in and his hips pistoned forward, resuming the brutal pace he'd set before as he drank deep. The pleasure from his bite rippled through me while the fingers that had been playing with my clit went back to clutching my hip as he pounded into me, still keeping a death grip on my braid.

I reached down to feel his hard length slipping in and out of me, the slickness coating my fingers before I teased the swollen and sensitive bundle of nerves. It felt like my mind was shattering when the orgasm I'd been denied finally erupted out of me. Seconds later, a low, wicked groan rumbled out of Mikhail's chest as he came hard.

Gradually, his thrusts slowed and he pulled his fangs out of my throat. I felt the warm blood trickle down my neck as I practically sagged against him. He let go of my braid, wrapping both arms around my waist to support me, and we stayed like that, partially dressed and slick with sweat in the middle of the living room for a couple of minutes before Mikhail pulled me to my feet and buttoned his pants.

"As far as punishments go," I drawled, "I don't think you really accomplished what you wanted to. If anything, I'm more likely to leave your ass in a realm in the future just so I can get a repeat."

17

His full mouth curved up into a sinful smile. "Hmm. Well, we still have several hours before we need to start getting ready. I'm sure I can come up with something else." I squealed when he grabbed me and threw me over his shoulder, my pants still halfway around my thighs, and smacked my ass. "We'll use your bed next. I've got some ideas that require a headboard."

"YOU SHOULD TALK to Kalen about your magic tonight," Mikhail murmured as he continued to run his fingers down my back in mesmerizing patterns, occasionally circling the flower tattoo between my shoulders.

Instead of responding, I just nestled in closer where I was half-sprawled across his chest. I let my eyes drift closed, enjoying how sated I felt. We didn't have to leave for another hour... Maybe I could nap a little bit more...

"Nemain?" Those lovely fingers stilled on my back, and I groaned, tilting my head up to look at Mikhail's pointed expression. He laughed when he saw my lips twisted into an annoyed frown. "Your magic hasn't been right since the dragon realm. You know this."

I huffed out a breath and shifted so I was on my back but still tucked against Mikhail's side with his right arm wrapped around me.

"It's just lingering aftereffects of the all-you-can-eat dragon buffet."

Raising a hand into the air, I let my magic out. Blue flames sprung from my fingers before sinking lower and wrapping around my wrist, making it look like I wore a glove of fire.

"Yes," Mikhail drawled. "I've heard Kalen's lecture."

Everyone had heard Kalen's lecture because he'd repeated it at least a dozen times. When we'd first returned from the dragon realm and Kalen had learned that I'd devoured the magic of countless dragons, he'd been a little pissed.

Badb's rage I was used to, since the two of us were constantly annoying each other, but Kalen had never been angry at me before, only patient and thoughtful.

That patience had evaporated the moment he'd found out what I'd done. Apparently, building up your tolerance for how much magic you could carry was something you had to do slowly and carefully. Not go *Wee!* and dive in headfirst.

I'd let him yell and rant for twenty minutes before telling him I was too old for a fatherly lecture and that we'd talk when he calmed the fuck down.

An hour later, he'd tracked me down, and we'd had a much calmer conversation. I was pretty sure it was because I'd made the father reference. It was taking time, but I was starting to accept Badb and Kalen as my birth parents. I still called them by their names, but I no longer corrected people when they referred to them as my parents. Macha and Nevin would always be my mom and dad, but I was realizing I could make space in my heart for Badb and Kalen too. I had no doubt it was what Macha and Nevin would have wanted for me.

"My magic levels have almost evened out." The flaming glove grew until it was more like a gauntlet. Most devourers were completely immune to magical attacks, but since I was only part-devourer, I could only block magical attacks with my fire. Kalen had been forcing me to practice making shields and armor out of it.

I'd gotten pretty good about creating armor to protect my entire body. The problem was, it still required a decent amount of concentration on my part, which I'd often let slip during sparring. In real life, that would be the absolute worst time to leave myself open.

"Did you tell him about extending your magic to me? And what happened when you did?" Mikhail reached out with his free hand and intertwined his fingers with mine, which were still writhed in blue fire. The flames happily leapt to him, wrapping around his hand and lower wrist.

My heart beat a little faster, and I nuzzled into Mikhail to distract him from hearing it. As much as I hated it when he made me purr in this form, if I could have started purring now, I would have. Anything to keep him from asking these questions.

Because what exactly was I supposed to say? *"Hey, babe. You cool with my magic locking us into a mate bond? Because that's what's happening, and I don't know how to stop it yet. Want some whiskey?"*

Mikhail and I had started as enemies, but the pull between us had always been there. Love wasn't an adequate word to describe what I felt for him. I would burn through every realm that ever existed to keep him safe, and he would do the same for me.

This wasn't just love. This was a bond. A fucking fae mate bond.

It never occurred to me that being part-fae, it was possible for my magic to do this. For the most part, my body acted like that of a typical feline shifter and my fae nature was intrinsically tied to my devourer nature. I'd stupidly assumed that most of the fun things that came with being fae didn't apply to me.

But here I was, with my magic trying to intrinsically tie our souls together for eternity. I'd only known Mikhail for a few years, and our relationship had started in the dragon realm. Six months. We'd been… involved… for six bloody months.

Seemed kind of soon to be *binding our fucking souls together*.

"I'm going to take your silence as a no." He tutted. "You'll have to tell him about how your magic is acting between us at some point. I've no doubt he or Badb have noticed your magic has been extra clingy around me lately."

I scowled. "It's not clingy."

Mikhail untangled his fingers from mine before pulling his hand away, and the crystal blue flames surged, forming a bridge between our two hands before slamming them back together. Then the flames twisted and danced until they resembled ropes binding our hands.

I yanked my hand out of his, forcing the magic rope to snap. Mikhail laughed, and my cheeks burned as I felt him staring at me. Meanwhile, the flames winked out of existence, and it felt like my magic was sulking inside my chest.

"Soon," I grumbled. "I'll ask Kalen about it soon."

I wasn't lying. The bond wasn't going to just stop forming, and I needed to ask Kalen about it and what the repercussions of letting it come to pass would be. He might have some suggestions on how it could be slowed down to buy me more time to come to terms with it, but I dreaded telling Kalen—and by default, Badb, because I knew those two told each other everything—about the bond.

They had always been a little wary of Mikhail. Now I wondered if it was because they'd suspected the bond had been forming before I had and they felt protective of their daughter.

Argh. I did not want to deal with this right now. Why couldn't my magic have just kept its greedy little paws to itself so I could have explored whatever this was between me and Mikhail at our own pace?

Mikhail bent down and kissed the top of my head. "Kalen will be there tonight. You will tell him everything so we can get his advice on how to deal with the odd behavior of your magic."

"You're not the boss of me." My defiance faded a little when Mikhail rolled out of bed and strolled over to the door, giving me a rather spectacular view of his perfectly chiseled body wrapped in warm, light-brown skin. His black hair was tousled in messy waves from the hours I'd spent running my hands through it.

He paused in the doorway and glanced over his shoulder, an arrogant smirk on his lips. "Want to join me in the shower?"

"Yes." I jumped out of bed and walked towards the hall-way. "Only because you always use up all the hot water though."

"Someday you'll admit I'm prettier than you."

I patted him on the cheek. "And on that day, you'll know that I'm lying."

Chapter Three

We arrived at The Inferno shortly before midnight. Cian told me to get there at 11 p.m., but my brother rarely arrived when he said he would, so I hadn't been the least bit concerned about getting there on time. After Mikhail and I had taken a ridiculously long shower that had ended with us pulling down the curtain rod, we'd realized that we hadn't cleaned up the living room, which had reeked of blood and monster bits.

Once we'd taken care of that and showered again, we'd collected Magos, Elisa, and Bryn. The grimalkins had elected to stay behind, and Misha and Damon had drawn the short straw over babysitting duties and wouldn't be joining us until Isabeau and Finn were asleep. Everyone else was meeting us there. Elisa had not so subtly informed me that if I had bothered to check my newly acquired cell phone, I would have known that Eddie and Cerri had already been there for an hour.

"Why do I have to be the one with a phone though?" I complained as Bryn held the door open for us and we all poured into the tavern. "Magos is the responsible one, and Mikhail... Well, Mikhail exists."

My vampire assassin gave me an exasperated look before reaching into his pocket and pulling out a sleek phone with a large screen. I gaped at him and then looked at Magos, who was holding up an identical phone. The two vampires winked at me before joining our friends who had already gathered in the back half of the bar.

I spun to face Elisa, and she just shrugged, a haughty expression stamped on her face. "No one else has complained about it, Nemain. In fact, they were *grateful* I took the trouble to acquire the phones for them. So suck it up."

Bryn patted me on the back before looping an arm around Elisa's shoulders, tugging her after the others. I looked towards the bar and found Pele, Asmodeus, and Zareen smirking at me. The first two handed over several bills of folded cash to the shorter, dark-haired bartender.

I narrowed my eyes and wondered what the bet had been on. No doubt whatever it was came at my expense. Rude.

"Nemain!" Eddie called from the back. "Get your ass over here!"

He held up a bottle of whiskey, and I grinned, annoyance at the cell phone already forgotten. I wound my way to the back of the tavern where everyone was standing in front of a few large tables that had various snacks laid out. Eddie immediately handed me a shot and a pint glass of amber-colored ale.

"Thanks." I tossed the shot back, enjoying the smooth burn, then placed the glass onto the table. "Told you Cian would be even later than us." I grinned triumphantly at Magos.

"Impressive, considering we're already an hour late." He took a sip from his cocktail that I was pretty sure was called an Old Fashioned.

"We were here on time," Cerri said, holding out her shot glass to Eddie, who gave her a healthy pour. I arched an eyebrow. It never failed to surprise me that Cerri loved whiskey almost as much as me. She was so classy that I wanted to peg her as more of a wine or fancy cocktail drinker like Magos. She caught me looking and grinned, holding up the shot glass before slamming it back in one gulp.

"Actually, we were here thirty minutes early," Eddie grumbled.

"Exactly." Cerri nodded. "On time."

"What'd I miss?" Misha popped into existence next to me, and a thin whip of fire flared out of seemingly thin air, smacking him right in the crotch. He groaned and grabbed himself before dropping to the floor as we sipped our drinks and watched him curl into a fetal position.

"What have I told you"—Pele joined our circle and narrowed her turquoise eyes at the young vampire on the floor —"about using magic inside my tavern?"

"That... the next time... I did it... " Misha ground out, "I'd regret it."

"And do you regret disobeying me?" She stepped closer and prodded him with her four-inch heeled boot.

"*Yes*," he squeaked.

"Good. Rules are rules. Even for my favorites." Her eyes darted to the whiskey bottle Eddie was still holding. "I'll get us more whiskey."

A stunning, blonde nymph with round hips and perky breasts slipped into the space Pele had vacated and knelt down beside Misha. "You okay?"

Misha gave the beautiful newcomer a pained smile. "She called me one of her favorites, Sten!"

The nymph laughed and held their hand out to the vampire, helping him to his feet and giving Misha a sympathetic look as he winced a little while getting up. "Come on. We'll get you a drink."

Misha nodded and looked at Bryn and Elisa. "Damon is still at the apartment. He'll swing by once Isabeau and Finn are sleeping. Aki just arrived to watch over them, and the two of them were chatting when I left."

Elisa snickered. "'*Chatting*.'" She held up her fingers to make air quotes.

"Can't believe I lost the shy one to that damn empath," Sten grumbled as they led Misha to a chair. I grinned at the loki's annoyance. Misha and Damon had spent most of their lives under the restrictive and watchful eye of the Vampire Council, but they were making up for it now. Sten had taken an interest in them six months ago, something I was pretty sure was Sigrun's doing, and the boys had been more than happy to engage in all sorts of debauchery with the loki.

Lately, Damon had been spending time with Aki, a Kalari empath who had moved to Emerald Bay last year. They weren't officially dating, but we all knew that's where it was headed. So far, Misha was enjoying the companionship of Sten… and the other lokis… and some of the daemons… and I was pretty sure I saw him flirting with a couple of mermaids last week.

Good for him. He deserved to live a little.

"Are your parents coming, Nemain?" Cerri asked. I'd given her the rundown of my family dynamics after we'd rescued her from the dragon realm, so she knew Cian was technically my cousin even though we'd been raised as brother and sister and still considered each other as such.

"You missed them earlier while you were chatting at the bar," Pele said as she joined our group. "They breezed in and stole Eddie's drink before heading upstairs to deal with some fae bullshit." Pele passed me a full bottle of whiskey, and I almost kissed her. I opened it and poured myself a double shot before setting the bottle onto the table.

"Are you trying to get drunk?" Mikhail arched an eyebrow at me.

"Please," I scoffed. "I'd have to chug this entire bottle to get drunk. I just need a little bit of a buzz to tolerate Dante."

"He's really not that bad." Bryn frowned.

"It's okay that you're wrong," I assured her. The valkyrie's frown deepened, and Elisa leaned over to whisper something in her ear before kissing her cheek, which instantly stained into a dark shade of red.

Gods, was Bryn ever going to stop being such an easy blusher?

"I agree with the blushing virgin," Eddie said. "Dante's actually pretty interesting to talk to. I think you're the only one who doesn't like him, Nemain."

"I'm not a virgin!" Bryn blurted out. We all looked at her, and the blush spread down her neck.

Elisa slipped her hand into Bryn's. "Well, just to assuage any doubts, I think we can take care of this upstairs."

We all watched in amusement as Elisa winked at her girlfriend before pulling her towards the stairs that ran up the back of the tavern to the rooms on the floors above. Kalen and Badb leaned against the wall as they came down the stairs, allowing the young couple to squeeze by them on their quest to find an empty room.

"What's that about?" Badb jerked a thumb over her shoulder towards the stairwell as she came to stand next to Magos with Kalen on her other side.

"Elisa is about to deflower Bryn." I shrugged.

"Not a virgin!" Bryn screamed from somewhere upstairs before a door slammed shut.

Badb rolled her eyes and grabbed the bottle of whiskey I'd set aside. She didn't even bother with a shot glass, just took several long swigs before passing it to Kalen, who poured his shot into a glass. Eddie laughed under his breath before Cerri not so discreetly elbowed him in the stomach.

"What?" I looked at him suspiciously.

"Nothing." His burnt-amber eyes lit up. "It's just that you're exactly like your mom, and it's a constant source of entertainment for me."

"I am not!" I crossed my arms as I glared at him.

"The first thing your mum did when she got here was threaten to stab me if I didn't hand over the whiskey. Sound familiar?"

Kalen glanced at Badb, and she just shrugged before snatching back the whiskey.

"That doesn't mean anything," I argued. "You just have a very stabbable face."

Mikhail laughed, drawing Eddie's attention.

"Even your relationship is a copy of theirs." He pointed to me—"Feline shifter"— and then to Badb—"feline shifter."

I opened my mouth, but he cut me off as he pointed to Mikhail next—"Worked as an assassin for the Vampire Council"—and then gestured to Kalen—"worked as an assassin for the Seelie Court."

"He does kind of have a point," Misha said from where he was still being doted on by Sten.

"I will never buy you pizza again," I promised him, and he gave me a wounded look, which I ignored. Fucking traitor.

"Kalen was sent to kill Mommy Dearest but fell in love with her instead." Eddie cocked his head at me. "Starting to sound familiar yet?"

"Technically, I wasn't sent to kill her," Mikhail pointed out. "I was sent to track down the vampire brats."

Eddie arched an eyebrow, giving my vampire lover a knowing look. "Were you *thinking* about killing her?"

Mikhail glanced at me and then at my parents, both of whom were watching him rather intently. "I'm going to decline to answer that, given our present company. Just feels like it would be in bad taste."

"And because you like having your dick still attached," I said dryly.

He wrapped an arm around my waist and tugged me close before whispering in my ear, "Pretty sure you benefit from that too, shifter."

"Also, you both dress the same way."

I looked down at my black pants that were made from a thick, stretchy material and the black leather vest tied over my long-sleeve grey shirt before looking at Badb and blinking. Other than the fact that her shirt was a dark blue, we were wearing practically identical clothing.

"And lastly"—Eddie held up both hands dramatically—"despite you both claiming to hate politics, particularly fae politics, you both volunteered to be the Unseelie Queen's bitches."

"I will kill you," I growled. Unfortunately, Badb said the same thing as she thrust the whiskey at Kalen to free up her hands for said killing. She also punctuated her words with a growl, which only furthered Eddie's point.

Kalen and Mikhail were unable to contain their laughter and lost it. Based on how Magos was rubbing a hand across his mouth, I was pretty sure he was trying to hide his own laughter.

I narrowed my eyes at Eddie. "We should have rescued Cerri and left your ass behind in the dragon realm. You are a terrible friend."

"The truth hurts sometimes, my surly bestie." He blew me a kiss.

"Not your bestie," I grumbled.

"That's easy to fix." Eddie grinned and plucked the whiskey bottle out of Kalen's hands before passing it back to me. "Who's your bestie now?"

"I FEEL like this is ridiculously late," Kaysea said an hour later. "Even for Cian."

I pursed my lips and once again glanced at the large clock mounted on the back wall of the tavern. It was a few minutes past 1 a.m., making Cian two hours late. Kaysea had arrived not long before, a troubled look on her face that she quickly wiped away when I asked her about it.

Kaysea's parents had stepped down as rulers of the merfolk fairly recently. While the Seelie and Unseelie Queens had ruled uncontested for thousands of years, the monarch of Tír fo Thuinn—the merfolk realm—typically changed every five to six centuries.

Sometimes, it was a forced change, with more powerful fae rising up to challenge the ruling king or queen, but in this case, the change had been peaceful. Her father, Aquilus, was nearly two thousand years old. The fae aged slowly, but they did age, and his magic was starting to weaken, which meant he was entering the last years of his life.

Kaysea had thought he'd had a decade left last I checked, but it seemed like it might've been less than that. Her mother, Eeada, could have continued to rule because she was several centuries younger and her magic remained strong, but she had no interest in carrying the crown on her own.

All of this meant I didn't see Kaysea as often as I usually did, and I missed my best friend. But I understood that between her family and helping the new Merfolk Queen step into power, she had places she needed to be.

Despite the turmoil in her life, Kaysea wasn't one to easily panic or become concerned. If she thought it was strange for Cian to not be here...

"I'm going to check on him," I announced, having to speak a little louder because of the rowdiness of the tavern. Daemons had adapted to being nocturnal long ago, and even though they no longer had to be, they still mostly kept to a night schedule, which meant the hours between 10 p.m. and 4 a.m. tended to be prime time for The Inferno.

We had taken over the back corner, but the place was packed with daemons, lokis, and a few other random species that called Emerald Bay their home. I'd even spotted a few fae in the mix.

I pushed my way through the crowd until I reached Pele's office and swept aside the dark purple curtain. As soon as I stepped across the threshold, the noise of the bar faded away. Pele and Mikhail followed in my wake, and I looked at them in question even as a gateway started to open in front of me.

"Magos is going to stay here. Misha went back to the apartment to check on things there," Mikhail said. "We're going with you."

"It's probably nothing." I forced my voice to remain calm despite the sense of dread that had taken root inside my chest. It was true that Cian was always late for things, but it was equally true that my brother absolutely adored a good party, and he was the one who had orchestrated this one for Dante. My relationship with both Cian and his lover was strained, but we'd been making a lot of progress lately. There was no way he would choose to miss this party.

The gateway parted, revealing a cozy-looking log cabin set in a field full of tulips with a small pond off to the side. A pair of black swans lazily swam about, occasionally dipping their heads beneath the surface.

Nothing was real in the death realm. If you had death magic, you could make things look however you wanted. Dante was likely the most powerful necromancer in existence, and my brother was no slouch either. The previous version of their house had been a very neat, modern design, but Cian had visited Sigrun a while back at her cottage and had been inspired, so he'd completely redone their home, and Dante had changed the landscape to match.

The swans flapped their wings and honked at us as we strode across the meadow before rushing through the front door. My heart hammered inside my chest as I remembered the last time I'd felt this sense of fear and apprehension while rushing through the front door of a cottage.

Sebastian had been the one who favored ripping out the hearts of my loved ones, and he was long since dead, but that didn't mean someone else wouldn't be inspired to follow in his footsteps.

"Cian?!" I yelled as Pele and Mikhail split up to check the different rooms. "Cian, I swear to the gods, you'd better fucking answer me!" My magic poured out of me, blue flames running down my arms and swirling around my waist as it felt my panic but didn't know what to do about it. There was nothing here for it to attack because nobody was home.

My brother was gone and so was Dante.

I couldn't stop the quick breaths escaping my lips over and over again. The living room and kitchen were empty, but it didn't look like any type of fight had taken place. Mikhail and Pele joined me, both wearing tight, worried expressions.

"Nothing," Pele said.

"I didn't see anything out of place," Mikhail said. "There are outfits laid out on the bed, as if your brother was picking out what to wear tonight." He tossed me something. I caught it, and the air in my lungs seized.

"He kept it." My voice cracked as my fingers carefully fondled the crown I'd wound together with bits of vine. Interspersed between the thick, dark green strands were black and purple flowers I'd plucked from the garden our father had grown. "I made this for him on his birthday when we were kids. It was shortly after I'd come into my magic and I'd accidentally hurt him."

"So sentimental," a smooth, rich voice said. All three of us whirled to face the front door where Lir leaned against the doorframe. "You really should have agreed to work with me; we could have avoided all this ugliness."

"Lir." His name was barely more than a snarl as I flicked my wrist to trigger the mechanism for a throwing dagger to slide into my hand. But there was no dagger because the daggers had been hidden in my silver bracers, which had been burned off me in the dragon realm. I clenched my fists. "What the fuck did you do?"

Lir gave me a taunting, close-lipped smile.

I hadn't even meant to do it, but blue flames shot from me towards him. My magic was just so desperate to make me happy that it was trying to take out all threats on my behalf. The fire reached Lir and went straight through his body before crashing into the wooden door, leaving behind frost and ashes.

The sidhe warrior tilted his head to look at the damage, long, steel grey hair slipping over his shoulder before he turned back to look at me. His pale blue eyes lit up with delight as he smiled broadly from an ageless face. "Even if I were actually here instead of just projected as an illusion, that wouldn't have damaged me." He looked at me like I was an idiot. "Devourer, remember?"

I gritted my teeth. "Where is my fucking brother?"

Once again, my magic surged, and this time, an eruption of fire burst in a circle around me. Mikhail didn't move a muscle, but Pele quickly took several steps to the side. Damn it.

"Control problems?" Lir eyed the flames. "Exactly how many dragons did you let yourself snack on? I, myself, have only had two, and they were quite filling."

"I'm going to carve you apart when I find you," I promised.

Mikhail's arm brushed mine, and I felt some of my magic stretch out to wrap around him protectively.

"Your brother is with the vampires." Lir's illusion flickered before solidifying again.

"Control problems?" I repeated snidely.

He shot me an annoyed look. "We may have given the warlocks a bit of a power-up, but they're still human at the end of the day. I only have so much to work with."

"Such a flattering portrayal you make of your supposed allies," Pele noted.

"Please, daemon," he chided. "Don't play games with me. The warlocks are blindly loyal to Emir, and he is only loyal to himself. If you think you can drive a wedge between me and the warlocks by informing them of my poor view of them, you're sadly mistaken. They're well aware of the fact that I'll get rid of them as soon as they're no longer needed, and they no doubt have similar plans for me, but for now, they need me because I can provide the power they so desperately crave."

"Why give my brother to the vampires?" I fought to keep the fear off my face. Maintaining a neutral expression was beyond me at the moment, so I settled for a mask etched in fury.

"Because they asked." Lir shrugged. "One of the Council members apparently has a history with your brother and wanted him back. Originally, I'd just been planning on killing him when we took his lover, but this worked out so much better."

No, no, no. The word chanted over and over again in my mind. Cian *hated* vampires. It'd taken him a very long time to accept Magos, and he was still wary of Mikhail. I'd never been able to get him to tell me why, nor had I been able to figure it out on my own. It was one of the few secrets my brother had successfully hidden from me.

"And Dante?" I couldn't keep the slight tremor from my voice. Wherever my brother was, I *would* get him back, but he would never recover if he lost Dante.

"Don't you mean Hades?" Mikhail and Pele both stiffened beside me. I kept my attention on Lir, but I could feel Pele staring a hole into the side of my face, probably noting my lack of surprise. "Ah, so you knew."

My gaze flicked to Pele before returning to Lir. "Figured it out a couple of years ago, but it wasn't my story to tell, so I kept his secret."

"We're going to have words about this later," Pele muttered.

"Agreed," Mikhail chimed in.

I ignored them both. They had every right to be mad, but I stood by my decision. Besides, as the soon-to-be ruler of the Daemon Assembly, Pele no doubt kept some things hidden from me. I accepted that, so she had no right to be pissed about this. And Mikhail surely had some secrets too.

"Hades is with his kin." Lir smiled. "They've missed him terribly. Although, they were a tad overzealous in their reunion and might have overdone it. It's going to be a while before he wakes up so they can welcome him back properly."

The vampires having my brother was bad. Hades being held captive by his fellow gods who had been on the hunt for him ever since he'd massacred several of them was infinitely worse. But what the hell had Lir meant about it being a while before he woke up? What had they done? In my mind, Hades had always been invincible, and he was the main reason I hadn't worried about my brother as much as the others.

I thought Cian and Hades were too difficult of targets for anyone to go after, so I'd focused on keeping others safe. Now, they were paying the price for me being wrong.

"Is this the part where you offer up a bargain?" I said tightly. "We give you Finn, and you return Cian and Hades to us?"

I wouldn't do it. No matter how much I loved my brother... and tolerated Hades, I'd promised Finn I would protect him, and I would never betray him like that. Besides, my brother wouldn't want me to. He liked the fae boy and wouldn't want to be used in such a way to get to him. I just wanted to know what Lir's game was.

"No." Lir tilted his head to the side. "There is no bargain."

"What?" I went absolutely still.

"I didn't arrange all this to make a deal." Lir strode forward until he was standing a hair's breadth away from me. As an illusion, he couldn't harm me, but even still, it took a great deal of effort to remain in place. I could feel the tension radiating off Mikhail and Pele as they pressed a little closer to me but otherwise didn't move.

"Then why?" I searched his eyes for an answer. "Why do you hate me so much?"

"You look like your mother. But your father"—an ugly sneer rippled across his face—"Kalen is the spitting image of his father, Rowan. Your grandfather," Lir spat.

My thoughts raced about what I knew about Kalen's father. Rowan was one of the first fae warriors who Balor had managed to get past the ward locking them in their realm. Not long after crossing into the fae realms, he'd met Shayla, a sidhe with a strong affinity for ice magic, and they'd fallen in love. Kalen had been both the result and price of that love. Both had died seconds after he was born.

Dread-laced curiosity rose inside of me, but I tried to keep it off my face. "What does my family have to do with any of this?"

"Rowan was the reason I joined Balor's army," Lir said. "We were brothers in every way but blood. I would have followed him anywhere, and I thought he felt the same. Instead, he abandoned his position and everything we had worked for, and for what? Some godsdamn sidhe whore?"

"Are you fucking kidding me?" I roared and threw my arms wide. "You're doing all this because you're pissed that my grandfather fell in love? What the fuck type of toxic bullshit is that?"

Lir's expression went flat. "I'm doing all this because my king commands it, and unlike Rowan, I don't trade my loyalties so easily." He leaned forward a little more, causing his illusion to ripple where it brushed against my chest, and a warning growl rumbled from my throat as I held my ground. "Hurting you in the process is just an added bonus. I'll break you, which will no doubt break your bastard of a father. I do believe this is what's called a win-win scenario."

"You'll lose." I raised my chin.

"I never lose." He smiled. "You've been meddling in my affairs. First in the dragon realm. Then the seraphim realm. This is a reminder, Nemain. You have a lot of people in your life who you care about, which means I have plenty of targets. You're welcome to try to get Cian back from the vampires. He might be a little broken, but I don't think they'll kill him right away."

Pain shot through my jaw as I clenched my teeth hard enough to crack bone, and Lir's eyes lit up as he saw his words had struck a nerve.

"While you might succeed in getting your brother back," he continued, "it will require all of your attention to do so, giving me a little bit of breathing room. And if you're foolish enough to try to get Hades back from the gods... well... even you might not walk away from that fight."

I swallowed. He was right. The gods were powerful and almost impossible to kill, and the ones known as the Olympians were the cruelest and pettiest of them all. Going after them was suicide unless you were another god, and with Hades gone, we were fresh out of those.

Lir's illusion started to flicker again.

"Ah, my time's up, I'm afraid." He bared his teeth at me. "Good luck."

Chapter Four

I STARED at the empty spot where Lir had stood seconds before, vaguely aware of Mikhail and Pele arguing about something. Magic flowed out of me until a gateway opened, and I stepped through it, back into our apartment, and strode over to the weapons wall on autopilot.

Dual swords were my preferred weapon, but I'd had shitty luck with them. The most recent set had been lost in the dragon realm during the chaos of the final battle.

Mikhail had offered to find me a new set, but I hadn't taken him up on the offer yet. I didn't know what I was waiting for, but it just didn't feel right yet.

My fingers trailed over the various blades and blunt instruments. Short sword. Kitana. Some weird daemon sword that was basically a bastardized version of a claymore. Silver spear dripping with fae magic. Hammer.

The last one was from Sigrun because she'd decided that every weapons wall needed a hammer. Lately, I'd been favoring the sword she'd made for me, but when my hand landed on its handle, I hesitated.

"None of these are what I need," I rasped. My vision was

blurred as I continued to scan the wall, and I didn't understand why. There had to be something here that would work that I just wasn't seeing. The world suddenly seemed to dim as my lungs struggled to expand, and strong hands clamped on my shoulders before spinning me around.

"Breathe." The command punched through me, and I sucked in a deep breath while staring into Mikhail's eyes as Pele spoke urgently to someone in the mirror that hung on the wall across the living room. "We'll get him back," Mikhail promised, wiping away the tears I hadn't even realized had tracked down my cheeks. "We'll get both of them back, and we'll slaughter everyone who gets in our way. Then we'll hunt down Lir and break him apart piece by piece until he begs us to kill him, and then we'll let him heal and start all over again."

He meant it. Every word.

"I think I might love you, vampire," I said softly.

"Of course you do, shifter." His hand wrapped around the back of my neck, and he kissed me hard. I poured everything I was feeling into that kiss. Rage. Desperation. Terror. Mikhail took it all and gave me back my strength and resolution.

"Magos is coming back with Bryn and the vamp brats," Pele announced just as Mikhail and I broke apart. "Eddie and Cerri are coming too. Your parents are heading back to their place. Badb wants you to meet her there so she can give you something."

"Why can't she just bring it here?" I turned fully away from the weapons wall and faced Pele.

She let out an exasperated breath. "If you want to argue with your mother, you're more than welcome to, but I've got more pressing matters to deal with." Pele sharpened her gaze on Mikhail. "Out of all of us, you're the best suited to find out what's going on with the Vampire Council. I'm going to do some digging into what Artemis has been up to. She's likely the ringleader on the gods' side of things."

"Agreed," Mikhail said, and Pele nodded at both of us before leaving.

"I can't lose him." I sucked in a harsh breath. "He's already suffered so much in life because of me."

"You won't." Mikhail grabbed a thigh holster off the wall and set about attaching it to himself. I plucked his favorite dagger up before sliding it into the sheath and then grabbed a second one and tucked it into the sheath hidden in his right boot. He held perfectly still while I worked, but I heard his heartbeat speed up.

I rose and bent my head forward, resting my forehead against his. The thought of him leaving was threatening to tip me over the edge I was precariously perched on. My magic was already overloaded these days, and now it felt like a live wire.

"Be careful."

"Of course." He brushed a kiss against my lips. "Don't do anything foolish while I'm gone."

When I failed to say anything, he gripped my chin tightly until his intense, twilight eyes bored into mine, promising me all kinds of wrath if I failed to obey his command.

"As much as I want to start hunting down every vampire I can find," I said, "I won't risk Cian's safety. He's my first priority. We get him back, and then we'll find Hades."

Mikhail didn't release my chin right away, continuing to search my face for any signs of deceit on my part, but I'd meant what I'd said—my revenge would have to wait until Cian was safe. Reading that in my expression, Mikhail's fingers let go and trailed up my jawline. "Go find out what Badb wants. She wouldn't ask for you to come see her unless she felt it was important."

I nodded. Cian's mother had been Badb's sister, and while my relationship with Badb and Kalen was strained, Cian had been quick to get to know his newfound aunt and uncle. The three of them had easily slipped into each other's

@jjflorentina

lives, and I knew Kalen and Badb wouldn't rest until he was rescued.

"Open a gateway to the alley outside The Inferno," Mikhail instructed, and a few seconds later, the air rippled, revealing a familiar alleyway.

"Where will you go?"

"I'll start with the daemon tavern in Bucharest." He stepped through the gateway and turned to face me from the other side. "I still have some contacts there who should be willing to talk to me."

"Keep in touch. If I don't hear from you in the next few hours, I'm going to get really pissed off at you," I warned.

He gave me a cocky grin. "When are you not pissed off at me?"

I flipped him off and let the gateway close. In the emptiness of the apartment, my anxiety and fear started to push at me again. That wouldn't help Cian though. I needed to stay focused for both his sake and Hades'. A light flared from the kitchen island, and I walked over, picking up the cell phone Elisa had left for me.

It was locked and required a four-digit code. I took a wild guess and entered the year I was born. 1621. The screen changed, and a bunch of icons I didn't recognize greeted me. I knew enough to tap on the one that had a number in the corner and saw a text message from Elisa. She must have added all the relevant contacts in before giving me the phone. I begrudgingly admitted to myself that this was handy.

Be there soon. Asmodeus is already working their connections.

Using my index finger, I typed back a message. *Mikhail is checking in with his contacts. I'm going to see my parents. Will return to the apartment afterwards.*

I started to put the phone back onto the counter but changed my mind and slid it into my pocket instead. My parents had a place in town, so the phone would work there too. I wasn't exactly sure what would happen if I took the cell phone through a gateway. It obviously wouldn't work in a different realm, but I didn't know if that would actually damage the phone or simply render it useless until I returned. Elisa probably already knew, but if I asked her about it, she would no doubt give me some self-righteous response. I'd just find out on my own. Her snobby ass could buy me a new phone if I broke this one.

The apartment door swung open before Jinx trotted in. He had his glamour in place, so he looked like a small, black, short-haired, domestic house cat. As soon as he reached me, I stretched my arm out to the side, and he effortlessly leapt onto it before slinking around my shoulders. It was centuries of muscle memory for both of us, and I instantly felt a little calmer.

Are you alright? His voice rumbled through my mind.

No.

Luna is with the others. Where are we going?

More of the tightness within my chest eased. Jinx and I had bonded shortly after I was born. We'd been inseparable for most of my life, but things were changing. He had Luna now, who I was pretty sure was his mate. It had been selfish of me to think I'd have Jinx to myself forever, but I was too much of a chickenshit to talk to him about how our friendship was evolving.

Badb wants to see me, I told him. *Let's go check in with her. Mikhail is trying to find more information about where my brother might be.*

With barely a thought from me, my magic opened a gateway to the building where Badb and Kalen's townhouse was. It was in the part of Emerald Bay that was protected by a ward, so I didn't have to worry about any humans seeing the gateway. At least, not any humans who didn't possess magic. There were relatively few of those in town these days. Even outside of the magically warded blocks, Emerald Bay was becoming a magic-only town.

I released my hold on the gateway after I stepped through and felt it close behind me. Jinx waited by the dark wood door of the townhouse, and I raised my hand to knock but stopped myself. Kalen had repeatedly told me I was always welcome in their home, so I let myself and Jinx in.

When Badb had confessed to getting this place, I'd been super annoyed with both of them, but now I had to admit it was kind of nice knowing they were so close, even though they usually split their time between here and their home in the fae realm. I'd yet to visit them there, as most of my time in the fae realm was spent at the Unseelie Queen's palace. Well, technically *palaces*. She had one in each of the Unseelie realms, plus the one she shared with her sister in Tír na mBeo.

Jinx's pace had a bit of eagerness to it, and I suspected he was hoping his mother was here. Nyx wasn't bonded to Kalen or Badb, but she was friends with them and was often in their company. Jinx had seen her more in the last year than he had in the previous four centuries. He was still more than a little pissed at her for not telling us everything and keeping my parents' secrets, but things had been improving between them.

I paused in the large archway that separated the hallway from the main living area. Badb was pacing back and forth, the old hardwood floor creaking beneath her heavy steps. Kalen was perched on the large, dark blue couch that ran along the back wall, his elbows on his knees and the tips of his fingers resting against each other as his black eyes tracked his mate's movement.

Tension filled the room.

"You wanted to see me?" I asked when neither of them acknowledged my presence, even though there was no way they hadn't heard me enter.

Badb abruptly stopped her pacing and stayed perfectly still

while she stared at the wall. Her shoulders were rigid, but with her back to me, I couldn't read her expression. I looked at Kalen, a clear question in my gaze.

Slowly, his depthless, obsidian black eyes left Badb and latched onto me. Most of the time, Kalen was calm and steady; Badb was the one who was wild and a little reckless. But it was moments like these, when I saw the *other* that lurked beneath my father's skin, that I was reminded he was The Erlking.

Power rolled off him in waves. Unlike me, he'd had over a thousand years to practice absorbing the magic of others and weaving it into his own. Like me, he'd been born a devourer fae hybrid, but he was first generation and a little more... unstable.

I looked away from him and jerked back when I found Badb standing in front of me. I hadn't even heard her move.

"Fuck!" I took a step back. "What's wrong with you two?"

"I'm sorry." Badb took a deep, shuddering breath. "Your father and I have done everything we could to protect you... and Cian. He's my sister's son, and I promised her I would protect him just as she promised she would protect you. And we've failed... again."

My gaze flicked back and forth between Badb's emerald green eyes, identical to my own, and Kalen's dark ones. I could see the pain of old wounds reflected on both their faces. They'd been unable to save Cian's parents that day so long ago, and I'd had to watch my adoptive parents burn while desperately trying to keep my brother alive. Badb and Kalen had learned what had happened far too late to do anything about it, and they carried that guilt with them to this day.

I'd blamed them too at first, raged against them when they'd shown back up in my life, but I didn't hold them responsible anymore. I'd never specifically said I'd forgiven them though, since the words always got stuck in my throat whenever I tried to voice them.

"How about we get Cian back, and then we can argue about whose fault it was he was taken in the first place?" I shrugged with a casualness I absolutely did not feel but hoped would help get Badb and Kalen to calm down. The three of us losing our shit wouldn't help my brother. "Personally, I'm more than willing to blame Dante once we get him back too."

Some of the tension bled out of Badb as she let out a dry laugh. "I can't believe he's really Hades." She looked over her shoulder at Kalen. "And that you had no idea."

"It's not like I spend a lot of time around him." Kalen pursed his lips.

"Mikhail is talking to some of his contacts to try to narrow down where the Vampire Council is keeping Cian," I told them. "Pele is finding out what she can about Artemis. Do either of you know anything useful about what the remaining Olympians have been up to?"

"No." Kalen shook his head, a grim expression on his face. "After Hades slaughtered Zeus and Hera, the rest retreated to their realm to lick their wounds and never really left it again. Artemis and a few of the others have occasionally made an appearance in the fae realms for some of the bigger events, but I could count those occurrences on one hand."

"I figured." I let out a frustrated breath. "I've met a few of the gods in my life but never the Olympians."

"While we wait for the others to get information, I have something to show you." Badb bit her bottom lip, and surprise flickered through me at seeing her look unsure. It was so at odds with her usually confident and annoyingly arrogant self.

"Okay," I said slowly. "What is it?"

"It's at our home—I mean—our other home." A gateway opened next to where we were standing, and she stepped through it. I glanced at Kalen, but he just smiled at me and remained seated. Jinx leapt up onto the couch, circled three times, and then curled up into a ball next to him. Apparently, this was a mother and daughter trip.

Do you know what this is about? I asked Jinx.

I have my suspicions. I think it's best you to go alone.

Alright. I hesitated in front of the gateway. It felt weird not to be doing more to help Cian, but there wasn't anything I could do at the moment, and I trusted Badb not to waste my time. *We won't be long,* I said to Jinx as I gave him a farewell nod.

An icy wind tore at me when I stepped through the gateway, and snow-capped mountain peaks stretched ahead of me. I looked over my shoulder as I felt the gateway close, finding a massive, evergreen forest in its place. It reminded me a little of the forest we'd trekked through while looking for Finn; the magic seeping from the ground was familiar. This was one of the fae realms.

"Wow." I tilted my head back so I could study the enormous house, which, in all honesty, was more of a castle. "This is a little bigger than the townhouse."

Badb's lips twitched before she strode up the steps to the tall double doors. They swung open at her approach, and I followed her inside, eyes wide as I took everything in. Light streamed in from several openings in the ceiling, and to my left, another set of double doors was open, revealing a sunlit library. Opposite that was another room, this one full of weapons and what looked to be a large sparring area.

Two sets of stairs curved in front of us, leading to the second floor, and I could see several hallways on this floor splitting off to more rooms. The floor, ceiling, and walls were all made of the same light grey stone, but interspersed here and there were open spaces in the floor. A tree with bright purple leaves and silvery white bark grew on each side of the stairs. In other places, smaller fruit trees grew with low-growing flowering plants covering the soil around them.

"This was built for the fae." I reached out and plucked what looked like an apple off the nearest tree. "It's beautiful."

Badb watched me peek my head into the library before doing the same with the weapons room. Then I tossed the round fruit up into the air, catching it over and over again as I studied the castle my parents had called home for centuries.

"It was one of Elvinia's winter getaways," Badb admitted. "Things were complicated when we defected from the Seelie Court to the Unseelie one. There had to be some type of punishment for the betrayal."

"What?" I stopped and whirled around to face her. "You never mentioned that." Rage and confusion were no doubt evident on my face. I'd always thought she and Kalen had been friendly with Elvinia.

"It's in the past." She shrugged as she spoke. "Once you joined the Unseelie Court, our restriction was lifted."

"What restriction?" I seethed.

"This castle"—she raised her hands, gesturing to every-thing around us—"was our prison. We were only allowed to leave when we accepted a task for the Unseelie Court. Those jobs always came with time constraints, but sometimes I'd be able to squeeze in a visit to Macha."

My heart ached at everything Kalen and Badb had sacrificed to be with each other and then to protect me later on.

"It must have been hard," I said truthfully, "to not be able to see your sister after everything the two of you had been through together."

Badb gave me a pained smile. "I thought it was the hardest thing I'd ever have to go through until you were born and I had to give you up."

My chest tightened. I still didn't agree with what Badb and Kalen had done, particularly about keeping me in the dark about my true heritage for so long, but I understood why they'd done it. Sometimes, there were no choices that didn't end up

47

with someone being hurt, and you had to do the best you could to keep those you loved alive, even if they hated you for it.

"Come." Badb headed up the stairs, and I trailed after her. We walked down the hallway to the left of the landing at the top of the stairs, passing several closed doors. "Most of these rooms are just extra bedrooms," Badb explained. "It was always just the two of us and occasionally Nyx."

"Where is that tricky grimalkin?" I asked lightly. "Haven't seen much of her lately."

Badb chuckled. "She and Jinx had a pretty major spat last month. She complained to me about it, and I pointed out that he was kind of right to be pissed off at her. So now I'm on her shit list too."

I snorted. "I'm glad Jinx and I are bonded. We piss each other off all the time, but thanks to the bond, neither of us can stand to be apart for too long."

Badb looked over her shoulder at me. "I know your father and I fucked up a lot of things when it came to you, just as Nyx did things poorly with her son, but I have no doubt our decision to bring you and Jinx together was the right one."

"It was." A small grin played across my lips. "Although, now I know who Mom was cursing all those times we got into trouble when we were young."

A matching grin spread across her face. "Macha used to reach out to me through the mirrors and tear me a new one. Did the two of you really tie Cian to the ceiling and shave off his hair?"

I laughed. "We absolutely did. I actually wanted to shave him while he was in his feline form, because he was taunting me about how much prettier his black and silver coat was than my golden one, but he refused to shift, so we shaved his head instead."

The amusement I felt at the memory faded as my thoughts turned to the present and what the vampires might be doing to him now. Badb's grin dimmed as she sensed the shift in my mood, and we walked in silence as we turned down another hallway.

"Here." We entered a room halfway down the hall. It was small and cozy with a few chairs and wooden chests scattered around, but what drew my attention was the balcony that stretched along the outside. Badb didn't say anything as I stepped through the doorway, which had been left open. As soon as I did, the cold, brisk air slammed into me. Some clever fae must have set a spell around the castle to keep the cold air out regardless of whether the doors or windows were open.

I inhaled sharply as I took in the snow-covered valley framed by a mountain range that stretched impossibly high, disappearing into the clouds. I placed my hands on the thick, stone railing and looked down... and down... and down. Wherever the bottom of the gorge was, I couldn't see it. Only mist swirling around in the depths and licking the edges of the rocky slopes greeted me.

Something told me Mikhail would love this place. I'd have to bring him here someday.

I let myself enjoy the view for a few more moments before rejoining Badb in the room. She was kneeling before a chest made of a deep red wood, her hands resting on the thick, metal latches. I knelt beside her but didn't push. Whatever she'd brought me here for was important.

"We haven't talked about my older sister much," she said softly. "Macha and I both agreed to name you after her."

"*Nemain*," I whispered. "I tried to get Mom to tell me about her when Cian and I were growing up, but she rarely did."

"The three of us were very close, but her death hit Macha particularly hard. I think she always blamed herself for not guarding Nemain's back in that final battle."

"It wasn't her fault." I shook my head. "Eddie showed me a

vision of the day Nemain died. There was nothing either of you could have done."

"Not true." Badb's jaw clenched and unclenched. "If I hadn't picked a fight with the Seelie Queen, that battle with the Formorians never would have happened."

I didn't say anything, because what was there to say? It was true. The decisions we made often had unforeseen consequences. That was just life.

"I only saw part of the battle, but she seemed like a brilliant fighter."

"She was truly the best of us." Badb swung open the top of the chest. "Her preferred weapon was a spear, but she practiced with many others. Including"—I inhaled a sharp breath as she pulled out two dual swords—"these wicked things."

With trembling hands, I took the swords Badb offered me. They were shorter than the ones I'd wielded before. Lighter too. Maybe a foot and a half long. They had been forged from some type of dark metal, and etched into the blades were elegant, silver markings. I recognized them as Unseelie make. I frowned when I looked at the hilt. It was made of the same dark metal, but instead of Unseelie markings, there were deep blue sapphires set into it that looked suspiciously like something the daemons would use.

I looked up at Badb questioningly.

"Your friends helped, and Elvinia." She swallowed. "The base swords belonged to Nemain, and they were forged in our home realm. Macha didn't want them, and I never felt right wielding them, so they've been sitting here all this time. When I saw you with your dual swords... I just knew you were meant to have them."

"Thank you," I rasped as heat built behind my eyes. "They're beautiful."

"Elvinia did these herself." She pointed to the silver markings. "Not even dragon fire will harm them. They're impervious to all elemental damage. The blades will also absorb your devourer magic, so if you're ever tapped out, you can still wield it through these. We don't know how much exactly they'll store —you'll have to experiment a little."

"And the daemon bit?" I raised one of the blades and peered at the gems.

"Pele worked with that cranky-ass daemon you all like." She held out a hand and gestured for me to give her one of the blades. I passed her one with only a little hesitation. They'd been mine for less than five minutes, but I was already feeling attached.

Badb's fingers had barely wrapped around the handle when she thrust it at me. I didn't even move—just stared at the attack like an idiot—but instead of piercing my stomach, the sword stopped a hair's breadth from my body. "They can never be wielded against you; they're bound to your blood."

"Well, that explains why Pele got a little aggressive last month during one of our play sessions and drew some blood."

Badb gave me a puzzled look before shaking her head. "I don't even want to know." She threw the sword across the room, and I flinched when it hit the ground. "Call it to you."

I shot her an annoyed look for treating my already beloved blade so rudely before focusing on the sword. *Call it to me...* I pursed my lips and held out my free hand. Instantly, the sword flew from the ground and the handle smacked into my palm, my fingers instinctively closing around it.

"These are amazing." I stared in awe.

"I was planning on giving them to you soon." She shrugged and rocked back on her heels before rising to her feet. "Elvinia wanted to look them over one more time to make sure her enchantments were solid, but honestly, she's just an obsessive perfectionist. You need them now."

Badb reached back into the chest and pulled out a harness. I took it from her and buckled it on before sliding the swords home. It felt like a part of me that had been missing was finally restored.

Before I could second-guess myself, I yanked her to me in a fierce hug. Her body went stiff beneath my grip before she slowly wrapped her arms around me and returned my hug tightly. After a second, we broke apart and took a couple of steps back as we stood there awkwardly.

"Time to head back?" I asked, rescuing us both from the aftermath of the brief, sappy moment.

"Yes." Badb nodded, and a gateway opened inside their townhouse.

I looked over my shoulder at the balcony that overlooked the mountain range before returning my gaze to her. "I'd like to come back here again if that's okay?"

Her eyes shone brightly before she blinked. "Of course, daughter."

Chapter Five

KALEN AND JINX were waiting for us in the entry hall of the townhouse. The gateway had barely shut before Kalen asked Badb to open another one, this time in my living room.

"Mikhail's back," he explained. "He knows where Cian is."

"Already?" I asked eagerly as we stepped through the gateway into my apartment.

"Here." Magos thrust a cup of coffee into my hand, and I blinked as I looked at everyone gathered. Pele and Asmodeus leaned against the wall between two of the floor-to-ceiling windows, standing as close as possible without touching. Eddie was lounging on the couch with Cerri tucked into his side. My brows rose when I saw Vizor and Lynette sitting on one of the other couches. Eddie's distant relative had his usual cold, arrogant mask firmly in place, but Lynette gave me a shy smile. Her fingers flew through several different motions that I easily followed thanks to months of practice.

We're here to help however we can. Pele filled us in on everything.

I swallowed and pushed back the tears building behind my eyes. It still felt so odd to have so many people in my life who were willing to come to my aid. Finally, I let my eyes go to where they'd wanted to as soon as I'd set foot in my apartment. The pull was constant and demanding. Mikhail was leaning against the back of the couch. His posture was casual, but I still saw the tension in it.

He tracked my steps with a predatory focus as I closed the distance between us, passing my coffee back to Magos on the way. Then I gripped the front of Mikhail's shirt, pulled him forward, and kissed him deeply. In an instant, his lips parted and moved firmly against mine, matching my need with his own. I pulled back after a moment and cupped his face gently.

"I might have been a little worried," I admitted.

"I can tell." He smiled and leaned forward to kiss me again, this one was quick but still kind of sweet. I'd never really been the type of person who engaged in PDA, but something about Mikhail made me want to touch him all the time, and I was over denying it.

His hand slipped into mine before he pulled me over to one of the empty couches. I snuck a glance at Pele and snickered as she stared at me like I'd grown a second head. Considering I'd just kissed my lover hello and let him hold my hand, I couldn't really blame her.

"Bryn and the vamp brats are downstairs. Sigrun and Niall are with them," Magos said, handing me back my coffee mug.

Cerri straightened where she sat on the couch so she could sign the conversation easier for Lynette. "Sigrun says to consider her on standby for whatever you need. Niall too," she said, her fingers easily twisting and flowing to translate her words.

I nodded, grateful for the valkyrie and fae warrior's support. I mean, sure, Niall had stabbed me once, but honestly, most of my friends had that claim.

"A member of the Vampire Council has Cian, and he's not hiding it," Mikhail said, his brows creased in concern. "In fact, he's throwing a masked ball to celebrate his return."

The mug I was holding cracked, and I set it down on the coffee table before I shattered it completely. "His return?" I asked tightly. Mikhail's dark eyes looked at me, and the pity I saw in them only ratcheted up the tension I was feeling.

"Did you know your brother was once the lover of a Council member?"

I squeezed my eyes shut and took a few deep breaths. Worry for Cian now combated the urge to strangle him for getting mixed up with vampire bullshit. Not that I had much of a leg to stand on when it came to past relationships... and current ones.

"No," I finally said, opening my eyes and staring up towards the ceiling. "I knew Cian had a past with a vampire, it's why he hated Magos and then you so much at first, but I had no idea that past involved a tryst with a member of the Council."

"It was more than a tryst," Mikhail said slowly, as if he were carefully planning out his words. That was never a good sign. My gaze dropped to him, but Mikhail was working very hard to keep his expression blank. "He and Adrian were involved for several decades."

"Why didn't you tell me?" I asked through clenched teeth.

"It was a long time ago." His brows bunched together once more. "Two centuries ago? The relationship you have with your brother seems complicated, and I didn't see how bringing up ancient history would help. He's with Hades now, and I had no idea Adrian wanted him back. I'm sorry."

I sighed. "Not your fault. I wish you would have told me, but even if you had, I would have assumed the same. Why would he want Cian now?"

Something dark flitted across Mikhail's eyes. "It *is* my fault. I should have seen this coming."

"What do you mean?" Dread formed in the pit of my stomach.

"Adrian and I… have a history."

"We *both* have a history with Adrian," Magos corrected his nephew. "He is Marius' younger brother."

Well, that explained the grief-tinged rage on Magos' face right now. Marius was the vampire who had led the attack against the city Magos had helped found centuries ago when his people had first arrived in the human realm after their own realm had fallen to devourers.

Marius had not only laid waste to everything Magos had desperately tried to save and protect, but he had also killed his wife, Hasina.

The Council had executed Marius afterwards, claiming they had no knowledge of his plans, but we knew Elisa was related to his bloodline and possibly Misha.

"Could he be Elisa or Misha's father?" The words tasted foul on my tongue. I didn't like thinking of the vampire kids as being in any way related to the bloodline that had caused so much pain, but Elisa could shift into a wolf exactly like Marius, and Elisa and Misha were too similar in appearance for it to be a coincidence.

"I can't be absolutely certain, but I don't think so." Mikhail shook his head. "They don't look like Adrian." Magos grimaced, and Mikhail's gaze cut to him before admitting, "They look like Marius, and Elisa shares his magic. I think it's more likely that Marius had a child we didn't know about, and that's who they're related to."

"Okay," Asmodeus cut in. "So Lir cut a deal with Artemis to take out Hades. Somehow, Adrian caught wind of this and seized the opportunity to kidnap Cian. He may have wanted him back all this time, but even when Hades was masquerading as Dante, he was still a powerful necromancer who would have crushed a vampire like it was nothing."

"Vampires may be weak on the magic level, but they're conniving, patient, and crafty," Pele noted. "Adrian would know Nemain would come after her brother. This was a calculated move."

"I'm going to that masquerade." I folded my arms across my chest. "And I'm fucking walking out of it with Cian."

"Calm your tits." Pele rolled her eyes. "I'm not telling you to not go, but there is more going on than we're seeing."

Vizor leaned forward from where he was sitting on the couch and gave Mikhail an appraising look. "You served this Vampire Council, yes?"

Mikhail's mouth twisted in distaste at the reminder, but he jerked his head in a nod.

"What do you think Adrian has to gain by this?"

"Unfortunately, I know very little about Adrian," Mikhail said reluctantly. "There are nine members of the Council, and the seats are always changing hands. Sometimes through violence, sometimes through political machinations, and sometimes just because the vampire in question is tired of all the political bullshit."

"I feel that," I muttered.

"Adrian is one of the original vampires, and he has held his seat this entire time because he is absolutely ruthless. Despite my history with the Council, I rarely interacted with him." A cold smile played across his lips. "He very publicly supported what his brother did and thought he should have been celebrated, not condemned. But he was outvoted, and Marius was put to death. I'm quite certain he and the Council believe I'd kill him given an opportunity."

"How did Cian end up with someone like him?" I half whispered and twisted to face Mikhail more, our hands still wrapped together. My brother could strike with lethal violence when he had to, but it wasn't his true nature; he took after our dad, Nevin, who had been kind and gentle. I didn't understand why he would have fallen in love with someone like Adrian.

"I don't know the story of how they first became involved.

They'd been together for a few years before I saw them at one of Adrian's masquerades." Mikhail hesitated, his full lips pressed into a hard, flat line before speaking once more. "All vampires have venom we inject with our bite that induces a state of relaxation. The strength of that venom actually varies based on the vampire—sometimes it's barely noticeable, other times it's extremely potent."

"Where does Adrian fall on that scale?" My grip on Mikhail's hand tightened to the point where I was surprised I didn't snap any bones, but he gave no indication he was in pain and let me maintain the death grip.

"His is quite strong, possibly the strongest," he said almost apologetically, but it's not like any of this was his fault. "He enjoys having lovers who are hopelessly addicted to his bite so he can withhold it as punishment."

I let my head fall back against the couch cushion and resumed staring at the ceiling as rage consumed me. *Why, Cian? Why the fuck were you with someone like that?* We already had toxic relationships covered between the two of us, considering my fucked-up history with Sebastian, but apparently, Cian had his own experience with cruel relationships that he'd never told me about.

He should have fucking told me.

Mikhail tugged my hand until it was against his chest, and I concentrated on the constant thud of his heartbeat. The rage clouding my thoughts cleared a little, enough that another thought occurred to me, one that sent a wave of guilt to sweep away the anger.

"When was this?" I looked at Mikhail urgently. If it had taken place when I suspected it had… it made all of this my fucking fault for being a shitty sister.

"I don't remember exactly. I was… " The steady thrum of his heartbeat quickened beneath my hand. "I was a different person back then." Out of the corner of my eye, I saw Magos shift uncomfortably. "But it was probably early eighteenth century," Mikhail guessed.

"This isn't your fault," I told Mikhail. "It's mine. After our parents died, things between me and Cian were tense. Even though we're the same age, I always thought of him as my responsibility," I explained quickly, the words just rushing out. "It's not like he's helpless or anything, but Cian has always been soft-hearted. The human realm was a dangerous place back then for anyone with an ounce of magic."

"And your devourer blood made the fae and daemon realms even more dangerous," Pele added.

"I'm sorry." Kalen's apology drew my attention to him and Badb. They both wore matching pained expressions. "We didn't know about Macha and Nevin until it was too late. Badb wanted to come get you, and I almost gave in... "

"But that Seelie Queen bitch started targeting us again," Badb said, her expression absolutely murderous. "Because of our allegiance to her sister, she couldn't come after us directly, but some of our acquaintances met rather untimely and grue-some deaths. I was never able to prove that she directly played a hand in my sister's death, but I've always suspected."

"We were worried that if we took you in, Áine would target you both as a way to hurt us." The muscles along Kalen's jaw clenched. "I thought we could protect you from a distance. I was wrong."

"*We* were wrong," Badb corrected.

"It's okay." I held both of their gazes with zero hesitation. "I was... so very angry back then. If you had shown up after —" I swallowed, blocking out the dying screams of Macha and Nevin that echoed through my mind. "I wouldn't have stayed. Probably would have tried to kill you."

Badb's eyes shone, and she blinked rapidly before jerking her head in a nod. Kalen tugged her against his chest and gave me a similar nod of understanding.

"What happened?" Eddie asked after several beats of silence. "Why do you think this is your fault?"

I stared at the worn wood of the coffee table and my cracked mug, unable to meet everyone's eyes. "We'd been fighting more and more at that time. I was so fucking pissed off. At everyone. Warlocks for stirring up the hatred, humans for being so fucking stupid, and the goddamn fae for once again failing to help anyone but themselves."

Memories of Cian's tear-stricken face flashed in my mind's eye. By that point, both of us had stopped aging. While I looked like I was in my mid-to-late twenties, Cian looked considerably younger, maybe nineteen, twenty, tops. My heart clenched as I remembered just how much I'd hurt him that day.

"He missed our parents," I said numbly. "But he was ready to move on. I wasn't. I'd met Sebastian, and the two of us were hunting down witches and warlocks across the human realm. Cian happened to find out what I'd done to one particular coven, and he was appalled. He begged me to stop."

The front door creaked open, and I didn't bother looking. I felt Jinx's presence as he leapt onto the back of the couch before slinking down and curling into my lap. With one hand still clenched around Mikhail's, I dug my other one into his fur, and he started purring.

You were both hot-headed back then, Jinx said. *Cian wasn't totally innocent in that argument.*

"Shocking," Mikhail muttered.

"Maybe, but I was still far crueler than I had any right to be." I squeezed my eyes shut. "In the years before our parents died, Cian had started pushing for more freedom. We'd grown up in a very rural part of France, only going into the village to trade. I didn't care because I had no interest in interacting with humans. Plus, my magic was incredibly unpredictable. I spent most of my free time roaming the forests in my feline form."

60

Pretty sure your wanderings around in that form inspired more than one folklore, Jinx noted. I snorted and opened my eyes once more.

"Probably. I did scare the shit out of that one traveling merchant. That was your fault for daring me that I couldn't steal something from his cart without being noticed though." Everyone cracked a smile, and Jinx's rumbling laughter filled my mind. The distraction helped ease some of the tension coiled around my soul. I needed to get the next part out, despite how much it hurt.

"Cian started sneaking off to the village—there was a boy there he liked," I said softly. "It was just foolish, young love, and he had his glamour in place to make him appear human. Although his skin was still dark, which drew some attention— neither of us really understood that back then. This village was small and remote, so they didn't really care; it was just more of a novelty to them to see someone who looked different. And I think most of them feared our parents, so they didn't want to cause any trouble… at least not until later when the warlocks started whispering that we were something else. Something not human."

"I've been catching up on things since we came here," Vizor cut in. "It's my understanding that the witch burnings were mostly done by the humans, but the warlocks instigated everything behind the scenes. I don't entirely understand why though?"

"Mainly to get the witches out of the way," Pele replied. "The two groups have always hated each other. The witches had more power, but that was mostly because of their grimoires and how they passed down knowledge. When the warlocks took out large family units, they wiped out a good amount of that history, and witches have never truly recovered from it."

"Other species were caught up in the witch trials too,"

Asmodeus chimed in. "Mostly the ones that had no realm to retreat to and weren't able to remain hidden. It's hard to say how many died, but it definitely impacted the population of nonhuman species drastically. The warlocks killed many in the mayhem."

Including my parents. I kept the thought to myself since everyone here knew how my parents had died, but I couldn't stop myself from looking at Badb. The same grief I kept locked inside was written on her face.

"I told Cian it was his fault," I said in a rush. Everyone's gaze snapped to me, and my eyes dropped to the coffee table once more. "I said that's why it was so easy for him to get over our parents' deaths, because he'd wanted them gone back then so he wouldn't have to obey their rules about keeping to ourselves and away from the humans. That he'd cared more about his stupid little trysts than our family."

The silence in the room was heavy. Mikhail's hand never slipped from mine, and after a few moments, I finally found the courage to look at everyone gathered. I'd been prepared to see judgment, but instead, I only saw sympathy and understanding.

"We've all said fucked-up shit to people we love." Pele shrugged, and I just stared at her.

"That was pretty fucked up though," Vizor said. Lynette elbowed him in the gut, her fingers flying almost too fast for me to keep up. Something about him calling her something on her birthday once… I didn't recognize the word, but given the death glares the daemons and dragons were giving him—and the fact that smoke was curling out of Cerri's nostrils—I guessed it was something really bad.

"You said WHAT to her!" Cerri lunged out of her seat towards Vizor, but Eddie was quick enough to grab her and pull her onto his lap.

"I was pissed off!" Vizor shouted, and Lynette rolled her eyes.

He apologized and groveled for months afterwards, she signed.

Cerri didn't seem the least bit impressed by this and was still staring daggers at Vizor, but she did settle back against Eddie's chest and raise her hands to continue translating the conversation.

My point, Lynetted continued, *is that we've all done things we regret. I'm sure your brother has forgiven you.*

"He has," I sighed. "But we stayed away from each other for a century after that. He was clearly hurting, and his only family had abandoned him, so apparently this fucker of a vampire found him to be easy prey."

"That is basically Adrian's type," Mikhail admitted. I lifted my hand from Jinx and rubbed my face, hating that I'd inadvertently caused my brother so much more pain.

"What matters now is rescuing Cian and figuring out what Adrian is up to," Magos said firmly. "He's flaunting this for a reason: ensuring you come to his masquerade."

"Who else do you think will be there?" I looked at Mikhail.

"It's impossible to know which of the other Council members will be there. They're constantly jostling for power, and alliances are always shifting." He cocked his head to the side, eyes going a bit distant as he thought through something. We all let him have a moment. "There have been rumors that Katrina has resurfaced. Nothing that concretely connects her to Adrian, but my source mentioned she was seen at a hotel in Paris that Adrian frequently visits."

"Fuck." I rubbed my jawline. Katrina had been like an older sister to Elisa and the other vamp brats when they'd all been under the control of the Council.

Until she'd betrayed them.

"Who is Katrina?" Badb asked.

"She was raised with Elisa and the others," I explained.

"She has compulsion magic. Strong compulsion magic. She tried to use it to force Elisa to be loyal to the Council. She's the reason the kids fled when they did."

"Compulsion magic," Badb spat, and even Kalen grimaced in distaste.

Pele and Asmodeus wore matching neutral expressions. There were all kinds of compulsion spells, each with their own strengths and weaknesses, but for a being to have actual compulsion magic was rare. Daemons were one of the few species that were known for it, although only a few bloodlines were particularly strong.

My devourer magic could block a lot of things, but mental-based magic was always more difficult. I didn't know for sure if Katrina's compulsion would work on me, and I really didn't want to find out.

"Any advice for combatting compulsion?" I asked the daemons.

Pele and Asmodeus frowned at each other before Pele answered. "There are a lot of factors. Age—the older one is, the more time they've had to develop their own mental shields—whether they also have a mental-based magic, and individual strength of will. Whoever is using compulsion is essentially forcing their will on another."

"If you're strong enough, you can fight it," Asmodeus said. "But depending on how powerful she is, it can take time. During which you'd be under her control."

Even if we fought free in seconds... a lot could happen during that time.

"Compulsion doesn't work well on dragons, at least not according to everything I've read." Cerri waved a hand at Eddie and then Vizor. "And it probably won't work on them at all."

"Because I'm amazing?" Eddie grinned at her.

"If you're amazing then so is Vizor," Cerri drawled.

Eddie frowned. "You know I choose to pretend I'm not related to him."

"Likewise." Vizor's lip curled.

"I know a daemon with strong compulsion skills," Asmodeus said. "Katrina isn't a daemon, so her magic might work differently, but we should at least confirm if what Cerri read is true."

"Do it." I nodded.

"If Katrina is at the masquerade, I don't think she'll use her magic," Mikhail said. "Most of those who were around her as a child are no longer amongst the living thanks to the Council. She's become something of a legend over the years. Everyone knows she is an Apex bloodline and that she has compulsion magic, but they don't know how much of a threat she truly is. The Council likes having her as a secret weapon."

"They're also likely worried about someone assassinating her," Kalen mused. "She might be loyal to the Council, but even knowing that, other vampires might not be keen on working with someone who can manipulate their minds."

"So if she does make an appearance at the masquerade, we have to make sure we're never alone with her. We also need to let Elisa and the others know Katrina might be back on the playing field," I said tiredly.

A plan began to form in my mind. At least for an exit strategy from the masquerade, but we still needed a way in. My eyes met Mikhail's. "Is there any way we can sneak into the masquerade?"

"It would be difficult," he replied evenly. "I know the place it's being held, but not well enough to give you an idea of where to open a gateway inside, which means we'd have to start on the outside and break our way in."

"Vampire hearing is second to none," I said, mostly to myself as I thought through the options. "Maybe one or two of us could get in undetected, but we'd have no idea where my brother was. Seems unlikely we could make it far without getting caught, and then it'd be our small number against every vampire there. Not great odds."

I'd still do it if we couldn't come up with another plan, but I'd rather have a plan that had a higher chance of succeeding. Kalen and Badb were whispering furiously at each other, and Badb's emerald green eyes were practically glowing as Kalen glanced at me.

"We have an idea about how you can get in," Kalen said reluctantly. "But you're not going to like it."

"I don't like it," Badb growled. "It's just as likely to get her kil—"

"I don't care about liking it," I interrupted. "All that matters is getting Cian out as safely as possible. I'd make a deal with the fucking devil."

"Rude," Pele and Asmodeus said at the same time.

"I suppose all things considered," Kalen drawled, "one could consider the Seelie Queen the devil."

Chapter Six

"I REALLY HATE THIS IDEA." I glared at the winding path that led further into the garden. As the Seelie Queen, Áine ruled over both Mag Findargat and Mag Ildathach, but Mag Findargat was her preferred residence. As my gaze skimmed the pale silver grass that the realm was named after, I couldn't entirely blame her.

Lilac flowers weaved throughout the grass, the trees had light green leaves with silver patterns that reminded me of frost, and soft pink flowers were starting to bloom on vines that wound around the trees' trunks. The plain white silver was truly unique and breathtaking.

"We all hate this idea," Badb said. The scowl hadn't left her face since we'd arrived. "But your father is right, this makes sense, and technically, Áine cannot directly harm you. You're the Unseelie Knight."

"Yeah... still kind of pissed about that."

Badb grunted in response, and even Kalen looked a little annoyed. Clearly, we were all in agreement that Elvinia had pulled some shady shit, and even if having the title of the Unseelie Knight awarded me some protection, she could have fucking asked first. Then again, she was the Unseelie Queen. Asking for permission was probably a foreign concept to her.

"Just remember what we talked about," Kalen said.

"Yeah, yeah, yeah." I set off down the path. "Don't threaten her life, don't promise her anything, and don't call her a useless fae bitch queen."

Badb chuckled.

"Yes. That." Kalen sighed.

This was why Jinx wasn't here with me. He'd refused to promise to play nice even when Badb threatened to leave his ass behind. I was pretty sure he had thought she wouldn't actually do it and was probably now focusing on making sure she suffered for it. It had been brave of Badb to piss off a being who could curse her with bad luck.

Sunlight filtered through the trees as I stalked away from my parents towards where Áine waited. Kalen had arranged this meetup, with the backing of Elvinia, of course. The only request was that I came alone, something that had sent Badb into quite the temper tantrum, but it wasn't like we had a choice so they waited.

The last time anyone had spoken to my brother was three days ago when Elisa had confirmed with him for the dozenth time what time he and Hades would be arriving at the party. It'd been over a week since I'd talked to him. We were on better terms these days and talked regularly, but I'd thought I'd be seeing him in person so I hadn't bothered reaching out over the mirror.

Panic gripped me once more as I tried to think about what we'd even talked about during that conversation but I came up blank. What if that had been the last time I'd ever speak to him and I couldn't even remember what the fuck we'd talked about?

Blue flames rolled down my arms before vanishing, and I forced myself to take a few deep breaths. I needed to stay focused for Cian's sake. And Hades'. While my brother was my first priority, I was still more than a little worried about how Hades was fairing. The last time he'd been with his kin, he'd slaughtered a bunch of them. There were fucked-up families… and then there were the Olympians.

A songbird let out a long stream of melodic chirps, announcing my presence as I entered a clearing. I'd been expecting a throne like the last time I'd met the fae queens in a garden, when I'd sworn my allegiance to the Unseelie Court. During that encounter, Áine had been regal and had made a rather dramatic entrance, making it clear just how much power she wielded as the Seelie Queen.

I had not been expecting to find one of the rulers of the fae realms covered in dirt and sweat and wearing a pair of very worn denim overalls and a plain, white T-shirt. It seemed so *ordinary* and was honestly kind of a letdown.

"Come on," she gritted out as her hand sank into the earth. First up to her wrist, then up to her elbow. "I didn't mean it!"

"Uhhh… " I halted a safe distance away from… whatever this was. "What are you doing?"

She brushed the long, brown curls out of her face with her free hand and scowled at me with green eyes the same shade as the outer ring of Finn's irises. There were other echoes of him in her face, but her skin was a rich brown to his lightly tanned complexion.

"Yeah, she's gonna be a minute."

I barely managed to contain my flinch at someone sneaking up on me and turned my head to glare at the Seelie Knight. The first time I'd met Olwen was when she'd arranged for my kidnapping. It had involved tentacles, a sunken tub, and a portal. I was still mostly pissed because I adored baths and that had scarred me for a while.

We'd met a few times since then, but I still had no idea

what to make of her. She reminded me a lot of Kalen but somehow even more devious.

"Are you actually here this time?" I arched a brow at her. "Or only deigning to honor me with your presence via illusion?" Most fae magic was rooted in nature and involved the elements, but there were exceptions. Being able to project an illusion of yourself was something several bloodlines of the Tuatha Dé Danann, the most powerful of the sidhe families, possessed.

It was particularly irritating because it meant I couldn't punch Olwen in the face when she was being an annoying twat.

Her light silver eyes lit up with amusement as she slowly raised her hand and poked me in the shoulder. "Boop."

I rolled my eyes but couldn't stop myself from grinning. While I would happily drop the Seelie Queen off a cliff and laugh as she screamed the whole way down, her eccentric Knight was growing on me, even if I did want to throttle her half the time.

"So what's the deal with this?" I waved towards where Áine had gone back to cursing at the ground. She now had two hands in the soil, almost up to her shoulders.

Olwen sighed. "There's a rare type of sentient carnivorous flower that she's trying to encourage to reproduce. The problem is, they have to go through a rather complex blooming sequence, and this one is rather sensitive about the whole thing."

I stared at her, waiting for the punch line.

"I'm not joking." She shrugged.

"There are more pressing things than getting a flower to nut up," I growled and took a step towards the fae queen, but I stopped when Olwen rested a hand on my arm. The light-heartedness on her face had slipped, and for a moment, the wild and beautiful sidhe looked sad.

"She needs this." The words were so quiet, I knew she was relying on my shifter hearing to pick them up. "Balor has been increasing the attacks on the ward trapping him in his realm. Áine has been working nonstop the last six months to strengthen it, but it's grown more difficult after the loss of the other human realms. "

My teeth ground together. Unbeknownst to me, the fae queens had plotted long ago to fill other realms with humans as backups in case the original human realm was lost.

Humans generated a ridiculous amount of magic, and the vast majority of them never used a single drop of it. A friend had once referred to them as magical batteries, and he hadn't been wrong. The ward the queens had placed around Balor's realm to lock him inside relied on the magic generated by the human realm. As did the protective wards placed around the fae realms and others to keep devourers out.

We'd only learned about these backup human realms when we'd stumbled across some humans in the seraphim realm who were very clearly not from the human realm we were all familiar with. Sigrun later uncovered that Lir had been specifically targeting those realms, using the seraphim to wipe them out.

Being the pricks they were, the seraphim had bartered to be allowed to take some of the humans to their realm because they enjoyed hunting them for sport and just terrorizing them in general.

Seraphim loved to play with their food.

"If you had told us about those other realms, we could have helped protect them." Even my parents hadn't known about their existence. Badb had lost her shit, but Kalen had looked hurt that Elvinia hadn't trusted him with this knowledge.

I would have loved to have given the Unseelie Queen a piece of my mind, but I hadn't seen her since returning from the dragon realm. She'd declared me her Knight in front of her court and then ghosted me.

The fae remained the absolute worst.

"I'm the Unseelie Knight." I flashed my fangs at her. "I should have been informed of their existence."

"You're like a Baby Knight, and you weren't exactly the savior of humanity before." Olwen shrugged unrepentantly. "Besides, there were half a dozen of these realms; obscurity felt like the best way to protect them. We had some protective spells in place but didn't anticipate Lir working with the warlocks to figure out a way around them."

"I could have warned you about that." I arched an eyebrow. "Had. I. Known."

A muscle in Olwen's jaw ticked, but she didn't admit she was wrong. Not that I'd expected her to. I was pretty sure it wasn't physically possible for a sidhe to acknowledge such a thing.

"It happened fast. The protective wards all dropped at the same time. By the time we arrived at the first realm, the seraphim had already decimated it along with all the others."

I thought about the children who had been rescued from the seraphim realm. A few dozen. That's it. There were still other humans there we hadn't rescued yet because it would take a fucking army to do so. But how many had died in the other realms? Hundreds of thousands? Millions?

As usual, the fae moved lives around on a chessboard as if they were pawns, and when some asshole flipped the board on them, the fae simply moved on to the next game.

"How bad is it without those fail-safes?"

The corners of Olwen's mouth tensed for a fraction of a second before she smoothed them.

"They weren't just fail-safes. For the last decade, the queens have relied on the magic generated by those realms to patch up the ward. Now they have to rely purely on their own strength."

I grimaced. "Do they have enough power to do that?"

"For now. The fae queens are strong, but even their magic has limits."

I looked towards the Seelie Queen and saw what I'd missed before. Her hair lacked its normal luster, and there were faint lines at the corners of her eyes and mouth. There was a rigidness to her movements as well. The sidhe were incredibly graceful beings, and Áine was exceedingly so, but right now, she just looked tired.

"For the record, I'm still pissed off at you and the queens for keeping me in the dark. But I'll let her play with the stupid plant," I conceded. "Five more minutes."

"Splendid!" Olwen said cheerfully. Then she tilted her head, making her waist-length hair, which was the same dark silver as her eyes, catch the sunlight. The sidhe tended to be a beautiful people, and Olwen was no exception, her silver features contrasting boldly against her deep brown skin. She had a feminine look to her that made her unique among the mostly androgynous sidhe.

With a dull ache, I realized that while Cian and I were actually related, Olwen looked like she could be his sister more than I did. Cian's skin was several shades darker than hers and the silver coloring of his hair and eyes was lighter, but they still looked like each other far more than I resembled him.

It was a stupid thing to be jealous over. If Cian were here, he would laugh about it, but he wasn't because I had failed to protect him like I'd promised I always would.

"You should visit me more often now that we're work buddies."

"Work buddies?" I forced a smile as Olwen beamed at me, unaware of my inner thoughts.

"Yeah! Seelie Knight"—she pointed at herself and then pointed at me—"Unseelie Knight. Things were kind of complicated when your parents were the unofficial Unseelie Knights because of… well… you know."

"My mother trying to murder your queen and then stealing my father from your court?" I raised both eyebrows at her.

"Yes!" She snapped her fingers. "That!"

"I think you might be insane," I said seriously. "And that's saying something coming from me."

Instead of being insulted, she grinned broadly like I'd paid her the best compliment imaginable. Suddenly, the ground rumbled, and we both looked towards where Áine was now backing quickly away from where she'd been kneeling.

"Finally!"

My jaw dropped open as the earth exploded. I didn't know exactly what I'd been expecting to happen, but it wasn't for a twenty-foot monstrosity to burst free from the ground. Kaysea had given me a fae plant as a housewarming present when I'd moved to Emerald Bay. The thing was now six feet tall and had a flower larger than my head, but it still more or less looked like a standard flower as long as it kept its mouth shut.

I would not describe the thing in front of us as a flower. Unlike my plant, which was basically a stem and vines with the electric blue and bright orange blossom on top, this thing mostly consisted of what I guessed was the flower. A vibrant, red bulb sat directly on the ground while thick, green leaves with jagged edges supported the sides that eventually opened up into long petals that curled at the edges.

Bryn was always buying Elisa flowers, and I thought this thing looked like a cross between a tulip and a hibiscus. The strangeness only continued from there. From the center of the flower spiraled up what I was pretty sure was called a stamen, but it split into a dozen different stems that rose another six feet above the flower. Each one ended with a bright yellow ball that had some type of substance dripping from it.

As I continued to gape at the strange plant, one of the

stamen pieces abruptly moved and flung the sticky substance directly into the tree above it. A songbird was abruptly cut off, and a moment later, its feathery body fell out of the tree and directly into the center of the flower.

Suddenly, I was very happy my fae plant was perfectly content with eating ground chicken.

Áine gave the bird-eating flower a content smile before striding over to us. By the time she stood in front of me, her haughty and cruel mask was firmly back in place. I blinked as I realized her grungy overalls had been replaced by a clean, forest green tunic and earthy brown pants. She remained bare-foot, preferring, like a lot of fae, to always be in contact with the earth, and green vines with delicate leaves wound around her hair. This was the Seelie Queen I was used to dealing with.

The one who may have played a role in my adoptive parents' deaths, and who I currently needed a favor from. My jaw clenched as I forced myself to keep at least a neutral expression on my face.

"The daughter of the traitor and the shifter whore." Her lips curved up into a ruthless smile. "Come to *beg* a favor?"

"I need to attend the masquerade being orchestrated by a member of the Vampire Council tomorrow night. My parents seem to believe you can help with that," I ground out.

"Why do you want to attend?" She cocked her head to the side.

"Adrian has my brother," I said reluctantly. She probably already knew, but I still hated admitting any sort of weakness or failure to protect what was mine.

"Hmm." She tapped an elegant finger against her chin. "And what do I get out of this?"

Badb and Kalen had cautioned me about entering a bargain with the Seelie Queen. We all knew she would ask something of me, and they'd made me promise I would walk away if her price was too high. I'd lied. While I wouldn't agree

75

to anything that would put the lives of those I loved in jeopardy, everything else was on the table.

"I have neither the patience nor the finesse to properly bargain. You are no doubt far more clever with your words than I could ever hope to be," I said truthfully. "What do you want?"

"So much like your mother." She huffed a laugh before giving me a thoughtful look. I thought I saw a hint of uncertainty in her eyes, but it was gone so quickly that I wasn't sure. "I want to see Finn more. I've barely seen him since he's returned to us."

"No," I said instantly. "The entire purpose of me joining the Unseelie Court was to keep Finn out of the fae realms. He gets fifty years without having to deal with bullshit fae machinations."

"I'll come to Emerald Bay," she pushed. "They can be supervised visits. We won't talk about anything Court-related. I just want to know my nephew." I opened my mouth to deny her again, but she cut me off. "Please." She twisted her hands together before letting them drop to hang at her sides, and for a moment, she wasn't a ruthless queen. She was just a person who had probably seen some shit throughout her long life and wanted to know her nephew.

Part of me still wanted to deny her this, not only because I didn't trust her, but a darker part of me knew it would hurt her. But I hesitated. She was Finn's blood, some of his only biological family, and while I knew better than anyone that family could be made of whoever you chose, it wouldn't be right for me to make this decision for Finn.

It also occurred to me that I knew very little about the fae queens themselves. I knew Elvinia and Áine had trapped their brother in a different realm and the immense power they wielded, and I knew about their history with Badb and Kalen and thus me. But I didn't know anything about them personally.

Most of my interactions with Elvinia had been at official court events. Her relationship with my parents was complicated, and I wasn't entirely sure if I'd count them as friends. I knew even less about Áine. Did she have anyone besides Olwen? Did I care?

"I'll ask him," I said slowly. "If he agrees, then you can visit him... with supervision. I still don't trust you, and I won't have you whispering bullshit into his ears."

Annoyance flashed in her eyes, but she jerked her head in a nod. "It's a bargain."

Magic flickered inside my chest, there and gone in a flash. I rubbed at it, not liking the sensation. Finn would likely agree to meet with her. For someone who had a dark prophecy about ending the realms floating around him, he was a surprisingly kindhearted person.

"So how are you going to get me and the others into the masquerade?"

"Adrian already extended an invite to me, and I said yes. I'm allowed to bring three others with me. Olwen will be one of them. You can bring whoever you want with you, I don't care."

"Why did he invite you in the first place?" I frowned.

Her smile turned wicked. "I've been pretending to court the Vampire Council away from my brother, suggesting I can offer them far more power than he can and help improve their standing in the magical community. Adrian has been the most receptive to my offer."

"He actually believes that bullshit?"

"Fuck no." That got a genuine laugh out of her. "But he's a *vampire*." She rolled her eyes. "Adrian knows I'm deceiving him, but he likely believes that he can somehow deceive me back and come out on top. Vampire politics are child's play compared to fae courts. I could run circles around him all day."

"Great." I eyed the enormous flower. Did it look hungry? I took a step back. "Mikhail and I will be ready tomorrow. Just let us know where to meet you."

Áine turned and walked away without another word. Apparently, I was dismissed. I opened my mouth to say something snippy to Olwen, but I halted when the fae queen's steps faltered and she placed a hand flat against a tree trunk for balance.

For the barest second, pain and despair radiated from Olwen, then the queen straightened and walked on. Olwen flashed a flirtatious grin at me like nothing had happened and sauntered after her queen. I stared after them for a long moment before heading back down the path to where Badb and Kalen waited for me. We had a masquerade to plan for.

THUNK. Thunk. Thunk.

"I don't think the Seelie Queen is going to appreciate you doing that to her tree," Mikhail drawled.

"And I cannot emphasize how much I don't give a shit. She's been keeping us waiting for an hour." I stalked over and pulled my throwing daggers out of the bark before stomping back to where I'd been standing. Mikhail was in front of me in an instant, halting my arm when I raised it to throw again.

"She'll be here soon." He plucked the daggers out of my hand. "You need to calm down."

"I just wish we knew what we were walking into." I stared past Mikhail at the tree with its now torn-up bark. "They clearly want me to be there, which means we're walking into their trap. I think our plan is a good one, but I'm still worried there is something else going on we're not seeing."

"There absolutely is," Mikhail agreed. My attention snapped back to him, but I didn't see an ounce of worry on his face. He'd lined his eyes with kohl tonight, and it made his already startlingly beautiful eyes that much more intense. "Nothing is ever straightforward with the Vampire Council, and Adrian is one of its most duplicitous members. I have no doubt he'll spring several things on us that we have no way to anticipate."

"Not helping." I gave him a pointed look and took the daggers back from him, sliding them into my thigh holster. I slid the remaining two daggers into their sheaths, one on my other thigh and the other across my chest.

Mikhail just grinned in that devilish way of his that always made my thoughts scatter and started playing with the end of my braid. "They're not going to see our surprise coming either."

I let out a raspy laugh. He had a point there.

The sound of light footsteps had us looking to the side entrance of the castle. This garden was tucked away from the rest of the castle grounds, and if I didn't know better, I'd say Olwen had told us to wait here because she thought I'd steal something if I were let into the Seelie Queen's castle.

She was totally right, of course. I'd bet that fae bitch had all kinds of fun stuff in there.

"You do know this is a masquerade, right?" Olwen scrutinized me from Áine's side. The Seelie Queen had opted for a gown that consisted of a light pink, fitted corset that flowed into a gauzy, white skirt. Her feet were covered, so I couldn't tell if she was wearing shoes or not.

I'd expected Olwen to be wearing practical clothes like me since the three of us were meant to be playing bodyguards for Áine, even though she was way more powerful than us and didn't need our protection. But it's not like the vampires were going to call the fae queen on her bullshit. Instead of the tunics

79

I always saw her in, Olwen was wearing a dark amber dress that showed a lot of her skin. The top piece was held up by one asymmetrical strap that went over her left shoulder, leaving her right shoulder completely bare as well as both arms. The sides of the dress had been cut away, putting even more of her on display. Like Áine's dress, Olwen's fell to the floor, but the fabric was slicker and shiny. It hugged her curves, leaving nothing to the imagination.

She smirked at me and did a twirl that ended with her popping out a hip, causing the high slit to reveal a good amount of her leg. "Want to have a go with me? The Unseelie Knight having her wicked way with the Seelie Knight would probably cause both courts to have a meltdown."

Áine shot her Knight an exasperated look.

"I'm good, thanks." I looped my arm into Mikhail's. "Sure it's a good idea for you to be in a room full of vampires looking like a tasty juice box?"

"That's kind of the whole point." She shrugged. "They no doubt are going to be messing with you and continuing to play whatever game they are with my queen. Me showing up looking like the *delicious* morsel I am is going to distract at least some of them. There's only so much they can do to fight against their instincts."

"Personally, I think the way *you're* dressed is going to cause far more of a stir." Áine waved her hand up and down at me. "Exactly how many blades do you have strapped to you?"

"Nine."

Both of them tilted their heads as their eyes studied me once more. I could practically hear them counting in their heads. I didn't give a shit that this was some fancy party. While I had to admit I hadn't hated wearing a dress to the Unseelie Queen's winter solstice ball last year, there was no way in hell I was going to walk into a ballroom full of vampires with my skin on display like Olwen.

I was covered from my neck down in thick, matte leather that absorbed any light thrown at it. It was daemon-made, and despite the form-fitting nature, the material had a lot of give so it was easy to move in, and they'd somehow made it breathable. A wide choker made out of enchanted silver protected my neck. I was going to kill some vampires and rescue my brother tonight while being dressed accordingly. I didn't give a fuck about the message it sent.

"I only count eight," Olwen said finally. "And that's assuming you have two in your boots that I can't see."

"Maybe I'll show you later." I winked at her, and she grinned back.

Mikhail pulled me closer, his hand lingering on the rise of my hip as he gave Olwen a cool look.

"At least the vampire understood the assignment." Áine's eyes darkened as she took in Mikhail, and the amusement I felt at Mikhail's flash of jealousy faded instantly.

Unlike me, Mikhail had opted to dress more in line with what one would expect at a masquerade. Since coming into my life, Mikhail had started to dress almost exclusively in daemon fashion, as their clothes were always a blend of comfortable and functional. He especially favored styles that blended femininity with masculinity like the khikri he was wearing tonight.

The garment blurred the lines between dress and robe. This one was a little more conservative than the one he'd worn to the fae ball. The indigo jacket perfectly matched his eyes, and the flared shoulders and narrow waist drew the eye, forcing your gaze to travel down to where the jacket flowed into a long panel that flared around him when he moved. At first glance, the pants he wore looked black, but when the light hit them, you could see they were actually a deep purple.

I'd also seen him in just the pants earlier before he'd put the khikri on and could testify that they molded to his ass perfectly. Matte leather boots reached up to just below his knees and were plated with silver similar to the choker I wore around my neck. The long sleeves of his jacket disappeared into silver bracers, completing the look.

Everything about him tonight was dark and dangerous, and even with the stress of everything going on, my blood still heated every time I looked at him. I saw an echo of the hunger I felt in the queen's eyes, and I didn't like it one bit.

My hand reached up and tilted Mikhail's face towards mine. Twilight eyes flared as my mouth crashed against his. I let my fingers wind around his dark hair that he'd left down instead of braiding back and pulled him tighter against me. A groan slipped from him as I continued to kiss him possessively. Finally, I broke the kiss and glared at Áine, still wrapped in Mikhail's arms.

Her lip curled in distaste before she looked away.

Olwen laughed. "Well, glad we got that settled." She tossed a mask to both me and Mikhail before adorning hers. "Let's go see how many fun traps the vampires have set for us."

Chapter Seven

"This feels a little on the nose," Olwen said as we all stared at the sprawling, gothic mansion just outside Prague.

"To be fair, Gothic architecture was quite popular in the fifteenth century, which is when most on the Vampire Council were born and later turned," Mikhail defended.

"Come on." I started walking up the wide steps to where two guards waited for us. "I need to find Cian."

Áine strode up the steps next to me, and I slowed a bit to let her go first. She was the queen, after all. Plus, if they decided to attack us straight away, might as well let them target her first. Olwen cut me a knowing look and sped up to walk slightly ahead. Olwen might play the mischievous trouble-maker, but her loyalties were to Áine. If she had to choose between saving her queen or us, I had no doubt who she'd choose.

It didn't bother me because I'd choose Mikhail and Cian over the two of them, and she was perfectly aware of that. We knew where each other stood and where the lines were drawn. I'd take that over someone who was less than honest with me any day.

I eyed the guards who waited for us at the top of the stairs. They wore identical black suits and gold masks that completely hid their features. On one hip, they had a long dagger and on the other, a gun.

I bit back my laugh and slid a sideways glance at Mikhail.

A gun? I mouthed.

The corners of his mouth quirked up into a grin. I almost wanted to provoke them just to see what would happen if they tried to shoot any of us. While I wasn't faster than a bullet, I was often faster than the person pulling the trigger. Even if I or any of the others got shot, bullets simply didn't do enough damage to keep us down. Large-caliber guns were a little more annoying, but still nothing any of us worried about.

I could only imagine the look on the Seelie Queen's face if someone pointed a gun at her. A snort escaped me before I could swallow it down. The attention of both guards snapped to me, and I gave them a smile that was really more of a baring of teeth. To their credit, neither reached for a weapon or looked intimidated in any way.

Behind them, the tall double doors were already open, revealing a wide, dimly lit hallway. Beyond that, I could see another set of doors, also open, and what I'm guessing was the main ballroom. Classical music flowed from the room, but I wasn't familiar enough with that type of music to know who the composer was.

Áine and Olwen strode past the guards without even acknowledging their existence. Mikhail and I trailed after them.

"You're going to need to control your temper in there," Mikhail murmured. "No matter what those in attendance say to you, stay calm."

"I am capable of self-control, vampire."

"You stabbed me three times today."

"Those were controlled stabbings."

"There's something wrong with them," Olwen mock-whispered to Áine.

The hallway ended, and Áine paused for only a moment before sweeping into the ballroom. I felt her magic gather around her like a protective shroud, but none of the vampires reacted in the slightest. They couldn't see or sense magic, so they had no idea the amount of power that had just rumbled through the walls.

My own magic shifted inside of me, not liking the walking threat that was the Seelie Queen, but she was in enemy territory and wanted to be ready for anything, so I couldn't fault her for it. I'd just have to grit my teeth and bear it for the night.

The conversations and dancing slowed as the vampires realized who had just arrived. The music abruptly cut off, and I got to experience how it felt to have hundreds of vampires stare at you. Because it was me they were staring at. Not the Seelie Queen or Olwen with her tantalizing outfit. Not even the former assassin of the Council.

Me.

Fantastic.

"Ah, good," a sensuous, masculine voice called out. The crowds parted, revealing a man with olive skin and midnight black hair. He was dressed in an all-black tux that was perfectly tailored to him, and two horns curled upward from the sides of his dark red mask. A devil's mask.

Mikhail went still beside me. Whoever this vampire was, he wasn't someone Mikhail had been expecting tonight. We knew that Adrian would be here, and Mikhail had taken a guess about who some of the other attendees might be, but the Vampire Council members rarely attended the same parties, both for safety reasons and because many of them hated each other. They worked together because they had to, but according to Mikhail, they were constantly playing games against one another.

"My apologies." The devil man bowed deeply to Áine. "Had I known the time of your arrival, I would have made sure you had a much grander entrance."

"No need to apologize," Áine said with a light casualness that was at direct odds with the magic swirling around her. "I must admit that, sometimes, it's nice to forget about all the formalities that come with the throne. It would be lovely to simply have an enjoyable evening."

"Of course." He gracefully rose from his bow and gestured to the band, who immediately started playing again. "I am Cassius. While my responsibilities as a Council member do not compare to what it must be like to be one of the fae queens, I can understand where you are coming from. We are delighted to have your company this evening. Perhaps I can take you on a turn about the room?"

"That would be wonderful."

"There are many who are eager to meet you." He held his arm out, and Áine slipped her hand into the crook of his elbow. His lips curved up into a sly grin as he leaned closer to her, as if they were sharing a secret. "I do look forward to keeping you to myself for as long as I can though."

She tilted her head back, a musical laugh spilling from her throat. Cassius' eyes flashed with hunger as he stared at her bare skin on display, and I felt Olwen's magic turn predatory even as she plastered a smile onto her face. Áine's laughter trailed off, and she let herself be led away from us. Cassius glanced over his shoulder, winked at Mikhail, and gave me a curious look before returning his attention to Áine.

"Well, I'm going to go fulfill my role as vampire bait as I keep an eye on my wayward queen." Olwen twirled a strand of her silvery hair around her finger. "Best of luck to you both."

Then she gave us a salute before sauntering after Áine and

Cassius. More than one vampire did a rapid head turn in her direction, and I was pretty sure I saw at least two drooling after her. I was still attracting ferreted glances, but no one else approached us.

"He's not here," I said tightly.

"Adrian is all about the drama," Mikhail said, unconcerned. He spun me around until my back was against his chest and nuzzled my neck. "He'll be here soon. We just need to keep you from burying those fancy new blades of yours into all these pretty vampires."

"Don't worry; none of them are even close to being as pretty as you."

"A compliment." He grinned against my skin. "You truly must be on edge to let one of those slip out."

"Hilarious." I twisted so I could nip at his neck and whisper into his ear, "Just so you know, you're gonna tell me what the deal is with you and Cassius when we're out of here."

The muscles along his jaw flexed. "Have I ever told you that your perceptiveness is annoying?"

"Likewise." I held his frustrated gaze, making it clear I wouldn't be letting this go. Mikhail was usually very good at hiding his emotions, but Cassius had thrown him off, and I wanted to know why. I had a lot on my plate right now, but if Cassius had done something to Mikhail, I'd kill him. I just needed to know if the death should be slow or quick.

"Well, isn't this adorable," a honeyed voice said. The faint accent sounded Romanian to me, but I was far from an expert when it came to accents across the human realm.

I turned to face the first vampire brave enough to approach us after Cassius had left, and my breath caught in my throat. She was absolutely stunning, with an ample hourglass shape wrapped in dusky brown skin that was practically glowing against the rich red dress she had on, which looked like it'd been painted on, considering how tight it was. Long, brunette locks fell in soft waves to her hips, and impossibly thick, black lashes framed dark brown eyes.

I'd never met Aphrodite in person, but I was pretty sure she would have paled in comparison to the vampire goddess who stood before me.

"Justina," Mikhail said in greeting. He smoothly maneuvered me so I stood at his side, and then he clamped an arm around my shoulder. I wasn't sure if it was because he was feeling possessive or to keep me from killing the walking sex symbol in front of us. "I'm surprised you're here, considering Cassius is too. You used to have to be physically forced to be in the same room as him."

She let out a laugh that was more like a purr. It would be so easy to rip out that pretty throat. Hard to make that sound without vocal cords. Mikhail's grip on me tightened.

"He's less tiresome now than he used to be." She gave a dainty shrug. "Plus, the rumors have been circulating that you're involved with this shifter, and when I heard she was coming tonight, I decided to crash the party in hopes you'd be here too."

Her eyes never left Mikhail's, and my hand trailed down towards the throwing dagger on my thigh. It'd be a little hard for her to look at him with my blade in her eye. Mikhail shifted his arm so that it was across my lower back, and he was able to reach around and clamp down on my arm just as I wrapped my fingers around the hilt of the dagger.

"So what you're saying is you owe me a favor," I drawled, and her exquisite, chocolate-brown eyes finally moved to me. "Seeing how *I'm* the reason he's here and all."

She tried to hide it, but I saw the flash of irritation cross her face as my words struck a nerve. Somehow, during all his explanations of what to expect tonight, Mikhail had left out some of his personal history with at least two members of the Council, because I had no doubt the vampire in front of us was part of the Vampire Council, considering the subtle gestures of respect every vampire who passed by us made towards her.

"I suppose I do." She gave me a polite smile and swiped a glass of wine off the tray of a passing servant. "Then again, I'm not entirely sure he's with you of his own accord. You're part-fae, are you not? Perhaps you've used some type of magic to bind him to you. Because the Mikhail I knew had no interest in politics. He only wanted to hunt and kill. It's why our nearly century-long relationship fell apart when I took a seat on the Council."

"*Taci!*" Mikhail snarled at her, and they traded more words back and forth in what I was pretty sure was Romanian. My damn translation mark couldn't make sense of it for me. The daemons had added a good amount of the human languages to the spell, but Romanian wasn't one of them.

"Hey!" I snapped, and they both shut up. Justina gave Mikhail a look that was equal parts lust and vexation before glaring at me. I wrenched my hand free of Mikhail's grip but remained at his side, feeling the tension and wariness radiating from him. "Congrats. You're super hot and you blindsided me with your love history. Up until this very moment, I was *convinced* he was a virgin before he met me. Granted, there were moments I had my doubts." I cocked my head to the side and furrowed my brows as if deep in thought. "That tongue trick of his is particularly good. Did you teach him that?"

The sultry expression she'd schooled her features into slipped, and her mouth fell open and shut rapidly as she tried to figure out how to react. Mikhail just laughed under his breath and brushed the back of his hand against mine, and I returned the gesture.

Despite the initial flare of possessiveness, I wasn't actually jealous of Justina. After four centuries, I had a rather complicated list of exes, both alive and dead. Not to mention the fact that Pele and I were still involved in our own unique and casual way. Mikhail was older than me, and he'd spent most of his time in service to the Council. I'd always assumed most of his past relationships had been with vampires. Plus, he was with me now, and that's all that mattered.

Her remark about their relationship ending because of her becoming a Council member troubled me though. Mikhail knew how involved I was with the fae courts. My life and my future was tied to Finn's, and he was the future king of the fae realms. I'd delayed *when* that would happen, but it would still happen eventually.

Mikhail had chosen me despite knowing all this... but what if he changed his mind once the reality of my future sank in? I shoved the doubts Justina had successfully planted in my mind aside. That was a discussion Mikhail and I would have to have at a later time.

Justina finally recovered and gave me a much more scrutinizing look than before, like I was a challenge she needed to figure out how to defeat.

Fucking try me. I grinned at her. *My claws are way sharper than yours.*

"She's not your usual type." Her gaze slowly swept down my body, and she clearly found me wanting. I wasn't lacking in curves, but I had considerably more muscle than her. No one would ever look at me and call me soft. Whereas Justina was nothing but enticing curves and alluring smiles. "But after everything you've been through, I think I can understand the appeal."

"How gracious of you," I deadpanned.

Justina tilted her head to the side and tapped a long, bright red nail against her pouty lips. I braced myself for whatever sore spot she decided to test next. "You're nothing like him. Not in personality, and definitely not in looks."

Cian. She had to be talking about Cian. Her barbed comments had mostly missed their marks when it came to

Mikhail, so she decided to go a different route. I bit the inside of my cheek until the metallic taste of blood spilled over my tongue. The plan couldn't move forward until my brother was here, which meant I needed to keep my cool. With deliberate effort, I removed my fingers from the dagger handle before I could give in to the temptation of using it.

"I'm the prettier one," I said lightly. "But I promise you, my brother can be just as wrathful as I." Cian might have eventually forgiven humans and warlocks as a whole, but he'd been standing by my side when we'd razed the village that had killed our parents to the ground. I had no doubt he would move heaven and hell to fight his way back to Hades.

"I'm going to have to disagree on the former." She smirked. "Your brother is quite pretty."

"No comment on the wrath part?" I gave her my best deranged smile.

She shrugged one shoulder, completely unconcerned. "He's always been a well-behaved pet."

The chains I'd been keeping on my temper broke, and not even Mikhail was fast enough to stop me. It wasn't my dagger that shot towards Justina but a spear made of blue flames, which slammed into her chest.

And winked out of existence.

Blood pounded between my ears as the band played louder and faster while the conversation around us died down. Justina casually brushed the spot on her dress where my flames had hit, even though there wasn't a trace of them ever being there.

"Apologies, was that supposed to do something?" Laughter broke out across the ballroom as she gave me a broad smile, showing off her fangs. "The world is changing, and vampires will claim their rightful place in it." Her eyes flicked to Mikhail. "Make sure you choose well, *Azuris*." Then she headed in the direction of Cassius and Áine, swaying her hips in that impossibly tight dress.

"Azuris?" I asked quietly as I scanned the room. None of the other partygoers approached us but they didn't give us nearly as wide a berth as before. I could feel their excitement and hunger. Seeing Justina easily deflect my devourer flames had emboldened them. I had no idea how she'd done it. Technically, devourers couldn't wield their magic against each other, but vampires and werewolves had always been the exception to that. Whatever magic the sorcerers had used to create them, they'd failed to instill that particular trait.

I had no way of knowing if this newfound skill was limited to the Council members or if every vampire in this room was immune to my flames. It could potentially mean that magic in general didn't work against them, in which case, Áine and Olwen would also be at a disadvantage. It was too late to do anything about it now. We'd just have to improvise.

When Mikhail failed to answer me, I turned my head to face him. Slowly, he turned his attention away from the rest of the room, his features fixed in an impassive mask that I knew meant he was trying to hide something painful.

He moved to stand in front of me, his hand cupping my jawline before he kissed it softly, then he shifted back to whisper in my ear. "It was the name my parents gave me when I was born."

Oh. She knew his original name. Because he'd told her, but not me. There was so much Mikhail knew about my life and history. It hadn't hit me until now just how little I knew about his.

A few more vampires headed our way. A woman in a pale pink dress and flowery mask flanked by men in identical white suits and silver masks. They exchanged pleasantries with Mikhail, but I couldn't be bothered to play nice right now.

"I need a drink." I walked off before Mikhail could stop me, though I felt him stare after me, a nearly scalding heat on my back.

Vampires murmured as I stalked past them, but I ignored their taunts. Cian would get here soon, our plan would go into play, and then we'd get the fuck out. It had been foolish of me to let Justina's words get under my skin, and I hated that she'd been able to find my weak spots so easily. I'd never really dwelled on how much I didn't know about Mikhail because I'd figured he would share it when he wanted, and I could be patient. Mostly. But it'd never occurred to me that he'd already shared so much of himself with someone else.

I didn't know if he hadn't told me about his past because he didn't want to talk about it, or if it was because he found me lacking in some way. I didn't think it was the latter... but he'd told Justina. I wished Pele and Kaysea were here. The two of them thought differently, but they both had a much better understanding of how relationships worked than me.

A vampire in a skintight white dress bumped into me, and she quickly retreated when I raised my lip in a snarl.

"I leave you alone for ten minutes and you look like you're about to incinerate half the people here." Olwen appeared at my side, and I barely contained my jump. Fuck. I couldn't afford to be distracted like this. She noticed my unease and held out an arm. "Come. Dance with me."

"I'm terrible at dancing," I grumbled but still accepted. She led me onto the dance floor, one arm slipping around my waist while the other held my hand up and to the side. We probably looked ridiculous, considering I was dressed like a mercenary heading into war while she took the lead in her fairy princess outfit, but seeing how I couldn't dance to save my life, it wasn't like I could lead.

"We all have to be terrible at something." She grinned. "Unless you're me. Then you're simply perfect."

"Gods, you might be worse than Eddie."

Ignoring me, she asked, "What happened?" Her hand slipped lower down my back, fingers brushing across the hidden dagger that rested against the center of my spine as she spun me into a low dip. "That a sword in your pocket, or are you happy to see me?" A salacious grin hugged her lips, and I rolled my eyes as she tugged me back up before our pace hastened with the music.

"That line is meant for when you're feeling someone up in the front." I pressed my hand against her back, forcing her tighter against me.

"See, this is why I like you." Her eyes sparkled. "Most people are too scared of me to flirt back."

I leaned forward so that it looked like I was kissing her neck but whispered into her ear, "Most people probably don't know you're in love with the Seelie Queen and that your flirtations are nothing but a cover."

She stiffened beneath me for a fraction of a second before forcing her body to relax. I pulled back and smirked at her.

"That's a dangerous accusation." Her eyes had taken on a predatory coolness. "Love is a weakness that many would seek to exploit."

"Yeah." I let my own inner predator shine through my eyes. "I'm well aware. Trust that I will never disclose my observation nor use it against you. I simply wanted to share why I have no problem returning your flirtations."

We danced another turn around the floor. I spotted Mikhail still talking to those three vampires, his gaze occasionally flicking to me before staring daggers at Olwen as she slid her hand lower on my back. She noticed and took the opportunity to spin me into another dip, and I felt the heated stare of Mikhail as he took in my body being stretched out on display.

Olwen laughed huskily against my skin. "You two are ridiculous. I can never tell if you want to fight or fuck."

"Both," I huffed. "Always both."

She smoothly pulled me back up, and I had to admit that

she was a hell of a dancer. "Want to tell me what had you so pissed off earlier?"

I chewed my bottom lip. Olwen spun me in two tight twirls, forcing some of the other couples on the dance floor to give us a little more space.

"It's occurring to me that, despite my age, I'm not particularly good at navigating relationships," I admitted. Most had been short-term flings. In my centuries of living, I'd only been seriously involved with two people: Sebastian and Myrna.

Sebastian and I had been toxic for each other and our love twisted. What Myrna and I had shared had been true and pure, even if it had only been for a few decades. Technically, Pele and I were also a long-term thing, but we had never been each other's primary lover. We were friends first and lovers second. Still, my relationship with Pele was important to me, and I appreciated that Mikhail understood and fully supported it.

"I hate to break it to you, sweet cheeks, but your relationships will likely only get more complicated. Particularly with the path you're on."

"I know," I said quietly. "Being with me is… a lot. I'm not an easy person to love, and my life is, as you put it, *complicated*. It might be selfish of me to want the things I do."

Sadness touched Olwen's features in understanding. "I'm not going to lecture you, and honestly, I don't even know what I would advise, but you should figure out your feelings soon before things progress too much further with your magic. You don't need that kind of pain in your life, not now."

My eyes flashed in warning even as I gave her a tight nod. I still wasn't ready to deal with that fun little detail and fully planned to push it off until after we figured out our current disaster.

"May I cut in?" a lightly accented, masculine voice asked.

Olwen looked at me in question, and I squeezed her hand

before releasing it. Then she gave me a flourished bow, a cocky grin back on her face. "I should probably see what Áine is up to anyway. Make sure she hasn't befriended any plants and fed the vampires to them."

Emir glanced after Olwen's retreating form before arching an eyebrow at me. He wore black slacks, a dark purple button-down shirt, and no mask. Either nobody had told him this was a masquerade, or he simply hadn't cared.

I didn't bother answering his unspoken question about how or why the fae queen would be feeding vampires to plants. Instead, I just took his arm and started leading us in a dance because I figured it would annoy him to have a woman lead, and poorly at that. I stepped on one of his feet within the first ten seconds. Only sort of on purpose.

"Wasn't expecting to see you here. Enjoying being Lir's bitch?"

Emir's pleasant smile didn't so much as slip at the jab. Creases lined his face, and his thick, dark brown hair was showing some silver around the temples. He'd been a member of the Warlock Circle for centuries. He and Sebastian had been enemies back when we'd first gotten together, so he was at least as old as me. This was the first time I'd seen him in person since he'd summoned me to the forest outside Emerald Bay and offered me Sebastian's life in exchange for serving him and the Circle.

I'd taken Sebastian's life but turned down the deal.

"Enjoying being the Unseelie Queen's bitch?"

Touché. "What do you want?"

Several curious glances slid our way, including Justina's from where she was standing close to Áine and Olwen.

"Don't react. I mean you no harm," Emir murmured a second before I felt magic spring out from him and hover in the air around us. My magic instantly came to attention, and he flinched slightly as flames flickered out from my palms and bit into his skin. "It's just a simple sound distortion spell so others don't overhear us."

The band changed to a new song, a slower one. Ugh. I slowed down but kept a couple of inches between us. The idea of being so close to Emir made my skin crawl, and I was having a hard enough time keeping my magic under control. The night Sebastian had died, my former lover had told me one last secret. He'd claimed Emir had been the one who had orchestrated the murder of my parents.

It could have been a lie. Sebastian had hated Emir. Maybe he'd hoped that, even in death, he'd get his revenge against him. In his final moments, he'd also given me a spell to undo the tattoos he'd forced onto my flesh. I had no idea what to make of that final act or the secret he'd shared.

Either way, Emir was an enemy.

"I want to discuss a truce between us."

I stared at him for several seconds before barking out a laugh. "That's a good one. Got any other jokes?"

"Lir will continue to target your family and friends. So you can either laugh at me while they die around you, or listen to what I have to say."

Magic roiled under my skin as more of it nipped at him. "You already have an alliance with Balor through Lir," I pointed out. "Sides have already been chosen."

He gave me a patient smile. "Please. Lir will betray and dispose of me and the rest of the warlocks as soon as we're no longer needed. Same with the vampires. At the end of the day, he is fae, and they're all arrogant fucks."

"Probably should have thought of that before you climbed into bed with them."

He shrugged. "We needed power, and they gave us that. Now I'm just planning our exit strategy."

"And you think I'm going to help you with that?" I cocked my head. "Given that you're talking to me about betraying your current ally, I'm not really feeling inclined to trust you."

"Trust"—he laughed—"is for fools and heroes."

"So why not bargain with the understanding that we'll both betray each other when the moment is right?" I didn't bother to keep the sarcastic bite out of my voice.

"Exactly." His fingers slid along my hand, and I felt cool metal slide around my pinkie finger. "It'll be a lot easier for you to protect those you care about if you know who Lir will go after next. I could provide that information for you. Perhaps sometimes, I might even be able to derail his plans before it gets to that point."

I wanted to tell him to take his offer and shove it up his ass. A week ago, I would have, but that was before my brother had been taken right out from under my nose. He was right. I had too many people I cared about to protect.

"Think about it," Emir said as the song ended and another started. He spun the dark silver ring he'd slipped onto my finger. "Spin it three times counterclockwise when you're ready to speak."

The spell dissipated around us as he walked out of the ballroom, disappearing down the hallway. Mikhail appeared at my side moments after I strode off the dance floor.

"What did he want?" he asked, an edge of violence underscoring his words.

Before I could answer, the atmosphere in the room suddenly shifted. The slow, melodic beat the band had been playing became bolder and faster, and all eyes turned to the doors we had entered through, my gaze following theirs.

The vampire who stood there practically dripped power and masculinity. A close-lipped, arrogant smile graced what hinted to be a very handsome face, drawing more attention to his square jawline. Only the dimple on the left side betrayed any sort of playfulness.

He wore a midnight blue suit that did nothing to diminish his broad build; he was nearly as big as Magos. An elaborate skull mask covered the top half of his face. Beside him, wearing nothing but a similar mask and a belt that held two panels of the same midnight blue fabric that barely covered him, was Cian. With chains wrapped around him.

I exploded.

Chapter Eight

THIS TIME, Mikhail had reacted fast enough to at least grab me, but that didn't stop my magic from exploding out in a circular wave. The vampires who had been closest to us stepped back even further. I had no way of knowing if that had been instinct, or if they weren't protected from my magic the way Justina was.

"Nemain!" Cian yelled and jolted forward, only to be yanked back by some invisible force. The thick chains that wound around his body and pinned his hands behind his back creaked and tightened before he let out a pained groan. My flames shot out a little further.

It was hard to focus on anything except the vampire who was holding my brother prisoner, but I saw Mikhail step forward between me and him, his mist sword springing into existence. On the edge of my peripheral vision, I saw Áine and Olwen standing separate from the vampires, waiting to see what was going to happen. I was setting our plan on fire, and they were all doing their best to adapt.

With a force of pure will, I pulled my magic back inside me, leaving only the barest hint of it out to periodically dance down my skin. My lungs filled as I pulled in a deep breath, centering myself as best I could. Mikhail glanced over his shoulder, his eyes bright with the promise of violence.

I read the question in them. *You good?*

When I jerked my head in a quick nod, he stepped back to my side, his sword vanishing instantly. I glanced quickly at Olwen, and she nodded in understanding. It was time to set our plan into motion.

Go time, I pushed the thought out as hard as I could. I was a weak telepath, but my friends weren't. There was no doubt in my mind they would hear me. We'd discussed the risks of a telepathic vampire being present, but Mikhail didn't know of any, so we'd all decided it was a chance we'd have to take.

We would find out in the next few minutes if we'd made a fatal mistake.

"Well," the newcomer who had to be Adrian rumbled, "I have to say, I'm not used to my entrance being upstaged by one of my guests. This is a novel feeling. I suppose I should thank you for that." Cian moved to his side as if someone had pushed him, and Adrian kissed his temple while wrapping an arm around his waist. "You also have my thanks for keeping my love safe for me all these years."

"If you have to kidnap someone and wrap them in chains to be with you, I don't think you get to call them your love," I said coldly. The blinding rage I'd felt before had receded just enough for me to look more closely at my brother and see the bite marks along his neck and bruises mottling his skin. "You hurt him."

"Oh, that." Adrian trailed a finger down Cian's sides, and my brother shied away from the touch. "I gave him the option of sharing my bed or pain. He chose pain."

"I should have killed you long ago," Mikhail said. "But I promise that error will be corrected soon enough."

"Always so arrogant." Adrian laughed as he tucked Cian,

who hadn't spoken a word since calling out my name, into his side. They strolled towards us, and the vampires parted to make way for them. I noticed Olwen pulling Áine towards the door. With everyone focused on me and Mikhail, no one paid them any attention.

Justina and Cassius emerged from the crowd to trail behind Adrian. It was clearly meant to be a show of support, but I didn't miss the dark look that passed between the two of them. Every part of me wanted to run to Cian and tear him away from the prick holding him captive, but I forced myself to remain rooted in place. Mikhail stood by my side, close enough that his arm pressed against mine, and I drew strength from the contact.

"This is meant to be a joyous occasion." Adrian beamed at everyone gathered. "Not only do I have this stunning creature by my side once more, but my nephew is here to make a very special announcement."

I was fairly certain that if my brother had access to his magic, he would have ripped Adrian's soul from his body and torn it to shreds. Whatever they were using to keep him under control must have been powerful.

"Thank you, Uncle." A vampire who looked barely past twenty strode into the room. On his arm was an equally young-looking woman with sandy blonde hair and large, blue eyes. They stopped to stand next to Adrian. "You're too kind."

Katrina. The only photo I'd been able to find of her was several years old, but there was no mistaking those blue eyes and pretty face.

"Fuck," I muttered and glanced at Mikhail. We'd known this had been a possibility, but I had still been hoping she wouldn't be here. On the plus side, if she tried to use compulsion on us here, every vampire in attendance would know what she was capable of. Given the lengths that she and the Vampire

Council had gone to keep her talents under wraps, I didn't think she would.

Katrina's appearance was concerning, but it was the young man whose arm she clung to that sent shock running down my spine. He looked down at her with adoring eyes that were the *exact* shade of dark indigo blue as Elisa's and Misha's. And he had their elegant, beautiful features as well as sharing their creamy, white skin and black hair.

Adrian had referred to him as his nephew. Beside me, Mikhail had gone completely still.

Five minutes, a voice rumbled through my mind.

We had to separate Cian from the rest, but not too soon, otherwise we'd risk getting overwhelmed. I didn't dare take my eyes off the vampires standing before us, but hopefully Áine and Olwen had just slipped through the doors and were heading outside to the point we'd agreed upon. Some of my magic slipped out, and with a few seconds of concentration, I opened the gateway for them. Hopefully anyway. I'd been practicing opening gateways where I couldn't see them, but sometimes I was off a little bit.

"Perhaps an introduction is in order," Mikhail said smoothly, recovering from his shock. "So that we all might know what it is we're celebrating."

"Ah, yes." Adrian toyed with a lock of Cian's hair before giving us a sly grin. "I believe you know Gabriel's half siblings, do you not?"

Siblings. Misha and Elisa were brother and sister, and this was their brother.

"How are dear Elisa and Misha doing these days?" Katrina asked lightly. "They left in such a rush. Not even a chance to say goodbye."

"You come near them, and I'll separate your head from your body faster than you can speak a word through those poisoned lips of yours," I promised.

103

We'd told Elisa that Katrina was definitely still alive and that it was possible she was part of whatever Adrian was planning. The young vampire had gone deathly pale as I spoke. She had attacked Katrina before, but she'd done it out of panic and a fierce desire to protect the others. She would hesitate to harm Katrina again, all the vamp brats would, because they'd grown up together and had loved Katrina.

I couldn't allow her to encounter Elisa and the others. Katrina would view that love they had once felt for her as weakness and exploit it.

Cian let out a pained cry and fell to his knees. I jerked forward, but Mikhail caught me, holding me back.

"Careful," Adrian warned. "Katrina is soon to be a part of my family, and I won't tolerate any threats. And I'd advise you to definitely not say such disparaging things around her future father-in-law. He's a bit… feral."

Mikhail sucked in a harsh breath. "Who is the boy's father?"

Adrian grinned wider. "You know who."

"That's impossible." Mikhail's jaw hardened. "He's dead. I saw him die."

"You saw what we wanted you to see." Adrian shrugged an elegant shoulder. "Come now, Mikhail. We all knew that, despite your rage, Magos always had your loyalty. You never would have agreed to work with us if you knew the vampire responsible for the destruction of Noua Zori was not only still alive but a member of the Council."

No. The denial was instant. That fucker couldn't still be alive. He had destroyed Magos' entire world. I refused to accept that he was still breathing.

"*Where is he?*" Mikhail's words were a throaty growl, and it was my turn to hold him back as he lunged towards Adrian.

You close? I shoved the words out as I strained to hold Mikhail back.

104

Here.

Do it.

Mikhail heard the silent conversation, and he stopped pulling against me even as rage rolled off him. Trusting that he had himself under control, I released him. I needed my hands free for what came next. We'd just have to grab Cian in the chaos, because I was officially done with this fucking party. I took a few steps forward, closing the distance a little between me and Cian, but I stopped when Adrian stepped in front of him.

"I think that's close enough. There is no reason for things between us to be so tense. We're practically family," he purred. "Perhaps we can come to an understanding."

"You tried to force my brother into your bed." The promise of violence dripped from my words. "You've hurt him. There will be no *understanding*. I'm going to shatter your bones, and when I get bored with that, I'll skin you alive. Then I'll stake you out in the sunlight and listen to you scream while your magic cannibalizes your body." I took another step forward, blue flames flickering menacingly down my arms. "And then, and *only then*, will I consider carving your heart from your chest *if* my brother asks me to."

The chains around Cian rattled, and he hissed in pain before leaning to the side and spitting out a mouthful of blood. A savage grin spilled across his bloody and cracked lips. "Love you too, sis."

"First you upstage my entrance, and now you threaten me in my own home." Adrian shook his head, completely unconcerned by my threats. "Rather foolish, considering I hold your brother's life in my hands, and given the particular talents of my favorite guests."

"We could go somewhere more private so I can make them more agreeable?" Katrina suggested quietly while Gabriel looked at us with a hungry expression that made me think he shifted into a wolf like his father and Elisa.

"Why don't we soften them up for you first, dear?" Adrian suggested. Several vampires in the crowd stepped towards us then, their faces still hidden by masks but their fangs on full display. Cian struggled to get to his feet only to be knocked back down. This time, I felt the pulse of power from Adrian. Telekinesis was common amongst daemons, and that's what his magic felt like, but there was an oddness to it. I wasn't sure if that was because he was a vampire or something else. Either way, at least we knew what type of magic he had now.

"Sorry," I said apologetically as more vampires drew closer to me and Mikhail. "But I only let one vampire eat me these days."

Phrasing, an amused voice.

Incoming, another slightly annoyed voice said.

"Afraid you don't have much of a choice in the matter," Adrian said confidently. "It seems the fae queen has abandoned you, and those lovely flames of yours won't work against any of us here, I assure you. You're outnumbered hundreds to one. Honestly, it was foolish of you to come, but I'm delighted you did."

I glanced over my shoulder to the wide, floor-to-ceiling windows behind us and the two dark forms in the night sky barreling towards them.

"Yeah... but I'd bet two dragons against a few hundred vampires any day."

Mikhail and I instantly grabbed a couple of vampires, holding them as fleshy shields in front of us. The windows shattered seconds later, sending glass shards hurtling across the ballroom as Eddie and Vizor crashed into the room. The vampires screamed as the glass cut into them, and we shoved them aside once it had stopped.

Adrian had been standing in front of Cian and had unintentionally shielded my brother from the glass barrage. A particularly large piece had impaled his stomach, and dozens of shallower wounds dotted his body. He gaped at the enormous, black dragons who were currently snapping up every vampire in reach. Honestly, I hadn't thought they'd eat the vampires, but apparently, I'd been wrong.

I sprinted towards Adrian, yanking one of my daggers free, but Gabriel barreled into his uncle and pushed him out of the way. They both fell and skidded across the floor just as guards spilled into the room. A frustrated growl ripped out of me, but I ran towards Cian instead of chasing down Adrian. My brother came first. We'd have to wait for our revenge.

By the time I reached him, Cian had already struggled to his feet. I yanked him to me in a quick hug before pulling back and quickly scouring the chains, looking for any type of lock or weakness but seeing none. Grabbing two links, I tried to see if I could pull the chains off him but immediately released them with a hiss. My skin burned where it had touched the metal, but there were no wounds I could see.

"Fuck, Cian," I swore. "How are you standing?"

"Not well." He swayed, and I gripped his shoulders, avoiding the chains, to keep him upright.

"Mikhail!" I yelled over my shoulder. "I need you!"

He was there in an instant, covered in blood with a wild grin on his face. A dragon roar drew my attention, and I twisted around just in time to see a vampire launch a spear at Eddie. It should have bounced off his scales, but instead, it sunk into his flesh, just above his left haunch. A pained snarl tore out of him, and I saw at least half a dozen more spears sticking out of his body. Vizor wasn't much better off, and there was a slowness to both of their movements.

"Carry him, and I'll cover you both!" Mikhail didn't argue. His sword vanished into mist, and he threw Cian over his shoulder. He let out a pained hiss as the chains came into contact with the skin on his neck, but as least he was wearing long sleeves, so most of his body was protected against whatever fucked-up magic they'd been enchanted with.

I slipped my dagger back into its sheath and pulled my short swords free before taking off towards the dragons. Mikhail followed close behind, leaving me just enough room to cut through any vampire who got in our way. The ballroom was in absolute chaos, and I didn't see any signs of Adrian, Katrina, or Gabriel. The guards must have forced them out of the room and left the rest of the guests to fend for themselves. Justina and Cassius were also nowhere to be seen.

Half the partygoers had fled, but the remaining ones were helping the guards target Eddie and Vizor. One vampire in a shimmering, blue gown and peacock mask swiveled her hands together as if she were rolling a ball between her palms. Purple mist formed between her hands, crackling with electricity. I yanked a dagger free and threw it just as she started to draw her arms apart.

My blade sunk into her throat a second before she let her magic loose, and it caused one of the purple orbs to crash into the wall and the other into one of the vampire guards. The spear fell from the guard's hand as their body went rigid. Bolts of what looked almost like lightning snapped out from underneath their gold mask and across their armor before they collapsed to the ground.

The vampire who had thrown the magic pulled my dagger from her throat, and blood poured from the wound. It wasn't enough to kill her, but it was enough to slow her down. We raced past her, and I maimed or killed anyone who got in our way. Suddenly, three guards appeared in front of me, and I skidded to a stop, causing Mikhail to do the same behind me, but a long black tail slammed into them and flung them halfway across the room.

Leave. Now, Eddie said. Even in my mind, his words were

slurred and full of pain. We had to get those fucking spears out of them.

He was closer to us than Vizor, who was busy taking out the guards who were trying to rally again. Mikhail rushed past me and leapt onto Eddie's extended front leg, scrambling up the dragon's body to the spines that ran down his back.

"Go!" I screamed at them before running towards Vizor. Eddie took off through the window, tilting slightly before righting himself. Two more spears sank into Vizor, one in his chest and the other in his underbelly. I rammed into a guard who was preparing to throw another one. There was nothing elegant about the move; I just slammed all of my body weight into them, sending both of us crashing to the floor.

Just as I scrambled to my feet, Vizor's black, scaly tail wrapped around my waist, and I found myself suddenly airborne. Vizor hurled himself through the window, his dark, leathery wings snapping open once we were through. My stomach lurched as he dove down and his tail flung me forward.

I bit back a scream as I arched upward and then free fell for several seconds before slamming onto Vizor's back, narrowly missing a spine.

I hate when you guys do that, I hissed even as relief poured through me at seeing Eddie flying ahead of us with Cian and Mikhail.

A raspy laugh filled my mind. *I know.*

Chapter Nine

Less than ten minutes later, the five of us collapsed onto the hardwood floor of my apartment. Mikhail and I were mostly fine, the various wounds we'd received during our mad dash to Eddie and Vizor had healed other than one deep gash across Mikhail's ribs. His entire right side was soaked in blood, but he didn't complain, only continued to support Cian, who was still bound in those damn chains.

Cerri and Lynette were instantly there, pulling their respective mates up and over to the couch. I rose to my feet with a grimace and half stumbled over to Cian.

"Nemain, I—" His words cut off when I yanked him to me and wrapped my arms around him. His arms were still bound so he couldn't hug me back,b and the enchanted chains burned into my stomach where a section of clothing had been torn away, but I didn't care. Cian's familiar scent swirled around me, and I let out a broken sob.

He was here. He was safe.

"It's okay," he said soothingly. "I never had any doubt that you'd come for me. Every time they tried to break me, I'd laugh in their faces and tell them they had no idea the hell that was about to descend on them."

With some reluctance, I pulled back and helped my brother over to one of the chairs beside the couch. We had to figure out how to get the chains off him so he could heal properly.

"That bastard Adrian got away," I growled.

"It doesn't matter," Cian said. "All that matters is finding and rescuing Dante—"

"They all know he's Hades," I cut him off. "Seemed like they should know all the details, given what's going on."

A muscle ticked underneath Cian's left eye, but he dealt with that revelation and continued on. "I know you don't like him, and I won't ask you to come with me. If you can just help me heal then I'll—oww!" He glared up at me after I smacked him on the back of the head. "What the hell was that for?"

"For thinking I wouldn't help you rescue the love of your life!" I crossed my arms. "There's nothing I wouldn't do for you, little brother."

"You're only older than me by one week."

"Still older and wiser."

Mikhail snorted, and I gave him a dirty look over my shoulder, which only made him grin.

"Make yourself useful and call Kaysea. Tell her to come over here and bring Zareen; they can help heal the dragons." I frowned at the chains encircling my brother. "And maybe help me with these."

I heard Mikhail walk over to the mirror, and a second later, Kaysea's voice filtered through. Good. I'd been worried she would be out and we'd have to find someone else to play healer.

"Where is everyone?" I asked Cerri, who was fretting over Eddie. For his part, Eddie didn't seem to mind the extra attention, and I was pretty sure he was playing up the seriousness of his wounds. True, they weren't healing like they should, but shifting back to his human form had helped heal the worst of it.

"There has been an increase of attacks in Acleonia," Cerri said. "Bryn, Sigrun, and Niall went to help and investigate. We're not clear if this was random or if it's part of some overall effort to force you to split your attention."

"Damn it." I slipped my fingers under the top loop of the chains that wrapped around Cian's upper back and chest. The burning was instant, but I gritted my teeth and tried to shift them up, yet there was no give at all. After a few seconds, I swore and yanked my hands free, and Cian sagged as best he could in the chair. "Are Taliesin and Lucan okay?"

Tal was Cerri's best friend along with Lynette, and Lucan was his lover. Not only did I like both of them, but they'd been very helpful in getting the dragons settled in their new realm.

"Yes, they're with Lucan's brother." Eddie tugged Cerri up onto the couch to sit next to him and wrapped an arm around her while holding a towel against the cut on his chest.

I knew my friends were more than capable of protecting themselves, and Eddie had volunteered to come with us to rescue Cian after Cerri and Pele had come up with the idea. I'd been surprised when Vizor had volunteered too, but didn't turn him down because the only thing better than one dragon was two. Still… I didn't like that they'd both been hurt and now the rest of the dragons might be being targeted because of their association with me.

"Wipe that look off your face, Nemain," Cerri said firmly.

"What look?" I arched an eyebrow.

"The one that says you're plotting how to continue onward and rescue Hades without any help from us." Eddie mirrored my eyebrow raise and gave me a smug grin. "We all know what you're thinking. You're very predictable."

"It's true," Vizor agreed. "I don't even know you that well and I could tell that's what you were thinking."

"Why are you here again?" I snapped.

"Because the options were to hang out in Acleonia and deal with all the political posturing there, or go munch on some vampires." He shrugged but instantly grimaced at the movement. "Seemed pretty obvious which one I should pick."

Cian shifted, drawing my attention away from the dragons, and I caught the wince that flashed across his face. Maybe we could physically cut the chains off? Did we have anything here that could do that? My gaze flicked over to our weapons wall, but nothing there would do it. We needed bolt cutters or something.

"Eddie, do you have anything at your shop that might help get these off?"

He pondered my question for a moment. "I don't know. The magic coming off them is strange. If I had to guess, I'd say it is a mix of fae, devourer, and warlock. I still don't understand how they're wrapping devourer magic into things, considering it destroys other magic."

"I don't remember much about how they were put on; it all happened so fast," Cian said in frustration. "Hades and I were taking a walk after dinner. Everything seemed fine… " His brows furrowed. "I smelled something. Cypress. I thought it was strange because there are no cypress trees in the forest surrounding our home, and I started to mention it to Hades when he grabbed me."

My brother looked at me with absolute devastation. It was the same expression he'd worn on the day our parents had died, and I hated seeing it on his face again. Knowing that once again, I had failed to protect him.

"He was *terrified*, Nemain." Cian's voice broke. "He shoved me away and told me to run, to find you, and then he was just gone. I don't know how or what happened, but he vanished right in front of me. Within seconds, these things"—he shifted the chains—"wrapped around my body, and the shock of it made me pass out."

I swallowed. "Have they been on you this whole time?"

Cian didn't answer for a moment, and tension roiled inside me. "Adrian said the chains would come off if I... if I let him... " Quick, panicked breaths started slipping through his lips, and he squeezed his eyes shut as tears leaked out of the corners. "I refused. So the chains stayed on and they tried their best to break me. He'd ask me if I'd reconsidered every few hours."

I felt my magic dance across my skin like liquid fire as my fists clenched and unclenched at my sides. Someone grasped one of my hands. Mikhail. He raised it to his lips and kissed it, not the least bit concerned about the flames. "Don't worry, love. We'll kill them all. But I'm going to need you to calm down so we can focus on getting your brother free of his bindings, okay?"

Between his touch and his words, I calmed down a little, my magic sinking back beneath my skin, satisfied for now.

"Kaysea might have some ideas," I said numbly. "We'll have her look them over when she gets here. If she can't help, I'll fetch Chamosh." The daemon amulet crafter wouldn't be happy about me dragging him here, but I wasn't taking Cian outside of the wards protecting our apartment building until he had access to his magic again.

"She'll be here soon," Mikhail promised. "In the meantime, maybe we ca—"

The apartment door opened, and Isabeau dragged Finn inside and over to Cian. Cerri frowned at the kids before glancing at the door. "Where's Magos?"

Isabeau waved her off impatiently. "He told us not to come up yet, so I distracted him and we snuck out."

We all stared at the eight-year-old girl who had somehow gotten past a vampire nearing eight *centuries* in age. She plastered a cherubic smile on her face but ruined it by rolling her eyes seconds later when she realized none of us were falling for her bullshit.

"Finn can fix it." She raised her chin defiantly. "Show them!"

Finn bit his bottom lip as he brushed his chestnut brown hair out of his eyes. It wasn't long enough to pull back into a braid or ponytail, so it was constantly getting in his eyes, but he didn't want us to cut it. None of us said anything as Finn took several careful steps forward until he was standing directly in front of Cian's chair.

A look of pure concentration settled onto his face as he studied the chains. He would be turning ten the following month, but he still looked so small to me. There was barely a size difference between him and Isabeau. Granted, her personality made her seem larger than she actually was. How something so tiny could be so loud was a genuine mystery to me.

For his part, Cian tried to stay calm when parts of the chain started being tugged in various directions by an invisible force. The silver links across his ribs shifted an inch lower, and he let out a low hiss before clamping his jaw shut. Then the chains stopped moving.

"Sorry," Finn mumbled.

"It's fine. Barely felt a thing," Cian assured him.

Isabeau moved to stand next to Finn, and the two of them exchanged a look that implied they were once again communicating telepathically and not sharing with the rest of us. After a moment, the two of them closed their eyes.

Seconds passed, and Cian glanced at me, but I shook my head, silently telling him to just wait. All four dragons snapped forward until they were on the edges of their seats. Blood started dripping to the floor from a wound on Eddie's leg, but he was so absorbed in whatever magic he was seeing Finn do that he didn't notice.

Mikhail caught my eye, and I gave him a baffled look. Whatever Finn was doing, I could feel it but not make any sense of it.

All at once, every single link snapped and shot away from him until they hovered in the air a few feet away.

"Oh, thank fuck," Cian breathed out as he rubbed his newly freed arms, wincing as he moved them around. They had to be sore as hell after being twisted behind his back like that for days.

Eddie rose from the couch and moved to crouch next to Finn, who had walked the floating chain links away from us and was now standing with them hovering in front of him.

"How did you do that?" Eddie gestured towards the remnants of the chain. "Before, there were three different types of magic woven into the links. Now, there is just one… and it's something I've never seen before."

"It's mine," Finn said shyly. "I've never encountered warlock magic before, that's why I couldn't undo them at first. It's so different compared to fae or daemon magic. The warlock part of the spell was cruel, and I was scared I would trigger it."

"What do you mean?" Eddie asked, keeping his tone gentle but encouraging.

Finn thought about it. "The chain didn't *want* to be removed." The floating links moved until they were once again part of a chain, although Finn didn't bother closing the links, his magic kept everything in place effortlessly. He wound the chain in the air as if it were wrapped around an invisible body. "If it wasn't all removed at once, it would have tightened until it cut through everything beneath it." The loose loops of the chain snapped together, sending a piercing metal *ting* throughout the living room.

Cian paled, and I was right there with him. If the removal

of the chain had gone wrong, I would have been holding pieces of my brother right now.

"Whiskey," Cian rasped. "Whiskey would be great right now."

"On it." Cerri hopped up and strode towards the kitchen.

"It won't hurt anyone now," Finn assured everyone before plucking one of the chain links out of the air and holding it out to Eddie. "Here."

Eddie cautiously extended his hand and let out a sharp exhale when Finn dropped it into his palm. Vizor and Lynette joined them, both looking at the remaining links with a mix of awe and bewilderment. Some of the pieces separated from the rest before joining together, twisting and elongating until a flower that resembled a daisy emerged. Finn waved his hand, and the metal flower flew over to Vizor, who caught it and raised a brow in question.

For you to give to her, Finn carefully signed.

In a rare moment of softness, Vizor smiled, and the cruelness that seemed to be forever etched into his features lessened before he handed the flower over to Lynette, whose face lit up with delight. She reached down and gave Finn a hug, keeping it brief because he was still not super comfortable with physical contact of any kind other than from Isabeau, and that was mostly because the vampire girl had left him no choice in the matter.

Thank you. Lynette smiled kindly at the young fae boy. *You are truly a wonder, Finn.*

"Crap!" Isabeau squealed and ran over to grab Finn's hand. "Magos knows, and he's pissed!"

"Language?" I drew the word out in a question and glanced around at everyone. "I feel like we should be saying that to the eight-year-old swearing?"

"I'm almost eight and a half!" Isabeau challenged as she proceeded to drag Finn towards the front door.

117

"Keep copping an attitude with me, and I'll tell Elisa," I warned. "Also, what are we supposed to do about those?" I gestured towards the remaining chains still floating in the air.

Finn waved his hand again, and the links shot over to the corner, where an old wine barrel had been repurposed as a pot for my fae monstrosity of a plant. Silver swirled faster than I could track, and soon, a stylized metal sculpture rested next to the barrel, a smaller replica of the plant next to it.

The enormous blue flower of the fae plant turned towards the newcomer, its petals vibrating rapidly as if it sensed the strange magic. Hopefully it wouldn't try to eat the thing. Something told me that wouldn't go well.

A door slamming shut echoed throughout the apartment, announcing the kids' departure. Cerri handed me a shot of whiskey before refilling Cian's shot glass and passing the bottle around. Eddie drank straight from it and passed it to Vizor, who wiped the rim off with his sleeve before doing the same.

"Finn's magic… " Vizor started before stopping and pressing his lips into a hard line. "I don't even know where to begin."

"Yeah." Eddie slapped him hard on the back, earning a glare, which he just rolled his eyes at. "Don't worry. According to the prophecy, Finn won't kill us all because Nemain is going to keep him from the dark side."

Everyone stared at me with completely straight expressions. Eddie was the first one to break with a laugh that was more of a snort. Cerri dissolved into adorable giggles while Lynette leaned into Vizor's chest, her shoulders shaking. Even Vizor's lips curled up into a grin.

"I don't know why you're all laughing," Mikhail said in amusement. "She sneaks him at least five cookies a day. That's definitely going to keep him on the good side."

"But doesn't the dark side have cookies?" Cerri said

between laughs. "I'm pretty sure I saw that on a bumper sticker."

My gaze dropped to Cian, who was smiling, but there was a tightness to it that drew me back to reality and away from our brief break of lightness.

"Hey." I sat on the coffee table in front of him. "Kaysea and Zareen will be here soon. We'll get you and everyone healed up and then we'll figure out our next move."

"I know." He let out a frustrated breath. "But I have no idea how long it will take for my magic to come back. I don't even remember the last time I felt this weak, and we have no idea where Hades is, and I'm not even sure where to start looking. Even dreamwalking hasn't worked! Whoever has him must be incredibly powerful. They're blocking me from reaching him while he's sleeping and somehow keeping him restrained. I don't think those chains they had me wrapped in would be enough to contain him. Maybe Lir… " He trailed off when he saw my expression. "What?"

"We know who has him, Cian," I said slowly. Lir had been the one to tell us, but they would have been my first guess anyway. I was a little surprised my brother hadn't pieced it together by now, but I suppose he had been through a lot. "I thought you knew," I finished weakly.

"*You know*?!" He bolted up until he was standing over me, his silver eyes practically glowing. "Why the fuck didn't you say something earlier? We've just been sitting around here wasting time when we could be going after him right now!"

"What exactly were you going to do?" I shoved to my feet, which put me eye-to-eye with Cian, although I outweighed him by a solid twenty pounds of muscle thanks to my brother's leaner build. "Up until five minutes ago, your ass was still wrapped like a fucked-up present!"

"Who. Has. Him?" Cian bit out.

I pursed my lips. It'd occurred to me earlier that Cian was

being relatively calm about all this. I'd thought it was because of the shock and trauma of being held captive by the vampires and everything that fucker Adrian had put him through, but now I knew it was because he hadn't known who had Hades, and he'd been racking his brain trying to piece together potential suspects.

We couldn't do anything. Not yet. Rescuing Cian from the Vampire Council had practically been a walk in the park compared to going up against Artemis and the rest of the Olympians. I had no firsthand experience with them, but I did have experience with some of the other gods. The only reason they didn't rule over everything was because they were so few in number and the majority of them had no interest in it. Really, it was only the remaining Olympians who were assholes, and they had their own realm to reign over.

Pele was gathering information, and I needed to check with some of my other sources, which meant I needed to keep Cian calm and prevent him from doing anything rash that would get him killed.

"I promise we'll go after him," I said, forcing myself to remain calm. "But first—"

"Now!" Cian snarled and gripped my biceps, jerking me in his grip. I felt the claws spring from his fingertips as he partially shifted. "Tell me right now!"

Mikhail was there in an instant, shoving Cian away from me, a deep growl of his own rumbling out of his chest. I slid between him and my brother, shoving them both back.

"Enough!" I barked.

"Brother or not, I'll still fucking break you if you hurt her again," Mikhail warned.

"It's barely a scratch and is practically healed already." I frowned over my shoulder at him. The stubborn look he gave me said he clearly didn't care. I just rolled my eyes and let it go.

I couldn't exactly complain about his overprotectiveness when I felt the same way.

Turning back around, I met my brother's outraged stare. Cian was a smart person, and while he wasn't as world-traveled as me, thanks to spending most of his life in one death realm or another, he should have figured out who had Hades already. He wasn't thinking rationally. Given that he'd been attacked, kidnapped, and tortured, that was understandable, but I needed him to get his head back in the game because Cian made stupid fucking decisions when he was in this state of mind.

"Think," I said forcefully. "You know who has him."

"If I knew," he ground out, "I'd already be on my way to get him back."

"Cypress." I let the word hang between us. "Earlier, you said you smelled cypress just before the attack. Those chains that held you never would have contained him, nor would anything the warlocks could cook up. Even with the boost of devourer magic. What kind of power is needed to capture one of the gods?"

"It's not her." He slashed a hand across the air. "We've been keeping close tabs on Artemis all this time. She's never so much as hinted that she suspected he might be alive."

I leaned forward. "She's the goddess of the hunt. Did you *really* think you could outrun her forever?"

The denial that he'd been stubbornly clinging to faded, only to be replaced by absolute terror.

"Open a gateway," Cian demanded.

"First of all, we are in no position to go rushing in without a plan." I tried to keep my voice calm even as panic started to rise inside me at seeing Cian so distraught. "Second, I can't, I already tried. Therrea isn't a realm exactly, and you know this. Even my magic doesn't work there."

121

"Don't give me that bullshit!" Cian shoved me. "I'm telling you to open a fucking gateway right now!"

"I don't give a shit!" I snarled and pushed him back. Eddie slid in between us, gripping Cian by the shoulders while Mikhail grabbed me around the waist and pulled me back. I kicked out like a feral cat for a few seconds, but his grip on me didn't slip. Stupid fucking vampire. "Let me go!" I growled.

He laughed. "It's cute you think your little growls intimidate me."

Cian tried to slip past Eddie, only to be firmly muscled back. A low rumble poured out of my brother, and I responded in kind. I should have left the damn chains on him until I knew he would be reasonable about all of this. Normally, Cian was the rational one between the two of us, but clearly, that wasn't the case right now.

Lynette glided across the room and tapped Cian's shoulder, drawing his attention. His body went rigid for a moment before he stepped back from Eddie and crossed his arms. Whatever she signed to him, I couldn't see because her back was to me, but Cian relaxed slightly and jerked his head in a nod. Then she took a step back so we could all see her clearly.

Nemain, would you mind explaining why you can't open a gateway to the realm? Some of us are a little behind on the intricacies of realm travel. Lynette gave me an apologetic look. I knew what she was doing. Cerri was the problem solver, but Lynette was the expert at dealing with people. She had to be to put up with Vizor.

I gestured at Mikhail, asking him to translate while I spoke because I didn't trust myself to adequately speak and sign at the same time for something like this.

"Asmodeus could explain this better than me, but basically, we believe the realms are alternate realities. These different realities came into existence at different points in time, which is why sometimes they're similar to most of the other realms and other times they're completely different. Also, events play out differently. You've met Aki before?"

The dragons nodded. The young empath was a frequent visitor to their new realm.

"The realm her people were originally from, Kalarilia, was devastated by volcanic activity. Those same volcanoes exist in the human realm, the largest of them is under Yellowstone National Park. Here, it hasn't erupted in a very long time, but in Kalarilia, that volcano and several others went off around the same time, resulting in a mass extinction."

Lynette nodded. *What makes the realm the Olympians are hiding in different from all the others?*

"Therrea isn't a realm exactly." I paused and pursed my lips. "This is where I have to admit that I'm really not smart enough for this."

"So you can walk between worlds but don't understand how they work?" Vizor asked. "Seems like you should have made that more of a priority."

I glared at him. "I've had other things on my mind."

"Like what?" He sneered, completely unimpressed. "How to get your vampire off quickly?"

Blue flames shot out from my hand as I flicked my fingers towards him, wrapping around his throat. "Like how to kill a dragon in ten seconds."

Vizor grasped at the flames but jerked his hands away as my fire burned him. "I... withdraw my... question."

With half a thought, I snuffed the flames out of existence, and Vizor gasped as he drew in ragged breaths, sending me dark looks in between. I smiled at him.

"'I withdraw my question?'" Eddie squinted at the other dragon. "Who phrases things like that?"

Lynette grinned. *He's been watching courtroom drama shows whenever he helps me babysit Isabeau and Finn.*

"Of course he has," I said dryly. "To answer your original

question before Vizor dickishly interrupted, pocket dimensions are a thing. That's how they're able to summon their swords from the mist." I pointed at the vampires. "Their swords never stop existing, it's just that their people somehow learned to access a particular dimension, and that's where their swords go when they don't have them. It's a tricky thing to do, and most beings never attempt to actually go into one of these dimensions because they're not stable."

"But Artemis did?" Cerri asked.

"Yeah," I said. "It's called Therrea. It's normally referred to as a realm, but it's not, it's technically a pocket dimension, and I can't open a gateway there."

"You're the Unseelie Knight," Cian said abruptly. "Surely the Unseelie Queen knows how to get there. You can ask her and—"

"First of all," I cut him off, "I'm assuming she's busy patching up the holes Balor is punching through the wards of the realm he's exiled in. Because after declaring me her Knight and then demanding my time at various events, Elvinia has completely vanished. So now I look like an asshole because I have no idea what I'm supposed to be doing as the Unseelie Knight."

"Don't be so hard on yourself," Mikhail said. "You look like an asshole regardless."

I pulled a dagger from my thigh sheath and hurled it at his face, but he plucked it out of the air and admired the blade as if it were a pretty flower.

"Can the two of you flirt later?" Cian hissed. "Do I seriously have to remind you that my mate is being tortured as we speak?"

"I'd appreciate it if you wouldn't refer to him as your mate," I said. "Because I'm still personally hoping that you'll change your mind about him." My brother glared at me like he was envisioning carving out my tongue, so I hastened on. "I have it on good authority that whatever Artemis used to capture him knocked him out and he's still unconscious. They won't start in on the torture until he's awake."

How can you be sure? Lynette signed.

"Torture is less satisfying if there's no screaming," I said simply. Both Mikhail and Vizor nodded, but everyone else just stared at me. "You asked, I answered."

"I still want *my mate* back," Cian ground out, his hard stare daring me to challenge his use of words.

I sighed. "Waltzing in through the front worked with the vampires because we already had an in through the Seelie Queen and we were reasonably sure that they wouldn't attack us straight away. I have no idea how pocket dimensions work. It's entirely possible that Artemis will know the second we set foot in Therrea. We need to figure out how that place works and plan accordingly, otherwise, we could walk directly into a trap."

"I don't care," Cian said stubbornly.

"Will you care if Hades pays the price for your foolishness?" Mikhail asked in that arrogant drawl of his that usually set me on edge. Apparently, it had the same effect on my brother because Cian was looking at my vampire lover like he wanted to tear his head off. "Say we figure out a way into Therrea and go in with guns blazing, so to speak. What if that's exactly what Artemis wants? She could capture us all just to slaughter us in front of Hades. Or maybe she thinks it would be fun to kill him as soon as we enter her realm and drop his corpse in front of us. Personally, if it were my mate at risk, I would be more cautious, but maybe you just don't give a shit."

Cian's jawline flexed as his chest rose and fell rapidly. Before I could stop him, Cian lunged forward, grabbed a dagger from my thigh, and hurled it at Mikhail, who easily slid out of its path. The dagger spun across the room and crashed into my mirror, and I cringed as the glass shattered and fell to the floor.

"Fuck you," Cian spat at Mikhail before he whirled and stalked out of the apartment.

"Damn it." My shoulders sagged.

"Let him cool off a bit," Cerri suggested.

"I don't trust him not to do something idiotic." I headed after Cian. "If he needs some space, he can use the second floor apartment."

Just as I reached the door, Elisa called out in alarm from somewhere downstairs. "Wait! Don't go outside!"

I flung the door open, Mikhail on my heels, and we raced downstairs. I hit the second floor landing just in time to see Magos race through the front door of the building.

"Stay inside!" I grabbed Elisa's shoulder when she moved to follow after him and shoved her back towards the apartment where the rest of the vampire kids were spilling out of the doorway. "Keep everyone inside."

"Vampires!" Elisa said as I tore through the front door. "They're here!"

Her warning came too late. My heart thundered inside my chest as I slid to a stop beside Magos, and for the second time tonight, I found myself staring helplessly at my brother on his knees in front of a bunch of vampires. Not Adrian this time. Someone far worse, at least for us.

"Hello again," Katrina crooned. "Miss me?"

Chapter Ten

"Katrina," Elisa said in a pained voice from behind me. Damn it. I'd told her to stay inside. Damon and Misha's scents floated in the air as well, and I bit back a growl. This situation was already bad, but with Elisa, Damon, and Misha out here too, we were totally fucked.

Jinx? Luna? Please tell me one of you has Finn and Isabeau? I pushed the thought out.

We have Finn, Luna said, *but Isabeau slipped out before Jinx could stop her.*

Godsdamn it all. *Keep the dragons with you. The guards have those fucking spears. The magic might weaken them enough for Katrina's compulsion to work against them.*

Okay. Jinx's voice vibrated with tension. *But if things start to go sideways, I'm coming out.*

I didn't bother arguing with him. Things had already gone sideways. I'd known there would be some type of retaliation from the vampires for the events at the masquerade, but I hadn't thought they'd be this direct about it. Foolish of me not to be better prepared. Katrina's power of compulsion probably wouldn't work on me. She wasn't the first person I'd met with the ability, and thanks to my devourer heritage, I could burn through it. It would work on the vampire kids though, and possibly Mikhail and Magos.

From everything I'd been able to find out about Katrina, she was strong, but so were Mikhail and Magos. Maybe they'd be able to fight through it.

I eyed Katrina and Gabriel. They'd left their masks behind, but they were both still wearing their masquerade attire, and almost a dozen vampire guards fanned out behind them, each armed with those damn spears tinged with devourer magic. Cian was skewered with a spear through his shoulder. It was far from a fatal wound, but it had to hurt like hell, and he was already weakened. The tip had gone straight through his body and had sunk an inch into the concrete. Gabriel held the other end and stood just out of reach of Cian, not that my brother was in any condition to fight back.

It would have been swell if Cian could have gone twenty-four hours without getting himself caught.

"What the fuck are you doing here?" Misha bit out. He took a step forward at the same moment Damon shifted to the side, probably trying to get closer to Isabeau, who I still couldn't see.

"No need to be rude, brother." Gabriel grinned. "It just seemed like we were overdue for a reunion, considering your history with my beautiful fiancée and our blood ties." He cocked his head to the side. "Although, if I understand it correctly, you don't take after our father, do you? I guess blood doesn't always run true."

"Brother? Father?" Misha shook his head. "What are you talking about?"

Gabriel hummed. "Not particularly bright either." His piercing blue eyes slid to Elisa, whose expression was guarded. "But you are. Word is already spreading about the clever vampire girl working for a daemon. You do the family name proud."

Misha and Elisa stepped closer together, and I wished we'd had time to tell them everything we'd learned about their heritage before this confrontation. I'd just have to hope they kept their cool and didn't let Gabriel bait them into doing something foolish.

"Fuck you," Elisa said coldly. "I already found my family. You're not part of it."

"Look at you," Katrina drawled sweetly. "All it took was ripping out my throat to put a little backbone in you."

Elisa paled, her fiery spirit fading. "Don't do this, Katrina," she begged. "Please. Just walk away."

"Sorry, boo." She trailed her fingers down Gabriel's arm and gave Elisa a pitying look. "You chose the wrong side."

"What are you doing here, Katrina?" I asked. Magos had gone completely still at my side. He'd done the same the first time he'd seen Elisa. I suspected Gabriel bore an even stronger resemblance to their father, and Magos was likely reeling over it. Not immediately telling everyone Marius was still alive was really biting me in the ass.

"We came for the boy." She leaned to the side, trying to peer around us. "Oh, hello, Isabeau. You've gotten so big! Have your powers finally come in, or did you turn out to be dud after all?"

"You don't speak to her," Damon said in a harsh tone I'd never once heard from him.

"Aww," Katrina pouted. "Don't be like that, sweetie. That crush you had on me when we were kids was so adorable. Although you'll have to up your gift-giving skills now. Stolen candy and flowers made of paper were cute when we were ten, not so much now."

"She does have rather expensive taste." Gabriel chuckled.

"Walk away," I said flatly. "You're not getting Finn, and I

sure as shit ain't letting you take my brother again. You stay, you die."

Katrina clucked her tongue in amusement and gave Damon an appraising look. "Damon, sweetheart"—then her lips curled into a cruel smile—"do me a favor: *carve your heart out.*"

"No!" Elisa and Misha screamed at the same moment Damon's hand smoothly pulled the dagger from his thigh holster and plunged it into his chest. The two vampires gripped his hands around the dagger, fighting to pull it out and prevent him from doing more damage. As a vampire, Damon could survive a stab to the heart, but he couldn't survive it being torn out.

As much as I wanted to help with Damon, Katrina had to be stopped first. Magos and Mikhail both vanished into mist and reappeared at Katrina's side while I lunged forward and tackled Gabriel away from my brother. He snarled in my face and stabbed me in the side. It was a solid strike to my liver, but I shoved the pain aside as I slammed his head repeatedly into the concrete.

The sharp whistle of metal piercing through the air sounded, and I threw myself back so the spear only grazed my shoulder instead of slamming into my chest. I sprung to my feet as Cian gripped the spear through his shoulder, trying to pull it out. Gabriel was out cold, a spreading pool of blood beneath his head. I hadn't killed the prick, but he was temporarily out of the fight.

Several guards raised spears as others stepped towards me, and in an instant, I had both of my dual swords in my hands as I stepped forward to meet them.

Katrina dodged a strike from Mikhail and twisted impossibly fast, placing one palm on Mikhail's chest and the other on Magos'. "*Stop,*" she commanded. They both froze, and my steps faltered.

No, I screamed internally. Mikhail and Magos were old, centuries older than me, and had solid mental defenses, their wills iron. They had to be able to fight this off. Damon hadn't stood a chance, but they fucking should.

"*Kill Nemain,*" she told Mikhail before twisting to Magos. "*Bring me the fae boy.*"

The two vampires remained frozen in place before turning towards me and the apartment, both of their expressions locked in fury. I begged every god in existence to give them the ability to shrug off Katrina's compulsion.

I could feel the power radiating off Katrina. I didn't know if she had always been this strong or if she'd somehow gotten a power boost. But Pele had said it could take time to fight off compulsions, even for those who were strong-willed and powerful.

I took a step back, my heart pounding rapidly. This was all spinning out of control too quickly. Behind me, Elisa and Misha were still frantically trying to keep Damon from ripping out his own heart. I had no idea where Isabeau was, and two of the most lethal warriors I knew were moving towards me. One with a command to kill me, and the other with a command to take something precious from me.

The only thing in my favor was that they were both fighting the compulsion and neither were using their abilities to turn into mist to their advantage. Compulsion magic had its limits. When you forced people to do something they didn't want to, they could fight against it in other ways.

"Stop me," Magos said as he deliberately stepped towards me.

"Get Finn and run," Mikhail commanded, even as he flung a dagger at my face.

I slid out of its way and raised my swords just in time to block his strike. Twilight eyes full of fury and fear met mine. He pushed against my blades, mist rolling off his sword, and I took another step back. He struck, I blocked, and we danced across the pavement, trading blow after blow.

Mikhail and I sparred almost every day, and we never held back. Neither of us had any illusions that the world wasn't an often cruel and fucked up place. Just like we both knew there might come a moment when we'd be on our own to defend ourselves. So we had this silent agreement to make each other better. Push one another to be lethal enough that if we were ever separated, we could fight our way back to each other.

It never occurred to me that I'd be fighting for my life *against him.*

A bark of pain ripped from my throat as Mikhail's sword grazed the side of my ribs. I leaned back, and the dagger he'd slipped into his other hand passed a hair's breadth from my jugular. He'd learned that move from me.

I really wish he hadn't been paying attention so well.

"Mikhail," I pleaded, "please come back to me, love."

His eyes darkened and tension danced along his jawline, but he still executed a lightning-fast strike at my femoral artery. My sword clashed against his before we danced apart.

Everything faded away. Misha and Elisa's frantic cursing over trying to keep Damon alive. Katrina and Gabriel laughing. The vampire guards taking bets on how long I would last.

The world shrank to just me and Mikhail. I could practically feel his soul fighting this with everything he had, but his movements never slowed and I was bleeding far more than he was. Then I realized I'd lost track of Magos and couldn't stop myself from searching for him.

Mikhail seized my momentary distraction. A sharp hiss expelled violently from my lips as Mikhail's sword sliced into my thigh, and I faltered.

"Move faster," he snarled.

Metal clanged as I blocked a strike to my stomach, and Magos was almost to the door now. Mikhail was cutting me apart because I couldn't bear the idea of hurting him seriously enough to slow him down, and the vampire guards were closing in around us, ready to finish the job at any moment.

Finn was guarded by dragons and grimalkins. They wouldn't let Magos take him, but there was no way someone wouldn't be injured or possibly killed in the encounter.

Think, damn it. Think!

Mikhail sliced a chunk out of my arm, and I whirled, one blade shoving his away while the other cut into the tendon behind his knee. His leg gave out, and he dropped to a knee, pain and relief flowing through his face. I had to figure out how to break them free of this fucking compulsion, and I needed to do it fast.

His eyes slid to the right, a warning flashing in them, and I spun just in time to knock aside the spear being thrust at my back. The guard yanked back the spear for another strike, but my sword found his neck first. Blood sprayed as his head rolled from his shoulders, and I danced to the side as Mikhail struck for my open back. Pain was etched into his face, and there was a tightness to his movements. He was fighting against the compulsion so hard but it still wasn't enough.

Out of the corner of my eye, I saw Magos approach the door as Isabeau blocked his way. Her eyes were wide in panic as she took in the chaos around her, but then a fierce determination settled over her features.

"Isabeau." Katrina's voice rang out in a clear, commanding tone. "*Step aside.*"

"*No.*" The snarl that came out of the young vampire would have put a werewolf to shame. Katrina stumbled back as if she'd been slapped while everyone else froze. I felt it then, a tug on my mind. Mikhail took a step towards me and wavered before Katrina's compulsion drove him forward again.

Magos took another agonizing step towards Isabeau.

That small tug suddenly turned into something fierce and

133

dark. I was dimly aware of my knees hitting the concrete along with everyone else. Then I knew nothing at all.

"WHAT THE FUCK JUST HAPPENED?" Misha looked around the small tavern we found ourselves in. Katrina and the vampires were nowhere to be seen, but I'd watched them hit the ground too, so whatever had happened to us had caught them as well.

"It's gone!" Damon clamped a hand to his chest as relief flooded his face. "The compulsion is gone."

I looked at Mikhail and Magos, and they both nodded their heads warily. Cian rose to his feet somewhat unsteadily, rubbing at his shoulder where the spear had been a moment ago as his eyes scanned the room for the next threat. The vampire kids were relieved, but the rest of us knew better. We weren't safe yet. Far from it.

"Isabeau?" I knelt in front of the small girl who had wrapped us all in her magic. She was still on her knees, hands folded across her lap. Her usually bright, brown eyes were now black with jagged, white lines running through them like lightning strikes.

Okay… That was a new one.

I gently touched her shoulder, but she gave no reaction, just continued staring forward with her freaky, unseeing eyes. A frustrated breath shoved past my lips, and I rose again to take in our surroundings. The tavern was mostly empty, except for a few patrons who took up some tables or sat at the bar, but none of them seemed to be aware of our existence.

"Illusion?" Mikhail guessed. "We know she trapped Sigrun's furball in one before. Could she have dragged us all into one?"

"I think so," I murmured. Something about this tavern was bothering me though. My gaze slid to the shelves behind the bar, which were filled mostly with brandy and wine. A disheveled man at the end of the bar raised his glass and called for another, a thick French accent coating his words.

"Was that French?" Elisa's brows furrowed together. "Why are we in an old French tavern? Everyone is dressed like we're at a ren faire."

Both Mikhail and Magos looked at me, and I swallowed. "This is where I met him."

"Who?" Damon asked, but I was already focused on the man wearing a clean, dark grey cloak at a table in the back corner. He was facing away from us, but I would have known who he was even without the strand of golden blond hair curling out from his hood.

"*Sebastian*," Cian spat.

Sometimes I would have dreams where it felt like I was falling. I would wake with a start and an odd, panicked feeling, like my body was still locked in a state of alarm and didn't yet realize that the dream hadn't been real.

That was exactly how I currently felt. Only, when I woke from those dreams, that feeling went away after a couple of seconds. Now, I was stuck in a perpetual state of dread and never-ending terror.

A loud creak announced the tavern door opening. I didn't bother looking, because I knew who had just strode in. *Me.*

Elisa sucked in a surprised gasp as a younger version of me strode across the well-worn floor, straight to the hooded figure at the table. Technically, I looked the same as I did now. Shifters settled fully into their magic sometime in their early to mid-twenties. Not only did we get a massive power boost, but our aging halted.

I watched myself stalk across the tavern. It was 1801, and I'd been 180 years old. My parents had been long since dead, and I'd been hunting and bathing in the blood of witches and warlocks for the better part of a century. The human realm

135

had been in upheaval with wars and revolutions breaking out everywhere. Violence had been in the air no matter where you'd gone, and streets had run red with blood.

I'd fucking loved it.

Violence would always be a part of who I was. I was a predator before I was anything else, but as I caught a glimpse of my feral eyes and the edged smile cutting across my face, I had to admit that I'd been more than a little unhinged back then.

"You have a death wish, warlock?" I half snarled from where I'd stopped a few steps behind Sebastian. A few drunk locals rose from the table and gave us some space. "Usually your kind tries to hide from me, not leave me notes to meet them at a shithole like this."

A familiar, charming laugh rang through the air as Sebastian rose and turned to face the younger me. He gave a shallow bow, a self-deprecating smile on his face.

I no longer felt like I was falling. Instead, it was like someone had sucker punched me and all the air had rushed out of my lungs. I didn't want to see this. Hear Sebastian's lies as he told me how much he hated his own kind and admired my work. Watch myself fall for it all and willingly go down a path that would lead to unimaginable heartache.

"Fuck this." I spun on my heel and headed towards the door. Elisa and the vamp kids were still staring at the unfolding events, but Cian and Mikhail got them moving while Magos scooped up Isabeau. There had to be some way to break us out of this, because I had no interest in going down my fucked-up memory lane. Not to mention, I was assuming this was all happening in our minds, which meant our bodies were just lying out in the open.

Hopefully Eddie and the others were picking us up off the concrete and dragging us behind the wards of the apartment building, and maybe parting a few vampires from their heads while they were at it.

I had no idea how this illusion worked or how much we could interact with it, considering nobody could see us, but when my hand slammed against the wooden door, it swung open. The scent of burning flesh immediately assaulted me, and my eyes watered as thick smoke curled around us.

Someone coughed as the others followed me out, and we found ourselves amidst the remains of a small village. A pained sound slipped from my lips and I didn't realize I was stepping back until I crashed into Mikhail's chest and he spun me around to face him.

"What is it?" His eyes searched my face. "What is this place?"

"It's the village our parents were murdered in." I looked to Cian, who was staring down at a burned-up corpse that had its arm wrapped around another in some failed attempt to protect them, or maybe just offer them comfort in their final moments. "After Cian and I returned."

"You two… " Elisa bit her lip as she surveyed the destruction. The absolute annihilation. "You two did all this?"

We nodded, a haunted look darkening Cian's silver eyes. He'd regretted our actions long before I did. My feelings about what we'd done were more complex. We'd been seventeen years old, and these people had forced us to watch our parents be brutally murdered.

They had cheered while our mother and father had burned.

Centuries later, I still had nightmares about how Macha and Nevin had died and the look of terror on Cian's face as a blade had been held to his throat to force his compliance. An identical blade had been at my throat. The townsfolk had forced us to watch everything, then they ran us out of town only to change their minds and send witch hunters on our trail. Everyone in this place had wanted us dead.

"Were there any survivors?" Damon asked.

It would have been so easy to lie to them. Isabeau's magic had brought us to the aftermath. I could have told them we'd allowed the villagers to flee and only punished the ones who had played a direct role in the death of our parents. The vamp brats looked up to me. I had saved them from the Council and continued to shield them all these years. They knew I had a dark history, but it was one thing to be told something and quite another to have all your senses assaulted with hundreds of burned corpses.

I was the bad guy in a lot of people's stories. They had a right to know that.

"Most of the children were in that building." I pointed to the only structure that remained unburned. "It was a school of sorts, although they mostly used it to keep the kids out of the way during the day."

"You spared the kids," Misha said with obvious relief.

Before I could point out the flaws in his assumption, Cian cut in. "They listened to the screams of their dying parents, older siblings, and everyone else they knew for hours." He tore his gaze away from the building where countless children were likely huddled together inside. "We may not have killed them that day, but make no mistake: we ended their lives all the same."

"Children are resilient," Magos hedged.

"Traders stopped by the town once a week, so they would have found the children." I swallowed past the lump in my throat towards the building that represented the only part of this I truly regretted. "But we seriously fucked them up for the rest of their lives, and it wasn't exactly easy to survive as a human orphan during those times."

"Wasn't easy as a shifter orphan either," Cian said bitterly.

Everyone fell silent as we listened to the fire crackling around us. I could feel the heat from the flames, and when I ran my hand through them, my skin blistered. Whatever magic Isabeau had running through her veins made her one of the most powerful illusionists I'd ever come across, and her true power hadn't even been fully awakened yet. What would she be capable of when her magic settled in a decade or two?

"Why this memory though?" Mikhail looked at Isabeau who was still completely out of it in Magos' arms. She looked so pale and tiny. Her magic had to be actively fueling this illusion, plus the ones Katrina and the other vampires were no doubt trapped in.

"Traumatic memories are often the easiest ones to pull." Damon furrowed his brows. "If I try to search through someone's mind, those are the memories that often come to me first, even if it's not what I'm looking for. Maybe Isabeau's magic works the same way?"

"There's got to be some way to get out of this." Elisa chewed on her bottom lip, her eyes taking on that unfocused glaze they did whenever she was quickly coming up with and dismissing solutions.

"Illusion magic is tricky," I said. "There are ways to see through it or work around it in the real world, but either we're trapped in Isabeau's mind, or she's linked all our minds together. I don't think we're going anywhere until we figure out how to help her wake up."

The building closest to us creaked, and the flames leapt higher as the walls collapsed and the roof tumbled down with a crash. Isabeau jerked in Magos' arms, and he carefully held her as she thrashed.

The smoke around us grew thicker, making my eyes water and scorching my throat and lungs. I lost sight of everyone but heard them coughing around me as they struggled to breathe.

Just as I was starting to panic about whether I could pass out in an illusion and what that would mean, the smoke dissipated.

Tears streamed down my cheeks, and I clamped my hands over my eyes as I squeezed them shut to try to will away the burning. After a few moments, I dropped my hands and blinked several times to get the last of the tears out.

Another village surrounded us now, this one not on fire or reeking of corpses, thankfully. A few dozen log cabins that looked like they'd been hastily built sat in the center of a wide clearing, and tall pine trees stretched above us, covered in snow. I was fairly certain this memory had been made in the human realm based on the type of trees and buildings, but I didn't see any other helpful markings.

It was strange… There were no shops or taverns. No roads leading in or out of the village. Just a bunch of log cabins built close to each other.

"I don't recognize this place." I pursed my lips as I continued to rack my brain. If Damon's theory was correct and traumatic memories were easier to pull from, then something bad must have happened here. But the more I looked around, the more sure I was that this wasn't my memory.

Elisa and Damon took a step forward towards the nearest cabin.

"Don't," Mikhail said in a deadly soft voice.

Both vampires halted in their tracks as Misha sent him a questioning look, but Mikhail didn't look at anyone, all his attention on the patch of snow in front of his feet. My eyes drifted to the ground, and I saw what I had missed when I'd first scrutinized our surroundings. Paw prints.

This was a werewolf village.

Now the setup and isolation made sense. We were probably deep in a forest somewhere, far from humans and civilization. They had no need of merchants or taverns because they could hunt for food in the surrounding woods and they would only bring in other supplies every few months as necessary. The whole point of places like this was to stay hidden from the vampires… and especially from the assassin of the Vampire Council who had dedicated his life to eradicating them.

"What did you do?" Misha asked. There was an edge to his voice that was usually only present when he was talking about the Council. A potent mixture of rage, disgust, and fear. I saw the same sentiment echoed on Damon's face. Elisa was doing a better job of hiding her feelings, but there was a tightness to her features, and I didn't miss her taking a small step away from Mikhail.

Magos remained standing by his nephew's side, Isabeau still lying in his arms. She was no longer thrashing, but her breathing wasn't as deep and steady as it was before. I hoped to hell she was trying to wake up, because between Mikhail and me, there was no shortage of dark and twisted memories to use as fuel for these illusions.

"What did you do?" Misha repeated. His voice was louder this time, and there was no mistaking the accusation in his question. A brief flicker of movement in the thick trees of the forest drew my attention.

"You're about to find out." Mikhail tensed.

On silent paws, a large werewolf with a light grey coat prowled into the clearing. I moved to stand by Mikhail's side, my hand slipping into his. He briefly looked away from the wolf, and I saw the pain in his eyes before the blank mask he wore like armor slammed back down onto his face. My fingers tightened around his.

The wolf halted outside a cabin, a low whine tumbling out of them. Then they took a step forward, stopped, and backed up two steps as another pained sound slipped from them. Misha swore and whirled away, stomping towards another cabin and flinging the door open. Damon and Elisa looked at each other before following him.

Magos and I remained in the clearing, standing on opposite sides of Mikhail, whose gaze was on the werewolf who had begun to shift back to human. The vampire kids walked slowly out of the cabin just as the woman finished her shift and rose on shaky legs. Sandy blonde hair tumbled around her lean and muscular frame. She shivered, but I was pretty sure that had less to do with the cold and more to do with whatever she sensed waited for her in that dark cabin.

"You killed them all," Damon said in a daze as the three of them moved to stand in front of us. "While they slept."

"I was an assassin." Mikhail's voice was cold and flat. "Did you think I was honorable?"

The woman walked on trembling legs and pushed the cabin door open with her fingertips, then a wolfish howl tore out of her human throat as she crashed to her knees in the doorway.

Mist swirled behind her, snapping into place and revealing a lean figure wrapped in matte black leather. The mourning werewolf whirled, still in a crouch, and snarled. "My brother! He wasn't even there that day, you bastard!"

She launched herself at the newcomer, but he merely vanished again into mist before reappearing behind her. I slid a glance at Mikhail to gauge how he was reacting to seeing this younger version of himself, but his emotions were locked down tight.

"None of you were particularly concerned with killing brothers or sisters at Speranța Nouă."

Even from where we stood, I could feel the cold fury radiating off this younger Mikhail. His dark red, cloth mask covered the lower part of his face, leaving only his eyes exposed.

I'd often teased Mikhail about how he currently looked like

a pretty fae prince, but this version of him looked like a walking nightmare. Despite knowing some of Mikhail's history, it'd never truly occurred to me before just how similar we were. We'd both traveled down a very dark path after losing everything, but while my fury had burned hot and volatile, Mikhail's had been cold and focused.

"That was a mistake," she started. "Everyone knew you and your uncle were the most powerful of the vampires. We went to that city to kill you, but you weren't there, and they refused to tell us your whereabouts. I didn't… We didn't mean to let things get so out of hand."

"Slaughtering thousands of innocent people is an odd way to describe something 'getting out of hand.'" Assassin Mikhail cocked his head to the side. "Did you know that over a quarter of the people living in that city were children? Did you hesitate before you feasted on their flesh?"

She flinched. "This beast inside us… it's hard to control, but we're getting better."

"I'm sure the dead will be happy to hear that."

"Please." She dropped to her knees and bowed her head. "Both of our people have done terrible things, but it's not too late to stop this. We came to this forest to get away from the war and to atone for what we've done. You can kill me, but let the others go."

Shit. I swallowed. She didn't know that it wasn't just her brother who was dead. There was nothing but death left in every one of these cabins.

Isabeau flinched in Magos' arms, her eyelids fluttering. Hopefully that meant she was close to waking up, because I was really fucking ready to be done with this.

The Mikhail standing before the prone werewolf let out a low laugh that sent a chill up my spine. "Don't worry. I've already released the other werewolves from this life."

"No." A choked sob broke from the woman. Mikhail just

laughed again, gripped her by the neck, jerked her up, and buried his fangs into her throat.

Isabeau screamed.

Chapter Eleven

THE VAMPIRE KIDS stood around Magos, who was still clutching Isabeau in his arms, and watched as silent witnesses to the bloody havoc that both Mikhail and I had inflicted on those we'd deemed our enemies.

Mikhail silently stalking through a dark forest and slitting the throat of a werewolf. Me hunting a coven of witches and killing every single one of them. Him weaving through a crowded street of what looked like Venice and stabbing a young man through the heart as people screamed, then vanishing into mist like a devil. An older woman on her knees, pleading for her life before I shifted to my feline form and tore her to pieces.

There had been more to these memories than what we were seeing. The coven I'd been tracking had been using dark magic that involved child sacrifice to extend their lives. It had made them easier to find, because I was able to follow the trail of grieving parents. The witch who had been begging for her life had been selling love potions that took away the free will of anyone who drank them.

It hadn't been the sole reason I'd hunted those particular

witches down. I was far from the savior of humanity. They'd also been involved in instigating violence against other nonhumans, and that was what had put them on my radar. Their sins had simply made them easier for me to track.

Werewolves had committed plenty of atrocities against the vampires and sometimes other nonhumans as well. Maybe Mikhail's reasons for killing them had been similar to my reasons for killing the witches. Or maybe he'd simply been ordered to and hadn't questioned it.

I'd never asked Mikhail about the specifics of his past. He'd seemed to want to leave it behind, and I'd respected that. But between Justina's snide comments at the masquerade and seeing him in action as the Council assassin, I was regretting not asking him about it a little bit more. Not because I was angry about it, more that it felt like I knew so little about him while he knew so much about me. I couldn't help but feel hurt that he didn't trust me enough to share the burden of his past.

There wasn't any time for me to give more context to the memories, because Isabeau's magic shifted us violently from one to the next, and it almost felt like the illusions themselves were sped up. My jaw clenched tightly as it felt like someone was wrapping a fist around my soul and viciously ripping it out of my chest.

"Fucking hell." I leaned over, panting with my hands braced on my slightly bent knees as one of the vampire kids hurled their guts up behind me. Once I was reasonably sure I wouldn't do the same, I stumbled over to where Magos was crouching in front of a now awake Isabeau.

Well, maybe not exactly awake. She was standing and her eyes were open and back to their normal color, but she wasn't exactly there with us. Normally, the young vampire girl was a force of nature. She breathed life into any room she was in and was impossible to ignore, but now, she just stood there, showing no reaction to anything Magos was saying as she blankly stared straight ahead.

Still... progress.

"Isabeau?" I knelt beside Magos, who had his hands out, ready to catch her if she fell again. "While I appreciate you breaking Katrina's compulsion, maybe you can snap us out of this fun jaunt down memory lane?"

No reaction. I sighed, already dreading what fun memory she'd pull from our minds next, and glanced over to where Mikhail was standing near Elisa and the others. Damon and Misha were looking at him with the same wariness they'd had when they'd first joined us and been terrified of the infamous assassin of the Vampire Council. Interestingly enough, Elisa was standing next to him. Not exactly relaxed, but more on guard against whatever this next illusion would bring.

"Alright," I said slowly. "Whose fun memory is this?"

"Not mine." Mikhail frowned as he looked around. We were standing at the edge of a tree line, a sparse forest spreading before us. Something about it seemed familiar. I inhaled deeply, and it smelled of my childhood. Of my first home.

"France," I murmured. "We're back in France, close to where I grew up. This must be one of my memories."

"It's both of ours actually," Magos said. He'd let the vampire kids take over watching Isabeau and had moved further from the forest. I followed his gaze and went still. *Oh.*

"Yours?" Misha looked to Magos. "What death awaits us in this place?"

I ignored him and looked over my shoulder to where Isabeau stood between Elisa and Damon, each of them holding her hands. She was still staring in that eerie, unblinking way of hers, but the corners of her mouth were pinched and her brows slightly furrowed.

"I think she's trying to break us out." I pursed my lips as I

147

tried to puzzle out what was going through Isabeau's head. "This is still a dark memory, but it's not the same as the others."

"What is it?" Mikhail moved to my side.

"It's the day Magos and I met."

His eyes snapped to mine before cutting over to his uncle, who was focused on the lone figure sitting on a boulder up ahead, facing a cliff.

"Let's see how this plays out. Maybe we can figure out how to help Isabeau end this." Magos strode forward, and the rest of us followed him. The trees fell away, leaving a sparsely covered landscape that ended abruptly in a steep drop-off. The sun was starting to peek out over the horizon, the early rays bathing the gorge below in its warm light.

We halted near the large, flat boulder, fanning out so we could all look at this version of Magos. Physically, he was almost the same, although his hair had been longer back then, the thick braids almost reaching his waist. He'd only decided to grow it out again recently, and currently, his braids barely made it past his shoulders.

Mikhail's expression was etched in pain as he took in the absolute devastation and hopelessness lining every inch of his uncle's face. Our Magos looked at his previous self with sadness, but his eyes drifted to the forest line once again.

"I don't understand." Elisa turned away from the illusion as she gave Magos a questioning look. "You only got the ability to be in the sun without it hurting you last year. What were you doing?"

"This was not long after my people were slaughtered." His voice faltered slightly, but his gaze never wavered from the forest. "I'd lost everyone. My sister." Mikhail flinched at the mention of his mother. "My wife, Hasina. And in many ways, I'd lost Mikhail too."

Mikhail said nothing. While I knew he might have some

regrets about his part in the war against the werewolves, it was moments like this that truly haunted him. He hadn't been there that day because he had already abandoned Magos to seek his revenge.

Elisa slipped her hand free from Isabeau's, Misha immediately moving in to take her place, and edged closer to the cliff to peer down into the gorge beneath.

"You don't mean... " She stepped back, shaking her head. "I had no idea."

Magos gave her a gentle smile. "It was a long time ago."

"You asked me once what I said to your uncle to bring him back from the brink." My fingertips brushed Mikhail's chin, and I gently turned his attention away from the Magos illusion to the trees, close to where we'd originally landed in this memory. "You're about to find out."

A flock of sparrows burst into the sky as a scrawny kid on the cusp of being a teenager burst out of the woods, running at full speed, ashen blonde hair streaming behind her. Suddenly, she spun around and screamed, "FUCK YOU, CIAN! I'M GONNA BEAT THE SHIT OUT OF YOU LATER!"

Cian huffed a laugh next to me. "Some things never change."

"Honestly don't even remember what you did that day to piss me off so much." I let out an amused huff of my own.

Teenager me stalked across the grassy field towards the boulder. If I remembered right, this was not long after my thirteenth birthday, and between my growing magic and hormones, I had been a walking nightmare.

Illusion Magos remained sitting on the boulder but twisted his head to watch the young shifter approach, grimacing when the younger version of me gave him an appraising look.

"What are you doing?" she asked. Several bruises marked her arms, and it looked like Cian had managed to give her a shiner. Our shifter healing had been a little slower when we'd

149

been young. She looked over her shoulder at the rising sun and then back at Magos. "You smell like a vampire. Ain't you lot sensitive to the sun and shit?"

Mikhail slid a glance at me. "Even back then, you had a mouth on you."

"Drove my father nuts," I said softly. "He didn't like us cursing."

"Especially around his flowers," Cian added. "Said it made them feel bad."

"I was looking for a quiet place to ponder my future," illusion Magos said slowly. "The humans aren't safe to be around."

"Because you're a vampire and they don't like being snacked on?"

"I'm sure they don't, but it's not that. They can't tell I'm a vampire by looking at me," he replied.

"Then why?"

My heart hurt as I watched this past version of Magos shift uncomfortably. He'd made up his mind when he'd come up here but had no idea what to do about a persistent young shifter girl and her pushy questions. Even when his soul was nothing more than broken pieces dragging behind him, Magos was kind.

"The humans think I am one of them, and amongst their kind, those who look like me"—he gestured towards his face with its dark, rich brown skin—"are treated cruelly. They would try to harm me, and I would kill them. I'm tired of killing."

Younger me thought about this for a moment before jerking her head in a sharp nod. "Hiding bodies can be difficult, and there are a lot of stupid humans you'd have to kill."

"I mean, she's not wrong." Elisa shrugged.

"That wasn't what I meant," illusion Magos said carefully.

"But I suppose it's true enough. You should run along. I'll be alright."

My chest tightened at the finality in his words, even though I knew he would be fine.

Teenage me chewed on her bottom lip, shifting her eyes back and forth between the sun and the vampire. Twigs and bits of dried grass were stuck in my hair that was hanging in tangles around my face. Must have been a pretty good brawl between me and Cian. She opened her mouth slightly and inhaled, green eyes widening as the small bit of magic that allowed me to read souls revealed Magos' dark thoughts.

It occurred to me then that, while it was the least powerful of my magic, paling in comparison to my ability to open gateways and devour the magic of others, in many ways, it had been the most important magic in my life. It had allowed me to get a glimpse into the souls of others and make decisions that I otherwise may not have made.

"My brother is a tattletale and is definitely running home to try to get me in trouble, which means I need to lie low for the day." The Magos on the boulder shifted as more of the sun rose over the horizon and started to burn his skin. Teenage me kept talking like she was oblivious, even as she moved to stand in front of him as if she could block him from the light. "It's actually kind of good luck that you're here, which is funny, because Jinx usually gives me bad luck."

"Jinx?" illusion Magos asked roughly. Vampires didn't immediately burst into flames in the sun, it was more of a constant, painful burn. As a child, I'd never witnessed this, but now I knew you could stake a vampire out in the sun and it would take them a few days to die—their skin burning, healing, then burning again until their magic wore out and they couldn't heal anymore. Then they would burn until they were nothing but ashes.

"He's coming now. Cian, my brother, stepped on his tail, so

Jinx is cursing him with bad luck for a week. Have you ever met a grimalkin? I've only met the one, and he's super grouchy. But he's my best friend, so I overlook it."

"Gods, I really talked a lot." I shot the teenage version of me an annoyed look. "Kind of surprised you didn't tell me to fuck off, Magos."

He looked at me as the illusion of our younger selves continued to converse. Well, it was mostly me doing the talking while he looked at me in bewilderment. "I can honestly say that I had no idea what to do with you back then, and I have no idea what to do with you now."

Both Cian and Mikhail snorted. The vampire kids were still watching the memory unfold with rapt attention, and Isabeau showed no signs of waking up further. We likely only had a few minutes before a new memory was thrust upon us. The last two places she'd taken us had been dark. This wasn't exactly a happy memory, but while it had started out bleak, it didn't end that way.

There had to be a reason she'd chosen this one, we just needed to figure it out.

A furry, black blur shot out of the woods, and seconds later, teenage me let out an oomph as Jinx slammed into her chest in his smaller, glamoured form. Her eyes widened to an almost comical degree as Jinx telepathically spoke in her head.

"We need to get out of here," she told Magos quickly. "Jinx gave my brother bad luck, which caused him to walk through a patch of stinging nettle, which he's super sensitive to. He's already broken out in a rash, and Momma is gonna blame me for it."

"You should go then," he agreed. "As I said before, I'll be fine." The sun was almost completely over the horizon, and several blisters were already forming on his skin, but the younger Magos dutifully ignored this, even as his jawline tightened in what had to be pain.

Jinx's golden eyes turned to the vampire, assessing the threat. I didn't remember precisely what was said, but I knew he was arguing with me in my head about what to do. He didn't want to leave Magos to die, but he also didn't want me to reveal my magic.

Finally, after a moment, teenage me stamped my foot down. "It'll be fine. We can trust him."

"You really trusted him that easily?" Mikhail asked me.

"I was different back then," I said. "Nothing truly bad had happened to me. Sure, my magic was scary, but I had parents who loved me and a brother who annoyed the fuck out of me but was still my partner in crime. The small bit of magic that allowed me to read souls told me I wasn't in any danger. That was enough for me."

"What would have happened if you'd met him later?" Elisa's sharp blue eyes fell on me. "After everything that happened with your parents? After Sebastian… and Myrna?"

I thought about it before answering. My first inclination was to say I would have left Magos there to die, but then I thought about Niall. Everyone had met Niall at this point since he was basically attached to Sigrun's hip now, but they didn't know that Niall had been in a very similar state of mind to Magos when we'd first met. My soul reading magic had spoken to me then, and I'd listened, even though Niall had been trying to kill me.

"Despite everything, I still listen to my magic when it speaks to me. It doesn't happen very often… but it's never steered me wrong before." Misha and Damon shot me skeptical looks, which stung, but I kept the pain off my face. Elisa just nodded, accepting my answer.

The air next to the boulder shimmered, and a gateway snapped open, shrank down, then blew open again. My control had been so shaky at first, sometimes I'd open gateways without meaning to. It was one of the many reasons my parents had rarely allowed me into the nearby village.

"What… " Illusion Magos slid off the boulder and peered through the gateway into the other world beyond.

"I can travel to other realms," teenage me said simply, as if this was no big deal. "I've been wanting to explore this one for a while, but it has some monsters roaming around that I think are too big for me to tackle on my own."

"Monsters?" He shook his head, still staring at the gateway in disbelief.

Jinx trotted through the gateway, and the younger me followed before glancing over her shoulder. "It's always night-time in this realm. I don't know why." With a slightly quivering bottom lip, she gave Magos an imploring look. "If you don't come with me, I might get hurt."

"You were such a manipulative little shit," Cian murmured.

"Learned from the best, bro."

He rolled his eyes but didn't disagree. My brother was *excellent* at guilt trips.

Magos' eyes glistened as he watched his younger self look at the rising sun one last time before slipping through the gateway and following the shifter girl and her grumpy grimalkin into a dark and alien world. The gateway slowly closed, leaving us alone in the illusion.

I waited to feel a tug on my mind, signaling that Isabeau was going to shift us again, but nothing happened. Frowning, I looked at the girl and noticed she was tapping her index finger rhythmically against her side. Everyone else followed my stare and caught on to the movement.

"Maybe she'll snap out of it this time?" Damon asked hopefully.

Her lips started to move, but I couldn't make out what she was saying. "Anyone know what she's trying to say?"

"'The dark is pulling.'" Magos stared at Isabeau with furrowed brows. "'Need light. Give. Path. Out.'"

"Light," I murmured, and then I snapped my fingers. "If Damon is right, our dark and twisted memories are easier for her to use. Maybe she's not strong enough yet to control these illusions, so she needs help. This memory started out bleak but ended in hope. This is a path out."

Magos moved to kneel in front of the girl and gently raised her hands to rest on either side of his face. "Follow this memory, Isabeau. Go to where I went after this. After I met Nemain."

We all held our breath as Isabeau continued to stare without seeing. Then she blinked. Another blink. The chaotic light that always filled her brown eyes came back as her gaze latched onto Magos' copper ones and a smile spread across her face.

"One more," she said.

I let out a sigh of relief as her magic swirled around us and the scene faded away in a bright light before fading in once more. This time, we stood in front of what was now a familiar dojo nestled in the Cardamom Mountains of Thailand. We were frequent visitors these days; Pele had even set up a daemon-constructed gateway so Bryn and the others could travel there regularly without having to rely on me to open a gateway for them.

The dojo was more than just a place to train. It was a sanctuary.

A couple stood in front of the simple but elegant structure with its dark wood frame, white walls, and sloping roof. The man looked as ageless then as he did now, somewhere between thirty and fifty, enough fine lines around his eyes to show that he'd seen at least a few decades come and go. His long, black hair was pulled back in a topknot, and the loose-fitting clothes downplayed his strong build.

The woman his arm was wrapped around was stunning. No lines wrinkled her face, giving her the appearance of being in her early twenties, but I knew she was at least several centuries old. She'd inherited her beauty and long life from her mother, who was a kinnara, but she had thankfully also taken after her father, who was a human, so her body appeared completely human instead of part-bird like most kinnaras'. Her brown skin was several shades darker than the man's with a golden undertone, and her eyes were a captivating mix of green, blue, and yellow. They were her only feature that truly marked her as *other*.

Gensai and Intira.

I might have saved Magos that day, but these two had given him a new life.

Like his wife, Gensai had been blessed with a long life, even though he was completely human. I didn't know the full story, but he'd been in a hurry to get out of Japan and had come across an injured kitsune. Instead of leaving the nine-tailed fox behind, he'd scooped it up and nursed it back to health as he hid from his enemies. The kitsune had blessed him and his bloodline with exceptionally long lives.

They patiently watched as a large man made his way up the winding, stone steps that led to their hidden paradise. When he stopped a respectful distance away and bowed his head, some of the tension in Gensai's posture eased.

"Can we help you?" Intira asked politely, as if they received visitors every day at their home hundreds of miles away from the nearest human village.

The hood slid from the traveler's head, revealing Magos sporting a freshly shaved head.

"I have been wandering for some time, trying to find my way," he said. "Recently, I heard about a couple who have provided assistance to those in need without ever asking for anything in return. Those you have helped are fiercely protective of you both, so it has taken me some time to find you."

"And now that you have found us?" Gensai asked.

Magos gracefully knelt on the ground. "I am... lost. And I ask for sanctuary to help me find my way."

"You are a warrior." A statement, not a question.

"I was."

Gensai gave Magos a small, close-lipped smile. "You are."

"Come." Intira stepped forward and extended her hand. Magos took it and rose. "Join us for dinner. Perhaps we can help each other."

The three of them walked down the path that wrapped around the dojo to the cottage they'd built behind it. They still called it a cottage today, despite having expanded it into three stories and building an entire separate apartment on the back. The extra space was required for their kids and grandkids.

Magos no longer lived with them, but he was still a regular visitor. We all were now. Gensai and Intira's doors were always open to those in need.

"Happy." Isabeau smiled, exhaustion clearly visible on her face. "You found your happiness."

"I did," Magos said gently. "Was this memory enough? Can you wake us all up now?"

In response, Isabeau just closed her eyes. I jolted at the sensation of falling and then scrambled to my feet, my mind still trying to catch up to my body as I stumbled over something. Mikhail let out a sharp exhale when I crashed down onto him, and around us, everyone else was sitting up with a groan.

"Thank fuck," I breathed out.

We were on the sparring mat in my apartment, and Kaysea was staring at us all wide-eyed. "What the hell was that?"

Chapter Twelve

"Isabeau," I rasped.

Mikhail got to his feet, his usually graceful movements absent as pain lined his face. Wordlessly, he extended a hand to me and helped me up, tugging me against his side and slinging his arm over my shoulders as if he needed the contact.

I knew exactly how he felt. A few months ago, a traveling fair had rolled through Seattle. Elisa and the vamp brats had taken turns begging me, Mikhail, and Magos to bring them, and we'd finally relented. It'd been fun. Magos had won all the carnival prizes and given them to Finn and Isabeau while I'd made Mikhail try every single type of fried food monstrosity. He claimed that he'd hated all of them and that I'd been inflicting some new form of torture on him, but I had seen him sneak off to get a second deep-fried Oreo.

Towards the end of the night, the kids had dragged us all onto a ride that'd looked like a spaceship. We'd leaned against walls that had been made of panels that could move up and down. I hadn't understood why the panels were there until the ride had started and the ship started to spin. Fast. Isabeau had squealed with delight as the panel had raised her up and down. Even Finn had cracked a smile.

When the ride was over, I'd bolted out of it and knelt on the ground, trying very hard not to heave up the three bags of cotton candy I'd eaten.

This was exactly like that. Only, it was my soul that had been thrown into that godsforsaken spaceship and spun around before being jammed back into my body.

"Isabeau what?" Kaysea frowned at the little girl who was still asleep on the mat. "Is she okay?"

Cian swooped down to pick up Isabeau. "She's okay, just asleep." He groaned as he straightened, even though the girl weighed practically nothing, and settled her on the couch before collapsing into a boneless heap in one of the chairs.

I looked longingly at the soft cushions, but the ten feet between me and them felt like too far of a distance to conquer right now.

"Katrina was here." I leaned further into Mikhail, letting his warmth seep into me. It helped a little. "She has compulsion magic and is strong as fuck. Damon was doing his best to carve out his own heart, Mikhail was trying to carve out mine, and Magos was going after Finn. Isabeau saved us by knocking everyone out and trapping us with her magic. She crafted an illusion based on our memories—the fucked up ones, not ones featuring a fun frolic through flowery meadows. Isabeau is powerful but clearly doesn't have full control yet, it took us a while to find a way out."

Zareen walked out from the hallway, a stack of clean towels and clothes in her hands. Her solid black eyes were tight with concern as she handed the supplies to Kaysea and looked over all of us before going to Damon. His T-shirt was in shreds and soaked with blood, but I didn't think he was still bleeding.

An hour ago, I would have been over there checking on

him too, but after what he'd seen in our memories, I could feel the tension between us. Both he and Misha were looking at Mikhail and me differently now, and I was trying very hard not to think about how much that hurt.

I'd seen that same look, revulsion mixed with fear, on Andrei's face and countless others' before him. I was a hard person to be friends with, let alone love. Somewhere along the way of picking up the vamp kids and learning about Badb and Kalen, I'd forgotten that.

"It's mostly healed," Zareen murmured as she looked at the angry, pink skin on Damon's chest. "Go get cleaned up and I'll finish healing it."

He nodded and left for the downstairs apartment. Misha looked at Isabeau, who was peacefully asleep on the couch, and then around the room, his gaze skipping over me and Mikhail before landing on Elisa.

"Go," she told him. "I'll watch over her."

In a blink, he was gone. I assumed to clean up in one of the other apartments. A shower sounded so nice. So did a nap. Every part of me hurt, and my brain felt like mush, but first I needed to figure out what had happened while we'd all been unconscious and if Isabeau was okay.

And the dragons.

I frowned at where Eddie and Vizor were passed out on the mat. Their chests were rising and falling in easy breaths, and their relaxed expressions implied they were in a pleasant slumber and not the parade of nightmares we'd been trapped in. It was a little odd to see Vizor looking almost... happy.

Every once in a while, he'd drop his harsh, sardonic mask when he looked at Lynette, and it'd be so clear just how in love with her he was. The fact that we'd all seen it at least once helped improve his survival rate, because Vizor was an absolute dick but we all adored Lynette and didn't want to cause her any emotional distress. So Vizor got to keep his head, even when he pissed us off.

"What happened to them?" I nudged Eddie with the tip of my boot. "Did Isabeau's magic knock them out with us?"

I glanced at Cerri and Lynette, who were both sitting cross-legged on the floor between the two dragons, their shoulders leaning against each other. My fingers flew through the words as I repeated my questions for Lynette, but it was Cerri who answered, adjusting her position so she could sign as she spoke.

"When all of you collapsed outside, we ran out and dragged your bodies in. A few of the vampire guards were unaffected—maybe Isabeau couldn't ensnare everyone and had to prioritize the major threats? They were busy grabbing Katrina and Gabriel." Cerri stroked Eddie's hair and gave me a wry smile before continuing. "The two of them thought they could undo whatever Isabeau had done to knock all of you out, so they went traipsing around in her mind."

My eyebrows shot up. "How'd that work out?"

I told them not to do it, Lynette signed from where she was sitting cross-legged next to Vizor. *Eddie argued that he didn't need Vizor's help. My brilliant and not at all arrogant lover*—I snorted as she added some dramatic flourishes to arrogant—*said Eddie was too much of an amateur to do anything useful.*

"So they both slipped into Isabeau's mind." Cerri and Lynette shared an exasperated look. "And they both got their asses thrown out ten seconds later. Eddie managed to telepathically send me an 'oww' before passing the fuck out. Vizor was knocked out immediately."

A little bit of pride slipped onto Cerri's face as she smiled down at Eddie.

Really? Lynette rolled her eyes. *Do not tell Vizor that. I will never hear the end of it if he finds out Eddie didn't pass out right away like him.*

161

"They're okay though, right?" My eyes scanned the dragons again, trying to look for any hints of wrongness. "Just sleeping it off?"

"Yes," Cerri said. "Jinx checked on them after it all went down, swearing at them for being fools and even attempting it. He says they're fine but will likely be out for at least another twelve hours. He's currently sleeping in your room with Luna and Finn. The boy is… worried about Isabeau."

Luna is doing her best to keep him calm. Lynette cast a worried glance down the hall. *He tried to wake all of you up with his magic but couldn't.*

Shit. Finn must be a mess right now. I had no idea how much he'd heard. Did he know that the vampires had come for him? Did he blame himself? I added that onto the list of problems I needed to deal with. Not for the first time, I wished Jinx had the ability to grant good luck instead of only bad.

We could really use a change in our fortunes right now.

"Alright, so we've got two dragons who are down for the count." I watched Kaysea tuck a blanket around Isabeau. "How's Sleeping Beauty?"

Kaysea frowned. "Okay, I think. Physically, she is fine, but my telepathic abilities are barely better than yours. We should ask Jinx to take a look at her."

Not a chance in hell.

"Jinx." I glared down the hallway where the door to my bedroom was barely cracked open.

That nightmare spawn knocked out two incredibly powerful dragons, Jinx growled. *Both of whom are stronger than me. So unless you want me to swoon like a Southern bell, I'll keep my mind to myself, thank you very much.*

Swoon like a Southern bell? What the hell type of movies had Isabeau been obsessing over and subjecting everyone to now? I'd missed the last few movie nights.

It was impossible to change Jinx's mind once he made it up.

Luna would probably do it, but then Jinx would be pissed at me for putting her at risk. While I didn't think Isabeau would hurt her, I could understand his concern. When Jinx had found Luna, her mind had been badly damaged and her memories wiped away. She'd eventually recovered most of them, but there were still significant gaps.

"Maybe Aki can help?" Kaysea suggested.

I nodded. "Good idea. I need to go to The Inferno anyway. If she's not there, I'll swing by her apartment."

"The Inferno?" Cian lowered his hands from where he'd been rubbing them against his temples and squinted at me. Unlike me, Cian actually had strong telepathic abilities because he was a dreamwalker. I felt like crap, but given how haggard Cian looked, I suspected he felt much worse. I wasn't sure if being subjected to Isabeau's magic had been extra hard for him, or if reliving all those bad memories was what had done it, but I was pretty sure if I tapped him with my pinkie, he'd fall over.

"Before I go with you to rescue Hades, I need to make sure everyone here is safe." I glanced at the ring on my finger. "Emir was at the masquerade, and he offered me a deal."

"What kind of deal?" Magos asked warily.

"The warlock kind." I grimaced. "He wants to play both sides. Continue to get more power from the fae who serve Balor and also be prepared to double-cross them when the moment is right."

"Or us," Magos pointed out.

I shrugged. "It could definitely go either way, but he's offering to give us warnings before the vampires or Lir make a strike against us." My chest tightened, and I focused on the dark knot in the wooden floor in front of me. "I can't protect all of you. Not all the time. Lir was right earlier. I do have too many people in my life who matter, who make for easy targets.

If the warlock can help me protect all of you, I'll do whatever I have to."

"He could lie." Kaysea frowned. "Or he could simply *not* give you a warning and claim ignorance."

"That's why I'll make him swear on a blood oath to pass on any knowledge of strikes against me and mine, no matter how small."

I waited for everyone to tell me how terrible of an idea this was, but no one spoke. Everyone had similar pinched expressions, as they were probably having the same internal arguments with themselves that I'd been having. This was a terrible idea. Emir would absolutely betray us. Blood oaths went both ways, and I wouldn't like whatever he asked of me.

But we couldn't afford not to make this deal. This time, two people I loved had been kidnapped. Okay, one person I loved and another who I begrudgingly tolerated because of that love. And while we still had to save Hades and somehow survive an encounter with the Olympians, both he and Cian had been taken alive. Next time, Lir might have someone I loved killed.

Pele, Kaysea, Magos... Magic stirred within me and I felt Mikhail's gaze on me, those twilight eyes seeing straight into my soul. Blue flames danced across my skin before I pulled my magic back.

Mikhail had asked me once if I was scared of being with him because it meant accepting what I would become if anything happened to him. He asked if I would burn the world for him, and I hadn't answered because I hadn't needed to. We both knew the answer. The two of us were capable of terrible things and had already committed monstrous acts in our pasts.

But what I'd done after my parents had been murdered and after Myrna had been taken from me were nothing compared to what I'd do if something ever happened to Mikhail. We were both monsters, and our souls were now tethered together.

There was nothing I wouldn't do to protect him and the others. Including making a deal with my sworn enemy.

———

ASMODEUS DIDN'T EVEN RAISE their head when Mikhail and I stepped out of a gateway directly into Pele's office. Usually, out of politeness, I opened a gateway in the alleyway outside, but I'd been feeling too on edge to take any chances.

"Pele isn't here." They set down the pen and pushed aside the scroll they'd been writing on. I wasn't the only one who wasn't a fan of human technology. Daemons didn't completely avoid it, but they still preferred handwriting on scrolls over typing into computers. Granted that scroll was enchanted and anything written on it was automatically copied onto other scrolls as backups in the daemon realm. I'd encountered several daemons who had spelled quills to write down anything they dictated. I'd asked Asmodeus once why they didn't do that, and they simply said they enjoyed the act of writing.

No wonder Pele was so in love with them. Not that she'd ever admit it.

"I was actually coming to see you."

Asmodeus tilted their head, stunning turquoise eyes studying me and then Mikhail. All daemons had a reddish undertone to their skin; Pele's was a deep red that blazed like fire in the sunlight while Asmodeus' was more of a mahogany reddish-brown. Up until recently, I'd had no idea what color their hair was because they'd always kept it shaved close to their scalp, but they'd started growing it out and must have used magic, because the silky, black strands were already midway down their back.

Today, they wore it pulled back into a sleek ponytail. It made their bright eyes and elegant bone structure stand out even more. Asmodeus was gorgeous, brilliant, and absolutely devoted to Pele. I used to tease her about it, but now I was getting annoyed on Asmodeus' behalf. Pele was not only attracted to them, she was every bit as in love with Asmodeus as they were with her. She was still determined to deny it though for reasons I thought were completely asinine.

I'd stopped teasing them both about it because I knew Pele's denial was hurting Asmodeus, and the last time I'd pushed Pele about it, she'd stormed off and avoided me for a month.

"Okay, I'll bite. What do you need?"

"Well, I'd prefer you to stop stealing my lines." Mikhail grinned at them, making sure to flash his fangs. "You might actually be prettier than me, and I don't like it."

Asmodeus stared at me. "Congratulations, you found a lover who is every bit as arrogant and annoying as you." They raised their hands and clapped slowly.

"I've got mad skills." I rolled my eyes. "I'm about to make a foolish bargain with the leader of the Warlock Circle, and I need your help to make it less likely to blow up in our faces. If I asked Pele, she would probably just set him on fire, because she's a little volatile towards people who have tried to kidnap me and enslave my will."

"Emir." Their lips twisted in disgust. "To be fair, he has it coming."

"He does," I agreed. "But I need to keep everyone alive, and having someone on the inside to warn us of incoming attacks could mean the difference between life and death for those I care about."

"You want to do a blood oath?" they guessed, already reaching into a drawer for another scroll.

"It's the only way to minimize the risk of him betraying us, but he'll no doubt try to word things to his advantage, and I admit that I'm not smart enough to always spot that. I would have asked Vizor since he's a devious bastard, but he's currently passed out at my place."

Asmodeus paused their searching of the drawer to quirk an eyebrow at me. "And why is he passed out at your place?"

I gave them a quick rundown of what had happened with Katrina and how Isabeau had stepped in to stop it while Mikhail added a few details here and there. Asmodeus leaned back in the chair, brows pinched in concern.

"Compulsion is vile magic. If this Katrina person continues to level up her abilities, she's going to be a major problem." They hesitated for a moment. "Do you have any idea what Isabeau is? We know she's an Apex bloodline, which means something other than human is in her lineage."

All vampires were descended from the same Romanian town that a couple of sorcerers had used for their experimentations. They'd created both the vampires and the werewolves. While all the werewolves were basically the same, there were anomalies among the vampires because some of those used for the original spell hadn't been human, or at least not entirely human. The sorcerers had disappeared back to their realm after having their little fun, so nobody knew if this had been intentional or not, but the vampires who had something other than pure human in their lineage came with extra perks and were known as the Apex bloodlines.

Magos and Mikhail were originally from the Cerulle realm before it fell to devourers. Elisa and the other vamp kids were all Apex bloodlines as well, but we didn't know as much about their lineage since they'd never met their parents. Until recently, we'd only suspected that two of them were related to Marius. We had confirmation of that now, but we still had no idea about Damon or Isabeau.

"I've been to over a hundred realms," I said slowly. "Met hundreds of different species. Encountered more than a few with strong telepathic or illusion magic. So I am saying this from my hundreds of years of experience: I have no fucking clue what Isabeau is."

"Does it matter?" Mikhail asked. "Whatever the sorcerers did to us to make us vampires changed our magic considerably. Before my uncle and I were turned, our magic was elemental based. We both had an affinity for water, which resulted in us being able to vanish into mist as vampires. I also inherited a gift of manipulating sunlight from my father, which translated into me being able to walk in the sun as a vampire. Whatever Isabeau's parents or grandparents originally were might have been similarly twisted."

"Valid points." Asmodeus sighed. "I'll think on it more. In the meantime, I can help you with the blood oath. Do you have a way of reaching out to the warlock?"

"Yes." I raised my hand and wiggled my finger with the dark silver band. "We should go somewhere else. I don't want to bring Emir here."

They nodded. "Give me a moment and I'll be ready to go."

"Do you know if Aki is here?"

"I believe she's with Sten and their band of miscreants."

I smirked and headed out to the main room of The Inferno. Asmodeus had even less patience for the lokis than Pele, which was unfortunate, since Sten was a regular here. Personally, I enjoyed the chaos they brought.

"So Sten has finally forgiven her for stealing Damon away from them?" Mikhail asked as we weaved through the tavern patrons. The Inferno was packed tonight.

"You remember Kuya?"

"Big, hairy dude." Mikhail grabbed me and tugged me to the side just as a young fae hit the ground, snarled, and leapt back at a laughing daemon. Mikhail spoke louder as the two brawling idiots smashed into a table, their friends cheering them on. "Makes really good smoked ribs."

"He's a kapre!" I practically shouted. Magic sparked from

the bar, and I saw the daemon bartender raise his hands and flick his fingers apart. His name slipped my memory. He was a relatively new hire, but he was a strong telekinetic. The sounds of the fight died down, and I glanced over my shoulder to see both the daemon and fae pinned to the wall by an invisible force. Strong telekinetic indeed. "Sten has been trying to get an invite to one of Kuya's barbecues forever. Aki spoke to Kuya on their behalf and got them in."

"She really can negotiate anything." Mikhail chuckled.

"Perks of being an empath." I shrugged. "Doesn't hurt that she hangs out with Elisa all the time; the two of them together are a dangerous force. Pele is thrilled to have them both on staff."

"I bet."

We finally made it to where a slender girl with light brown skin and pretty features sat with a bunch of tall, burly looking men. I scrutinized all of them before my eyes settled on one with ice-blue eyes and a gnarly scar snaking its way down their face. There was something aesthetically pleasing about the scar. The placement emphasized their strong cheekbones and put them firmly in that dangerous but gorgeous category.

"Sten, I need to borrow Aki. You'll have to find a new wench for your barbarian horde."

They shot me a pouty look that seemed very out of place on their current face. "Really? I thought for sure you'd think I was that one." I glanced to where they was pointing, and another barbarian with a truly obscene amount of muscles and harsh, masculine features gave me a leering grin.

"Nice try." I snorted. "But you're too vain to ever let your face be that ugly."

"She has a point," Aki said with a laugh and rose from the table. "See you later, Steni-boo."

The barbarian who was Sten turned a bright red at the nickname, and the rest of the lokis erupted into laughter.

Mikhail and I steered Aki away from them and up the stairs to where meeting rooms lined the walls. I grabbed the first open one and shut the door, activating the silencing spell.

"What's up?" Aki asked.

"Kind of a long story." I leaned my butt against the stone table that took up most of the room. "Isabeau used her magic to help us out of a really bad situation, and we're dealing with the fallout of that."

"Is everyone okay?" Concern lit up her warm, brown eyes. "Damon?"

"He's fine," I said quickly, my gaze sliding to Mikhail's and back to hers. "Remember when we first met and you saw into the truth of my soul?"

She nodded. "I told you it didn't scare me, and I meant it then just as I mean it now. Just because I'm an empath doesn't mean I only care about people who are full of light. There are valid reasons for your darkness, Nemain. You are fiercely protective of those you love, and I will never fault you for that."

A lump formed in my throat, and I struggled to speak.

"Damon feels otherwise," Mikhail said, an edge to his voice. "As does Misha."

"It's fine," I finally managed to say, sending Mikhail a warning look. He liked the vamp kids, and I knew he was upset by their reaction just as I was. He was just also pissed off that they'd hurt me in the process. "But we have to leave soon, and I don't want them to do something stupid like run off on their own."

"You really think they'd do that?" Aki asked in surprise.

I thought about the unease in their expressions after we'd woken from the illusions and the distance they'd put between us.

"I'd rather not find out," I said evenly. "If they want to live somewhere else after we get back, I'll figure it out, but I don't have time to deal with that now."

"Don't worry," she said quickly. "I'll handle it."

"Thanks, Aki. Can you check on Isabeau too?"

She nodded and I turned to leave, Mikhail at my side, but she reached out to stop me. "It'll be okay, Nemain. I'm sure they'll understand once they get over the shock of whatever happened."

"Of course." I jerked my head in a nod and gave her a smile that I knew didn't reach my eyes. The vampire brats had finally seen just how much of a monster I could be, and I didn't think they'd ever accept it.

Chapter Thirteen

"How are you doing, my friend?" I patted the wide trunk of the fae tree that stood in the center of the clearing in the forest just outside of Emerald Bay. Glowing, yellow lines ran up the dark brown bark of the tree, widening in some spots and narrowing in others, and they pulsed brighter at my words. "You're overdue for a snack; I'll make sure to bring you something soon."

A thick, twisted vine rose from the ground and patted my foot before sinking back into the soil. I smiled at the tree and patted it one more time before going to join Asmodeus and Mikhail, who were standing a safe distance away. Asmodeus' eyes were wide, and their mouth had parted slightly. Apparently, I'd finally managed to shock them.

"You do know that tree is sentient, right?" they asked. "And extremely grouchy and vindictive?"

Branches creaked above us, and Mikhail took a step away from the daemon, as if he wanted to make sure the tree didn't target him by association.

"It likes me." I shrugged.

"Because you spoil it with treats." Mikhail shot me an accusing glare.

"Treats?" Asmodeus kept their attention on the tree, as if they expected an attack at any moment. As far as I knew, the tree required direct contact to launch its mental assault. I glanced down at the forest floor. Its roots extended quite a bit though; I wondered how far its reach was now.

"If you're brave enough to get a little closer, you'll probably be able to see some bones in the soil around its base," Mikhail said dryly. "Nemain has been bringing it tasty snacks in the form of warlocks, vampires, and dragons."

"You're feeding it?!" Asmodeus stared at me like I was the dumbest person on the planet. "This tree is already a freak of nature. Something went wrong with it when the fae worked their magic to have it serve as a gateway. Even the fae prefer to use the gateway at The Inferno instead of their own."

"I don't know why they made such a big deal about it eating one measly fae." I raised my hands, palms facing up. "From my understanding, that guy was a real douchebag who had it coming."

Before we could continue arguing about the fae tree that may or may not have been evil incarnate, magic from my ring pulsed. Then the air before us shimmered, revealing Emir.

"Let me guess." His lips stretched into an arrogant smile. "Katrina paid you a visit, and now you're rethinking my offer?"

"You knew she was going to attack?"

"Of course."

Asshole. I ground my teeth as my magic rumbled inside of me. Mikhail stepped closer, and his presence helped soothe it, which drew a curious glance from Asmodeus.

"I'm ready to deal." I forced the words out. "But it has to be now. I'll open a gateway so you can come here."

His projection flickered briefly as he pondered this. "Fine, but two of my allies from the Vampire Council will be joining me along with some bodyguards."

"What?" I drawled. "Don't trust me not to cut you up into little tiny pieces and scatter your remains in the forest?"

"Shocking, I know." He looked over his shoulder, clearly communicating with someone I couldn't see or hear, before facing me again. "I'm not familiar with how your magic works. That ring I gave you is connected to mine. Can you follow the magic back and open a gateway at my location?"

I glanced down at the ring on my finger and concentrated. The amount within the ring was minuscule, but it would be enough. A seam formed in the air next to Emir's illusion and widened into a gateway. The illusion snapped out of existence, and the real Emir appeared on the other side of the gateway in what looked like a combination of an office and a workshop. There was a simple wooden desk shoved into a corner and a much larger table taking up most of the room. Various trinkets and jars were stacked on it, and I could see some herbs drying in the window beyond it.

Emir's gaze flicked around the clearing for a moment before he stepped through, and three warlocks were hot on his heels, fanning out protectively around him while giving us the evil eyes. All were men, and I thought I recognized one from the first time Emir and I had met in this very clearing, when he'd offered up Sebastian to me on a silver platter and tried to bind me into servitude. I wasn't surprised when Cassius and Justina followed a second later. They'd bailed shortly after Emir at the masquerade and they were both on the Council, so I'd suspected they'd been the two allies he'd been referring to earlier.

Cassius was in a black suit that looked expensive as hell. He held a hand out to Justina who was struggling to stand in the soft soil with her six-inch heels, but she merely sneered at him before reaching down and unbuckling her shoes. Without them on, she was almost half a foot shorter than me. She should have looked ridiculous standing in the middle of a forest wearing a sparkling green gown made of dark blue and purple sequins with her shoes dangling from her hand, but somehow, she made it work and even sent Mikhail a sultry grin.

Maybe the fae tree would be getting a snack tonight after all.

"Great, we're all here." I let the gateway close. "Asmodeus has already written down what I want out of this. They'll work with you on what you want. Then we'll agree to it over a blood oath."

"A blood oath?" Emir's thick, dark eyebrows rose.

"Do you have a problem with that?"

"Not at all," he said smoothly. "Truth be told, I had my doubts about you agreeing to an alliance with me, but there is no breaking a blood oath without serious consequences. I'm merely surprised at your devotion."

"She's probably got her panties in a twist over how to keep lover boy safe." The familiar, blond-haired warlock sneered. "Should have taken our deal that night instead of surrounding yourself with weaklings you have to protect. No wonder Sebastian found you so easy to manipulate." He smiled as he gave me an appreciative once-over. "Although, if you miss having a warlock between those thighs of yours, I could—"

A crack echoed through the trees as Mikhail snapped the warlock's neck, twisting his head until it was almost completely turned around. Then he vanished into mist and reappeared at my side, his hands slipping into his pockets with an arrogant smirk across his lips.

"I think you'll find my *lover boy* can keep himself safe," I drawled. The remaining two warlock bodyguards glowered at Mikhail but made no move against him.

Cassius chuckled. "I'm sure the two of you would fare

better against him. Not like he was a ruthless assassin for centuries or anything. Go ahead. Try your luck."

"That won't be necessary," Emir said. His gaze lingered dispassionately on the dead warlock for a moment. "Nathaniel was never particularly smart; I'm honestly surprised he survived this long. I apologize for his behavior. I know there isn't much you wouldn't do to protect your family"—a hint of cruelty slipped into his eyes—"even if it comes at the cost of your vengeance."

I went predatorily still as something dark and angry tried to claw its way out of my chest. An old memory surfaced, one that had also happened in this clearing: Sebastian's dying words as his bloodied face stared up at me.

"Emir killed your parents."

Sebastian had told me many lies throughout our time together. I'd mostly dismissed his dying declaration as a way to point me in the direction of the warlock who had orchestrated his death. He'd used me as a weapon for most of his life, and I'd refused to let him do the same in death.

But maybe, for once, he hadn't been lying.

"Did you kill them?" My voice sounded flat and emotionless, and I barely recognized it as my own. Emir didn't ask for clarification about who I was referring to. Instead, he just flashed me a bright smile.

"Oh, yes. Tried to kill you and your brother too, but those damn villagers decided to draw the line at murdering children." His lip curled. "I had several witch hunters on retainer back then. They had no idea what I was, of course, so I sent them after you. Obviously, they were unsuccessful."

The beast within me screamed for blood, and I felt my magic roil beneath my skin. After all these centuries, the warlock who had killed my parents was right here. Emir was clever and no doubt had some type of protection in place he likely believed would save him, along with the two vampires he'd brought if I attacked, but whatever it was wouldn't be enough. He couldn't begin to understand the depths of my wrath.

I could have my vengeance. He was right fucking there, godsdamn it. Pain sliced into my palms as fingernails shifted to claws and bit into flesh. Warm blood dripped through my clenched fingers.

A ring of blue fire erupted around the clearing, locking us all in. Justina and Cassius snarled, each sliding closer to Emir. Asmodeus and Mikhail remained by my side, Mikhail's mist sword snapping into existence and two short, curved daggers with an odd, purple sheen appearing in Asmodeus' hands.

"Ah, there's the real you." Emir glanced at my flames, not a hint of concern lining his features. "I realize I'm the villain in your book, but I do believe in entering agreements such as ours with all the cards on the table, and I suspected Sebastian might have hinted at my role in your parents' death. He was a sniveling coward, but he was always good at playing the long game."

"Personally, I'm fine with keeping secrets like this locked down," Cassius said tightly. "Honesty is overrated."

"Given that you'd probably drop dead if you ever told the truth, that's not exactly shocking," Justina snapped.

"Why them?" My gaze never left Emir, but I felt the attention of the vampires as more of my blood fell to the ground. The power in it called to them, and a deep growl tore out of Mikhail as he took a step forward, angling himself between me and them.

"It wasn't personal," Emir replied. "We were mostly targeting witches, but sometimes other supernaturals made it too easy. Your family lived in a rural area and you had no allies nearby. Villages like the one close to you were easy to rile up. I didn't even know about your history with the fae queen back then. You really do have the worst luck, don't you?"

The crystal blue flames shot up another ten feet, and frost stretched across the ground as my control slipped a little more. The Seelie Queen had been the reason my parents had chosen to live in such isolation in the human realm. She had been the reason they'd had no allies and why Kalen and Badb hadn't known what was happening in time to stop it. I still didn't know if she'd played more of a direct role in things, but that hadn't stopped me from making a deal with her to save my brother.

Humans might have been the ones to set the fire, but Emir was the reason my parents were dead. He could also be the reason everyone I loved remained alive though. I'd spent most of my life avenging the dead, and it had only brought me more pain. Asmodeus and Mikhail would support me no matter what path I chose.

Maybe it was time for me to choose them.

The flames winked out of existence, leaving a ring of frozen ash around us, but I felt it swirling around inside of me, still desperate for blood. It wouldn't be getting that tonight. Though the Olympians had no idea what was heading their way, because as soon as Hades was safe, I would let my magic tear into them, and we'd find out just how immortal the gods truly were.

"Our deal stands," I said harshly. "Tell Asmodeus what you want, and once we're in agreement, I'll take a blood oath with you."

The barest glimpse of surprise flickered across Emir's face before he gave me a polite smile and gestured for Asmodeus to begin. The two of them stepped away, Asmodeus' scroll and quill floating through the air as Emir's requirements were added.

Warm fingers slipped around my bloodied hands, and I turned my head slowly to watch Mikhail raise them. Justina and Cassius remained perfectly still as they tracked the movement, their mouths slightly open, allowing their fangs to show.

Mikhail held my gaze as he brought one palm to his lips and licked the blood away before repeating the gesture with the other.

The magic that had felt like it was pressing against my skin settled deep within my chest with a contented sigh. Mikhail kissed my now clean palm and then the other before facing the two vampires, who were now looking at me with outright hunger.

"Mine." A growl punctuated his claim.

Cassius immediately backed down, but Justina held Mikhail's stare, her eyes almost seeming to glow.

I didn't like the way she was looking at him, and in a flash, I stood between them, my clawed fingers gripping her throat. "Mine." She clawed frantically at my arm as a strangled hiss escaped her throat, but I tightened my hold around her neck and shook her a little. "MINE."

"Are you gonna do something about this?" Out of the corner of my eye, I saw Cassius waving a hand at me and Justina. His tone was curious more than anything.

"Wasn't planning on it," Mikhail drawled. "Honestly, I kind of like it when she gets all territorial."

Justina's sharpened nails dug into my arm, and fresh blood flowed across my skin. Cassius inhaled sharply. "Her blood," he ground out. "I've heard rumors about shifter blood being intoxicating, but there are so few of them left, I've never experienced it for myself. Keep her away from me, Mikhail."

The Council member quickly backpedaled away from us even as he gazed hungrily at my bloody arm. The two remaining warlock bodyguards watched us cautiously from where they stood close to Emir.

Justina's struggles to get free became weaker. It wasn't actually possible to strangle a vampire to death; she'd pass out but then she'd wake up and be fine. Pissed off, but fine. She was probably old enough that she'd survive a broken neck too. I tilted my head as I pondered this, her body going limp in my grasp.

Spreading my fingers, I let her drop to the ground. Cassius didn't even notice, all of his attention on me. As if waking from a dream, he blinked slowly and then took another step back, keeping his eyes fixed on the ground. Satisfied with the distance between me and the other vampire, Mikhail whirled to face me and inspect my arm.

Blood was smeared all across my forearm, but the shallow wounds were already healed. He frowned at my arm before shrugging off his leather jacket and helping me into it. I arched an eyebrow at him in question, and hesitation flashed across his face.

"Vampire instincts drive us to protect our food source. It hasn't been a problem for me because I don't view Magos or the vamp brats as competition." He tugged his jacket closed around me. It was a cool, late fall night, and I hadn't bothered to grab something warmer earlier, so I snuggled into the warmth of the leather. "My scent will help cover up the smell of your blood, and it will keep Cassius a little calmer and help me resist tearing his head off for the way he looks at you."

It didn't escape my notice that Mikhail was carefully avoiding my gaze as he explained all of this.

"Hey." I ran my fingers along his smooth jawline and tilted his face towards mine. The moon was barely a sliver tonight, and in the darkness of the clearing, his twilight-colored eyes were almost black. "You don't have to hide your nature from me. I accept every part of you."

His eyes searched mine. "I know you have a history with vampires, and it's not exactly a good one."

I leaned forward and brushed my lips against his. "We do not hide from each other."

"As you wish, shifter." He smiled before kissing me back.

Chapter Fourteen

"How DID IT GO?" Magos asked when Mikhail and I entered the apartment an hour later. I'd opened a gateway for Emir and his people as soon as the blood oath had settled because I'd wanted them the fuck out of my town. Asmodeus had requested I open a gateway to the daemon realm, Meenri, because they wanted to check in with Pele, and I'd obliged.

Now I was both bone-weary tired and amped up with pent-up aggression.

"It's done." I raised my hand with the back towards Magos and sent out a little pulse of magic. A bloodred circle made of chain links appeared on my skin for a few seconds before fading away again.

Blood oaths were tricky because a certain extent of them were at the whim of magic. While magic wasn't exactly sentient, it was still a force of nature to be reckoned with. My fae blood complicated things because my very being was drenched in magic.

Some believed the fae could not lie. This was false. They loved to lie. False words dripped from their lips like honey. But they did have to be careful about *how* they lied. More than one fae had accidentally locked themself into an agreement or binded their powers because their magic decided to act on the words they spoke.

The fae were arguably the most powerful species when it came to magic. No other species could directly interact with it the way they could. It was the reason the fae queens had been able to lock away their brother and his army. But that power came with a cost, and they were as much beholden to magic as it was to them.

Luckily for me, I was only half fae, but I still had to be careful. Having things spelled out so clearly in the contract Asmodeus had crafted would help, and the mark would warn me if I started to stray into dangerous waters and give me time to correct my course.

If either of us broke the oath completely, our magic would be ripped from our souls. I wasn't entirely sure if it would kill Emir because I'd never encountered a human who had taken a blood oath before. The more magic you had, the more painful it was to lose it, and I had a lot of magic.

Breaking the oath would almost certainly kill me, but this was far from the first time I'd lived my life with a sword dangling over my head. At this point, I'd probably be more concerned if I couldn't see the blade.

"He will warn us of any threats, even if they are merely possibilities. Neither of us will physically harm or knowingly set things in motion that will bring harm to the other or the people we specifically named in the deal." I eyed the coffee maker and then glanced out the floor-to-ceiling windows that took up most of the living room wall. The night sky had lightened enough to bathe the world in a bluish light, the last of night giving way to a new day. "I did stipulate that Katrina, Adrian, Gabriel, and Marius were fair game."

With a sigh, I turned away from the coffee machine. I needed to get what sleep I could while I had the chance.

"What was the price?"

Letting the man who murdered my parents walk free.

My jaw clenched hard enough that I felt a tooth crack. I focused on making myself relax and fixed my expression into something as close to neutral as I could get before facing Magos. "Helping both the warlocks and vampires increase their magic. Basically the same thing Lir promised them."

"So we're helping our enemies get stronger." Magos' copper eyes held no judgment, and I knew he was likely already thinking about how to adapt to this new development. I didn't like it either, but it was the cost of keeping him and everyone else safe.

"Yes." I rubbed my face. "The vampires are particularly unhappy. Lir promised them quite a bit, and while they've definitely gained power, there are some major promises that, so far, haven't come to fruition."

Mikhail glanced at his uncle. "They want to walk in the sun again."

Magos made a noise of agreement. "Obviously they know Nemain did something to ensure Elisa, the others, and I could do that." Magos' brows furrowed before he sent me an apologetic look. "In helping us, you drew the attention of Emir's vampire allies."

"It was worth it." I stepped forward and patted him on the shoulder. "I explained it would be challenging to do the same for them, given that it would rely on the daemons agreeing to help with the spell. Emir implied that he had another idea, but he was cagey about it."

"Our alliance is off to a great start." Mikhail scoffed.

I shot him an annoyed look. "It is what it is. Emir will contact Asmodeus directly if he learns of any useful information, and they will act accordingly. Given how often I'm traveling between the realms, they were the best person to serve as the contact between Emir and me."

Magos nodded in agreement. "Get some rest. Most of the others are sleeping. Aki checked on Isabeau and the dragons; we're all in agreement that they're fine and will wake up soon."

"And Cian?" I was a little surprised my brother wasn't here demanding we leave immediately to rescue Hades.

Magos' face went carefully blank.

I narrowed my eyes at him. "What did you do?"

"Technically, it was Cerri's idea. I just went along with it." When I continued to stare at him, he gave me a sheepish look. "Turns out KO balls work on shifters."

"You used a knockout ball on my brother?" I choked on a laugh.

"He was clearly exhausted but wouldn't sleep." Magos shrugged helplessly. "It was in his best interest. He's on the couch downstairs."

I should have probably been mad about them knocking Cian out, but I couldn't really disagree with the logic.

We still needed to figure out a way to get into Artemis' pocket dimension. I had a few ideas about who we could talk to about that, but I was practically dead on my feet.

"Was the KO ball daemon- or fae-made?" I asked. They both knocked out the person or persons they were aimed at, but the magic behind them was different. From my experience, the effects of the daemon-crafted ones lasted a little longer.

"Daemon," Magos said.

"Perfect." I let out a tired sigh. "He'll probably be out for at least ten hours. You should get some sleep. Tomorrow afternoon, we'll visit some friends of mine and go from there."

"See you tomorrow, Uncle," Mikhail said as he tugged me down the hallway towards the bedroom we shared. Prior to us getting involved, he'd been sleeping on the couch. When we'd returned from the dragon realm, he just sort of moved into my room. I enjoyed his company, so I'd allowed it.

Okay, maybe I more than enjoyed it. Waking up with Mikhail wrapped around me every morning brought me a peace I hadn't even known I'd been missing. It was worth giving up a couple of drawers. Plus, we were similar in size and often wore each other's clothing. Apparently, we both had enough animal instincts in us to like seeing the other drowned in our scents.

Gods, we were such territorial assholes.

Instead of going to the bedroom, Mikhail took us straight to the bathroom and turned on the shower. Steam rose from the hot water, and I practically moaned in anticipation.

"Easy, shifter." Mikhail laughed. "I'm not even naked yet."

"As if you could ever get such a response from me." I slid out of Mikhail's jacket before pulling off the rest of my clothes. "My first and truest love will always be hot water. At our next place, we're definitely going to have a giant soaking tub like the ones at the fae queen's castle. Just without the tentacle monster."

Mikhail froze. His shirt dangled from his fingers, giving me a lovely view of his lean, chiseled chest. I had the sudden urge to lick it, until his next words snapped me out of my blatant ogling. "*Our* next place?"

It was my turn to freeze. I hadn't even realized what I'd said, the words had just naturally slipped out. My magic practically purred beneath my skin, which only made me panic more. I shouldn't have been talking about future places we'd live before I talked to him about what was going on between us. He deserved to know everything. To decide if this was something he truly wanted before my magic trapped him.

"I was just saying—*hypothetically*—if we were to move somewhere else for whatever reason, it'd be nice to have a tub." I yanked my bra off in what was rapidly becoming a blind panic. My pants, underwear, and socks followed next, and I kicked them all over into a pile. Mikhail wasn't the least bit distracted by my nakedness as he continued to ponder my words. "Obviously, it wouldn't just be our place. I mean, Magos would be there too. He can't be left to his own devices. Plus, who would make me coffee? And Bryn and Finn are a package deal. Plus the vamp br—"

"Nemain." His voice was a deep purr that sent shivers down my spine.

I swallowed. "Yes?"

"Shut up and get in the shower."

I did as ordered and practically ran him over to get under the hot spray. Mikhail finished undressing and slipped in behind me. I felt his fingers tug the band off my braid before he started unraveling my hair. I tilted my head to give him better access because I was born shameless. Then he leaned against me, his chest brushing against my back as he reached for the shampoo.

Lavender and rosemary filled the air as he poured some into his palm and returned the bottle to the shelf. This time, the moan that slipped from my lips was thanks to his nimble fingers and not the hot water. He didn't say anything else while he finished washing my hair, then we traded places so I could do the same for him. Gradually, my panic faded. I couldn't avoid this conversation forever, and I didn't intend to, but rescuing Hades came first.

And on the off chance that I would die during the attempt, I wouldn't have to worry about it at all.

I huffed a dry laugh as Mikhail shut off the water, and and we wrapped towels around ourselves and headed to the bedroom. I dropped my towel as soon as Mikhail shut the door behind us, and then I crawled into bed, not even caring that my hair was still wet and would be a tangled mess in the morning.

The sound of Mikhail's towel hitting the floor came from behind me, and I flipped onto my back so I could get a better view. His midnight black hair curled slightly the way it always did when it was damp. The way it stuck to the sides of his face and neck made his chiseled cheekbones and full lips stand out even more.

Damn it. He really was prettier than me, the bastard.

"Like what you see?" he asked as he prowled around the side of the bed.

"It's not bad." I licked my lips as my eyes trailed down his body. Broad shoulders tapered down to a narrow waist and long, strong legs. All of it wrapped in warm brown skin a few shades darker than my golden brown. Mikhail was beautifully lethal. I kept waiting to not be so captivated by him, but the attraction only grew. I didn't just want Mikhail. I *needed* him. Always.

And based on the hunger in his eyes as he drank in my body, I knew he felt the same.

"See something *you* like?" I teased him when his eyes snagged on my chest.

"Yes." A smile of pure sin spread across his face. "Want me to show you how much?" He knelt on the side of the bed and leaned down to kiss me. His lips on mine were hot and demanding, and I lost myself in the taste of him. One of his hands trailed down to grip my breast, and I moaned into his mouth.

This was exactly what I needed right now. A good fuck followed by a solid ten hours of sleep before we marched to our possible deaths.

Mikhail sensed just how much I wanted him and wasted no time. He ran a thumb over my nipple before sliding his hand down between my legs and sinking two fingers into my aching, hot core. I broke our kiss and thrust my head back into the pillow as I let out a satisfied sound.

His fingers pumped inside me, dragging more whimpers from me before pulling out and swirling around my clit. I arched my back, raising my hips as Mikhail used the slickness from my own pleasure to bring me closer to the salvation I desperately wanted. He brushed a finger directly over my clit, applying just the right amount of pressure, and I almost detonated right then and there.

"Yes," I panted. "Fuck, Mikhail."

Soft lips brushed against my neck and then across the top of my breasts before roughly sucking a nipple just as he pushed down on my clit again. A mangled sound tore out of me, a mix of wanton need and desire. Every muscle in my body was tight in anticipation of the bliss that was about to come.

Then it stopped. His lips and fingers abruptly left my body, leaving me right on the edge. What. The. Fuck.

Not again. I was really not liking this new habit of his.

My eyes flew open, and I glared up at Mikhail from where he was still perched on the side of the bed leaning over me. He raised one hand and licked his fingers clean, his dark blue eyes flicked with purple were bright with amusement.

"So"—he trailed a finger down my neck, between my breasts, and stopped inches away from where they'd been a second ago—"when were you planning on telling me about the fae mate bond forming between us?"

My heart, which had been thudding rapidly, suddenly felt like it stopped altogether.

"What—" My voice came out raspy, and I swallowed past the lump in my throat. "How did you know?"

Mikhail arched an eyebrow and gave me a wolfish grin. "You're skilled at many things, my violent, wondrous love, but lying to me isn't one of them. The fact that I can always sense where you are was a bit of a clue." His fingers drifted back up my body to tap over my heart. "Also, our heartbeats sync up whenever one of us is experiencing strong emotion."

"Oh." I raised my hand and placed it flat against his heart. His beats were in unison with mine.

"Why have you been lying about this?" he asked softly.

"I haven't lied," I said quickly and bit my bottom lip. "I just haven't told you yet."

"Why?" His grin never slipped, but I saw the flash of uncertainty in his eyes. Neither of us was capable of hiding anything from the other, it seemed. "Is it because you don't want the mating bond?"

He thought I didn't want him for the long haul. Stupid vampire.

In a flash, I hooked my arm around him and pulled, twisting my body with all my strength so that he flipped over me and landed on his back in the center of the bed. I followed the movement so I sat on top of him, straddling his hips and planting both of my hands on his chest to hold him down.

"Listen very carefully." I tried to keep my voice calm, but I couldn't hide the growl that underlined my words. Mikhail didn't even try to get out from under me, he just lay perfectly still. The grin was gone, but his lips were still tilted up in that arrogant way of his, twilight eyes glowing as they held my gaze. "I love you, Mikhail. You are *everything* to me, and I no longer see a future without you in it."

His expression softened a little, and he raised his hands to rest over mine on his chest. I took a deep breath and continued.

"That terrifies the shit out of me, but I'm coming to terms with it the best I can. I do not doubt your devotion to me, but I also recognize we've only known each other a few years and we've only been… together… for less than a year. There's still so much for us to figure out." I lowered my gaze. "You've been very accepting of my relationship with Pele, which I appreciate because it would tear my soul in half if you asked me to choose between you two. I know it's confusing, my feelings for you both, but I—"

"It's not," he interrupted. "You and Pele have been involved with each other for centuries. The relationship between the two of you is unique and different from ours, and I'm not the least bit threatened by it."

"Really?" My gaze flicked up to his, trying to catch a hint of a lie, but there was none.

He smiled softly. "I've already spoken to her about this."

I groaned. "She already knew about the mate bond, didn't she?"

"Do you even have to ask that?"

No. Of course Pele fucking knew.

He raised a hand to cup my face. "There is no doubt in my mind that without Pele, you would not be sitting here today. Just because neither of you are each other's primary relationship doesn't mean what you have isn't valid and important. I will always be thankful to her for keeping you alive long enough for us to meet."

The knot of tension that had been tightening in my chest unfurled as I felt the truth in his words. I raised a hand from his chest and pulled the hand from my cheek to kiss the back of his knuckles.

"Shifters have mates, but there's nothing magical about it," I continued. This conversation was far from over, and I might as well get it all out there. "It's the equivalent of human marriage. A fae bond is something else entirely."

"How so?" He threaded his fingers with mine. "I know a little of how it works but clearly not enough, because I don't understand why you're so freaked out by it."

"I'm *freaked out* because fae bonds are difficult to undo, and honestly, given my fucked-up magic and the fact that you're not fae, I don't even know if we would be able to undo it once it

190

settles into place." My eyes dropped to our intertwined hands. "I don't want to trap you with me and have you regret it later on."

Mikhail pivoted his hips up, and my world tilted sideways as he changed our positions. I gasped slightly as the breath went out of me with how hard he'd slammed me onto the bed. Before I could recover, he had me gripped by the throat, his pissed off face snarling over mine.

It probably said a lot about me that I was turned on rather than scared in this particular moment.

"Get it through that thick head of yours," he growled. "I will *never* regret you. I love you with every part of my fucked-up soul. There is no one else I would rather have by my side or guarding my back. It's you. It's always been you."

My eyes burned, and I blinked back tears. Rationally, I'd known Mikhail loved me. He'd sacrificed himself for me in the dragon realm, and nothing he'd done since should have made me doubt his devotion to me, but hearing the words from his lips was like a salve for my soul. Still, I needed to get the rest of it out there.

I tapped his hand, and Mikhail loosened his grip on my throat but kept it there, as if he was anticipating having to pin me down again to make a point.

"Justina said you ended things with her because she joined the Vampire Council. Up until now, I've kept you separate from the Unseelie Court as much as I could." I let my magic flow out of me. It'd been chomping at the bit ever since Mikhail had dropped the l-word, and the light blue flames lovingly wrapped around him and caressed his cheek. "Sooner or later, my magic *will* bind our souls together. The fae will see us as one, which means you'll be an official member of the Unseelie Court. You will be stepping into the life you tried so hard to avoid before."

Mikhail had seen my devourer flames turn beings to ash,

191

but he didn't look the least bit phased by the fire dancing across his bare skin. His trust in me and my magic was absolute, and that warmed my soul almost as much as his words.

"I didn't love Justina. Nor did she love me. We were simply what each other needed at the time, and the Council was always a means to an end for me. I wanted my revenge, and they provided a way for me to do that. I might be a vampire, but I never really belonged with them." He relaxed the hand that had been at my throat and ran his fingers down my jawline. "I was always something else, something that didn't belong. Magos held to the old ways even after he was turned, but that didn't appeal to me either. I didn't know what I was looking for until you crashed into my life."

"I'm glad I found you, vampire," I repeated the words I'd once said to him when we'd been bound and on our knees in a bloody arena.

"I'm glad I found you too, shifter." He smiled as he clearly remembered the moment. "You are my home. Wherever you go, I will happily follow."

My flames burned brighter for a moment before sinking back beneath my skin... and his. The bond between us strengthened as we both accepted it. I had no idea what that would mean for the future; it usually took fae mate bonds years to truly form, but my magic had never played by the rules, so we'd probably be in for a wild ride.

"Now that we have that settled... " Mikhail dragged his fingers across my clit, and I let out a harsh breath as my hips jerked upward. "How about I give you that fuck you were begging for earlier?"

"I wasn't beg—" A deep, throaty moan cut off whatever else I was going to say as he sunk three fingers deep into my pussy. This wasn't a gentle teasing. My body stretched around him and Mikhail fucked me ruthlessly with one hand while the other wrapped around my throat.

"You were absolutely begging." His thumb brushed lightly over my clit in rhythm with his fingers, and my eyes rolled to the back of my head. The release that had been building erupted, and I arched off the bed as Mikhail kept fucking me through it all. Every part of my body trembled and I bonelessly sank back onto the bed after, and Mikhail slowly withdrew his fingers, swirling through the slickness that coated my pussy and thighs. "Don't get too relaxed—I'm far from done."

I lazily smirked up at him. Two could play this game. I slid out from beneath him and moved down the bed. He exhaled sharply when I wrapped my fingers tightly around his cock, and I laughed under my breath. He might know how to play my body, but I was intimately familiar with every inch of his too. My hand slid up and down his shaft before I brushed a thumb over the precum beading at the tip. Mikhail's eyes darkened as I slowly leaned forward and licked him from base to tip.

"Fuck," Mikhail swore.

"Care to beg?" I teased and swirled my tongue along the sensitive underside of his head. He groaned, and I almost swallowed him whole, wanting to feel him come undone on my tongue. A frustrated noise spilled from my lips before I could pull it back.

"I don't have to." He laughed smugly. "You're impatient. It's why Pele always ties you up. You want my cock in your mouth as much as I do."

Damn it. He was right. Whatever.

I licked him one more time before taking him as deep as I could. Fingers gripped my hair, his hips thrust forward, and I almost came again as he hit the back of my throat. Just like with his fingers, Mikhail didn't hold back as he fucked my mouth. Neither did I. His cock thickened as I sucked and licked for all I was worth. Desire burned between us, and I could feel it pouring into the mate bond. We were definitely past the point of no return now.

Suddenly, Mikhail pulled me off and maneuvered us so I was on top of him again. He didn't waste any time. I felt his cock push against my slick entrance and then he slammed home. I pivoted my hips, and he slid deeper, both of us letting out low satisfied groans.

"Consider this me begging you to fuck me." He shoved his hips up, making me gasp, and grabbed my hand, guiding it down to my clit. "And fuck yourself too. I want to watch you unravel."

Fingers dug into my hips hard enough to bruise, and Mikhail thrust into me again. I swirled two of my fingertips around the edges of my pussy until they were dripping and then rubbed them against my clit.

Another low moan slipped from my lips, and my legs started to tremble. Mikhail's fingers kept digging in with their punishing grip as he matched every one of my thrusts.

"You are fucking perfect," he growled roughly as he watched my fingers work my body while my pussy clenched around his cock.

"I know," I panted.

"Harder," he begged.

The word was my undoing. I leaned forward, changing the angle, and a strangled scream tore from my throat as his cock hit an entirely new spot. My free hand wrapped around his throat, fingertips shifting to claws that punched through the soft skin. Mikhail's eyes glazed over, and I could feel how close he was.

I lifted myself higher, allowing more of him to slide in and out of me each time our bodies came together. My legs quivered as pure ecstasy rippled down my spine, and Mikhail roared at the same moment I screamed, both of us sinking into oblivion as magic burned between us.

After what felt like an eternity, I released my grip on his throat and leaned down to lick the blood clean before lying on his chest with his cock still inside me. Neither of us seemed inclined to fully break apart yet.

"You're mine, Nemain. Now and always."

"Same, Mikhail." I kissed his chest where his heart was still beating in rhythm with mine. "Same."

Chapter Fifteen

THE EARLY AFTERNOON sun bathed my room as I lounged in bed, tucked into Mikhail's side. We'd collapsed into a tangle of limbs and passed out hard after round two... and then three. Both of our bodies had needed the rest, and all my aches and pains from the last few days were gone now. I'd felt so good when I'd woken up an hour ago that I'd slipped under the covers and taken Mikhail in my mouth.

He'd been very enthusiastic about being woken up like that, and after he came down my throat, he had expressed his gratitude quite thoroughly. My thighs and core had only stopped trembling from the aftershocks of pleasure a few minutes ago. We both knew we needed to get up, but neither of us seemed willing to make the first move.

I snuggled further into him and inhaled his rich, spicy scent. Five more minutes.

Mikhail softly traced the blue flower tattoo on the center of my upper back. He always gravitated towards that spot, somehow finding the tattoo even when he couldn't see it. The first few times his fingers had brushed against the electric blue petals, I'd almost flinched from the contact and the guilt it stirred.

The tattoo had been a birthday gift from Myrna. She'd painted it on my skin with her magic hours before she'd died. For a long time, Sebastian had wielded the tattoo as a type of torment against me. When I'd claimed my vengeance, Sebastian had restored Myrna's gift to what it once was. I was still surprised by that, but maybe some part of his twisted love for me had shown through at the end.

A part of me felt guilty that I loved Mikhail so much. It felt like a betrayal to Myrna and what I had shared with her. Now confusion joined the guilt, because in the decades we'd spent together, a fae bond had never snapped into place between us. Back then, I hadn't known I was fae—I'd just assumed it hadn't happened because Myrna's fae nature hadn't recognized a shifter as a mate. That it'd sensed the devourer magic I'd kept smothered inside of me and deemed me unworthy.

It hadn't mattered, because Myrna had found me worthy. She'd loved me absolutely, and I'd been completely devoted to her. So why hadn't we bonded?

Considering how much I'd lost my shit in the years after her death, it had probably been for the best. If we'd had a bond in place, I probably would have died with her, but not knowing why it'd never happened still nagged at me.

"We should get up," Mikhail said begrudgingly. "If your brother isn't up yet, he will be soon."

"I know."

No doubt he'd be pounding on my door as soon as the KO ball wore off, and I wouldn't be able to fault him for it; his mate was in the hands of the enemy. They wouldn't kill Hades, of that I had no doubt. I'd never personally met Artemis or the remaining Olympians, but their reputation as vengeful assholes was pretty well documented.

It was unlikely they were throwing a picnic for their long

197

lost relative, but he was alive, and we had time to come up with a plan that had at least a chance of succeeding.

Instead of getting up, I twisted my head so I could look at Mikhail. "Tell me something about your life before the Vampire Council. Before you came to this realm."

"Justina knowing my birth name really bothered you, huh?"

"Yes."

His hand flattened on my back, pressing me tighter against his body while he bent down to kiss the top of my head.

"My father's name was Taegen. I don't remember much about him." I felt our hearts slow, as if the memory didn't want to surface, and I kissed his chest. "I suppose that's the curse of living a long life. Despite how much we try to cling to our memories, they still leave us."

"How old were you when he died?"

"Fourteen. It was hard for both me and my mother, Rania. My father was such a force of nature that it left this hole in our lives we didn't know how to fill."

"It was the same for me and Cian when Macha and Nevin died." I rested my head on his chest again. "She was so fierce and he was so steady. Growing up, I thought the two of them were invincible."

"As hard as it was losing my father, at least we had Magos and Hasina. You and Cian only had each other in a world that was trying to kill you."

"We had to Jinx too." I smiled. "That cranky-ass grimalkin is probably the reason we survived that first year."

"I'll keep that in mind next time he annoys me and I think about chucking him out the window."

I huffed a laugh.

"My mother and Hasina got off to a rough start. They both had strong personalities and were very... opinionated about how best to run our township." I could hear the smile in

Mikhail's voice as he reflected on his past. "But they were friends by the time my father passed, and after that, Hasina was there constantly for us. Magos was too, but he was often traveling.

"One morning, Hasina stopped by our place bright and early. She knew my mother had been working late the previous few days in preparation for the upcoming harvest and wanted to do something nice by making us breakfast." Mikhail's chest started to shake beneath me, and I realized he was trying and failing to suppress a laugh.

"I'm guessing this didn't go well?" I grinned up at him.

"Let's just say that you and Hasina have your lack of cooking skills in common. We woke up to her swearing up a storm in the kitchen as she frantically tried to open the windows to air out the smoke."

I chuckled. "That does sound like me."

"When Magos got home, he made us all breakfast and pointedly did not say anything about the scorch marks in our kitchen."

I listened while Mikhail recounted a few more anecdotes about the hijinks he got up to in his teenage years while giving me little bits of information about Hasina and his mother, Rania. I'd never get to meet them, but I liked knowing a little more about them all the same.

Finally, with great reluctance, we both got up, showered, and quickly dressed. Cian was waiting for us in the kitchen, sitting on a barstool at the island and staring at the coffee Magos had probably made for him.

"I'm going to chat with Hecate and then whatever other gods I can track down to see if they know of a way into the Olympian realm," I said, nodding my thanks to Magos when he handed me a steaming mug of caffeine and sugary bliss. I took several long sips before setting it down and getting out the part I knew Cian really wouldn't like. "You're staying here."

199

"Are you fucking kidding me?" Faster than I could track, Cian sprung from the stool and stood in front of me, breathing aggression. "You really think I'm just going to sit here on my ass and do nothing while they're—" His voice broke as pain erupted across his silver eyes.

"Hey." I gripped both sides of my brother's face. "I know it's hard, but one of them must know something useful. You're a little volatile right now, and we both know the gods are sensitive little bitches. If you say something to piss them off, they won't help us out of spite."

"You have no idea what they'll do to him." His voice trembled. "They're beyond sadistic, Nemain."

"True, but it's no fun for them if he's not awake, and I asked Lir about it yesterday," I said softly. "Hades is still unconscious. Whatever they did to knock him out when they kidnapped him worked a little too well. Apparently, Artemis is real pissed off about it."

"It might complicate things if we have to carry him out." Mikhail frowned as he sipped his espresso.

"There's a chance I might be able to undo whatever they did to him. I was able to use my devourer magic to remove the binding Cerri had placed on Eddie to hide his dragon side. But I won't know until I see him."

I could see the despair spreading across Cian's face. He needed something to do while I was gone to keep his mind distracted. He didn't fight me as I led him back to the kitchen island and pushed him onto one of the stools.

"I already know the history between Hades and the others." I walked around the island and leaned back against the counter. "But why don't you give us another rundown. It'll be useful for these two"—I waved to Magos and Mikhail—"and you can strategize while I'm gone. I'll find us a way in, and you lot can figure out how to keep us alive once we're there."

"Love your optimism," Mikhail said dryly.

Magos just nodded and placed a new cup of coffee in front of Cian along with some fruit and freshly baked bread. I eyed the food and then arched a brow at him.

"I was bored, and I find baking helps center my thoughts," he said almost sheepishly. "Finn and Isabeau also enjoy helping me."

"I fully support anything that involves food magically showing up in front of me."

Mikhail grabbed a thick slice of bread, slathered butter on it, and passed it to me. I gave him an adoring look, and he just rolled his eyes.

"Which gods do you think we'll be up against?" Magos asked. "Aside from Artemis."

Cian put down the melon slice he'd been nibbling with a grimace. "Probably all the major players who aren't dead."

"So Ares, Hermes, and Poseidon. Maybe Hephaestus." I tore a chunk of crust off my bread. "Unless something has changed, Aphrodite and Dionysus are in the wind."

"They still are," Cian confirmed. "According to everything Hades has told me about them, they just want to have a good time. I wouldn't say they're good people, but they didn't really have a lot of choices when Zeus and Hera were alive. Those two ran before the dust settled and haven't been seen since. I suspect they figured out a way to hide their identities like Hades, but none of the other Olympians cared about finding them."

"Weren't Hephaestus and Aphrodite married?" Magos asked.

"In name only," Cian said. "Zeus dictated the marriage; neither of them had any interest in it."

"You think Hephaestus is helping the others?" I chewed on my crust, not loving that idea. Hephaestus was known for his metalsmithing skills. As much as I loved magical weapons, I preferred to be the one wielding them, not the one being stabbed with an enchanted blade.

"Hard to say. While he hated Zeus, he adored his mother."

The vampires glanced at me, and I gave them both disappointed looks. "Do we need to draw you a family tree? Did neither of you watch Xena?"

Mikhail gave me a flat look, but Magos smiled. "It's on the list, according to Isabeau."

"Hera was his mother," Cian supplied. "Zeus could have been his father, or it could have been any number of Hera's other lovers. The two of them thrived on creating drama and making each other jealous. Hephaestus was there the day Hades killed his mother. He isn't a fighter, but I have no doubt he would be more than happy to donate some of his inventions to keep Hades contained or protect their realm."

"Great." I sighed.

"Hades managed to kill half a dozen of them in one go?" Mikhail gave Cian a calculating look. "How?"

My brother shook his head slowly. "It's not something any of us could do. I'm skilled in necromancy, and even I couldn't do it."

"It'd still be useful to know," Mikhail pushed.

"The gods' physical bodies aren't immortal—it's their souls that are," Cian explained. "They use magic to protect themselves physically, but if their bodies are destroyed, their souls will still remain out of the death realms. They'll float around collecting magic until they have enough to regenerate themselves. In order to kill them, you have to destroy their souls."

"And Hades did that?" Magos guessed.

"Yes." Cian nodded. "It's not an easy thing to do. Removing a soul from a body isn't hard, but usually, it'll just find its way to a death realm, or in the case of the gods, fly around for a bit before creating a new body. Necromancy is deeply tied to souls, and Hades is very possibly the most powerful necromancer in existence. Even so, he was only able to do what he did because he was so furious over what they did to Persephone."

"So," Mikhail drawled while tapping his fingertips on the counter, "is the whole 'Hades kidnapping Persephone and forcing her into marriage' thing true?" His gaze flicked over to me. "Even I know that story."

"Good of you to not be completely useless," I said lightly.

Mikhail's eyes brightened, and the corners of his lips curled into a smile. I grinned into my coffee cup. He'd definitely make me pay for that comment later.

"The marriage part isn't true, but the kidnapping part is." He rushed on. "But that was for a good reason."

"Which was?" Magos arched a dark eyebrow.

"Persephone's mother was Demeter, but her father was a human, so she was only a demigod. The only people the gods loved to fuck with more than humans were their own children, particularly the ones who had human blood." Cian clutched at a black ring that hung around his neck on a chain. "Hades met Persephone when she was only a year old. He actually helped raise her because Demeter had no interest in her... not until the girl was older and Demeter saw an opportunity to hurt Hades."

His fingers twisted absently around the ring, and I narrowed my eyes. Even from where I stood across the kitchen, I could feel the cold death magic rolling off the small object.

"Demeter started doing horrible things to Persephone." Cian swallowed. "Hades tried to protect her, but Demeter maintained he had no claim over her daughter... unless he married her."

"Demeter and the others must have enjoyed the perversion of it." My lips pressed into a flat line.

"The marriage was never consummated," Cian said. "Persephone was like a daughter to him. Even then, the deal

203

was that he could only have her for half the year. He was trying to barter a way around it when he angered Zeus and Hera over something else, and they used Persephone to make a point. I don't know the specifics of what happened that day, only that whatever they did enraged him enough to kill them and some of the others."

More familiar, cold magic leaked from the ring. "Is that Hades' ring?"

Cian blinked at me and then glanced down at the ring as if he hadn't realized he'd been holding it. "Yes."

"Was he wearing it the day he killed Zeus and the others?"

"Most likely. He used to wear it all the time before he gave it to me." Darkness flashed across Cian's silver eyes as he stared at the ring, his fingers tightening around it. "Nobody can remove it but me or him. Adrian was pissed and kept threatening to cut off my finger."

"We won't ever let him get you again," Magos promised. I was thankful he'd said that, not only because of the relief in Cian's eyes, but also because I was too pissed off to speak. Adrian was going to die. Painfully.

"I'll be right back," I said in a clipped tone and headed down to the second-floor apartment where Bryn and Finn lived. Vizor and Eddie were still passed out on the couch while Bryn and Cerri chatted in the kitchen, but they both paused when I walked in. "Cerri, do all dragons have the ability to pull memories from magical artifacts, or is that just an Eddie thing?"

"We all do," she answered without missing a beat. "Some of us are better at it than others."

"Do you happen to be one of the ones who are good at it?"

"Better than Eddie," she said without a trace of humility.

"Perfect. Can I borrow you for a moment?" I turned to head back upstairs, but Bryn stopped me.

"Nemain?"

A Shift in Death

"Yes?" I pivoted back around to face her.

Her solemn, grey eyes darted down the hallway. "Would you mind talking to Finn? He's taking everything that happened with Isabeau really hard." She rubbed her chest and shuffled her wings. "I can feel his anxiety, but he won't talk to me about it."

Valkyrie bonds worked differently than fae mate bonds, but they had some things in common. Bryn and Finn would always be able to find each other unless someone used particularly strong magic to dampen the bond. They would also feel more of each other's emotions as the bond continued to strengthen. Sigrun was teaching them how to control that so one of them didn't overwhelm the other, but strong feelings would always bleed through.

I'd been planning on talking to Finn before I left, might as well do it now. "Sure. Isabeau sleeping downstairs or up here?"

"Here," Bryn said. "We were going to put her downstairs in her room, but Finn... didn't like that idea."

Oh boy. Finn and Isabeau had fallen into a friendship almost instantly when he came to live with us. Even though he was almost two years older than her, Finn usually followed Isabeau's lead. She was the one who threw tantrums or made her opinion known... loudly.

We regularly joked that the fae prophecy must have gotten it wrong. Surely the quiet and kind fae boy wouldn't be the one to bring about the fall of the realms. That seemed more like an Isabeau thing.

"I'll head upstairs and speak with Cian," Cerri said.

She grabbed her coffee and left as I walked down the hallway. "Finn?" I knocked on the last door on the right. "Cool if I come in?" Ten seconds passed, and I waited, shifting back and forth on my feet. Patience really wasn't my thing. "Kid?"

"Yes." He'd answered so quietly, I barely heard the word, even with my shifter hearing.

I twisted the handle and entered the room. Technically, Isabeau had a room downstairs, but they had both requested bunk beds in their rooms, and it was rare that they slept apart. Instead, they just bounced back and forth between each other's spaces. Finn liked to draw sketches of mountains and strange-looking creatures then use them to decorate the walls. We all assumed it was from his childhood in the exiled realm of his father, the fae king, but he didn't want to talk about it and none of us were willing to push him on it.

Isabeau was tucked into the bottom bunk. Her caramel brown curls were fanned out around her head, and someone, I assumed Finn, had placed her favorite stuffed animals around her. She looked a little paler than usual but appeared fine otherwise.

Finn was sitting on the bed with her, his back against the wall and knees tucked up to his chest. He didn't look at me when I came in, just continued to stare at Isabeau like he wasn't convinced she was okay. The green outer ring of his eyes was darker than usual, making it contrast sharply against the inner golden yellow. I was used to his strange, two-toned eyes, but they still attracted attention whenever we took him somewhere.

Which wasn't all that often. Finn didn't always handle new people and places well and became overwhelmed easily. Technically, he shouldn't have come into his magic for at least another two decades. We didn't know if he was just going through magical puberty early, or if this was only the tip of the iceberg for his power. Something told me it was the latter. Kaysea's vision had implied Finn was destined to destroy the realms... unless I could prevent him from going down that path.

So far, I'd mostly been bribing him with cookies. Seemed to be working fine, despite Elisa and Bryn's concerns over too much sugar. The two of them really couldn't wrap their heads around not needing to be concerned about diet when you had supernatural healing.

I grabbed one of the books off the nightstand and took a seat at the foot of the bed. Finn watched as I flopped my legs down close to Isabeau, but not touching. I felt a little flare-up of his magic, but he returned his watchful gaze to Isabeau. I started flipping through the pages. Loudly.

After a few minutes, the book slammed shut in my hands. Finn scowled at me, and I smiled.

"She won't wake up," he finally said. "And she's blocked me from her mind."

"Aki and Kaysea have both looked at her," I said calmly. "Isabeau used a lot of magic to trap us all in those illusions— more than she should have, considering her age. She'll be fine. Just give her a couple of days."

Finn chewed his bottom lip. "But what if—"

"Do you see Elisa freaking out over Isabeau?"

"No."

"You know what Elisa went through to protect her." I had no doubt Isabeau had told Finn everything about her experience growing up under the Vampire Council's "care," and who knew what Isabeau had learned since then, considering she had the ability to traipse through most of our minds without us being the least bit aware. Keeping secrets from her was impossible. "Do you seriously think Elisa wouldn't be tearing down the walls if she thought Isabeau were in trouble?"

He thought about this before nodding. "Okay." Though his expression remained dark and haunted.

"What else is bothering you?" When he didn't answer, I stretched a leg across the bed over Isabeau and poked him with my toe.

Frustrated eyes snapped to me. "Bryn just leaves me alone. You're really annoying."

I poked him again. "I'm *persistent*."

He let out an angry breath. "Why can't I help her? I was able to get those chains off your brother. When you broke that table at Pele's, I fixed it. But I can't fix *her*."

I moved until I was sitting next to him on the bed, my legs curled underneath me. "You might be a little badass, kid, but you're not all-powerful."

"Language," he said in a hushed voice.

"Ass doesn't count as a swear word." I rolled my eyes. "We don't know exactly what your magic is, but you are fae. Even with the devourer bit, that's still what your magic is, and fae magic is mostly elemental-based. Obviously you can do more than that... but so far, nothing you've demonstrated leans towards strong telepathy skills." My eyes slide from Isabeau's face to his. "She's the reason the two of you can communicate mind-to-mind, isn't she?"

He nodded.

"You two are quite the pair," I murmured. "I have no idea what Isabeau's lineage is, but she's already the most powerful telepath I've ever met. We'll find someone to help her learn to control her magic better so it doesn't hit her so hard next time."

"Next time?" Fear flickered across his face. "She can't do this again."

"She can," I said calmly. "And she will."

The bed frame rattled as Finn struggled to deal with this, and I held my hand out, letting my flames flicker to life.

"Trust me, kid. Nothing good ever comes from denying who you are."

AFTER PROMISING Finn that both Aki and Kaysea would be by again to check on Isabeau, I headed back upstairs. I wasn't sure if we'd get anything useful out of the memory of Hades killing the other gods, but it was worth a shot. Anything that might give us an advantage was worth it, because I highly doubted we'd be able to get into their realm, rescue Hades, and get the hell out without a confrontation.

"We ready?" I asked as I breezed back into the apartment. Everyone had gathered into a circle on the sparring mat with Cerri in the center. Mikhail and Cian moved further apart to make room for me, and I slid in between them.

"Yes," Cerri said. "Everyone needs to be in physical contact with me, and I'll pull you in."

"This isn't going to be like with Isabeau is it?" Mikhail grimaced as he placed his hand onto Cerri's shoulder. Magos and I did the same, but Cerri held out a hand to Cian. He didn't hesitate, clasping her forearm, and she did the same, bonding them together.

"It's not like that," she answered Mikhail. "I can't pull memories from people, only from objects that have a lot of magic." She held up the black ring pinched between her index finger and thumb. "The magic in Hades' ring feels like some type of illusion spell. It was in contact with his skin for centuries and soaked up additional magic from him. During that time, he imprinted some of his memories onto it."

"I've done this before with Eddie," I told the others. "Trust me, it's nothing like the fun memory tour Isabeau took us on."

"Everyone ready?" We all gave a chorus of agreement, and Cerri closed her eyes. "Here we go."

Between one blink and the next, the world around us changed. My apartment vanished, and a sprawling throne room appeared. White marble columns stretched up to an impossibly high ceiling, and one side of the room was completely open to the sun-drenched mountainside. Most of the other walls were made up of the same brilliant white marble as the columns and were covered in murals of what I guessed were the various exploits of the gods.

I wandered away from the others, unable to resist my curiosity about how the gods had once lived. Golden lines raced through the teal-tiled floors. It should have been gaudy, and I wanted to hate it, but something about the design just worked. It not only spoke of power and magic, but of a bygone era in the human realm. I'd been born long after the gods and other supernatural powers had either left this realm or faded into obscurity. Now, I lived in a world where most humans had no idea what walked among them, so caught up in their technology and short, simple lives.

Humans no longer feared or worshiped the gods, but they had once, and everything around me was a reminder of that.

"What is the meaning of this?" A cool, arrogant voice rang out across the room, drawing my attention. Hades. He sounded the same as he did now, but I couldn't see him from where I was standing. I walked over to where Cian and the others were gathered. Similar to Isabeau's illusions, we could move around here, but unlike them, we couldn't interact with anything.

Nope, we'd get to be front-row spectators to whatever fucked-up event was about to go down. Joy.

Cerri was hovering protectively around my brother while Mikhail and Magos were scouring the faces of everyone in the room. I moved to stand next to Magos so I could see better.

Two people, who could only be Hera and Zeus, were sitting on thrones on top of a raised dais. Her golden blonde hair was wrapped up in some intricate bun, and a simple but refined gold crown rested on her head. A soft pink dress wrapped her body, making her lightly tanned skin practically glow. Beside her, Zeus was only wearing a pleated skirt, leaving his broad shoulders and chest on display.

In my mind, I'd envisioned the two of them appearing older, thanks to all the depictions I'd seen of them over the years. They both had to be over a thousand years old at this point but appeared to be in their thirties. Zeus had light brown hair that he'd haphazardly pulled back into a ponytail, and his handsome features were fixed into a mask of boredom-tinged arrogance.

In front of them were the rest of the gods, the major players anyway. Something about all of them drew my eye, even if they weren't classically handsome or beautiful. Even in this memory, I could feel the power dripping off them.

"What's the matter, Uncle?" A man with jet-black hair and rough features sneered. "Lose something?"

"I'm guessing that's Ares," I murmured, eying the large dual swords strapped to his back.

"Wondering just how good the god of war is with those things?" Mikhail saw me studying the blades. "I'll let you have the first go when we meet him later. Consider it a gift."

"Thanks, love."

We fell silent as Hades strode further into the room, stopping a few feet from Zeus and Hera, who remained seated in their thrones, not the least bit worried about a very pissed off god of death. It was a little unsettling to see Hades appear then exactly as he did now. Same wavy, black hair, dark eyes, and olive-toned skin. The only difference was there was a hint of softness to him now that I attributed to my brother. This Hades was nothing but cold fury.

"Where. Is. She?" he bit out. Magic flared out of him, and most of the gods wisely took a step back. Even Zeus shifted slightly in this throne, although his haughty mask didn't slip.

Ares remained where he was standing, a cruel smile stretching across his face. "We're just having a bit of fun, Uncle. No need to be so dramatic."

Hades slowly turned his head towards his nephew, eyes brimming with fury. "I'm done with your fucking games." His gaze drifted across those gathered, settling on a woman with startling green eyes and flowers woven into her hair. "Yours too, Demeter."

"You brought this upon yourself." She shrugged a dainty shoulder. "And her."

He took a step towards her but halted when lightning crackled across the floor. Zeus finally deigned to rise from his throne and slowly stepped down the dais towards Hades. The arrogant indifference was gone from his face, replaced by cruelty.

"I grow bored of you interfering with us," he said. "If you don't want to partake in the lovely delights we find in this realm, that's fine. You can go sulk in one of those many death realms you love so much." Zeus took another step into Hades' space and looked him right in the eyes. "Let today be a reminder that I am not to be fucked with."

A terrified scream tore through the room, and Hades whirled, only to slam to his knees when Zeus shocked him with a bolt of lightning. In an equally fast movement, Ares drew his swords and thrust them through the backs of Hades' legs and straight into the ground.

I was so enraptured with everything going on that I jolted when Cian dove forward, only to be pulled back by Cerri and Magos. He fought against them, his screams blending in with that of his lover's.

"Just a memory," Cerri soothed. "This pain is no longer. It's okay, Cian." She repeated the words over and over and kept her arms wrapped around my brother.

Whimpers slipped out of Cian, but he stopped fighting to get free. I returned my attention to the memory unfolding, studying the way Ares had his arm wrapped around Hades' throat, holding him in place. A woman with dark brown hair stood towards the back of the room with a bow on her back and a predatory look on her face.

Artemis.

On her left stood a blond man who seemed really young, appearing closer to twenty than most of the others. His expression was blissed out like he was drinking in Hades' pain. To her right was a man the exact opposite of the young blond man. Physically, he looked like he was in his early thirties, but his solid grey hair made me think he was older. There was a regal handsomeness to his face with its square jaw and strong nose. I wasn't sure who either of them were, but if they made it out of this room alive, it'd be easy enough to narrow down.

Three large men dragged in a young woman, who was screaming her lungs out as she frantically struggled.

"No!" Hades rasped. He fought to pull free, but between Ares' grip around his neck and the swords pinning his legs to the ground, he was well and truly trapped.

The guards threw the girl to the floor and then grabbed her arms, yanking them back and keeping her in place. Words tumbled out of her mouth, fast and tangled together. Our translation marks must not have been working or something must have been wrong with the memory, because nothing she said made any sense.

"Persephone." Pain lit up Hades' dark eyes before he glared at Zeus. "What did you do?"

"Relax. Nobody touched her." The king of the gods shrugged. "You're always keeping her away from us; I thought maybe she should get to know our family a little better."

"My boys kept her entertained with some lovely dreams," Ares drawled into Hades' right ear. He laughed when Hades tried to fling his head back to hit him before he tightened his hold around his uncle's throat.

Two men stepped forward in unison, both dark-haired like their father but with handsomer features. They leaned down to stroke Persephone's cheeks, and she trembled and stopped whimpering for a moment before trying to hurl herself backwards, but the guards held her firmly in place. One of the men laughed while the other gripped her chin and forced her to look at him.

Something in his sickly, yellow eyes stirred, and she started to scream.

Magos clenched his jaw and looked at me. "Who?"

"Deimos and Phobos, I'm guessing." I grimaced as one of the guards shoved a cloth gag into Persephone's mouth when her screaming showed no signs of stopping. "They were some of Ares' children and strong empaths."

"They could invoke fear, dread, and panic," Cian said numbly. "Ares used them often in battle."

Persephone finally quieted, slumping in the guards' holds. Her green eyes were dull as they stared forward, not focusing on anything and definitely not recognizing Hades.

"Hmm," Zeus grunted. "I think we might have broken her."

Ares sneered at the shattered girl. "Thought your daughter would have been a little tougher, Demeter."

Demeter just twirled her hair around her finger. "She always was a disappointment."

"Please," Hades whispered past Ares' choke hold.

Zeus flicked his eyes towards his son, and the god of war loosened his grip around Hades' throat enough for him to speak. Hades stared at Persephone, eyes shining with love and fear. "Just let her go, and I swear I will never interfere with any of your plans again."

"Alright." Zeus smiled triumphantly, and electricity crackled through the air. Hades surged forward, flesh ripping as he pulled his legs free. Ares redoubled his efforts to hold him, his sons coming to his aid. Hades made it halfway to the still prone Persephone before they managed to get him under control. Deimos and Phobos each wrenched an arm back, and Ares punched him hard, snapping his head to the side with a resounding *crack*.

All I could do was watch with an odd feeling of detachment and horror as Zeus strolled over to Persephone and placed a hand on the girl's head. For one brief moment, she seemed to come back to herself, the confusion leaving her eyes as she blinked and looked around the room before whispering one name.

"Hades?"

Lightning erupted from Zeus' hand, burning straight through Persephone. She didn't even have time to scream. Her body jerked as it arched back, and within seconds, she was nothing but ashes. Zeus waved a hand through what was left of her, sending the ashes scattering across the floor.

"There." Zeus brushed his hands together. "She's gone."

Hades stared at the ashes that had stopped in front of him. I thought of how much I'd hated him at first. How much I'd tried to convince my brother not to get involved with him. I hadn't even known who he truly was back then. He was just a hot guy Cian and I had met at a tavern. When it'd started to become clear Cian had feelings for him that went beyond a casual fling, I'd tried to talk him out of it.

Hades—Dante back then—had been so cold. The only emotion he'd seemed to show was arrogance with a hint of cruelty. My brother was a softhearted person, and I'd been worried that this mysterious, dark-haired stranger would hurt him. I'd thought Hades hadn't been capable of loving someone the way my brother deserved.

But as I watched Hades looking at the ashes painted across the floor, I could feel every part of his soul break. It wasn't that Hades had been incapable of love when I'd first met him, it was that he'd been heartbroken and terrified of ever caring about another person again. As someone who had lost her parents, friends, and lovers over a long and often cruel life… I could understand that.

"They broke him," Cian said softly. "And now they're going to do it again."

No, I thought. *You are the key to breaking him. And they'll never get you.* "Don't worry, brother," I said instead. "We'll get him back, I promise you. Mikhail is very eager to kill a god, and I'm feeling a little wrathful myself."

"Speaking of wrathful," Cerri said, eyes burning as she watched the air around Hades stir. "His magic is really something."

Ares turned from where he had been conversing with his father towards Hades, a frown on his face. I inadvertently took a step back as I felt an avalanche of icy magic roll through the room. Then Ares' eyes widened.

"Let go of him!" he commanded his sons.

It was too late.

Phobos and Deimos stiffened before their arms went slack, releasing Hades. Thin, silvery tendrils stretched from their bodies as they collapsed to the ground and Hades rose. Their souls swirled around him before diving into his chest. Hades' dark eyes glowed white as he absorbed the souls of the fallen gods.

"I'm going to cut you apart." Ares pulled his swords free and prowled towards Hades.

Hades raised his hand, and Ares staggered to a stop. His arms trembled as his swords slipped from his grasp and clanged to the floor. The remaining gods watched in shock as Hades strode forward like an unstoppable force and thrust his hand into his nephew's chest.

"STOP!" Zeus commanded, lightning dripping from his fingertips. Hera rose from where she'd been lounging on her throne this whole time, watching the events unfold with unrestrained glee, but the amusement was gone from her face now.

Several of the gods, including who I guessed were Aphrodite and Dionysus, had clearly seen enough and fled. A woman with rich brown hair and sharp eyes stood behind Zeus, hands clenched at her sides. Her gaze darted across the room to where Artemis was surrounded by most of the remaining gods. Some sort of unspoken communication passed between the two, and Artemis shook her head stubbornly. The sharp-eyed goddess looked to the gods on either side of Artemis, and they slowly nodded.

Artemis screamed as they grabbed her and dragged her from the room. "Athena!" She struggled to get free. "Let me go! I'm not leaving her behind!" The gods pulling her out of the room paid her no mind, and soon, her screaming became nothing but faint echoes.

"Artemis was saved by her sister," I murmured.

"Athena had the gift of foresight," Cian said. "It was rare that she would see visions very far into the future, but she almost always knew how things would play in the present."

The room became thick with angry magic as the gods remained locked in their standoff. Golden lightning rolled off Zeus' fingers as he glared at Hades, who still held Ares in his grip. The god of war didn't look all that impressive anymore. His skin had paled to the point that he already looked like a corpse, but I could still hear his labored breaths.

Hades looked past Ares to where Zeus was standing, cloaked in his power. "I saw Persephone take her first steps. I was there when she fell out of an olive tree and broke her arm. I listened to her cry when the boy she had a crush on broke her heart." He twisted the hand that was still inside Ares' chest, causing the god to writhe. "She's the closest thing I've ever had to a daughter. *To an actual family*. I went along with all of your fucked-up demands." Hades' dark eyes glowed with fury. "Although, telling me to marry someone I loved like my own child was particularly fucked-up, even for you."

"That was Demeter's idea." Zeus glanced at his sister. "Even I thought it was in poor taste."

"No, you didn't," Demeter hissed. "You laughed and said you were disappointed you didn't think of it first."

"It doesn't matter." Zeus cut a hand through the air. "We all knew you wouldn't actually do anything with the girl. It was just a bit of fun."

Cerri shifted from where she was still supporting Cian. "What the fuck was wrong with these people?"

"I don't know," I said, my lip curling in disgust. "I've met some of the other gods, and while they're a little terrifying, they're not completely fucked in the head like the Olympians were."

"Let my son go, Hades," Zeus commanded. "You will be forgiven for what you did to Deimos and Phobos if you release him now and leave."

"No," Ares ground out. "He pays."

"Silence!" Zeus barked.

"None of you are leaving," Hades said matter-of-factly, cocking his head slightly as he watched Ares struggle weakly to get free. "She was the only thing I gave a shit about. Even if I find her soul in the death realms, you made sure she was absolutely destroyed. It will take centuries for her to heal, and even then, I don't know if she'll ever truly get past what was done to her."

"Hades," Athena warned, finally speaking up. She placed a hand on Zeus' shoulder before stepping past him. "Think about this. Even you cannot fight all of us."

For a moment, I didn't think Hades would respond. Ares seemed to be shrinking in on himself; his muscles had lost definition and his skin had begun to shrivel. Hades watched with mild interest as the body before him decayed. Everything I knew about the Olympians had been passed through others. Athena was a bit of a mystery to me, and I was curious as to why she died that day. From everything I knew about her, she didn't seem as bad as the others.

"You knew," Hades said quietly, still not taking his gaze off Ares' slow demise. "Not only that things would play out this way, but everything else. Every other bit of cruelty they would bestow on me. On Persephone. On everyone. You knew it all" —his gaze cut to her—"and you did *nothing*."

"Humans don't matter."

"Persephone did."

Athena said nothing.

Faster than I could track, a form darted behind Hades, a dagger aimed at his throat. I took a step forward, forgetting for a moment that this was merely a memory. Not that it mattered. Hades' hand, the one not buried in Ares' chest, shot out from his side and caught the figure by the throat.

He released the god of war, who collapsed to the floor but then began crawling away.

"You're insane." The god in Hades' grip struggled to breathe but still managed to bury the dagger into Hades' shoulder. "All this," he gasped, "over some stupid, half-blood bitch."

"Apollo!" Athena cried out.

Magic erupted from Hades, and he dropped the corpse of the golden god at his feet. The ghostly silver outline of his soul swirled around him for a moment before Hades' cold magic latched onto it and pulled it into his body. Athena screamed, and Zeus bellowed. All the gods converged on Hades, but he just let out a cold laugh as his magic struck at everyone in the room. Zeus' lightning shot out, and I saw something dark spill forth from Hera, but none of it mattered.

Death magic poured off Hades, and any other magic that came into contact with it was destroyed instantly. Even in this memory, I could feel the magnitude of magic he had unleashed that day.

We looked around the room full of dead gods. "Well… " I drawled, "the god of death certainly delivered on that front."

Chapter Sixteen

"We'll be back soon," I promised Cian. He still wasn't thrilled about being left behind while I went to chat with Hecate and potentially some of the other gods, but I refused to take him with us and risk having him mouth off to the wrong god.

Not that there was a right god to be a smartass around.

After pulling us out of the memory, Cerri had gone to sit on the couch, a little unsteady on her feet. Thankfully, the rest of us felt fine, no massive after-sickness like from Isabeau's magic.

"Use this time to prepare and pack anything that might be useful," I instructed Cian. "Talk to Badb and Kalen, see if they have any suggestions for weapons or anything else useful we can bring. With any luck, we'll be leaving as soon as I get back."

Magos looked at me. "Who's going on this particular adventure?"

I pursed my lips. If Eddie had been awake, I'd have probably invited him along because the dragons were particularly handy, but he and Vizor were still passed out, and I wasn't comfortable bringing the other dragons. Cerri was perfectly capable of taking care of herself, but Eddie would have skinned me alive if I took her with us while he was asleep.

"Mikhail and I can handle it." I looked at Magos. "Can you keep an eye on Cian while I'm gone and make sure he stays safe?"

"Of course." He gave me a reassuring smile.

Cian's expression had morphed into one of determination, which was better than the hopeless look he'd worn before. Mikhail handed me my various straps and harnesses for my blades, and I strapped them all on before stepping further into the living room. With minimal effort on my part, a gateway split open in front of us. I still wasn't on Badb's level—she could open them rapidly and leap through them with infinite ease during a fight—but I was getting there.

"Be back in a bit," I said before striding through the gateway. As soon as Mikhail joined me, I started to close it, but a large, black blur leapt through it and crashed into my chest, knocking me to the ground.

I gasped as I tried to suck in a breath even as claws pierced the flesh beneath my collarbone. Golden eyes glowed with rage.

Right. Jinx had told me that morning while Mikhail and I had been lounging in bed to let him know when I was leaving. I'd gotten caught up in everything else that had happened, and I'd forgotten.

You. Idiot! He snarled in my face as his claws dug in deeper. In his fae form, he was close to a hundred pounds, but he could use his magic to make himself denser so he easily held me down.

"I didn't know you wanted to come with us!" I said in defense. "You only said to let you know when I was leaving."

And did you? Luna asked, and I blinked as she patiently sat next to us. Like Jinx, she was also in her fae form, which was

221

rare for her. She preferred to keep her glamour up. I was pretty sure she did it because she only weighed about ten pounds in her glamoured form, so it meant Finn could carry her around and she could sleep in his lap. He took comfort in her presence, which was why she rarely left the apartment. The two were damn near inseparable.

"What are you doing here?" I gaped at her. Jinx sunk his claws deeper, but I was so surprised by Luna's presence that I barely noticed.

It's time I started contributing to the safety of the group, she said. *Besides, I know so little of this world after being locked away in the exiled realm for so long. If I'm going to help Finn in the future, I need to start building alliances now.*

"Plus, you're far easier to get along with than Jinx, and therefore less likely to get us all killed," Mikhail added helpfully. Jinx's head swung around to glare at the vampire. "Tell me I'm wrong," Mikhail taunted.

I hissed as Jinx withdrew his claws from my flesh only to extend them again. "Quit antagonizing him!"

You just had to mate with him, didn't you? Jinx accused before leaping off me.

My stomach muscles flexed as I drew my knees up before pushing off the ground in one smooth motion and landing on my feet.

"You knew?" I rubbed my shoulders. The puncture wounds were already healed, but this was one of my favorite long-sleeve black shirts, and now it had holes in it. Stupid grimalkin.

Obviously. Jinx sneered. *You two might as well have had a flashing sign above your heads that said, FUCKED-UP FAE BOND HAPPENING.*

"I thought I was doing a good job of hiding it." I frowned. The vampire and two grimalkins stared at me. "Whatever. You guys are assholes." I glanced at the silver grimalkin. "Sorry,

Luna. You've been around Jinx for too long so his assholery has officially worn off on you too."

She walked over to Jinx and rubbed her head against his. *He is perfection.*

Jinx purred. Fucking spare me.

"Let's go before Jinx's head gets too big for him to move." I started back up the path.

Mikhail scrutinized the isolated stretch of beach before looking towards the winding path that led up a hill. "So this is where *The Mother of All Witches* lives?"

"I really suggest you don't call her that," I said dryly. "Hecate has a complicated history with witchcraft, particularly with witches and warlocks in this realm. I haven't had nearly enough coffee, or whiskey, to get into it with her."

"You know her that well?" Curiosity tinged his voice.

"My history with her is *also* complicated," I huffed. Above us on silent wings, a large eagle soared, banking down to get a better look at us before flying off. "In the human realm, 'gods' is a somewhat catchall term, or at least, that's what it's become. But back in the day, it specifically referred to beings from Nineveh. They were part of the original cataclysm where multiple realms fell to the devourers at the same time. Those from Nineveh settled around North Africa and the Mediterranean region and founded most of the major cities during ancient times. They wanted to recreate what they had lost, and I think they did, for a while at least."

Mikhail eyed an odd-looking plant with gold leaves and bright purple berries but wisely didn't touch it. I'd warned him before that Hecate loved her poisons, and apparently he remembered. "It's my understanding that the gods are quite powerful. What type of devourers were able to force them out of their realm?"

"Viral." I grimaced. "It's the only known case of a devourer strain of a virus, thankfully, but it's hard to fight what you can't see, and it spread rapidly. The gods used their abilities to set off volcanoes as they fled to wipe out all life in the realm and thus provide no hosts for the virus, but the fae and daemons have forbidden anyone from ever returning there just in case."

Mikhail looked at me sideways. "Tell me you didn't do something foolish like take a job that required breaking into the realm?"

"Okay." I grinned at him. "I won't tell you that."

He rolled his eyes. "You are a menace."

Two deep, baying sounds came from further up the trail. Hecate's hounds.

"Don't hurt them," I instructed. Jinx and Luna both slipped into their glamours, and he leapt onto my shoulder while Luna leapt onto Mikhail's. "They're harmless."

Mikhail glanced at me as he scratched Luna's head.

They're disgusting, and they drool a lot, Jinx complained.

"You were the one who wanted to come," I pointed out. "The hounds adore you, and they don't understand why you won't play with them."

Loud and enthusiastic canine sounds greeted us as we passed through the open gate of a white picket fence and into a garden that looked like something from another world. Vibrant flowers of every color under the sun stretched upwards, releasing intoxicating scents that sent my mind whirling. My nose crinkled as I fought back a sneeze. Hecate's garden was full of deadly, otherworldly beauty, exactly like her.

Her hounds however…

"Who's the best boy?" I crooned at the nearly two-hundred-pound dog dancing around me joyfully. Hecate had always had hounds for as long as I'd known her. These were descendants of the original ones she'd saved from Nineveh and bred into specific breeds from the human realm. Dogs weren't really my thing, so I didn't know much about them aside from the fact that she occasionally called them mastiffs.

The second hound, who was a brindle color like the other one but much darker, finally grew impatient with not getting any attention and barreled into my legs. Jinx abandoned me and leapt to Mikhail's chest, who, on instinct, caught the grimalkin as he watched me and the hounds in intense fascination.

My legs went out from under me, and my ass hit the dirt. Immediately, the two dogs were all over me. Jinx was right; they did slobber a lot.

"Okay, okay, okay!" I tried in vain to push them away, but they weren't having it, and I wasn't willing to hurt them.

"Philo! Zephyr!" a powerful voice rang out. "Enough, my loves."

After giving me one last slobbering kiss, both hounds obediently trotted away to stand by their owner's side. I sat up and wiped away the foul-smelling drool from my cheeks as best I could. Ugh. So gross. This was why cats were superior. Jinx never drooled on me; he'd just occasionally give me bad luck that resulted in me breaking a leg and falling down a mountain into a bramble of thorns. Much better.

"Are they ever going to not do that?" I waved towards the dogs who were still shooting me looks of complete adoration.

Hecate shrugged. The wispy white color of her eyes swirled as if someone had captured the essence of a misty morning over the ocean and gifted it to her. "I bred them to be empathic and loyal. You're responsible for saving their ancestors from Nineveh."

Mikhail arched an eyebrow at me. "*That* was the job?"

Yes, Jinx spat. *We had to go to that godsforsaken realm to rescue some stupid dogs.*

Instead of being insulted, a bemused grin played across Hecate's lips. "Come." She turned and walked towards the sprawling, two-story house. She'd lived here for as long as I'd known her, but the architecture of the house had changed every century or so.

The outer walls consisted of different-sized stone pieces in a variety of tones ranging from a dark, earthy brown to light beige. It made the enormous building blend into the surroundings better than the previous iteration, which had been made of lighter limestone. A black, wrought iron gate in the center was ajar and led to an open space that I'd always thought of as the heart of the home. The structure was built to wrap around the garden with patios and balconies opening into it. Personally, this was my favorite of the houses she'd built so far, and I'd hoped she'd kept it.

"How did the dogs survive?" Mikhail asked as we followed Hecate into the inner garden. "I thought you said they used the volcanoes to wipe out everything in the realm?"

"First"—I held up a finger—"I've been to realms that have been decimated by volcanic activity. Something always finds a way to survive."

And that something usually wants to eat you, Jinx grumbled.

"You weren't even there that time." I glared at the grimalkin. "Your ass got to stay at a tavern eating sushi while I had to deal with overgrown worms."

And whose fault was that? he sniped back.

I sniffed at him before holding up a second finger. "Two, the answer is always magic."

Hecate chuckled, brushing her fingers along one of the hounds' backs—Zephyr, I thought—as the large dog gently nudged her in the direction of a stone table set up near a shallow pond. If not for her distinct eye color, most folks would never know Hecate was blind, considering how confidently she moved around.

"When it became clear we were going to lose the realm, I put my dogs and some of my other pets into an enchanted sleep and buried them deep within the earth. It was the only thing I could think of to protect them. My plan had been to go back for them, but the need to evacuate happened faster than I thought it would and I couldn't go back."

When we approached the table, Mikhail pulled out a chair for Hecate, and she smiled at him. "Thank you. I'm not used to vampires with such good manners." His eyes flicked to mine, a dark brow raised in question, but it was Hecate who answered him. "Did Nemain not tell you about my abilities?"

I shrugged as I took a seat across from her. "I told him nothing about you other than your love of poisonous things, and that was mostly because I didn't want to deal with him touching the wrong flower and passing out on me."

"Wise move." She patted the head of the hound who had helped guide her, and he let out a soft woof before going to join the other, who was stretched out on the ground, soaking up the sun. A familiar-looking raptor landed on the olive tree closest to us. It ruffled the white feathers of its chest as it took us all in before settling down and giving me a death glare.

"Nice to see you too, Boreas." I raised my upper lip so he could see my fangs, and he puffed his feathers again. The Bonelli's Eagle had never liked me. Somewhere around here was his mate, Lyra, and she liked me a little more.

"Don't antagonize him," Hecate chided.

Mikhail looked from Hecate to the eagle and then to the sunbathing hounds. "They do more than just guide you… " he guessed. "Can you use them to see?"

"Polite and perspective." The ancient goddess grinned at me. "I can see why you mated with him."

"Can we not talk about that?" I groaned.

The snort that came from her didn't seem very godlike, but I refrained from pointing that out.

"To answer your question," Hecate said, "I can form bonds with animals, and while I can see through their eyes with this bond, I don't actually use it all that often. Only to get glimpses here and there. It can be rather disorientating, so I prefer to only do it when I'm sitting. Otherwise, I know where most things are around here, so it's easy for me to walk around, and when I leave my home, Philo and Zephyr provide excellent guides."

"It's my understanding that gods such as yourself are basically indestructible," Mikhail said carefully.

"You want to know how I could possibly be blind when I can survive literally any wound?"

One of the glass patio doors slid open, and a young woman with strawberry blonde hair stepped out, carrying a tray with glasses and a pitcher. She glanced at the grimalkins, who had settled in the same tree as Boreas and were looking at him like he was a tasty treat, before her light green eyes fell on Mikhail, where they lingered for a moment before moving to me. If the smell of herbs hadn't given her away as a witch, the way her eyes narrowed at me definitely would have.

Still, she didn't say anything as she poured us each a glass of iced tea.

"Thank you, Maria," Hecate said, sipping some of her tea.

"Of course. Let me know if you need anything else." With one last wary glance at me, the young witch retreated inside.

"Still teaching witches, I see," I mused.

"I turn most of them away," Hecate replied. "But Maria was both stubborn and promising."

We sipped our tea for a moment, and I enjoyed the milder weather. It was far warmer here than on the Washington coast, and I was silently glad Hecate hadn't left Greece. I subtly glanced at her while her head was tilted back, clearly enjoying the weather as well. Today, she wore a simple, loose-fitting, sleeveless dress, the deep purple tones complementing her olive skin and chestnut-colored hair. While she remodeled her house every century, Hecate's appearance had never changed once in the time I'd known her, but the last time I'd visited, she'd seemed... tired. I was glad to find her looking a little happier.

The only thing that hinted at her age were the fine lines that crinkled around her eyes and the corners of her mouth when she smiled. I had no idea what her exact age was. She'd been part of the original crew that had come to the human realm after Nineveh fell over five thousand years ago. I regularly joked with her that she was older than dirt, which she took as a compliment.

Which was lucky for me, because she definitely could have kicked my ass when I'd been younger.

She'd have a harder time now, at least in a straight-on fight. Hecate was powerful, but most of that strength came from the spells she was capable of crafting and the wisdom she'd collected over her long life.

And her insane collection of poison-coated weapons.

"Not all gods from Nineveh are the same," she finally said, her cloudy eyes somehow finding Mikhail. "I had very little magic when I was born, aside from my affinity to animals. There were beings in Nineveh who were... " She pursed her lips as she pondered her words. "I suppose they were similar to some of the spirits here in this realm, like the lwa."

"Lwa?" Mikhail asked.

"They're spirits worshiped by humans, specifically practitioners of vodou," I explained. "As far as I know, they have always existed in the human realm. The lwa are not... " I struggled for the right words. "They're not people. Fae, daemons, vampires, warlocks—whatever species you choose, we have some baseline of commonality. That is not the case with lwa or most spirits in general. It makes them tricky to deal with. Some of them are benevolent... but the ones that aren't... " I shuddered. "Even I steer clear of them."

"And you sought out the aid of such creatures in your

home realm?" Mikhail looked at Hecate curiously. "What did you want that was worth the risk?"

"At the time, I wanted everything. While I was good at crafting spells, I wanted more." She laughed. "I was young, brash, and arrogant."

"Seems like we were all that way once," Mikhail said in understanding.

"I suppose," Hecate agreed. "I performed a ritual, calling on the spirits of Nineveh, specifically one who was known for making deals. She asked what I wanted, and I said, '*The knowledge to craft any spell I desire and the foresight to always find what I seek,*' to which she asked what I would be willing to give for such a thing." She raised her glass to her lips but didn't drink. "I waved my hand at all the offerings I had collected and said, '*Anything you see before you.*'"

"She took your sight?" Mikhail guessed.

Hecate set her glass down. "She said if I couldn't see the value in what was around me, perhaps I would do better without seeing it at all. Then I might truly appreciate it." She cackled. "Sixteen-year-old me did not handle this particularly well. One month later, our realm fell, and I found myself in a strange new land. My family was dead, friends were also dead or scattered to places I didn't know, and I struggled to walk across a room without bumping into something."

"But you survived," Mikhail said.

Hecate flashed her teeth. "God or not, I am a survivor." She picked up her glass again and turned her head towards me. "Not that I don't enjoy your company, Nemain, or that of your polite vampire, but somehow, I doubt you've stopped by to enjoy my tea and discuss my history."

No point in drawing it out.

"Artemis has Hades."

The glass she'd been raising to her lips froze halfway. Hecate's cloudy, white eyes darkened to black for a split second before returning to their normal, albeit strange, coloring. "Impossible." She slowly lowered her tea back onto the table. "Hades died shortly after he slaughtered Zeus and the others. I personally visited the underworld after it happened. I felt his absence. His soul was irrevocably tied to our death realm; it's why they are *both* named Hades."

"I don't know how he did it, but he faked his own death."

"How do you know this?" she demanded.

"Because he's been in a relationship with my brother for over a century," I admitted. "Although, to be fair, I didn't know his true identity until a couple of years ago. I just thought he was an arrogant asshole."

Takes one to know one, Jinx grumbled.

"Why didn't he tell me?" Hecate whispered, and I saw genuine hurt flash across her face. "We were friends."

I shook my head. "I don't know. You can ask him after we rescue him, but if I had to guess, he was probably trying to protect you. He had to know the wrath Artemis and the remaining Olympians would rain down if they discovered he was alive."

She pursed her lips, and one of the hounds rose, sensing her distress, ambling over to bump her hand with his enormous, square head. Hecate absently patted his muzzle as she continued to deal with the bomb I'd just dropped on her.

"Do you know of any way to get inside Therrea?" I asked, doing my best to keep my tone gentle. "There are no fae or daemon gateways leading to it, and I don't know of any way to open one there."

"No," she drew out the word. "Olympia was created by Zeus, and it collapsed onto itself with his death. Artemis is considerably smarter than that jackass ever was, so she no doubt made their home even more secure."

"The pocket realm Zeus created fell apart after he died?" Mikhail asked, sitting up a little straighter. "How quickly?"

Hecate thought about it. "Less than an hour. Pocket dimensions are created by forcing space in between the realms. They require a continuous feed of magic to remain in existence. Zeus' Olympia was bound to his soul. When Hades destroyed Zeus, there was nothing to prevent the realms Olympia was sandwiched between from gobbling it up. Having your soul ripped apart and pulled into dozens of different realms is bad enough, but you'll likely never find peace in the afterlife after that."

Mikhail and I shared a look. "So we have to be careful about who we kill while we're there," I said. "At least until we find Hades and a way out."

Well, fortunately, they can't die, so we don't really have to worry about that, Jinx helpfully chimed in.

"They can," Hecate said. "For all their blustering, the Olympians aren't true gods. Not the way I am or Osiris and his lot are."

"Uhhh… " I said eloquently. "Come again?"

Hecate gave me a small smile. "In Nineveh, there were gods and mortals. There weren't many of us gods, and our magic and lifespan were different there because our realm actually had very little magic. Osiris was king, and for the most part, benevolent, although he had his moments. There was a group of mortals led by Zeus who wanted more power. They found a way to increase their magic, and it caused a civil war in our lands. That's why we weren't able to do anything about the devourer virus until it was too late; we were a bit distracted."

She sipped some tea, and I did the same. Hecate was always tight-lipped about what things had been like in Nineveh; she'd only told me about it before because she'd hired me to rescue her beloved hounds. As much as I wanted to pester her with questions, I bit my tongue and allowed her to speak at her own pace.

"When we arrived in the human realm, the magic here mixed with ours, and suddenly, we became so much stronger than we were before. The humans began to worship us, and we discovered that only increased our power." A phantom wave ran through the garden, and I noticed some of the flowers stretched towards her. "It was the time of the gods."

"And then Hades went on a killing spree and the humans abandoned the survivors." I grinned at her. "Womp, womp, womp."

Mikhail shook his head while Luna gave me a chiding look and Jinx's deep laugh rumbled through my head. At least someone thought I was funny.

"You know you would have been killed for your insolence back then, right?" Hecate arched an eyebrow at me.

I raised a hand and let my blue flames flicker to life across my fingers. "There are a number of things I would have been killed for."

"True." She cocked her head, and I felt the barest brush of her magic against mine. Not a hint of fear on her face, more curiosity than anything.

"So the Olympians aren't truly immortal then?" Mikhail asked. "They can be killed?"

"Well, Hades already killed Zeus and a few others, so we knew that," I pointed out.

"He did that by drawing their souls out of their bodies and consuming them," Hecate said. "It was a risk on his part, because if he'd failed to overwhelm Zeus' or any of the others' souls, they could have consumed his instead and inhabited his body."

"Okay, aside from having their souls sucked out and eaten, they're basically immortal right?" Mikhail pushed.

"Yes." Hecate nodded. "Their bodies are basically immortal. No matter the damage, they will eventually regenerate."

"How did they become that way?"

"Apples."

"Apples?" He stared at her before glancing at me. "I honestly never know if I'm being fucked with whenever we meet up with old friends of yours."

"In Nineveh," Hecate explained, "Hera crafted a dark spell to elevate them to gods. None of us have ever been able to determine the specifics, but it relied heavily on sacrifice and the blood from it. When they fled Nineveh, Hera dunked several apples into her cauldron and brought them with her. They were planted in the human realm and then later moved to Olympia. Given that they all still have their power, I have no doubt Artemis has some apple trees tucked safely away somewhere in Therrea."

"No immediate way to turn back their immortality then?" Mikhail asked.

"Unlikely." She shook her head. "They probably have to eat the apples regularly to maintain their power, but that's mostly a guess on my part based on how protective they are of those damn trees."

"Interesting but not helpful." I frowned.

"I'm sorry I can't offer more," Hecate said. "I've never had the desire to visit them in Therrea, so I don't know a way into it."

"It's fine," I said with a sigh before downing the rest of my iced tea. "You're just the most pleasant of the gods, so I was hoping I wouldn't have to talk to any of the others." She laughed. "Any suggestions on who to try next and where I might find them?"

"Horus." She thought about it. "He's currently in Prague at some fancy new daemon tavern that just opened. VIP section on the third floor."

I blinked. "That seems oddly specific."

"Maria follows him on some social media app," she said.

"He posted about it today, and she was very excited by this news. I think she has a crush on him."

She pulled out a sleek, black phone from her pocket and held it in front of her face. A clicking sound announced the phone unlocking, and she placed it on the table. As her fingers glided across the screen, a pleasant voice said words out loud that meant absolutely nothing to me. After a moment, she spun the phone around and nudged it in my direction, a smug look on her face.

I glanced down at the phone and saw a picture of a young man with a mischievous smile holding a cigarette in one hand and a bottle of bourbon in the other. The words below the image read, *"Getting the party started at Salvation."*

"You have a cell phone?" My lip curled in disgust. "And you stalk people from it?"

"It's not stalking, it's social media." She rolled her eyes.

Mikhail laughed, and I shot him a dirty look.

"When we find a way in, do you want to come?" I asked her. "Once we secure Hades, you can have the first shot at giving a little payback to Artemis."

Her eyes flashed black, and it took several seconds of deep breathing before the darkness faded. "Thank you for thinking of me, but no. I have no interest in starting things with them again. He's gone, and there's no bringing him back."

Chapter Seventeen

"Who was the 'he' Hecate was referring to?" Mikhail asked as he scanned our surroundings, looking for potential threats.

I'd opened a gateway straight from Hecate's garden to a rooftop in Prague. It'd been a while since I'd been here, but this particular building was owned by daemons, so I wasn't worried about any humans seeing us and losing their minds. It still felt weird not hiding my abilities from all the other nonhumans, but thanks to my title as the Unseelie Knight, the cat was out of the bag, so to speak.

The locals of Emerald Bay had eventually gotten over it, but whenever I traveled outside of my town, the whispers would always start when I entered a room. Most didn't know the specifics of my power, but they knew I could open gateways and that I wielded devourer magic. I didn't give a shit about what they thought. If anything, their fear of me could help keep those I cared about safe, but I absolutely *loathed* being stared at.

I headed towards the fire escape on the side of the six-story building and started climbing down. "Hecate prefers to stay in the Mediterranean area—she's had that house in Greece for as long as I've known her—but she does occasionally go wandering around to see the rest of the world. Sometimes she'll spend months in other realms. She was on one of these walkabouts a long time ago when she heard rumors about a tentacled monster wrecking ships near Norway and decided to investigate."

Mikhail stopped halfway down the steel stairs. "The kraken? The friend she's mourning was the bloody *kraken*?"

"He was actually very sweet, just"—I raised my hand with my index finger and thumb almost touching—"a little bit terri-torial. It was actually Kaysea's father who helped to move him to one of the fae realms, which is where I met him." I smiled at the memory. "Hecate named him Leviathan. We called him Levi for short. He thought it was really fun to throw me up into the air and catch me with his tentacles. Only dropped me a few times."

Mikhail looked at Jinx.

She's not kidding. But, I mean, Nemain naps against a psychotic fae tree, thinks lokis are amusing instead of deviant liars, and for some reason, enjoys your company. I think it's been well established that she's insane.

"Pretty sure you should include befriending yourself on that list." Mikhail narrowed his eyes. "Given your *winning* personality."

Ever fallen down a fire escape and had the unfortunate luck of hitting every single stair on the way? Jinx's eyes glowed malevolently.

What happened? Luna interrupted, her lilac eyes on me.

"Hecate had a disagreement with Artemis," I said softly. "I don't know the specifics, but I've gathered it was over a minor thing. She thought Artemis had graciously accepted no as an answer, but the next time she went to visit her friend, all she found was a tentacle staked to the pier where she used to sit while spending time with him. A note was sitting next to it that read, 'Thanks for the treat. He was delicious.' It was signed by Artemis."

The amusement we'd all been feeling faded at the reminder of how petty and cruel the Olympians could be. That had been their reaction to a small disagreement. We were about to go into their world and steal back someone who they very much wanted to torture for the next thousand years.

"Yeah." I sighed. "We're going to have to kill them all."

Mikhail's eyes lit up. "I've never killed a god before."

I'll bet I can kill more than you, Jinx boasted.

"You wish," Mikhail sneered. "Unless they're allergic to hair balls, I don't think you'll do much damage."

Magic from Jinx sparked, and the stair Mikhail had been standing on collapsed. He barely managed to jump across to the landing as the metal snapped off and fell to the level below us.

Luna's head swiveled between Mikhail and Jinx before settling on me. *I think they might be crazy.*

"Cleary." I nodded sagely. "It's obvious I'm going to kill way more gods than either of them."

She sighed. *We should put our glamours up. Jinx is going to get annoyed if the humans try to pet him.*

Conversations from the sidewalk below us drifted up. Since Prague was a major human city, there wasn't a dedicated section for nonhumans like there was in Emerald Bay. Instead, the daemons, fae, and others simply owned buildings here and there. This meant we needed to at least blend in a little bit until we got to the daemon tavern.

My fingers brushed against the dark blue gem of the leather necklace around my neck. I didn't wear it much these days because I didn't have to worry about standing out in Emerald Bay. Most of the humans who lived there were at least somewhat aware of the magical community, and the few who weren't just wanted to be left alone. If they noticed anything odd about some of the locals, they kept it to themselves.

An itching sensation immediately spread across my skin as the glamour took effect. According to Kaysea, I shouldn't be able to feel fae glamour, but I absolutely could. I thought maybe it had something to do with my devourer magic; it probably didn't like the feel of foreign magic being so close and wanted to nibble on it.

Mikhail frowned at me and then the spot where he'd last seen Luna and Jinx. Most fae had some ability to glamour, but it wasn't all that useful. Grimalkins could glamour themselves so they appeared like a smaller version of themselves, but they could also make themselves invisible. Anyone who could see magic, which was a common ability amongst nonhumans, would notice the obvious signs of a glamour being at play. Unfortunately for my lover, vampires did not have that ability.

"If I step on you, it's not my fault," Mikhail warned before flinching slightly when Luna leapt onto his shoulder.

Sorry, she murmured. *But I don't want to get stepped on.*

I felt Jinx land on my shoulder but didn't flinch because I'd expected it. "Don't smile." I pointed a finger at Mikhail, and he flashed his fangs in a wide grin.

We made it off the fire escape a minute later, and I looked around to orientate myself before heading down the street. A group of tourists bumped into me, and I fought back a snarl. Someday, I'd have a fortress like Kalen and Badb in the middle of nowhere. Maybe with a drawbridge and a moat.

"Where are we going?" Mikhail asked, ignoring the group of three young women who were outright ogling him. This time, I did snarl.

"The only place a hip new daemon bar would be in this city." The street we'd been walking on opened up, revealing a large, cobblestone square. At the opposite end was a monument of a man standing tall and people gathered at his feet.

Hordes of tourists walked around the locals rushing through, trying to get to their jobs or homes. A church dripping in Gothic architecture rose across the square to tower over all the nearby buildings. "Old Town."

"THIS MUST BE IT." I waved to the building across the street. The four-story structure sat sandwiched between two taller buildings yet somehow managed to look more intimidating than both of them. Human tourists walked by, not even glancing at it while they scurried in and out of the shops on either side. Large, arched windows with frosted glass and iron bars took up most of the dark grey stone front. A dark wood door identical to the one at The Inferno stood in the center, and the sign above this one read, *Salvation*.

We strode across the street, and I shoved the door open. For the first few steps, nothing but darkness greeted me, and I slowed, but as soon as the door closed behind Mikhail, the shadows vanished, and we were inundated with loud music, boisterous conversations, and waves of magic.

I froze, letting my senses catch up to everything around me. The Inferno could get chaotic at times, but it was mostly all locals. Emerald Bay was a small, daemon-run town. The beings who lived there generally wanted to live a quiet life amongst other nonhumans. Their idea of a rowdy night was drinking beer around a table and maybe playing some pool or darts.

Daemons and others came to cities like Prague to party and cut loose. Bodies swirled around us, slamming into each other as magic danced in the air. Music pulsed, rapid and seductive, trying to pull me in. If I were in my feline form, my hair would have been standing straight up.

Too many people. Too loud. Too much *everything*.

The rules and atmosphere of daemon bars varied by the daemon who ran them, but there was one rule they all shared. No glamour. You came as you truly were, or you didn't come at all. The spells around the doorway had stripped away our glamours immediately, which was why I'd grunted when Jinx's hundred pound frame pushed off me.

"VIP section is probably upstairs!" I shouted and pointed up. Mikhail nodded, and we started weaving our way through the crowd.

"Pretty kitty!" a dryad with eyes so wide she had to be on something screamed. She stretched a delicate, olive-toned hand towards Luna, her pastel pink hair falling in a curtain around her.

Jinx whirled, ready to tear into the presumptuous but ultimately harmless girl, but Mikhail beat him to it. He grasped the dryad's hand and pulled it away from the silver grimalkin, who shot him a look of thanks before darting further into the crowd.

"Sorry," Mikhail said, leaning closer so the dryad could hear. "She's not friendly."

Large, pretty green eyes blinked at him before her lips curled in an appreciative smile. "That's okay." She slipped her hand free from his so she could place both on his chest. "I'm friendly."

I shoved myself between them, gripping both of her wrists. "I'm not."

The girl burst into tears, and her friends, who had been dancing around us, quickly came to her rescue. They pulled her away from me, cooing soothing words to her while giving me dirty looks. I rolled my eyes. Freaking dryads. They were such drama queens.

Mikhail slipped his hand into mine and pulled me in the direction the grimalkins had headed. "Was that really necessary?" he chided. "I was going to let her down gently."

"I don't like crowds," I grumbled, knowing he'd still be able to hear me with his vampiric senses. "Plus, I'm feeling a little extra territorial these days. Sorry."

He released his grip on my hand and whirled, cupping my butt and lifting me up. Instinctively, I wrapped my legs around his waist, and his amused, twilight eyes bore into mine. "I like it," he purred. His mouth crashed against mine, and for a moment, nothing else existed but the taste of him. Then someone bumped into us, and he tore away from me to snarl at them.

"Now who's overreacting?" I teased. He kissed me again and nipped my bottom lip hard enough to draw blood. A groan slipped out of me as he kissed me harder and I felt his tongue run along the cut he'd made. When we broke apart a minute later, I felt a little breathless, and he smirked at me before planting one more quick kiss on my lips and setting me down.

"Really, Nemain." He grabbed my hand again and pulled me forward. "Now isn't the time for such things. We're here for a reason."

I scowled at his back.

Just as the crowd parted in front of us, someone brushed by me, and I went still as I stared at the back of his blond head.

"You coming?" Mikhail asked over his shoulder, his brow furrowing as he tried to figure out what had distracted me.

"Take the grimalkins upstairs," I said, not taking my eyes off the retreating man. "I'll be there in a minute." When he didn't move, I glanced at him. "Trust me."

Mikhail pursed his lips. Clearly, he didn't like this, but he did as I'd asked and continued on. I trusted him to find Jinx and Luna and guide them upstairs to where the VIP section likely was.

I made my way towards the bar where the blond man was

drinking an amber-colored liquid in a short glass with a blocky square of ice in the middle.

Stunning, blue eyes looked at me from a classically handsome face. Despite his attractive appearance, the other patrons had given him a wide berth, as if they sensed something off about him.

"My dagger." I held out my hand, palm up to him.

Through a sleight of hand that even I couldn't follow, one of my throwing knives appeared in his palm. Instead of handing it over, he twirled it around his fingers a few times, studying the way the light caught the silver blade.

"It's customary to present a god an offering."

"How about I offer to shove my boot up your ass, Hermes."

The Olympian tilted his head at me like I was a puzzle he couldn't figure out. "You have no fear of me whatsoever." A cruel smile stretched across his lips. "What a nice change. Usually when our enemies finally meet us face to face, they break down sobbing and beg for mercy. You'll be a fun one to break."

"You were the god of messengers and thieves." I curled my lip at him. "From all the stories I've heard, you were a pathetic coward who only preyed on those weaker than you."

His smile grew sharper. "I'm a god. Everyone is weaker than me."

"Last I checked, the other gods didn't have to munch on magical apples to stay powered up." I shrugged. "So, really, you're kind of a poser."

The smile slid from his face. "Artemis sent me here with a message. The sum of it is that you should be happy you got your brother back in one piece. That will not be the case if you come after Hades. She suggests you take your win and walk away. Because if you go up against us, you and everyone you care about will know suffering like you've never known before."

He set his drink down and slid closer to me. I forced myself to stand my ground, even as my muscles tensed, preparing to move quickly if I had to.

"Personally"—he jammed my dagger back into the holster on my thigh—"I hope you come. Because it'll be my pleasure to break you." His lips brushed against my ear. "And then you'll be on your knees giving me all kinds of *offerings*."

I snapped my fangs an inch away from his face, and satisfaction rolled through me as he flinched. "See you soon."

Hermes' expression smoothed over, and he let out an amused snort before strolling away, the crowd parting for him quickly. I waited until I felt his magic fade and I was fairly confident he had left before heading upstairs.

I had no idea how he'd known we would be here. But he was the herald of the gods. Finding people was kind of his thing. Still, if he didn't know we were here to speak with Horus, I didn't want to clue him in on that little detail.

Mikhail and the grimalkins were waiting for me at the top of the stairs. My lover shot me a questioning look, and I shrugged.

"Hermes decided to pay us a visit in person to warn us off."

"Let me guess." He fell into stride next to me. "He threatened you with pain, torture, and death. And you snarled back in his face and made him flinch."

I flashed my fangs at him. "Technically, I didn't snarl."

Mikhail laughed as we approached two identical daemons with fiery red skin and green eyes. They waved us through a set of glass doors, and I breathed a sigh of relief at the less crowded room we walked into.

It didn't take me long to spot Horus. Hard to miss the six-and-a-half-foot god sprawled on a couch with a group of adoring nymphs waiting on him. I rolled my eyes. Clearly, Hathor had dumped his ass again.

"Hello, friend." I stopped a few feet away. "Got a minute?"

"Nemain." His rich voice rumbled through the room and slid across my skin. "Long time no see. *Are* we friends? I thought we parted on bad terms last time?" He tilted his head, and his straight, black hair slid over his shoulder. Piercing, brown eyes looked at me from a face that was neither pretty nor handsome. It was simply striking.

His sharp nose and cheekbones sat above full lips, and he had a strong jawline that practically begged you to trace your fingers against it. Hathor may be the goddess of love, but Horus should have been named the god of lust. Everything about him drew you in, and the arrogant bastard knew it.

He'd chosen to sit in the corner of the room where the sun was shining directly in, and it caused the gold specks in his umber brown skin to shimmer.

"We had a slight disagreement over who those sets of rings belonged to," I admitted. "But seeing how you wanted them for Hathor, and she's clearly not in the picture… " I pointedly looked at all the nymphs who were trying to sink unnoticed into the sofa. Except for the one rubbing his feet—she kept right on going, humming to herself without a care in the world. "Seems like that's water under the bridge."

"I dumped her six months ago." He shrugged.

Sure you did, Jinx laughed.

"Careful." Horus glared at where Jinx sat by my feet. "My mother's the cat person. I prefer raptors."

For a second, something crawled beneath his skin, making his features even sharper and more predatory. His mouth contorted, stretching into a hard, curved beak before magic popped and he was once again reclining on the couch in his human form, wearing a nonchalant expression.

"So touchy," I drawled, reaching down to scratch Jinx's head. "She really did dump your ass."

Mikhail's eyes glinted in amusement. "I think, going

forward, I should be the one who does the talking in situations when we're asking a favor."

"Really?" I arched an eyebrow at him. "What was the first thing that went through your mind when we approached?"

"A month ago, Elisa was trying to explain to me what a 'fuck boy' was, but I didn't quite get it." He waved a hand at Horus. "Now I do."

"This is a real interesting strategy to ask for a favor," Horus said flatly. "Got to say, I'm not really feeling inclined to grant one."

"We're going to beat the shit out of the Olympians, Artemis in particular, but probably the others too." I gave him my best feral smile and held up a hand, letting the blue devourer flames flicker to life. "Current plan is to carve them into pieces and burn them one by one. See if that takes."

"Oh." His crazy smile matched mine, and he waved away the nymph at his feet so he could lean forward. "You should have led with that. What do you need?"

"A way into Therrea. I can't open a gateway there, and Hecate doesn't know how to get in either."

Horus looked at the nymphs and others gathered around us, and they all scattered. Then he reached forward and tapped a red gem embedded into the table, and I instantly felt the familiar magic of a silencing spell rise around us.

"I take it you know Therrea isn't a true realm?"

I nodded.

"Good, that will make this a little easier. The death realms are also not true realms, despite being referred to as such."

"They're not pocket realms though." I furrowed my brows, not really sure where he was going with this. "I can open gateways to the death realms. I can't to Therrea. I tried, trust me."

"Not pocket realms." He rested his elbows on his knees and leaned forward more.

Horus looked like he was no more than twenty years old,

and most of the time, he acted like it, but there were moments when his true age leaked through his eyes and held you in place. He wasn't as old as some of the other gods—he'd been born in the human realm after Nineveh fell—but he was still over five thousand years old.

"There are few absolutes in life. Death is one of them. We all die eventually, even us immortals, and all roads lead to death.

"Duat, Underworld, Hel, Mag Mell." He raised his fingers, counting off the realms. "We give them individual names and we call them realms, but that's not what they are. They're all the same place. Ever expanding, all encompassing. It has no beginning. No end. There is no fighting the inevitable. Death claims us all."

Silence stretched, then Horus frowned, breaking the moment.

"Sorry. I've had a lot of vodka." He pinched the bridge of his nose. "There will be a back door to death from Therrea. As soon as it was created, the connection to death was formed. Where there is creation, there is *always* death. Artemis' idea of death is Hades, so that's where the door will be."

"Okay," I said slowly. "How do we find it?"

"Ammit is excellent at finding doors. She's currently mad at me, so she won't answer my summons." Horus dropped his hand from his face as he thought about it. "I'll find a way for you to summon her—you just have to get yourself to one of the death realms. Doesn't have to be Duat; she'll find you anywhere."

"So, just so I have this right… " I rubbed my face. "Your proposal is that we wander around the most chaotic of all the death realms with a cankerous beast who bears the fun nick-name 'Devourer of Souls' as our guide until we stumble across the specific door we need?"

"Yes, that's exactly what I'm saying." Horus gave me a judgmental look. "Are you saying you're scared?"

"No." I grinned. "I was worried you were going to suggest something boring."

"We hate to be bored," Mikhail drawled.

Luna turned her head to look at both of us before focusing on Jinx again. *I always thought you were exaggerating when you said they were insane. I'm staying home from now on.*

Wise move.

Chapter Eighteen

My PHONE BUZZED on the kitchen counter, and I tapped the screen.

"Horus is ready."

I shoved the last piece of my roast beef sandwich into my mouth and ignored Elisa's gloating expression. Mikhail, the traitor, had been the one to tell her I'd given Horus my number and told him to text me when he was ready for a gateway to be opened. Elisa rarely said "I told you so" out loud, but she had the ability to capture it in her expression down to a science.

At this point, even I had to begrudgingly admit that having a cell phone was handy in the human realm, but I was still betting I would break the damn thing within a week.

I slid off my stool and stepped away from the kitchen island. Horus and I weren't particularly close, but his magic was so unique that it wasn't hard for me to focus on it and direct a gateway to open between us. It was hard to believe that, five years ago, I'd been struggling to control my devourer side and thought the most I could do with my shifter magic was open gateways between two realms. Badb and Kalen were frustrating as hell, but they were excellent teachers.

Horus appeared on the other side of the gateway and leapt through as soon as it was large enough. "Close it! Close it! Close it!" he shouted in panic.

"What'd you do?" I asked even as I closed the gateway, though not before a booming voice came through.

"YOU'D BETTER BRING THAT BACK!"

Oh, shit. I recognized that voice. Even I had the sense to avoid its owner as much as possible.

I gaped at Horus. "You stole something from your dad?" Osiris was a pretty chill guy who mostly just wanted to stay home and worship his wife, but he was definitely on my Do Not Fuck With list.

And that was saying something, because I usually didn't give a flying fuck about who I messed with.

Horus stumbled to his feet and held up a slender, gold cylinder with holes running along its top. It looked like a whistle of some kind. "All of our summons are unique. Ammit might ignore my call, but she would never ignore one from The King of Duat." He glanced over to the kitchen island. "Ooo! Sandwiches!"

"Help yourself," I said dryly. He tossed the whistle to me and sauntered over to the kitchen. His eyes brightened when Elisa handed him a plate with a sandwich and some chips.

"Thank you, beautiful." He took the plate from her and not so discreetly checked her out. "Any interest in showing me around this lovely town later?"

Bryn scowled from where she was leaning against the sink, her golden wings wrapped around her like a cloak. "She's busy."

Horus glanced at her and then back at Elisa. "You two a thing, I take it?"

Elisa nodded. "*We* would be happy to show you around once things are settled here. I'm working tonight at The Inferno, and I'm sure you could find some company there."

"None as beautiful as you though."

Bryn growled. Like actually growled. I was kind of proud of her.

Luckily, Horus was generally easy-natured, so he just held his hands up in defeat before tucking into the sandwich.

I glanced at Jinx. *Want to let Cian and Magos know we're ready?* He trotted towards the door, which swung open for him, and then looked over his shoulder at Luna. She looked at me, and I nodded, knowing she probably wanted to check on Finn. She was a bit of a mother hen and didn't like to be apart from the fae boy. Given all they'd been through together while they were locked away in the exiled fae king's realm, I understood.

The two grimalkins headed downstairs. Cian had been packing our bags in the second-floor apartment. We didn't really need much, just the basics and backup weapons, but Cian worried, and when he worried, he over-engineered everything. I had no doubt he'd probably packed and repacked the bags at least a dozen times in the last hour.

"This sandwich is amazing," Horus said between bites. "Anyway, after this, I definitely need to go drown myself in alcohol. Maybe pour some directly into my eyes to block out what I saw while getting that damn summoner."

"What'd you see?" Elisa asked, perking up as curiosity lit her indigo blue eyes.

"My father having my mother for dinner." He grimaced.

Bryn frowned. "Why is that a bad thing? Haven't they been together for thousands of years? It's kind of sweet they still have dinner together."

A sly smile curled the corners of Elisa's lips. Unlike Bryn, she hadn't misunderstood.

"They weren't having dinner together," he said slowly. "He had my mother spread out on the table with her legs over his shoulders and was *having her for dinner.*"

Bryn turned a shade of red I'd only seen on tomatoes,

which only made Elisa smile wider. For once, she wasn't the one making the valkyrie blush.

"They're still like that, huh?" I chuckled.

"It's not funny!" Horus' mouth twisted into an impressive scowl. "It's been over six thousand years! How are they still this in love and obsessed with each other!"

"Yes. How dare your parents love each other," Mikhail deadpanned.

"Look, I just want to be able to go over to their house without being scarred for life." He crossed his arms. "They're my *parents*."

Mikhail and I looked at each other, and then we both broke into laughter. Horus just shook his head and went back to eating. Elisa poured him some coffee, and he looked at her adoringly, which only had Bryn scowling harder. It would have looked more intimidating if her cheeks weren't still so flushed.

Cian stalked into the apartment and tossed some bags down. Magos followed, a calm wall at his back.

"I'm ready," my brother said, not even sparing a glance at the ancient god sitting in the kitchen.

"We'll leave as soon as Sigrun gets here."

With me, Magos, and Mikhail being gone, I'd wanted at least one heavy hitter staying in the apartment to watch over Finn and the rest of the kids. Bryn was a strong fighter, but she was still young and learning. The dragons would pop in and out, but Eddie was the one who came over most, and it might be a few more days until he was back to his usual self.

"A word of advice," Horus said around a mouthful of sandwich that he swallowed in one gulp. "Artemis has the uncanny ability to sense magic, but that doesn't extend to animals, including shifted forms."

I glanced at Cian before turning back to Horus. "So if we are in our feline forms, she won't be able to feel us?"

"Nope. It's why she became known as the huntress. She

252

viewed any beings capable of shifting into animals as a threat and would hunt them down if they crossed into her territory."

"Thanks."

He nodded and went back to his sandwich. This information didn't change our plans, but it did increase their chances of succeeding.

I opened a gateway to the realm Sigrun called home, and her cottage appeared on the other side. A moment later, the door swung open, and she stepped out, armed to the teeth. She strode through the gateway, Niall at her back, looking similarly armed.

"We're not expecting to defend against a siege, guys," I said wryly as the gateway closed. It's not like Sigrun needed any other weapon besides the hammer she had strapped to her back. I'd always known she had Mjölnir, but until recently, she rarely carried it. I didn't know the specifics as to what had changed, but I suspected some of it had to do with the dark-haired fae standing at her side.

"Hello, Nemain. You're looking particularly lethal today." Niall grinned at me.

He wasn't wrong. In addition to my dual swords, I had almost a dozen knives strapped to my body. I'd changed into matte black leathers that, thanks to daemon ingenuity, were quite flexible. Normally, I wore my hair in a long braid down my back, but I'd opted to wrap it in a tight bun today.

Mikhail was dressed in a similar fashion. Only Magos wasn't armed to the teeth. He wore his normal, loose-fitting black pants and a simple, long-sleeve green shirt that did their best to slim down his ridiculously broad build. Magos exuded civility, while Mikhail and I always looked like we were dancing on the knife's edge of violence.

"You look… " I trailed off as I scrutinized Niall. He belonged to a fae race that was basically extinct outside of those still in Balor's army. The sciatháin. He'd glamoured his inky black wings away, and, like me, he was armed as if he were going to war. Several inches over six feet, Niall was a beast, which was hilarious, because he was actually kind and sweet.

He did not look sweet now.

Dark brown leathers wrapped around his frame with extra protection around vital areas. A dark gold spear drenched with magic was strapped diagonally to his back, and two curved daggers hung at his sides. I narrowed my eyes at the blades. They were curved like half moons. The tips were thin, and I would worry about them snapping, but, like the spear, I could feel the magic within the dark silver.

Sigrun could make amazing weapons, but she couldn't enchant them. Interesting.

"You both know you're staying here, right?" I looked back and forth between them. "We should be alerted about any future attacks from Balor going forward, so I'm not expecting any trouble."

"Whether you expect it or not, trouble always finds you," Sigrun said. "Also, I'm staying here, but Niall's going with you."

"Absolutely not," I said immediately.

"Told you she wouldn't like this plan." Niall smirked at Sigrun, who just rolled her eyes at him, before he refocused on me. "If you want to get out of Therrea alive, you need me. Thanks to the devourer magic running through my veins, their magic won't work on me." His gaze slid to Magos and Mikhail. "No offense to your vampire friends, but I'm a much stronger fighter than they could ever hope to be."

I sighed. "You really need to let that fae arrogance go, Niall."

"It's the truth. I'm just sa—" He froze when he realized both Mikhail and Magos had vanished, leaving only trails of mist in the air. To his credit, Niall did dodge both of their strikes when they materialized around him. Magos had aimed for the back of his knees while Mikhail had gone for the throat. They hadn't summoned their swords, but they definitely weren't pulling their punches either.

Sigrun came to stand next to me as the three of them traded blows across the apartment, moving away from the furniture and towards the open space of the sparring mat. Neither of us made a move to break up the fight. Niall had brought this upon himself, and they all had excellent healing abilities.

"Why?" I looked at Sigrun. Her jaw was set in a stubborn line. "You don't owe me anything, and neither does he. And you definitely don't owe Hades anything. The two of you just found each other, and now you're willing to risk that?"

Niall had defected from Balor's army and had been in a dark place when he'd crashed into our lives. He was doing better now, and I was pretty sure that was largely due to Sigrun. My friend was also in a better headspace than she'd ever been. She had Bryn as an apprentice, had formed an odd friendship with Badb that I'd decided not to question, and she had Niall.

Valkyries formed a bond with one other person when their powers awoke. It was said that the bond was unbreakable, and that if one bonded died, so did the other. This wasn't exactly true. It was excruciating, but it was possible to survive a broken bond. Sigrun had chosen to do so and been exiled from the Yggdrasil realms and the rest of the valkyries for it. I hadn't thought it was possible, but I was pretty sure the beginnings of a bond were forming between her and Niall.

I wouldn't let them risk that.

Sigrun looked at me through dark, cinnamon-colored eyes. The gold bands in her braids practically glowed against her rich, dark brown skin.

"Tell me, my friend," she said in her calm, Nemain-is-being-foolishly-obtuse tone. "If Lir managed to steal Niall from me and whisked him away, what would you do?" I clamped my jaw shut and refused to answer, and one side of her mouth tilted up. "You'd grab your swords, those two vampires,"—she waved a hand at where Niall was trying to break out of the choke hold Magos had him in while Mikhail just smirked at the fae warrior and taunted him with a dagger—"and ask me who we were killing and where."

She was absolutely right, and it pissed me off.

"Niall and I discussed it. One of us needs to stay to help here, even if there is a low risk of attack. With his devourer heritage, Niall is the best suited for this mission." She rested her hands on my shoulders. "Cian is your family, and Hades is his mate. That means they're our family too."

I slumped my shoulders in defeat, because what she'd said made sense. I had to trust my friends knew what they were signing up for, but I would bring Niall back to Sigrun no matter what.

"Thank you," Cian murmured after he walked up to us, having heard everything with his keen shifter hearing. "I feel the same, and I know Hades does too. Anything you need in the future, we'll be there for you."

"Alright," I said loudly. "Leave the poor delicate fae alone."

Magos and Mikhail both vanished into mist before reappearing at my side. They were trying to hide it, but I could tell by the way they were standing that Niall had gotten some solid hits in.

"Don't pick on him anymore," I continued. "Sigrun's in a much better mood these days, and I'm pretty sure it's because she's getting laid on the regular."

Sigrun let out an exasperated sigh while Niall's cheeks darkened. Wow. Another easy blusher. Elisa and Eddie would have a field day with this.

"To be fair, I was just distracting them so you and my love

could have a chat." Niall grinned. For someone who had been gasping for air a moment ago, he seemed perfectly fine now. "I take it you two came to an understanding?"

"Yes, you're coming along," I huffed.

Magos simply nodded in acceptance, but Mikhail frowned at Sigrun. "Can't you come instead? I don't like him."

The valkyrie stared at him, her golden wings ruffling slightly. "No."

"But—"

"No."

He looked at me, and I shrugged. "You need to get over him stabbing me that one time. I stabbed him back, so we're even." Mikhail's lips curled, but he didn't argue any further. Honestly, he chose the weirdest things to get upset about. "Alright," I said. "Let's do this. We're going to start at Cian's home in Mag Mell. We'll summon Ammit from there and then head into Hades."

"Ammit is excellent at traveling through the death realms." Cian strapped one of the packs to his back. "Hopefully she can limit how much time we spend in Hades. It's one of the more unstable death realms, so we really don't want to be there long."

Jinx, I pushed the thought out. *We're leaving.*

Be right there, he replied. *Also… incoming.*

What?

The apartment door swung open, but it wasn't Jinx who came through. It was Kalen. I blinked at my father as the gateway opened next to me. "What are you doing here?"

"Coming with you."

"What the fuck is with everyone inviting themselves on this suicide mission?" I threw my hands up in the air just as Jinx trotted in and followed the others through the gateway. I moved to stand in front of it, blocking Kalen. "We already discussed this. You and Badb *agreed* to stay here. Someone needs to be responsible for Finn if I don't make it back."

I would fight like hell to make it back, but in case I didn't, it was important to me that Finn didn't feel abandoned. Not because of the dark prophecy surrounding him, but because he'd already been through enough in his short existence. He deserved to be loved and surrounded by people who cared about him.

"You were very adamant before," Kalen agreed. "Your mother and I *agreed* that it wasn't worth causing you undue stress by arguing, so we devised our own plan. She will remain here. I will go with you to make sure you make it back."

Depthless, obsidian eyes looked at me, and I could see he was set on this path. Badb was stubborn but impulsive, and it was easy to trigger her rage as a distraction, but I'd learned over the past year that Kalen could not be swayed once he made a decision. He would remain calm and determined no matter what I said.

Sigrun was watching us both closely. She was my friend, but she'd also become close with both Badb and Kalen. If I had to guess, she'd support Kalen's decision to come with me. No help there.

"I understand why you want to come. It's natural for parents to want to protect their children from harm." I slipped one of the special daggers Pele had crafted for me from the holster on my forearm and palmed the blade. Kalen saw the movement and tensed slightly but remained where he was. He was five feet away from the gateway, with only me in his way. I couldn't let him get through it because I'd never get him back out.

"But I already watched my father die once protecting me. I'm not going to do it again." The blade was flying through the air before the last word was out, and Kalen darted to the left, exactly as I knew he would. When we sparred, he favored going to the right. I knew he did it on purpose so he could surprise me in the future.

Unfortunately for him, I wasn't born yesterday. He let out a pained grunt as my knife sunk between his ribs. Normally, he would have laughed off being stabbed with a barely four-inch blade, but this one was enchanted to be specifically effective against devourer-fae hybrids. Magic didn't work against Kalen thanks to his devourer nature, but poison did.

He sank to his knees while trying to pull the blade free, but his muscles were spasming, and he couldn't close his fingers around the handle.

"Sorry." I held his pained gaze as I stepped back through the gateway and shut it. After sucking in a deep breath, I turned to face the others. "We need to get out of here before Badb finds out what happened and both of them tear after us."

"You mean tear after *you*," Mikhail said helpfully.

"Yes." I gritted my teeth. "That."

"I'm sorry... " Niall stared at me wide-eyed like he'd never seen me before. "Did you just stab your father with a poisoned blade?"

"He's the freaking Erlking." I shrugged. "He'll be fine as soon as Sigrun pulls it out."

Magos sighed. "I really wish stabbing people weren't your go-to solution for everything."

"If it ain't broke, don't fix it." I looked to Cian. "Can you bring us somewhere away from here so I can summon Ammit without having to worry about a very pissed off Badb and Kalen crashing our party?"

"Yeah." He furrowed his brows for a few seconds. "I'm not as good at traveling around as Hades, but there is one place I can manage. Let me just grab some things real quick."

He darted into the house while we all waited outside.

"So this is the fae death realm?" Niall looked around curiously. "It's more colorful than I would have thought. Almost like it's blending different aspects of all the fae realms together."

"Most of the death realms are a reflection of life. 'As above, so below.'" I plucked an orange from a nearby tree and tossed it to him. Niall caught it and studied it a moment before his eyes flicked to mine in question. "You can eat it." I shrugged. "It's not real, but this one won't do you any harm."

"This one?" He arched a dark, thick eyebrow at the fruit.

"Everything around my brother's place is safe." I waved at the bright garden full of fruit trees and colorful flowers. "And in general, Mag Mell is one of the least treacherous death realms, but even here, there are things dangerous to anything still living, so we'll definitely have to be careful in Hades. The fae are generally peaceful, which is why their death realm is. I think we all know what the Olympians are like in life, so you can imagine their death realm."

Niall processed all this while he quietly munched on his orange. Cian strode out of the house a moment later, and I went absolutely still at the sword hilt poking out over his shoulder. It was Macha's sword. My adoptive mother had been a lethal swordswoman, and she'd carried that sword with her everywhere. After we'd returned to the village where she and Nevin had died and razed it to the ground, we'd begun searching everywhere for the sword.

After a few hours, we'd pulled it from the ashes of the town leader's house. Cian had offered it to me, but I couldn't bear to wield it, so he'd kept it all this time.

Cian's silver eyes met my emerald green ones. "It's a fitting use of our mother's blade," I said, my voice rough.

"I think she would have approved," he replied, his voice equally rough, before turning his attention to the others. "Everyone needs to get close to me."

Ugh. I hate doing this, Jinx complained.

"Same," I muttered. Niall and the two vampires gave me a

questioning look as we all gathered around Cian. "Nothing here is actually real. It's all manifestations brought about by the magic and souls who reside here. Things get weird when it comes to time and distance. Anyone with death magic can use that to their advantage."

Cian's pale grey eyes glowed white, as did the silvery rosettes patterned across his dark skin. My own magic retreated deep inside to the furthest reaches of my soul to get away from the necromantic magic Cian was manifesting. As a fae-shifter-devourer hybrid, it was probably hypocritical of me to call death magic something unnatural that shouldn't exist, but it made my skin crawl. Given how Jinx was hunkered down on the ground and Niall's normally cheerful face was fixed into a grimace, I took it they felt the same.

Meanwhile, Magos and Mikhail seemed no worse for wear. Freaking vampires.

My stomach churned, and I swallowed down bile as it felt like someone reached inside me and yanked me forward by my intestines. With one final pulse, Cian's death magic faded away. I bent over, flexing my knees slightly and placing both hands on them as I took several deep, steady breaths.

Mikhail reached over and rubbed my back, and I concentrated on his touch until the urge to vomit left me. Magos was checking on Jinx, who was trembling on the ground. He hated traveling like this even more than I did.

"What, no one is going to check on me?" Niall grunted. He was standing, but based on how pale his tanned skin was and how tightly his arms were clutching his stomach, I was pretty sure a gentle breeze would have knocked him over.

"You're the one who decided to crash our adventure party," I told him.

"Too bad you weren't around for the last one," Magos said, his copper eyes lighting up with amusement. "Going up against the dragons was a lot more fun."

Mikhail glared at his uncle. "You got your ass lit on fire and seriously injured."

"You got yourself captured." Magos' lips tilted up.

"Someone had to save Nemain!"

"Hey!" I slapped Mikhail's hand away from my back. "I was perfectly capable of saving myself."

"Sure you were," he said skeptically. "Your brilliant plan for saving me was to surrender, *have silver melted off your skin*, and then free me before saving your-godsdamned-self!"

"It worked, you ungrateful asshole!"

"Should we?" Niall waved a hand back and forth between me and Mikhail.

"No," Cian and Magos said at the same time.

"Well, this is amusing," a soft, feminine voice with a slight lilt said from behind me. "Glad to see you haven't changed at all, Nemain."

My breath caught in my throat for half a second before I whirled around and saw familiar, warm brown eyes that always seemed to be laughing at me. The word slipped from my lips like a lost dream.

"*Myrna.*"

Chapter Nineteen

I STARED at the woman before me, noting the slight differences between my memories of her and how she now appeared. She and Kaysea were twins, and although they weren't identical, the similarities had always been a bit uncanny with their seafoam green eyes and delicate, pretty features. Myrna had the same soft, curvy build as her sister but was a couple of inches taller. When we'd been together, she'd glamoured her dark green hair to be a light chestnut brown to differentiate herself from Kaysea.

It had bothered her being compared to her sister because she had been the least magically gifted of the family and had always felt like she'd been lacking. I'd made it a goal every day upon waking to make sure she knew just how much I loved and cherished her.

Myrna had loved me, and that love had gotten her killed.

My knees trembled, and heat built behind my eyes until burning streaks trailed down my cheeks. Something broke on Myrna's face, and she stumbled forward, wrapping me in her arms.

"Don't cry, my love," she murmured. My arms slipped

around her waist, and I buried my face against her neck, inhaling her scent. Even here, she smelled like the oils she'd loved to paint with and a hint of the sea.

We held each other for a few minutes before I pulled back and cupped her face in my hands. "What are you doing here?"

She twisted her bottom lip and bit it lightly, glancing at Cian before her gaze fell back to mine. "I've always been here." She waved a hand at the colorful bungalow with purple shutters and a wraparound porch full of blue flowers. "Cian built it for me when I arrived. There is a town just over the hill, and the ocean is a ten-minute walk away. He offered to rearrange things so I was closer to the water, but I enjoy the walk."

"What?" I let out a sharp exhale and glared at Cian. "You *knew* she was here and didn't tell me!"

Soft fingers trailed across my jawline and directed my face away from my brother, who was returning my glare with a stubborn and defiant expression. Myrna stroked my face soothingly.

"Don't be mad at him. I asked him not to tell you," she said evenly. "Dying is rather confusing for the soul; even those who die peacefully can take a while to come back to themselves here. And for me… " She winced, and my jaw clenched. "Well, you know my death wasn't peaceful. Cian and Hades helped me heal."

I swallowed, nodding slowly. "But why didn't you want him to tell me he'd found you? I asked him to search for you." My voice cracked. "I would have come."

"I know. That's why we didn't tell you." A sad smile stretched across her lips. "It wouldn't have helped you heal. Years had passed by the time I was myself enough to understand what was going on, and by then, you were so hurt and angry. Cian promised me that, despite everything, you had Kaysea and Pele." She chuckled softly. "I had faith in those two to bring you back from whatever darkness you found yourself in."

"They tried," I rasped. "But I got captured… It was Magos who saved me. In more ways than one."

Myrna beamed at the vampire. "I knew you would. It only took a little nudge."

He tilted his head in confusion, copper eyes landing on me with a question, but I had no idea what she was talking about.

"What do you mean? What did you do?"

"It was more of a team effort," she hedged.

The door of the bungalow opened, and four women stepped out. One of them walked over to join us while the other three leaned on the railing of the porch and watched. I got the impression that, if they could have, they would have made popcorn for this.

"Hi!" The newcomer gave us all a bright smile. She looked like she was barely eighteen, but it wasn't like appearances mattered down here. She could have been older than me for all I knew. She reminded me a little of Hades with her olive skin tone and dark eyes. "I'm Persephone."

"Like *the* Persephone?" Mikhail raised both eyebrows at her. He'd been quiet this entire time, just watching as things played out while hiding whatever he was feeling behind an emotionless mask. I'd been so caught up in Myrna that I hadn't even introduced them. It hadn't been an intentional slight, but I worried that I'd hurt him all the same.

Gods, I was so bad at navigating all this relationship shit.

The young woman, who was apparently Persephone, lightly smacked Myrna's shoulder. "I get a *the* in front of my name now! Suck on that, Hera!"

Myrna rolled her eyes, and the three women on the porch chuckled.

"What did the five of you do?" Cian narrowed his eyes at

Persephone, who squirmed under his attention before scurrying back to the porch.

"Nemain was missing, and none of you had found her," Myrna said defensively. "I was worried, so I asked Stheno and Euryale to... uhhh... see what they could *see*."

The names echoed in my mind, and I turned sharply to look closer at the three women. All of them had the same olive-toned skin as Persephone, but they had golden blonde hair and sharper features. The one in the middle looked to be maybe twenty while the two hovering at her side appeared a decade older.

Amusement danced in their eyes, and they all blinked in unison. For a second, their pupils changed to vertical slits and their eyes glowed a bright green before shifting back to their normal soft brown.

My head whipped back to Myrna. "You're friends with Medusa and her sisters!"

She shrugged sheepishly. "Hades has saved a lot of people who were hurt by his family. Since he's with Cian and Cian wanted to help me, I'm sort of friends with most of them. Stheno and Euryale have been particularly... helpful."

Medusa's two older sisters snorted at that, and Myrna blushed.

Before I could question what that was about, Cian interrupted. "Why didn't you tell me what they saw?" His voice was edged in pain. "I was going out of my mind looking for her. I thought I'd lost my sister."

Guilt rippled through me. Cian and I were always fighting over something. When I'd first gotten free of Sebastian, I'd often thrown it back in his face that he hadn't been the one to save me. It had been a real dick move on my part. I'd never apologized for it either.

"Because he was the solution." Myrna pointed to Magos. "We didn't know how or why, only that he was the one with the best possible chance of finding Nemain." She walked over to my brother and clasped his hands. "I knew how you felt about vampires. You never would have gone to him, but then you would have blamed yourself if Nemain… didn't make it. So I told Hades, and he tracked down Magos and made sure he heard the rumors of a shifter with unusual gifts being held by vampires."

Cian stared at their clasped hands as shame flickered across his face.

I closed the distance between us and placed a hand on his shoulder. "Hey." Slowly, he turned his head to face me, still not letting go of Myrna's hands. "I don't expect you to be perfect. Gods know I'm not. You had valid reasons for not trusting vampires. If our positions had been reversed and I had to ask a warlock for help, I'm not sure what I would have done."

"But you did." Cian dropped his gaze to the dark silver ring on my finger. "You made a deal with Emir to protect all of us. Jinx told me."

"Sure, now I did." I gave him a light shove, and he let go of Myrna to fully face me. "But the me from three years ago would have told Emir to take his offer and shove it up his ass. Call it a moment of growth for me."

Mikhail snorted and muttered something under his breath that I couldn't make out but would have no doubt annoyed me. I sent him a cool look, and he just grinned unrepentantly.

"How about we both accept that we've fucked up in the past and we'll try to be better going forward?" I gave Cian another shove, slightly harder this time. "You're my little brother, and I love you no matter what, you dumbass."

A lopsided grin tugged at his lips, and he shoved me back. "Love you too, sis." Then he frowned and looked over my shoulder. "I'm not sure, but I think someone just opened a gateway near our house."

"Badb and Kalen." I grimaced before reluctantly saying, "Which means we need to move."

Cian nodded in understanding and moved to wait over by Magos, giving me space. Niall stood next to them with a polite expression stamped on his face, but his brows were creased slightly. I had no idea what Sigrun had told him about Myrna and my past. He was likely confused about what was going on but too nice to say anything.

Standing apart from everyone else, Mikhail waited patiently, eyes scanning the environment for threats. The way he held himself was too relaxed to be natural. My magic, which had been silent since we arrived in the death realm, unfurled from my chest. One small tendril stretched out, so thin that the crystal blue flames were almost translucent, then wrapped around his wrist and up his forearm. The relief he felt at the contact echoed in my soul, and for once, I didn't panic at the growing bond between us.

"It's okay," Myrna said, pulling me in for one more hug before drawing back and holding my gaze. "I owe so much to Hades. We all do." She waved at the women on the porch. "You have to save him, Nemain."

"We will," I assured her. *Even though I couldn't save you*, I thought.

Sadness touched her eyes as she likely guessed what I was thinking.

"You need to stop blaming yourself for my death. It wasn't your fault."

"It really was," I countered bitterly. "I should have known better than to think Sebastian would have let me go so easily, but I didn't want to let you go, so I convinced myself I could keep you safe. You died because of my selfishness."

"I knew what I signed up for." Myrna's eyes lit up in defiance. "The day I met you, Kaysea had a vision. She grasped my hand when it happened, so I saw it too. In the vision, I was holding my own bloody heart in my hands with my chest ripped open. My sister repeated six words over and over again: '*To love her is to die.*'"

"No." Claws shot out of my fingers as I shook my head violently in denial.

"You think yourself selfish for not letting me go, but I'm my own person," she pushed, not backing down as steel coated her words. "I knew my fate, and I tried to stop it. Not only to save myself, but because I knew the kind of pain my death would cause you." My heart hammered inside my chest, and I knew my expression was something dark and terrible. Still, Myrna didn't stop, even as her bottom lip trembled slightly. "You may have been selfish, but so was I, because I could have told you. Knew that I should. But you would have left if I'd told you the truth."

"Of course I would have!" The last of my resolve broke, and I screamed, the barest hints of my magic coming to life and coating my skin in shimmering, blue flames. "He never would have been able to get to you if you'd returned to the sea. Back to Tír fo Thuinn."

"But you couldn't have come with me." A wry grin tugged at her lips. "You've got a lot of skills, but alas, none of them let you breathe under water."

"This isn't funny," I snapped, clenching my hands into fists until my claws bit into my skin. "You didn't have to die."

"I know, and I'm sorry." She wrapped her hands around my fists, not caring about the blood leaking out or my flames that simply wrapped around her hands, careful not to harm her. "I've had a lot of time to process everything that happened. I did try to find a way to be with you and survive; it's not like I just gave up and resigned myself to my fate. The time we had together was a gift, Nemain. Even an extra day was worth it."

"You can say your pretty words all you want." I inhaled a

deep breath and tried to let out some of the anger when I exhaled. My flames retreated back inside, but I still felt like I was going to explode out of my skin. "I'm still beyond pissed at you."

"Fair." She gave me a small, unrepentant grin and raised my hands to her mouth, kissing my knuckles softly. Then she spun on her heel and walked up to Mikhail, who turned to face her with a close-lipped smile curling at the corners of his lips. I remained rooted in place, unsure what exactly I was supposed to do about my dead lover confronting my current one.

"If you ever—" Myrna started.

"Is this where you threaten to cut off various parts of my body if I hurt her?" Mikhail drawled as he smirked down at Myrna. "I appreciate the sentiment, but it'll be a little hard for you from here, won't it?"

He. Did. Not.

I was going to *murder* him. Couldn't he pretend to not be an asshole for once? A growl slipped from my lips, and I tried to recall the little bit of my magic that was still wrapped around his forearm, but the blue flames simply burned brighter. My magic was a fucking traitor.

"I see you and Nemain share the same trait of hurling barbed comments when you're feeling emotionally over-whelmed. The two of you are so alike."

Mikhail's smirk slipped for a moment.

Myrna matched his smirk with one of her own and closed the small distance between them. She was over half a foot shorter than him but still managed to look ferocious as she stretched one hand up and traced her fingers across his jawline.

"If you *ever* hurt or betray her, Kaysea will drown you on dry land and Pele will burn your body to ash." Myrna brushed some of his hair behind his ear. "And then Cian will show me the way to your soul, and I will rip whatever is left of you to shreds. I'm sure if I ask Hades, he'll piece you back together so I can do it again."

"And we'll help!" Medusa called out from the porch, her sisters smiling darkly next to her.

"I can see why she loves you." Light danced in Mikhail's twilight eyes, and his smirk turned into a genuine smile as he placed a hand on his chest. "I would rip out my own heart and give it to you before I would ever harm or betray Nemain."

Myrna let her hand fall lower, slipping it underneath his to rest directly over his heart. "I believe you." Then something passed between the two of them, and I felt the barest whisper of magic before Myrna let her hand fall away. "Keep her safe."

He nodded deeply, not a hint of arrogance in his expression for once. "With my life."

"Yeah, no one else is sacrificing themself for me." I stomped a few feet away, swearing under my breath about all the frustrating people in my life. Reaching into my pocket, I took out the summoner and raised it to my lips. When I'd asked Horus how it worked exactly, his super helpful instructions had been, *"Just wrap your lips around it and blow real hard."*

Over four thousand years old, and he still had an adolescent sense of humor. Honestly, I was impressed.

I blew into the summoner, expecting it to let out a whistle. Nothing. I pulled it away and frowned at it. "I think it might be brok—"

Darkness formed in the air in front of me, and the icy punch of death magic slammed into my chest. I stumbled back a step and immediately bumped into Mikhail, who steadied me. A deep, guttural, hissing sound that caused the hair on the back of neck to stand up rumbled from the center of the dark cloud.

I slipped my hand into one of the three pouches I'd tied to my belt and wrapped my fingers around the warm, slippery object it contained. The bags had been enchanted to keep their contents fresh. Ammit was part feline and could be a finicky asshole about these things.

"Hey, girl," I crooned. "Sorry for dragging you out of Duat, but I need a favor."

A rumbling bellow was her answer, and I winced as it felt like my eardrums would burst. A quick glance over my shoulder, and I saw Magos had pulled Myrna back and pushed her towards the others on the porch. Jinx went with her, leaving Cian, Magos, and Niall standing guard.

"Don't be like that," I warned and pulled my hand free, holding it out in front of me so she could see what I had to offer. "I brought you snacks. We need to find a door, Ammit. It's in Hades and leads to its true king." Ammit understood things based on how they related to death. Artemis meant nothing to her, but Hades was forever connected to the death realm that bore his name, so Ammit would sense the connection between them.

Something between a cough and growl sounded from the shadows before they started to dissipate, revealing a beast not much larger than Hecate's hounds. Dark, intelligent eyes latched on to the bloody heart resting on my palm, and the chuffing sound once again flowed out of the crocodilian jaws.

I tossed her the heart, and she snapped it out of the air, then tilted her head back and swallowed it in one gulp.

Glittering, black eyes looked at me and then to the remaining pouches on my belt before she settled down into a sphinx position.

I smiled. "And that, my friends, is how you strike a bargain with the Devourer of Souls."

"Where'd you get the hearts?" Cian asked, still eying Ammit warily.

"It's not exactly hard to find humans who have done fucked-up shit." I shrugged. "Literally just walked around for ten minutes and used my ability to read souls, discovered half a dozen within a two-block radius."

"They were a little unnerved by a random woman walking up and sniffing them." Mikhail snickered. "Can't argue with the results though."

Niall, bless his soul, wasn't the least bit afraid of Ammit. Instead, his blue eyes lit up as he excitedly shouted, "Something new!" Then he practically skipped over to the strange beast and crouched in front of her before holding out his hand.

Mikhail looked at me. "I'm having flashbacks to Andrei trying to smell all the flowers in the fae realm."

I huffed out a laugh. My werewolf ex-lover had known almost nothing about things outside the human realm. I missed the way his entire body had practically shaken with excitement over seeing the smallest thing.

While I had no regrets about ending things with him, I still missed having him in my life. I hoped one day our paths would cross again and we could figure out some sort of friendship. Maybe when being in my life was less likely to get him killed.

Unlike Andrei, Niall wasn't some naive youngster looking at the world with rose-tinted glasses. Niall was somewhere around four thousand years old, so he'd seen a lot, but for most of that time, he'd been locked away with the exiled fae king. Now, he cherished every new thing he saw like it was a gift.

Even if said gifts were as likely to bite his hand off as they were to sniff it.

"Niall," I said warningly, "she's not like Gunnar."

Sigrun's wolf was a bit standoffish but wasn't prone to random acts of violence.

"What is she?" Niall asked in wonder as hot breath shot out from the nostrils resting on the top of Ammit's crocodilian jaws. I held my breath for a moment, wondering if those sharp teeth were going to sink into fae flesh, but she just pulled her head back and resumed her statue-like pose as her eyes once again focused on the pouches at my side. Ammit had a bit of a one-track mind.

"A manifestation of the death realm Duat," I explained. Niall finally pulled his hand back but remained crouched in front of Ammit, studying her strange body. "Osiris and his lot landed in Egypt when they fled to the human realm. They fell in love with the land and remained there for thousands of years. They influenced Egypt and its people, but the gods themselves were also influenced."

"Egypt," he said slowly, as if tasting the name on his tongue. "I haven't been there yet."

"Aki grew up there for part of her childhood. I'm sure she'd be delighted to take you sometime." The young empath absolutely adored playing tour guide. "Duat existed before the gods came to the human realm, but it changed over time to reflect Egypt more and more. Osiris created Ammit based on some of the beasts that prowled Egyptian lands, the ones its people feared the most.

"Crocodile." I waved a hand at her reptilian head before pointing to her furry upper body. "Leopard." My hand lowered to where the fur melted away and turned into rubbery, grey skin that wrapped around thick hindquarters, muscular legs, and a short tail. "Hippopotamus."

"Sometimes the leopard part is replaced with lion," Cian added. "It all varies based on the whims of Osiris."

Ammit's jaws opened, and a low hiss filled the air. She was probably growing impatient about being called away from Duat. She may be able to wander all the death realms, but Duat was where she belonged.

"It's time." I forced myself to walk over to Ammit, and the others joined me, forming a half-circle behind her. Jinx had wisely decided to perch on Magos' shoulders away from Ammit's long jaws. I looked to where Myrna was now standing, nestled between Stheno and Euryale. Both of them had an arm looped around her waist. I thought of her blush from earlier and gave them a smile. "Thank you for making her happy. She deserves nothing less."

They grinned before planting a kiss on Myrna's cheeks, causing her to blush again. Shadows rose from the ground beneath Ammit's feet, swirling around us. I hoped her way of traveling wasn't as bad as Cian's because I was pretty sure I would hurl if it were.

"Nemain," Myrna's voice called out, and our stares locked. "Be happy too."

I swallowed and nodded once before everything went dark.

Chapter Twenty

I squeezed my eyes shut, waiting for the feeling of my insides being yanked about to come, but it never did. Cautiously, I cracked open one eye and then the other. We stood on the edge of a forest, a meadow spanning before us. Long, sturdy stems stretched out of plants with thin, elongated, green leaves, rows of white blossoms lining the stems.

"Asphodel Fields," Cian said what I was thinking. "Glad it's not Tartarus."

"Same." I eyed Ammit before giving my brother an appraising look. "She's way better at moving around here than you."

He rolled his eyes. "I have death magic. She *is* death magic."

"Excuses, excuses." I opened another pouch to pull out a heart, and Ammit's reptilian eyes watched with rapt attention. "Find us the door leading to Hades," I commanded, trusting that she would understand I meant the god and not the place.

I waited until she let out that strange, coughing sound that I decided meant she agreed before tossing her the heart. She swallowed it in one gulp and then trotted forth into the meadow, her stubby tail swinging rapidly as if it were propelling her forward.

Both my mind and heart were still dealing with seeing Myrna again, but I didn't have the luxury to dwell on that now, so I wrapped all my complicated feelings together, shoved them into a box, and tucked it away in my soul to unwrap later. Preferably with whiskey.

Mikhail fell into step behind me with Cian following in his wake, and Magos and Niall guarded our rear. I didn't sense anyone or anything around us, but that didn't mean much. My instincts were almost as useless as my magic in the death realms. Nothing here made sense, and it always put me on edge.

An annoyed hiss from behind me was my only warning before Jinx landed on my shoulder, sinking his claws in deep to get purchase. The asshole could have landed mostly on the leather vest I wore, but of course he'd made sure that at least one paw landed on the exposed skin at the base of my neck.

I reached up and nudged him, forcing him to settle into a perch and latch on to my vest for stability instead of my skin. Out of habit, I scratched him behind the ears, despite my annoyance. Jinx had been my one stable companion throughout life, and as much as I wished he were home safe, I took strength from his presence.

This feels wrong, he said after I dropped my hand away. *Seems a little too convenient that the door leading to Therrea would be in such an empty part of Asphodel Fields.*

"Agreed." My eyes scanned the tall grasses around us. "Even considering how large this part of Hades is, I would think there would be at least some souls around here. Can you feel anything, Cian?"

A pause, and I felt my brother send out a wave of his magic. "There's something here... Just one, I think." Another cold pulse of death magic. "Wait. Something here is *alive*. Besides us."

"Where?" I asked, keeping my voice low and even. We all knew there was a chance Artemis had discovered the door between Hades and Therrea, but I was really hoping we would luck out for once.

Ammit continued her steady trot. Occasionally, she would pause and go perfectly still before letting out a snort and continuing onward. If she sensed something around us, she wasn't bothered by it. Then again, it's not like she could die. As a manifestation of Duat, she would simply be reborn again if her current body was damaged. None of us had that luxury though.

"Somewhere ahead of us," Cian murmured.

"There's a cavern," Mikhail said.

"Just throwing it out there that I really hate caves," Niall said, still sounding really upbeat about everything despite this turn of events.

"Not a fan of them myself." I squinted. "Could be a coincidence. Maybe the doorway is somewhere else?"

Spoiler alert. It was not.

"You were saying?" Mikhail drawled as we all peered into the darkness of the aforementioned cavern.

"I hate you."

"You wish."

Magos sighed. "Can we concentrate for a few minutes?" Mikhail and I gave him looks of complete innocence, and I got the distinct impression he was counting to ten in his head. Then he looked at Cian. "Is whatever you sense in there?"

Death magic rolled off Cian, and his silver eyes sharpened. We all waited patiently, including Ammit, who was once again doing a sphinx impersonation.

I'd only encountered Ammit a couple of times before. She wasn't exactly a normal animal, but I was pretty sure she was watching something in the darkness of the cavern by how keenly she was focused. There was something she sensed that none of us could. And whatever it was, she didn't like it.

Which really didn't bode well for us.

The mouth of the cavern was at least twenty feet wide, and it towered far over our heads. Just looking into the inky blackness set my nerves on edge. We should have been able to see a good way into the cavern given the size of the entrance, but less than a foot inside, it was like someone had dropped a curtain made of shadows. I couldn't see or sense anything from a foot in front of me.

I turned slightly to my right where Magos was standing. "Can you hear anything?" My hearing was excellent but not as good as a vampire's.

He shook his head. "Nothing in the darkness."

To my left, Mikhail grimaced.

"Whatever is alive is in there, but where or what it is, I can't tell," Cian growled. "I think there is something else in there too, but I can't get a lock on it. It's not alive."

"Ammit, is the door in there?" I glanced at her, and she nodded her head deeply. "Can you show us where exactly?"

She rose and slowly moved towards the shadows, almost like she was fighting against an invisible force. When one paw crossed into the darkness, Ammit bellowed in pain and yanked it back, but the shadowy tendrils followed. They swirled around and struck at her flesh, even as her feet swiftly carried her away from the darkness. Panicked noises pierced the air as the living embodiment of Duat tried to break free.

"Shit!" I dove towards her, not exactly sure what I could do to help. She was spinning around rapidly, trying to get whatever this magic was off her, but the shadows just reformed. I tried to call my magic forth, thinking maybe my devourer flames could help, but it wouldn't respond.

Fucking death realms. Gods, I hated it here. I felt totally

useless. My magic didn't work, and everything here was already dead, so it wasn't like I could threaten it with violence.

"Move!" Cian shouted and forced me aside before sinking to his knees in front of Ammit. The silver rosettes running down his forearms glowed against his dark skin as his magic poured out. The air turned frigid, and I took a step back, goose bumps rising on my skin. Cian shoved his hand into the swirling shadows, and they solidified into obsidian glass before he clenched his fingers into fists and twisted them sharply. Then the magic that had been engulfing Ammit shattered.

"You good?" I stepped forward and rested a hand on my brother's sagging shoulder.

"Yeah," he said through panted breaths. "Just give me a minute."

Ammit released a deep groan that seemed to vibrate up her throat before she rested her head on Cian's thighs. Jinx bumped his head against mine before leaping down and settling next to Cian. Jinx and I might be the bonded ones, but he'd grown up with Cian too and cared deeply for my brother. Not that he'd ever admit it.

I glanced back at the others. Mikhail and Magos had taken defensive positions in front of the cave; both of them had called their swords forth and mist was still trailing off them. Niall stood slightly behind them, but when he sensed my attention, he walked over to me.

"Your brother is a necromancer?"

"Yes." I took in his pinched brows and the tension around the corners of his mouth. "That a problem?"

"What?" His expression relaxed a little. "No. Sorry. It just threw me off is all. Balor has some necromancers in his army. I've never been able to determine what they are exactly. At some point, they were fae, but not any kind I've ever encountered."

"And now?"

"Now, they're dark creatures." His usually jovial face darkened. "I've seen a lot of fucked-up shit being locked in that realm for thousands of years, but what he's twisted them into... Those creatures are nothing but walking nightmares now."

"Lovely." I grimaced. Fae had a variety of magic, but I'd never encountered any that had necromancy. Given that Balor had been locked away thousands of years ago, it was entirely possible that species no longer existed in the fae realms. Niall was the only sciatháin I'd ever met. "Exactly how many unique monstrosities does Balor command in his army?"

Niall tilted his head back and looked towards the sky, shifting side to side a few times while he contemplated my question. "I don't think you want me to answer that until you have a bottle of whiskey in your hand."

"I was worried you'd say something like that." Here's hoping the fae queens could keep Balor locked away forever and I'd never have to worry about him releasing his army of nightmares on us all. Something told me I wouldn't be that lucky.

Cian finally rose, giving Ammit a pat on the head before walking over to us. "I think those shadows are part of some type of spell to keep away the denizens of Hades. Being a manifestation of Duat, Ammit can't enter, and I probably have enough death magic flowing through my veins that it'll attack me as well."

My lips curled into a grin as I glanced at Niall and then the vampires. "Sounds like we're up, boys." I looked to Jinx. "Stay with Cian and Ammit. I'll try to communicate with you once we're inside."

Not a fan of this plan.

Same, my friend. Same.

Then I pulled both my swords free and strode towards the shadows, Mikhail and Magos at my sides with Niall trailing behind me. Air filled my lungs as I took a deep breath. Nothing ventured, nothing gained. Then I stepped forward into the dark.

———

As soon as we crossed through the shadowy barrier, the darkness fell away, courtesy of the golden-flamed torches lining the cavern walls. I only had a split second to notice this before something large barreled into me and sent me flying into the wall I'd just been looking at. Pain exploded when my shoulder slammed into the rock-hard surface. I'd just barely been fast enough to keep my head from taking the brunt of the hit. As it was, my shoulder was definitely dislocated, and I could feel blood running down my back where a jagged edge had sliced through my leather vest.

Mikhail was there in an instant, helping me to my feet. I could hear the sounds of Niall and Magos battling whatever had attacked me. With careful, steady movements, Mikhail held my injured arm and extended it slowly. Our gazes connected, and I jerked my head in a nod, trying to force my muscles to relax. Then he slowly pulled my arm forward, and I ground my teeth as the pain intensified before my shoulder slid back into place.

The relief was instant, and I let out a long breath before flicking my hand towards the sword I'd dropped. It instantly leapt to my hand. I *loved* these swords.

A deep, rumbling growl tore across the cavern, and someone—Niall, I guessed, based on the cadence—let out a hiss of pain. My back still hurt, but I could already tell the bleeding had slowed. I took off towards the others. The fight had moved further in and around the bend, so I couldn't see what type of fun beastie we were up against.

Just as I turned the corner, Niall flew back and crashed into me. We both tumbled to the ground, barely managing not to stab each other with our blades. Mikhail moved to help Magos as I dragged Niall up with me.

"What the fuck is that thing?" A nasty cut ran down the side of his face, narrowly missing his left eye.

"Oh, shit," I swore when I saw the enormous, two-headed dog squaring off with the vampires. It looked similar to Hecate's hounds, only significantly larger, at least fifteen feet at the shoulder. Black fur covered its bulky body with a ridge of dark red running down its spine, and glowing, red eyes latched on to me. I had no doubt it remembered me. "Fuck. Me."

The hulking nightmare of a dog snapped at Mikhail with one head and Magos with the other, but both vampires vanished into mist before reappearing next to me.

"Now's not really the time, love." Mikhail grinned at me. Of course he'd be enjoying this. "I thought Cerberus had three heads?"

"He does." I pointed one of my swords at the dog. "That's not Cerberus. That's his brother, Orthrus. I... uhh... sort of killed him way back."

"You killed a *dog*?" Niall frowned at me even as he swayed slightly. Must have been some head wound to give a fae a concussion.

"He was trying to eat me!" I yelled defensively. Before I could argue my case more, Orthrus let out an eardrum-shattering bark and charged after us. Mikhail and I went right while Magos grabbed Niall and yanked him left. In a very much not shocking turn of events, the two-headed monster thundered after me.

"If you killed him, he's dead!" Mikhail shouted.

A shadow above me was my only warning before I dove to the side and rolled just as a large paw slammed into the spot I'd just vacated. Another paw landed next to me, and I thrust my sword right through the tendon on the back of his leg before darting forward. Orthrus let out a pained yelp and leapt back.

"That's usually how *killing* something works," I said between panted breaths as Mikhail and I raced across the cavern.

Something dark glimmered on the surface of the far side, and I realized it was a large, underground lake. *What the hell?*

I glanced over my shoulder to where Magos and Niall were harrying Orthrus, who was still limping. Whatever spell was pushing out the death magic was likely interfering with his ability to heal. Look at that, a lucky godsdamn break.

"I mean"—Mikhail sent me a pointed look—"something in here is *alive,* and if it's not Lassie, then where is Timmy?"

I gave him a blank stare. "You really need to stop watching whatever shows Isabeau and Finn drag you into. Also, I don't even think that reference makes sense."

"Whatever. My point still stands."

With Orthrus temporarily distracted, I ran over to the water to see if it could offer any clues as to what was going on here, and a dark form rippled beneath the glassy surface. Something very, *very* big.

"It can't be," I breathed out and fell to my knees at the lake's edge, dropping both my swords.

"Do you really think you should be touching that?" Mikhail asked when I reached my hand out, but instead of dipping beneath the surface, I met a solid resistance, like a pane of glass sat on top of the lake. The magic it contained bit into my skin, but I held the contact, trying to coax my magic to rip into whatever this was.

"Damn it," I growled. It wasn't just death magic that was suppressed in this cavern, so were my devourer flames. Artemis had covered her bases. A long tentacle with suction cups the size of dinner plates slipped beneath the surface to rest on the underside of the barrier, directly below my hand.

Emotions that weren't mine pierced me like a spear. Fear, pain, and a never-ending well of loneliness.

"Nemain," Mikhail warned before yanking me to my feet. I barely had time to summon and catch my swords before he pulled me into a run as Orthrus pounded across the cavern after us.

I glanced over my shoulder just as Magos appeared in front of Orthrus and struck at his right leg. From the other side of the angry canine, Niall thrust his spear, aiming for the left leg, right at the knee joint. Both of Orthrus' front legs folded, and he flipped head over heels, the ground shaking as he tumbled.

Mikhail and I halted while Magos and Niall caught up to us, both of them covered in blood and breathing hard.

"Did you come up with a brilliant plan while you were fucking around?" Niall held a hand to the side of his head and winced.

Orthrus struggled to his feet. His healing was slowed drastically, but it wasn't completely gone. We had minutes before he was on us again. Based on the death glare he was giving me with both pairs of eyes, I would definitely be his primary target.

"We need to get him out of here." I gestured at the pissed off dog. "Despite being the one who killed him, I don't actually want to keep hurting him, and it's not like we can kill him again."

"Agreed, but how?" Magos asked. "He won't leave us alone while we work on taking that barrier down, and it's too narrow in that area of the cavern to fight. He'd be all over us, and I don't particularly want to be used as a chew toy."

I bit the inside of my cheeks. "That barrier is mostly keyed to death magic," I said thoughtfully. "That's why it hurt Ammit, but Orthrus doesn't actually have any death magic. He's just tainted with it slightly because he's dead, but it's a bare minimum amount. It would hurt him to pass through the barrier, but I think he could if properly motivated."

"And how exactly are we going to motivate him?" Niall asked.

"The same way you do any not-so-bright predator," Mikhail said slyly before jerking his head towards me. "Bait."

"How quickly can you get the two of us into the air, Niall?" I cocked my head from side to side, cracking my neck as I shook the muscles of my body loose. I would need every bit of my speed and agility to pull this off.

"Fast enough, hopefully." The old fae warrior grinned happily.

Magos sighed. "Why do your plans always give me grey hair?"

"You don't have any grey hair," I pointed out.

"I feel like I do."

Shudders ran across the cavern floor as Orthrus finally managed to lumber to his feet, drool dripping from his jaws as he lowered his head and prepared to charge us again.

"Niall, get to the barrier and wait for me. I'll be coming in hot." Black wings flowed out of his back, and the sciatháin leapt into the air. With the way the cavern walls angled inward the higher up you went, he didn't have much room to maneuver, but he managed. Seconds later, he disappeared around the corner. "Okay, the two of you, pop in and out around him. Your job is to piss him off but not injure him seriously or distract him away from me. Got it?"

They both nodded and vanished into swirls of mist.

"Come on, boy!" I slapped my palms down on my thighs and then clapped my hands. "Come on! You're not still mad at me for killing you that one time, are you?"

Growls vibrated through the air and echoed off the cavern walls as Orthrus charged, and I waited until the last possible second to dive out of the way. I couldn't just run straight for the barrier, because I needed to get him so enraged that he didn't think about where he was going.

All my friends regularly told me I had a true talent for pissing things off. Time to put that to the test.

As he barreled past me, Orthrus twisted one giant head around, and a gaping maw full of sharp teeth started to close around me. Mikhail appeared and spun us both out of the way as the jaws slammed shut. Then he dropped a kiss on my lips before vanishing, only to reappear beside the overgrown hound and yank on his ear hard.

Orthrus snapped, but my mate was already gone, and an enraged bellow flew out of the hound only to end on a yelp when Magos appeared and sliced at his shoulder. The cut was shallow but long. Orthrus rose up on his hindquarters before slamming both front paws down, causing dust to fly several feet into the air.

Oh, yeah. He was pissed. I just needed to do something to push him over the edge.

Before I could think better of it, I slid both my swords into the sheaths on my back and darted forward, straight at the two-headed beast. He saw me coming and lowered both heads to meet my charge. Just as I reached him, I feigned going right, and he committed, his left head lunging and snapping closed, but I'd already adjusted my course and slid left to smack him on the nose.

"Thanks for the idea, Elisa!" I cackled as I sprinted away. The walls shook as Orthrus bellowed in rage again before tearing after me. My lungs burned as I pushed myself to run as fast as I could. Orthrus wasn't particularly fast, but he covered so much distance with each stride that, in a straight line, he was almost as fast as me.

Almost.

JINX! I telepathically screamed as loud as I could as I

turned the bend and the barrier came into sight. Here was hoping he'd be able to hear me as I got closer. *JINX! MOVE!*

Niall was crouched down, balanced on the balls of his feet directly before the wall made of shadows. I could hear Orthrus gaining on me. No time to slow down. I flung myself forward, and Niall did the same. We collided midair, and the wind was knocked out of my chest from the impact. For a second, we just hung there as I felt the hound's hot breath on my neck.

Then, enormous black wings swept down, and we shot upward. Some part of Orthrus smacked my lower legs, but it wasn't his teeth, so I didn't care.

"Shit!" Niall tried to bank left, but he'd been so concerned with getting us the hell out of there that he hadn't paid attention to where we were going. A long stalactite loomed in front of us, hanging several feet down from the cave ceiling, and we bounced off it. Niall lost his grip on me, and I plummeted to the hard cavern floor.

I twisted midair, trying to at least land on my feet, but I overcompensated, making my back parallel to the ground. My eyes squeezed shut as I braced for impact, only for a pair of strong arms to grab me. I slowly opened my eyelids and looked into twilight eyes dancing with amusement.

"I can't believe you booped that overgrown mutt on the nose." He set me on my feet, slipped one hand around the back of my neck, and kissed me deeply. I wrapped my arms around his neck and kissed him back, not even caring about the blood and dirt covering both of us.

Someone cleared their throat behind us. "We should probably check on your brother and the others to make sure they handled the sudden appearance of a two-headed beast of legend alright."

"To be fair, he's barely a legend," I said, detangling myself from Mikhail. "His brother got all the attention. Apparently, three heads are better than two."

Chapter Twenty-One

Luckily, Jinx had heard my warning, and he told me everyone had managed to get out of the way of Orthrus' rampage. They'd watched the hound bolt towards the forest without a backwards glance; clearly he'd been excited to get the hell out of that cave. I had no doubt if I ever ran into him again, he'd be even more pissed off at me, but at least he was free now. Although the grimalkin was very much not pleased about having almost been trampled by a dog.

Unfortunately, with the barrier up, Cian and Ammit were still trapped on the outside, and we needed the latter to tell us where exactly this door to Therrea was because I couldn't sense it.

Either the natural doorways to the death realm worked completely differently than the gateways I could open, or Artemis had used some serious magic to hide it.

There was also the small problem of the kraken.

"Thoughts?" I asked Niall, who had been crouched on the glass-like surface of the lake, studying the magic for the last five minutes. Levi was reaching up with his tentacles and flattening them against the underside. Now that I had more time to investigate his watery prison, I could make out the manacles clamped around his tentacles.

I hadn't ever met Hephaestus or encountered anything he had made, but I was willing to bet this was his handiwork. If we didn't see him when we confronted Artemis and the others, I'd be tracking him down to repay him in kind for this.

It broke my heart that the poor guy had been trapped here all this time. The Olympians were such assholes. But some of the fear and sadness I'd initially felt about Levi had faded and been replaced by hope.

The ancient fae warrior pursed his lips as he rose and faced me. "I can only see magic. The sciatháin never had much magic compared to other fae. So I'm not the most well-versed in understanding spell castings, but I can tell you there is a direct line from this lake to the center of that wall." He pointed to a section of the cavern wall ten feet to the right of the lake. "Magic is flowing towards there and vanishing. I don't sense anything, but if I had to guess, that's the doorway we're looking for."

The four of us walked over to the spot Niall had pointed out and stared at the rocky surface. My fingers skimmed the cool stone, and I concentrated, trying to pick up any trace of magic.

"Nothing," I murmured.

"We need Hecate," Mikhail said. "She could probably understand the spell and give us more information." He pointed his thumb over his shoulder back towards the lake. "And she'll definitely want to know about our buddy over there."

"I know." I sighed. "She's going to lose her shit when she sees him like this. I'm going to see if Kaysea is available; Hecate might need some help to manipulate the water." Two gateways opened beside us, one revealing the trail leading up to Hecate's home, and the other to a cottage built into the rocky coastline just outside Emerald Bay. I glanced at Mikhail. "I'll keep the gateways open. You go get Hecate, and I'll grab Kaysea." My eyes moved to Magos. "You and Niall can update the others."

Everyone nodded, and we went our separate ways. I jogged up the stone steps to the simple home Zareen and Kaysea shared just outside of town. If neither of them were there, I'd try The Inferno next or my place.

"Kaysea!" I called out and knocked loudly on the door. "You here?"

Heavy footsteps sounded, and I frowned, taking a few steps back. Definitely not Kaysea or Zareen. My hand hovered over one of the daggers on my thigh as I eyed the door.

"Come back, later," a tall, well-muscled man with green eyes so pale they were almost white growled as he yanked the door open. "Or better yet, just don't come back at all."

"I cannot begin to tell you how much I don't have time for your bullshit, Connor." I shoved Kaysea's older brother aside and quickly dodged his attempt to grab me. "Kaysea!" I screamed again. "I'm going murder your brother if you don't get your ass out here!"

"Nemain!" My friend rushed in, her long, green hair flowing behind her. "What's going on? Why are you back already? I've been pacing back and forth all day," she rushed on, her eyes going wide as she took in my roughed-up appearance. All my wounds had healed, but I was still covered in dried blood. "Pele promised to update me the moment she knew anything, but we assumed we wouldn't hear from you for a while. I was just talking to Qu—"

"Kaysea," I cut her off and placed a hand on each of her shoulders. "Focus. I need you to come with me. We found something in Hades. Turns out Artemis didn't kill the kraken all those years ago. He's trapped in a cave in Hades, and Artemis is using his magic for some type of spell.

Mikhail is getting Hecate now, but we might need your water magic."

"Levi is alive?" Kaysea blinked.

"Doesn't matter." Connor slid between me and his sister, his hulking frame blocking her from my sight. "She's not going."

"Excuse you?!" Kaysea darted around him to stand by my side. "You don't get to tell me what to do, and if I want to go and save the godsdamn kraken from some shitty death realm, you can't stop me!"

Connor opened his mouth to argue when the sliding door to the back porch opened and a woman strolled in. She was taller than Kaysea, but still a few inches short of my almost six feet, and had a lithe build. Between how she was built and her light, quiet movements, I suspected she could be quite stealthy when she put her mind to it. Dark blue hair stood out vividly against her pale white skin, and a salty scent drifted over to me. Another mermaid then.

"Who the fuck are you?"

"Nemain," Kaysea warned at the same time Connor growled, "She's the Merfolk Queen, you idiot."

I cocked my head to the side as I studied the newly crowned leader of Tír fo Thuinn. Kaysea's father had willingly stepped down because his magic was fading, which meant his long life would be coming to an end soon. I didn't know the specifics of the new queen's rise to power other than it appeared entirely peaceful. Pele didn't trust her, but Pele didn't trust most people, including the Unseelie and Seelie Queens.

"Ashling, right?"

"It's Qu—"

The Merfolk Queen waved her hand across the air, cutting Connor off. "Ashling is fine. No need for titles here." Her eyes, one a brilliant green and the other a golden yellow, slowly took in every inch of my appearance, cataloging every detail. "Your magic is… interesting."

"Sorry, I don't have time to do a little dance for you." My gaze cut to Kaysea, who was shifting uneasily as she looked back and forth between Ashling and Connor. Clearly, I'd walked in something, but I didn't have time to deal with it now. "Come on, Kaysea."

I grabbed Kaysea's hand and tugged her towards the door. Connor snatched his sister's other wrist and tugged her back, leading Kaysea to yank out of both our grips and cross her arms. "You two are fucking impossible."

"Kaysea's coming with me. Try to stop me, I dare you," I growled at Connor, letting my flames ripple down my arms. He sneered at my challenge and took a step forward.

"I'll go." Ashling walked on silent feet towards the front door where my gateway waited for us.

"What?" My flames winked out of existence as I twisted to stare at the Merfolk Queen. "That's not… that's not necessary. Kaysea is who I want."

"I don't care about who or what you want," she said coolly. "Kaysea is one of my subjects, and I say she's staying here. I was magically gifted before I ascended, and now that I bear the mantle of Tír fo Thuinn"—power rippled from her, cool and unstoppable like a tidal wave—"you'd be hard-pressed to find someone more powerful than me when it comes to water magic. Perhaps you should take what you are given, Knight."

We stared at each other for a long moment before I forced myself to unclench my jaw. "Nemain will do. No need for titles, as you said."

A close-lipped smile flashed across her face, and her striking eyes went to Connor. "Won't you escort *your* queen?"

What in the flying fuck had I walked in on? When Kaysea had first told me her father had stepped down, I'd panicked because I'd thought Connor might take the throne, but he'd apparently had no interest in it and had been trying to distance himself from the new Merfolk Queen. Clearly, that wasn't working because Ashling was here. In Kaysea's fucking living room.

For a moment, I could see the conflict in Connor's pale eyes, and I felt bad for him. He blamed me for Myrna's death, but he also blamed himself. It's what drove him to be so over-protective of Kaysea and was the main reason I hadn't killed him all these years. He could hate me all he wanted. I knew he would give his life to protect Kaysea, and that was worth dealing with his bullshit.

But he was also stupidly loyal to Tír fo Thuinn and would never disobey its queen. There was something else in his face when he looked at Ashling, which he never did for long, always averting his gaze. *Desire.* I laughed under my breath. Connor had a thing for the new Merfolk Queen. No wonder he was trying to avoid her. Connor didn't like complications when it came to relationships.

And Ashling was a walking complication.

"Kaysea, why don't you go to my place?" I said, taking pity on Connor. The wards around my apartment were no joke thanks to the machinations of both Pele and my parents. "You can stress walk back and forth there just as well as you can here. I'll open a gateway for you."

"Fine." She sighed. "Zareen bakes when she's stressed, so I'll have her come over after her shift at The Inferno and maybe we can distract Finn. Poor kid is still worried over Isabeau, and with you all being gone, I'm sure he's extra upset. Not that he'll admit it."

Ashling didn't hesitate, just strode outside and walked straight through the gateway into the cavern. Connor waited until Kaysea went through the new gateway I'd opened and watched as she walked into my apartment building. As soon as she was inside, I closed the gateway and took a step towards the remaining one to join the others in the cavern.

Connor shoved me aside and stomped through on his own, muttering something under his breath that I was certain was about me and also very unflattering. I counted to ten in my head, and once I was sure I wouldn't stab Kaysea's brother in the back with one of my poisoned blades, I followed after him.

Hopefully Mikhail's trip to collect Hecate had gone smoother than mine.

TENSION WAS high in the cavern when I closed the gateway behind me. Connor had moved to stand in front of his queen, who was waiting a safe distance away from the lake and the extremely angry goddess who was kneeling on top of it. Her loyal hounds stood on either side of her, not looking the least bit concerned about the giant monster lurking close by.

"How's it going?" I asked quietly when I reached Mikhail's side.

"Magos and Niall went to wait with the others outside," he murmured back. "Hecate is… a little upset. I figured having less strangers around her right now would be best. Who is that?" He nodded towards Ashling. He'd had the unfortunate experience of meeting Connor already at Kaysea's birthday party last year.

"That," I drawled, "is the Merfolk Queen herself, Ashling."

"Huh." He watched the queen step around Connor and stalk towards Hecate with her chin held high and not a hint of fear on her face. "She moves like an assassin."

"Yeah." I watched Ashling walk with perfectly balanced, even steps. "Methinks the queen has led an interesting life. I also can't shake the feeling that her being at Kaysea's place today wasn't a coincidence."

He slid me an amused glance. "You do love getting involved in fae politics."

I watched Connor stomp after the queen, who was now arguing with Hecate, and my brows furrowed. "I'm not sure if I'm the target of a fae's plotting this time."

We walked towards the ancient goddess and the freshly minted queen. Connor was hovering behind Ashling, clearly unsure about what to do in this scenario. Hecate was a little out of his league, but the stupid bastard would still try if she attempted to harm Ashling. I could see it in his eyes.

"So what's the plan for helping our friend out?" I asked lightly when we reached them. "And dismantling the barrier at the cavern mouth?"

"I think I have enough understanding of the spellcasting to break this apart." Hecate tapped her knuckles against the clear, solid surface of the lake. "But it won't stop the flow of magic into the doorway. The lake water is slowly leeching magic from him, and that's what she's feeding into Therrea. There is enough magic in the water to sustain it for quite some time."

"And how do we get him out of here?" I kneeled down and flattened my palm on the surface. A tentacle rose from the murky water to meet my hand. *Relief. Excitement.* He trusted us to free him. "Soon, buddy," I promised.

"I can help with that," Ashling said confidently. "I don't care what magic that bitch laced the lake with. If it's water, it's *mine.*"

Hecate rose to her feet and ushered us to the shore, then reached into a leather pouch on her belt and pulled out a handful of what smelled like dried flower petals mixed with herbs. Magic crackled in the air as words from a long dead language poured forth from Hecate. The more she chanted, the thicker the magic in the air grew until it felt like every breath coated my throat with the power of her spell.

The last word slipped from her lips, and she opened her

hand before blowing a steady breath across her palm. The flower-and-herb mixture flew through the air, multiplying as it went. Then the pieces scattered across the lake until the entire surface was covered with purple and yellow blossoms.

I'd forgotten how beautiful Hecate's magic was. No wonder the witches worshiped her.

Magic in the air flowed after the flower petals, and there was an audible crack. Followed by another. And another. The magical barrier on top of the lake shattered into a thousand pieces, and they sank into the water, taking the flower petals with them.

A single tentacle rose out of the water almost hesitantly and stretched towards Hecate. Sensing its approach, she reached out , and they bumped into each other. Levi's tentacle carefully wrapped around her waist, as if he were hugging her.

"I missed you too, friend," she said in a rough voice. "I'm so sorry I didn't find you sooner."

Another tentacle shot out of the water and gripped me, flinging me up and over the lake.

"Nemain!" Mikhail yelled in alarm.

I felt the moment he summoned his mist sword and quickly called out, "I'm okay! He's just saying hello!"

Just before I hit the water, another tentacle wrapped around me, taking care not to squeeze too hard. Then the water churned as the bulk of the kraken's form rose, and an enormous eye looked at me, its shade that of the deepest ocean blue.

"We'll have to play later, Levi," I said. "I have another friend who needs me." He gazed at me for a long moment, and emotions of gratitude poured into me. I patted his tentacle in return. Reluctantly, he stretched his tentacle back towards the shore and set me down. Mikhail was there in an instant, looking me over, and I arched a brow at him. "I told you he was friendly."

"Sorry, but I question your definition of friendly."

"Fair." I grinned and patted his cheek before walking over to Hecate as she quietly talked to Levi, who had removed his tentacle from her waist and was currently trying to stroke her hair. "I'm sorry to rush you, but can you take a look at the other barrier? The one at the entrance?"

"Show me." She nodded briskly. Mikhail walked over and took her arm, looping it around his, and guided her towards the barrier. Philo and Zephyr trotted obediently behind them.

"Can you really get him out?" I asked Ashling.

"Yes." Her mismatched eyes took on a cunning edge. "For a price."

"Of course." My lip curled. The fae and their damned bargains. "And what, pray tell, do you want from me?"

"From you?" She arched a perfectly sculpted eyebrow. "Nothing." Connor stiffened behind her as if he knew what her next words would be. Sure enough, she smirked at him with an expression of victory. "I want him to agree to help me with a task of my choosing. He will be bound to me for the duration of that task and then free to go about his business."

I squeezed my eyes shut. There was no way Connor would agree to this. He clearly didn't want to be around Ashling. There was drama there I didn't understand and had no interest in learning about.

Okay, that was a lie. I was wickedly curious about it and would be gossiping with Kaysea later, but it was obvious that, while this bargain would be between Ashling and Connor, it was being done as a favor to me.

Connor didn't do me favors. Ever.

"Agreed."

"What?" My jaw dropped as I stared at Kaysea's brother. Surely I had misheard.

"This isn't for you," he said flatly. "No creature of the sea should be caged and used like this."

"Shall we seal the bargain with a kiss?" Ashling winked at Connor, and his expression went cold as ice even as heat flared in his eyes.

Yeah. I'd definitely be talking to Kaysea and Pele about this turn of events later.

Ashling's lips curled into a triumphant smile, and she flicked her fingers towards Connor. Water droplets formed in the air and splashed against his forearm. The water darkened to black ink, and a stylized water serpent wrapped around a spear settled into his skin.

"Can you open a gateway, Nemain?" Ashling asked.

"Not in that water with all its strange magic and definitely not big enough for him to get through."

"That's fine." She waved me off. "It'll just speed things up if I already have a gateway to work with. You can open it anywhere in Tír fo Thuinn, and I can change the destination as long as it's within the water."

Voices filtered in from the front of the cave. Hecate must have broken the barrier. "What task do you need Connor for?" I asked Ashling.

"Sorry, Nemain," she said in what seemed like a genuinely apologetic tone. "I like you, but you're the Unseelie Knight, and while I know that wasn't a title you actively sought out and more one that was thrust on you... your loyalty still lies with the fae queens."

"And?" I tilted my head as I studied her, trying to glean any sort of motives from her face but getting absolutely nothing. "You may be merfolk, but you're still fae, and last I checked, all fae, even those in Tír fo Thuinn, ultimately submit to the fae queens."

For just a second, the bemused arrogance slipped from her face, and something dark and twisted rose in its stead. "I submit to no one."

The others filtered in, Cian and Ammit leading the way.

The Duat creature went immediately to the wall where we suspected the doorway to Therrea was, and the rough, grayish-brown surface shimmered at her approach, becoming more opaque. She sat down, and her eyes latched on to the bag hanging off my belt, drool dripping through the jagged teeth of her jaws.

Hecate strode confidently back towards us, one hand resting on Philo's back while Zephyr hovered by her other side.

"Thank you both for your assistance." I touched Hecate's shoulder and nodded at Ashling. "Connor, I suggest you keep an eye on that doorway after we go through it in case Artemis sends someone to investigate."

"We'll be out of here soon," Ashling said. "Just open that gateway for me before you leave."

I did as she'd asked, opening a gateway to one of the few places in Tír fo Thuinn I'd been to. A vast coral reef stretched out on the other side of the gateway. Ashling would have to move it somewhere deeper for Levi, but she'd said she could, so I left her to it.

Cian was standing in front of the doorway to Therrea, and I could tell by the way he was flexing and unflexing his fingers that my brother's patience was at its end. It was time for us to go. Reaching into my bag, I pulled out the last two hearts and tossed one to Ammit.

"Thanks, little beastie." Then I tossed her the second heart. "The bargain is complete." She swallowed the second heart, and black shadows swirled around her. Within seconds, she was gone.

I looked to Cian. "Time to shift, brother."

He shrugged off our mother's sword and the sheath and handed them to me before quickly removing the rest of his clothes. Magos and Mikhail pointedly looked away, but Niall just watched with a puzzled expression. I passed the harness and sword back to him, and he slipped them back on before dropping to all fours and shifting to his panther form.

Just like in our human forms, Cian's panther form was slimmer than mine. He was made for stealth; his black coat with its silver rosettes could slip through the dark forests like a ghost.

Our mother's sword had been made in the shifter realm, Kanima, and had the ability to shift with us. Or it might just disappear into a pocket dimension like Mikhail's and Magos' mist swords. I shrugged my shoulders, feeling the weight of my dual blades. I'd have to ask Badb if mine were capable of the same or if all the spells placed on them undid that. It would be handy to have weapons that shifted with me.

"Do not stray from the plan, Cian," I said firmly. "Stay in your animal form until you absolutely have no other option. We'll distract Artemis and the rest of the gods. Your one task is finding and freeing Hades."

Understood. He snagged his pants off the ground. *Stay alive, sister.*

Then he bounded through the doorway, vanishing from our sights.

Jinx leapt off Magos' shoulder, dropping his glamour as he hit the ground. The sleek, hundred-pound feline trotted through the doorway next.

"Time to kill some gods?" Niall asked, holding his enchanted spear so it rested on his shoulder.

"Yeah." I glanced behind me to where Hecate and Ashling were working on getting Levi out of this cursed place. "Let's make them hurt first though."

Chapter Twenty-Two

CIAN AND JINX were nowhere to be seen when we stepped into a lush jungle on the other side of the doorway. The vibrant green of the trees, ferns, and other plants was almost over-whelming in its uniformity. I had to look hard to find another dash of color in the fauna. A salty breeze wound its way through the branches, and everyone stood perfectly still and alert as we scanned our surroundings for any type of attack, but none came. I was a little surprised Artemis hadn't had an ambush waiting for us here.

"Not what I was expecting." I frowned. "This doesn't look like Greece at all."

Can you hear me? Jinx asked.

Yes, I answered. Cian had a short range when it came to telepathy, which was why I'd sent Jinx with him.

Cian says he can feel Hades' death magic now and took off towards the south as soon as we got here. I followed and convinced him to at least travel in the treetops with me to keep us out of sight for as long as possible.

Okay, I replied. *Keep me posted on where you are.*

"There's a note." Magos stepped towards a tall palm tree and plucked a folded piece of paper off its trunk. He scanned its contents, deep grooves cutting into his face as he read. "Artemis welcomes us to Therrea. She invites us to visit her at her home so she can give us a proper greeting." He turned the paper to face us. "There's a map."

"Huh." Mikhail grabbed the paper from Magos, reviewed its contents, and then passed it to me. "I don't think I've ever been so politely invited into a trap before."

"The spot she's telling us to go is southwest of here. Not far. Should be able to get there in less than two hours." I thought about our options. Our job was to be a distraction so Cian and Jinx could search for Hades. It was possible that he was also at this location, or close to it, but it'd still be better if they arrived separately from us. If we didn't go to this location, Artemis would likely send someone to fetch us, and there was a chance they would discover Cian and Jinx in the process. "We play along for now, but we won't rush getting there."

I updated Jinx on the note and told him to try to come from the west if Cian continued to feel the pull south. Although I suspected my brother would be hard to steer off course, even momentarily, the closer he got to Hades.

"Alright." I started down a narrow path that cut through the jungle. "Let's go see what fun activities Artemis has planned for us."

We traveled in silence for the better part of an hour until Niall suddenly stopped and took a step off the path, head cocked as he studied something none of us could see. Mikhail and Magos fanned out a little more, swords in hand, looking for possible threats while I tried to focus and figure out whatever Niall had sensed.

It was hard to pick up on anything specific because Artemis' magic saturated this land, but I concentrated in the direction Niall was looking and felt it. Something that was not Artemis' magic.

It felt dark, ancient, and chaotic. My instincts told me to stay far, far away from it.

Niall looked over his shoulder at me. He'd glamoured away his dark, feathered wings because there was no room for flight with how dense the trees were. His deep blue eyes were serious when they found mine.

"I think I've found another prisoner of our esteemed hosts."

"Do we have time for this?" Magos asked. "We could come back for whoever this is after we get Hades freed."

I chewed my bottom lip, looking away from Niall to the path we'd been on and then back to him. "We'll make time. I have no interest in ever coming back here, and there's a solid chance we'll be making a hasty exit from this realm. We'll at least investigate whatever this is and decide from there."

The last update I'd received from Jinx was that they were still trying to pinpoint Hades' location, but he had managed to get my brother to go further west before cutting south. I was fairly confident we had some time to spare, but not much. If it came down to freeing whoever this mysterious prisoner was or Hades, I'd choose the latter.

Here's hoping whatever Niall had sensed was close by.

Ten minutes later, we stood in front of a temple that seemed like it was in the process of being swallowed by the jungle. It was a simple rectangle building, and the front facing us was narrow and had a single open doorway at its center. There were no statues or other adornments I'd come to expect from the Olympians. Clearly, this wasn't a temple devoted to the worship of the gods.

"A creepy-looking temple in the middle of a jungle. What could go wrong?" I spun both my blades, loosening my wrists.

"Don't be such a scaredy-cat," Mikhail said with a completely straight face.

I pointed one of my swords at him. "You'll pay for that later."

Niall strode into the temple, and we all cursed as we ran after him, but I slowed as soon as I passed the threshold. Hidden from the outside view was the fact that the roof was completely open to the sky above. Bright beams of sunlight poured into the temple, lighting up the golden apples hanging from a dozen trees.

"Looks like we found their fancy apples." I spun around in a circle. "No sign of a prisoner though."

A dark form glided above us on silent wings, and we all turned to face the newcomer as they landed between us and the trees. They were covered head to toe in black armor that devoured light, and a tattered cowl with a deep hood hid their features. Wings stretched behind them, the only hint of color. They reminded me a little of the falcons Hecate favored—dark brown feathers interspersed with white ones.

"Who are you?" Niall asked, letting out his own black wings. "You are not here willingly."

"What makes you say this?" The voice was soft and feminine, but something about it made the hair on the back of my neck stand up.

"The collar around your neck."

I had no idea what Niall was talking about, but the figure went completely still for a few seconds before she pulled back her hood. Her eyes were solid black, and dark red lines were inked vertically down her face, starting on her forehead, going through both eyes, and then trailing off midway through the cheeks into a thinner line. Her skin was pale like moonlight.

Slender fingers tugged on the cowl, revealing a gold band around her neck.

"I am Nemesis."

"Fuck," I swore, tightening my grip on my swords.

Nobody took their eyes off the warrior before us, but

Mikhail murmured, "I take it that name means something to you?"

"She's not a god," I said quickly. "Remember when Hecate talked about spirits like the lwa? There are others, including manifestations of human ideas and emotions that were born in the Mediterranean region. They were called mageía. Nobody knows how they came to be or where they went."

"Nobody *cared* where we went." Her dark eyes brimmed with fury, and the collar glowed before she shrieked, gripping her head as she shook it violently.

Niall stepped forward, but I grabbed his shirt and jerked him back. "She is the offspring of Nyx and Erebus. Darkness and literal *chaos* run in her blood. She is retribution in the flesh."

"I thought you said spirits don't have mortal forms," Mikhail said, eying Nemesis. "She looks real to me."

"The mageía were always a little different. They can manifest physical bodies, but destroying their physical forms means absolutely nothing; they'll reform within seconds." I pulled Niall back a little further and stepped forward. "How did you come to be here?"

Nemesis' hands fell to her side, and she straightened. Only the tightness around the corners of her mouth revealed the pain she still felt from whatever that fucking collar did. Then she tilted her head back and displayed the collar more.

"Hephaestus wanted to be free of Artemis' scheming, so he struck a bargain. He would craft collars that could enslave my kind and trap us in our mortal forms in exchange for being left alone. One by one, either through trickery or violence, we became prisoners and were bound to Artemis. I cannot disobey her commands as long as I wear this collar."

"And what is your current command?" I angled my body slightly, adjusting my balance.

The manifestation of vengeance and retribution pulled up

her hood, hiding her face once more as her voice echoed across the temple. The entryway we'd passed through was gone, trapping us inside. "To kill anyone who sets foot in this temple."

She lunged, her wings propelling her forward, and a long sword with a wide, black blade formed in her hands. The air whistled in front of my face as I barely managed to dodge the strike. Magos was there in an instant, meeting Nemesis' next attack with one of his own. Mikhail appeared on her other side, forcing Nemesis to divide her attention.

Which she did. Easily.

"Happy now, Niall?" I panted as Nemesis broke from the vampires and thrust her obnoxiously long blade at my stomach. I trapped it between my dual swords and twisted sharply, trying to knock the weapon from her grasp, but she just followed my movement, forcing me to rapidly step to the side so I didn't completely lose my balance.

The five of us danced across the temple, weaving in and out of the rows of trees. It was four against one, but we were losing. Our blood coated the temple floor, and Nemesis' last strike to my thigh had been deep enough to hit bone. The wound burned as my body frantically tried to knit itself back together. Her armor blocked any vital strikes, and the way she was dancing around told me she was just playing with us.

Magos struck a beautiful move with his sword, and Nemesis leaned back until her back was practically parallel with the ground. Mikhail seized the opportunity and sliced at her exposed neck. She twisted to the side and kicked out, catching him in the chest. He flew backwards towards a tree with a broken branch jutting out.

I abandoned my attack on the mageía and threw myself towards Mikhail. My body slammed into his a second before the branch would have pierced his heart, slicing through my arm instead. I grunted as we both hit the ground.

"We need to get the fuck out of here," Mikhail hissed.

307

"There is no defeating her, and eventually, she's going to get bored and cut us to pieces. My blood is too precious to water some damn trees."

"The only way out is up, and she can fly, so that's not going to help us much," I growled. My devourer flames were still on lockdown—whatever spell Artemis had used in the cavern to block devourer magic, she'd done here as well. Mikhail and I both started forward to rejoin the fight when I saw the glyphs on my swords flare with a blue light.

Badb's words floated back to me, *The blades will also absorb your devourer magic.*

"Loophole," I whispered with glee as I pushed my will into the blades more, and blue flames sprung to life. Artemis' spells blocked me from accessing my devourer magic, but they did nothing to objects imbued with it.

I spun to Mikhail. "I need a shot at her neck."

"Then you shall have it." We sprinted towards Nemesis just as her sword caught Niall in the ribs. The only thing that kept her blow from cutting him in two was Magos slamming his sword against hers. The winged fae warrior pulled himself free, blood pouring from his side as he bared his teeth at Nemesis, who did the same in return.

Magos struck at her exposed side, forcing her to block and concentrate on him while Niall stumbled away before collapsing. Nemesis refused to be muscled back, and for probably the first time in his life, Magos was losing a sword fight.

"Mist, Magos!" I screamed.

A split second before she would have claimed his head, my friend vanished into a swirl of mist. Mikhail did the same from my side. Nemesis focused on me, rotating her body and the angle of her sword.

I dropped one blade, clasping the remaining one with both hands as I raised it for an overhead strike that I would have to pour all my strength into, trusting Mikhail to give me the opening I needed. There would be no do-overs. Either I did this, or she would cut me down.

Mikhail snapped into existence directly behind Nemesis, one arm wrapped around her chest, and the other knocking the hood away so he could grab a fistful of hair and wrench her head back. She reversed her sword and stabbed backwards. My heart hammered within my chest when Mikhail screamed as the sword impaled him through the gut, but I didn't hesitate as I struck.

The mageía pulled her blade free to block me but was a second too late. My sword coated in blue flames struck the collar, and an audible crack echoed throughout the temple.

Mikhail staggered backwards. Magos appeared in a swirl of mist and dragged his nephew away as Niall moved to stand by my side, still a little unsteady.

We watched as Nemesis stood there in shock, her fingers trembling as the long sword coated in all our blood fell to the floor. In a daze, she reached up and clasped the collar with both hands, her expression strained as she pulled. The crack I had formed with my strike snapped, and she wrenched the collar off her neck and threw it clear across the temple where it smashed into the wall before falling to the floor with a final *clang*.

The living embodiment of retribution threw her head back and screamed.

ALL FOUR OF us dropped to our knees and clutched our ears. I felt something warm and sticky flow through my fingers. Ruptured eardrums. Great.

After what felt like an eternity, the screaming finally stopped. I dropped my hands away from my ears but remained where I was, feeling more than a little light-headed. Gradually, my senses came back to me, and sound started filtering back in. I struggled to my feet and helped Niall do the same. Mikhail and Magos both vanished from the other side of Nemesis and reappeared next to us. I summoned my swords from where I'd dropped them, and they both flew to my hands.

Nemesis eyed them. Her expression wasn't exactly friendly, but it wasn't murderous either, so I'd take it.

"How." Not a question. A command.

For one hot second, I thought about giving her a smart-ass answer, but Mikhail stamped on my foot. I gave him a cool look before replying, "Do you know what devourers are?"

She nodded.

"I'm part-devourer. It's complicated." I shrugged. "Artemis has spelled this pocket realm to block me from accessing my devourer magic, but my weapons already contained it. The magic within them is still accessible."

"You will come with me to free the others." She nodded and took a step forward.

"Yeah, that's not going to work for me." We all raised our swords against her. It was pretty clear she could kick our asses, but we'd make her work for it.

She halted and furrowed her brows. "Why?"

"We are here to rescue someone important to us." I purposely didn't say Hades' name because I had no idea what his history was with the mageía. "He's family."

"Family," she said slowly, pondering my answer.

She wouldn't just let us go. The mageía weren't exactly family, but it was my understanding they were all loyal to and respectful of each other. Being careful to appear unthreatening, I slid one of my swords into the sheath on my back and flipped the other in my hand so the hilt was facing her.

"If you swear to return this to me, I will allow you to take it and free those important to you." With a thought from me, flames once again danced across the blade. "It should contain enough magic to finish the task."

"Do you know where they are?" Niall asked.

"Yes." Nemesis' black eyes studied my sword, but she made no move to take it. "They are locked in a prison just north of here. Artemis only lets them out when she has a task for them, which is rare."

"Do I have your word that you will bring my sword back to me?"

She wrapped her fingers around the hilt and took it, holding the blade up in front of her face, and reflections of blue flames danced in her eyes. "Beautiful." Her gaze snapped to mine. "I am in your debt. Where can I find you to return what is yours?"

I jerked my head over my shoulder. "We'll be south of here, saving our friend and slaughtering some gods."

"We're big fans of Slaughter Parties," Mikhail added helpfully. A stupid grin appeared on Niall's face while Magos just sighed.

Nemesis looked at each of us carefully before her lips split into a terrifying smile. "This sounds like a wonderful way for me and mine to celebrate our freedom. Might we join you in this... Slaughter Party?"

Did we want the manifestations of Night, Chaos, Darkness, and Retribution to fight on our side against the Olympians? Hmm, let me think...

"We would be honored if you would join us," I said. "Just know we are on our way there now."

"I will make haste then." She bent her knees and launched herself into the sky.

"See?" Niall slapped my back. "It all worked out just fine!"

Mikhail had a hand clamped over his stomach where blood was still leaking out through his fingers. His uncle wasn't faring much better. Magos swayed slightly on his feet, and the two of them stared flatly at Niall.

"Congratulations, Niall." I slapped him equally hard on the back. "You get to add another new experience to your list."

"Really?" He looked at me in confusion. "What?"

"Feeding vampires." I shoved him towards Magos while I rolled up a sleeve for Mikhail. They'd heal on their own within an hour, but we'd already spent too much time here. We'd have to pick up the pace for the rest of the trip.

Mikhail kissed my skin gently before his fangs pierced it and he drank my blood down, being careful to only take enough to heal. Despite our situation, I couldn't stop the heat pooling between my legs and the way my breath quickened. Mikhail drew his fangs out and tilted his head enough to look at me while he licked the remaining drops of blood away.

"Oh," Niall said. "Is that how it's supposed to be done? Because the big guy didn't do that."

Magos let out a bone-weary sigh. "Niall, please stop talking."

I laughed and kissed Mikhail deeply before heading for the doorway that had reappeared at some point. "Come on. We need to make up for lost time."

We set out at a brisk jog, our brief moment of levity slipping away.

Jinx? Update?

We've made it to the shoreline, and now we're making our way up it. There was a tension in his voice that instantly put me on alert.

What is it?

There are humans here. They're just lined up on the beach. I think they're maybe servants or something by the way they're dressed. When we walk by, they give no reaction to our presence at all.

I supposed it made sense Artemis had brought humans here to serve them. It's not like she or the other gods were going to do anything as pedestrian as making their own damn meals. Still… the humans would have needed food and basic necessities…

Cian thinks they're ghosts Artemis has figured out how to pull out of Hades and control.

Of course she would discover a way to force people to serve her and also not have to worry about their physical well-being. I thought back to how empty it was in Asphodel Fields. This would explain why the area around the cave had been so deserted. How was she doing it though? Neither she nor any of the gods most likely helping her had any skills when it came to death magic.

Tartarus, I thought, and then quickly filled Jinx in on us finding and freeing Nemesis.

Well, hopefully either Tartarus gets his ass down here, or we manage to wake up Hades. Otherwise, we'll have hundreds of ghosts to contend with on top of the gods.

Be careful, and make sure Cian doesn't go barging into anything. We'll be at the spot on that map within thirty minutes.

Try to make it twenty. We're definitely getting close to Hades, and I don't think I'll be able to hold your brother back if he lays eyes on his mate.

We'll run. See you soon.

My stride lengthened until I was flat-out running. The vampires easily kept pace behind me. If Niall struggled with the speed, he didn't complain about it.

By the time we reached the edge of the tree line, all of us were breathing a little hard. The tropical theme of Therrea continued, and an impossibly white, sandy beach stretched before us as bright turquoise waves gently brushed against the sand. Fifty feet from the shoreline, a palace of white limestone rose from the water. The two-story structure had columns on the bottom half that supported an open balcony on the second level.

Jinx, I pushed out, *we're here. No signs of Artemis or any of the other gods, but there's… a freaking palace floating on the water. It's directly in front of us.*

We're a little further down the beach. Do you see the small building to the east?

I looked to my left and saw a solid stone structure rising up out of the sand. It looked like a tomb.

Yes.

Cian is positive Hades is in there. He paused, and I could sense his hesitation. *I don't see anyone guarding it, but that can't be the case. Whatever distraction you provide, it's got to be good.*

No problem.

Nemain, don't die.

Oh. Well, I did specifically have it planned out that we'd all have horrific deaths, but just to make you happy, I'll cross out our names and write the gods' names in instead. Happy?

Ecstatic.

"Alright, boys," I stepped forward onto the sandy beach. "All we have to do is stay alive until Hades is woken up, and then maybe he can do that fun soul-ripping trick of his. Or we can all beat a hasty retreat and let the mageía take on clean up duty."

"Solid plan." Mikhail grinned as he walked next to me.

Niall nodded, keeping his wings out but tucked tightly against his back. "Very detailed."

"Somehow, all of your plans always boil down to who's the better killer." Magos' copper eyes danced with amusement.

"Spoiler alert." I pulled my remaining sword free and plucked one of the poisoned blades from my thigh sheath. "It's always us."

Chapter Twenty-Three

THE FOUR OF us walked across the beach side by side with enough space between us that we could react quickly if needed. I kept my eyes straight ahead, away from the tomb to my left and wherever Cian and Jinx were hiding in the trees, waiting for an opening. We halted just before stepping into the water. I noticed there seemed to be a steep drop-off after only a few feet, which hurt my brain a little to think about, because the way the tide was rolling in and out implied the water here was shallow.

I guess when you created a pocket realm, you got to decide when physics came into play.

"Stay out of the water," I said quietly, and everyone gave barely perceptible nods.

"Well, that would be a shame." Artemis strolled out onto the palace balcony. Her dark brown hair was pulled back into a tight braid, and her white tunic with its thick, gold belt fluttered in the gentle sea breeze. No bow to be seen, but she still moved with perfect balance. The same two men we'd seen standing beside her in the memory joined her on the balcony.

I'd already had the pleasure of meeting Hermes. Given

that there were only so many Olympians of significant power left, I assumed Grey Beard was Poseidon. Yeah, definitely staying the fuck out of the water.

Unease ran through me when Ares failed to make an appearance. Mikhail either felt the same, or he'd picked up on my emotions, because he turned slightly to keep an eye on our backs.

"The water here is quite lovely, I assure you," Artemis said. She didn't shout, but her voice easily carried across the waves to us. "When I made this realm, I decided to model it after our home realm, Nineveh. We may have called Greece and the Mediterranean 'home' for a time, but my heart always missed Nineveh. It was mostly water there, even more so than in the human realm. Tens of thousands of islands littered the realm, surrounded by a glittering jewel of an ocean."

"Sounds lovely," I drawled. "Want me to open you a gateway there? Because I'd be happy to do that for you." And let it hit you on the ass on the way out.

"You do realize I am a god, yes?" She took two steps forward off the balcony and dropped straight to the water below. Instead of a splash, there was only a ripple as she landed on the surface as if it were solid, and she walked towards us at a leisurely pace until she was only ten feet away. "You should bow and worship at my feet."

"I don't even bow to him, and he makes me coffee every day." I pointed with my thumb at Magos.

"You think because you belong to the Unseelie Queen that you are untouchable?" An arrogant laugh poured out of her lips. "Her time is coming to an end. Neither she nor her sister will survive the war against their brother. Even now, she grows weak." I fought to keep my face carefully blank. She had to be messing with me—the Olympians were not to be trusted. "Don't believe me?" She gave me a coy smile. "My sister rarely had visions so far into the future, but the few she had all came true. The demise of the fae queens was one of her last ones."

"Pity she didn't see the one about Hades ripping out her soul." I grinned, putting my fangs on display. "Might have been useful."

"I admit, your demeanor and role in this surprises me." I tensed when she reached behind her back and pulled out a familiar-looking dagger. It was the one Hades had made for me that I'd lost in the dragon realm. I couldn't stop my jaw from clenching, and Artemis' eyes lit up at my tell. "Ah"—she tapped the flat side of the blade against her palm—"I thought it strange Hades would imbue his magic into an object and then carelessly lose it, knowing it would give away the fact he was still alive. But he didn't, did he?" She pointed the blade towards me. "This blade was in your possession... and you lost it. Everything that has come to pass is your fault. Tell me, how does it feel to know you will be responsible for the deaths of everyone you love?"

"You're not the first person to threaten such things," I answered coldly, refusing to give her the satisfaction of knowing her words had struck true. "If you want to ask the others how their threats went, you'll have to make a trip to the death realms."

"It's easy to be a big fish in a small pond." She tossed the blade over her shoulder, and it disappeared beneath the waves. "You should have heeded my warning. We're a little out of your league."

The water churned where the knife had sunk before an enormous serpentine head rose from the depths on a long neck, its blue and green scales glittering in the bright sunlight.

Another head rose next to it. Then another. And another. Until nine heads towered above the palace.

The lernaean hydra.

One of the heads stretched forward to rest next to Artemis,

and she placed a hand on the side of its snout. The remaining heads all looked hungrily at us through fathomless, dark blue eyes.

Mikhail turned and narrowed his eyes at me. "Sure would be nice if we had some dragons right about now."

"It's not my fault their delicate asses got knocked out by a nine year old!"

"We know other dragons," Mikhail countered.

"Argue later, children," Magos said tightly.

Artemis was staring at us with amused interest, like we existed only for her entertainment. We were out of our league here. We all knew that. Regardless of how they'd acquired their magic, they were still gods, and they had the fucking hydra as a pet. I knew this was a fight we were unlikely to win.

Wouldn't stop me from trying to carve out her heart though.

"I saw a vision of the day Hades wiped out half your family." I bared my teeth in a feral smile. "Your siblings died like the little bitches they were. Not very godly, I must say."

The corners of her eyes tightened, and she raised her hand off the hydra's head and made a waving gesture. It rose and joined the others. I had no idea how she'd even gotten this thing here. The hydra hadn't been seen in eons. Most of the legendary monsters had been killed off or relocated to other realms when the daemons and fae started caring about human survival. Maybe the hydra was dead and Artemis had snatched it from the death realm and brought it here.

It didn't really matter. The creature was massive, and those scales looked thick. Not to mention, it had nine freaking heads all loaded with sharp teeth. Going up against it with nothing but swords would be suicidal. Mikhail was right. I wish we had a dragon. One monster to fight another.

"I'm glad you came," Artemis said, waving her hand airily. "We've been having a little trouble awakening Hades, and toying with you will help pass the time until we solve that particular problem."

Faster than vipers, streams of water shot out of the waves and wrapped around our necks and wrists. I fought as hard as I could to get free, but it was like fighting against steel. There was no give, and it only took seconds for the watery ropes to pull me to my knees with my head bowed, my sword and dagger slipping from my grasp into the sand in front of me.

Jinx, I gritted out. *Distraction managed. Wake Hades the fuck up.*

Whatever he'd said was lost to me as my panic surged at being bound. I'd gotten better about working through it over the years, but the lingering trauma of being tied up while my parents died and then again when Sebastian had me held captive and tortured had left lingering scars. I concentrated on breathing through it, knowing it was just my initial reaction and it would pass. Fingers wrapped around mine, and I saw Mikhail had managed to fight his hand to the side to grab mine, knowing I would be losing my mind over being bound again. The panic eased, still there but manageable.

Someone crouched in front of me, and I was able to raise my head enough to meet a pair of bright blue eyes on a pretty face framed by blond hair.

"Hello, again. Didn't I say you would be kneeling before me if you came here?" Hermes reached out and trailed a finger down my cheek. "Delicious," he said thickly.

Mikhail growled at my side, gripping my hand tighter.

"These two will be fun." He remained crouched but twisted to look up at Artemis. "You know how much I enjoy breaking lovers in front of each other."

"Hmm," Artemis hummed as her sharp eyes scrutinized each of us before settling on Magos and staying there. "I'm curious about this one."

Fear clamped down on my heart. Whatever magic Hermes had was clearly empathic in nature, and I hated giving him a taste of my fear after he had dined on my panic. But the idea of Magos being the target of Artemis' wrath broke something inside me.

Jinx, I pleaded. *Hurry.*

No answer. I reached for my devourer magic and felt it trying to respond, but it remained out of my grasp.

"Oh… oh!" Hermes laughter had a maniacal quality to it that set my teeth on edge. "So much grief wrapped in a pretty package. His wife died tragically a long time ago, and he's still desperately clinging to his love for her," he crooned with mock sympathy. "Added bonus: he's important to the two lovebirds. My guess is a stand-in father figure. Hurting *him* will hurt *them.*"

"I thought as much." Artemis smiled. "Curses are my specialty, and Hermes has always had a special talent for reading souls. Hades wanted him to use that skill to guide the dead to their appropriate resting place, but we found a much funner use for it."

Hermes rose before whispering in Artemis' ear, and she laughed gleefully. "Oh, that's good."

"Don't," I growled. "I'm right here! I'm the Unseelie Knight, and I'm the reason everyone is here! It was me who mouthed off to you. Punish me!"

I'd expected us to get bloodied in a fight with them; that was something I could handle. I should have fucking known better. The Olympians never went for the easy kill when they could inflict suffering instead.

"Hurting me will hurt them both!" Mikhail shouted loudly.

I was distantly aware of Niall fighting on the other side of Magos, but it was no use. We were all at the gods' mercy, and there was still no sign of Cian, Hades, or Jinx.

"You're a vampire," Artemis purred. "I've come across your kind before. You must drink blood regularly, otherwise, you'll weaken. After a while, you'll start to go mad without it. I once experimented with a few of you; some lasted over a decade before their minds started to unravel."

I struggled helplessly as she ran her fingers across Magos' jawline. He stared at her solemnly, saying nothing.

"All these years, you've been shackled to the memory of your poor, dead wife. I'm really doing you a favor." The watery ropes tightened, and Magos groaned as his back bowed painfully before Artemis slammed a hand onto his forehead, forcing his head to tilt back. Words poured from her lips, and I had no doubt it was from the same dead language Hecate had used earlier.

"STOP!" I screamed. Mikhail bellowed next to me, but neither of us could do anything to help the man who had done so much for us both.

The last word slipped from Artemis, and she removed her hand. Magos sagged as much as the bindings would allow and panted, "What… what did you do?"

"Every time you drink blood, you'll lose a memory of her." She knelt in front of him and used two fingers to tilt his head up to look at her. "Maybe it will be the smile she gave you every morning upon waking. Maybe it will be the first day you saw her. Whatever it was, you'll know you lost something because your love for her will not fade even as you begin to forget what her face looked like. What her voice sounded like. Every little detail you cherished will die with every sip of blood you take."

Magos was so still, I wasn't sure if he was breathing.

Artemis ran a thumb across his lips. "You'll find your thirst has increased as well. So you can try to deny your nature all you want, but your choices are forgetting her… or madness."

Something in me broke. I didn't know how to fix this. I could carve Artemis into a thousand pieces, but the curse would remain. My friend was damned.

And I am the reason.

All of this was happening because I'd left that fucking dagger behind.

"There is always another path, even if we can't see it right away," Magos said, not a hint of a tremble in his voice. "But I promise you, your path will end today."

Annoyance flashed across Artemis' face at him refusing to break before her. "Perhaps you had the right idea, Hermes." She pointed one long finger at Mikhail. "Cut out that one's pretty eyes. The Hydra could use a snack."

Clanging steel rang from behind us, followed by the sound of someone hitting the sand hard and rolling. I tried to twist around to see what was going on but couldn't turn my head enough. I took several deep breaths. Cian. If Jinx or Hades were with him, I couldn't smell them.

"About time, Ares," Poseidon said in a bored tone. He'd left the balcony but had remained on the water, letting the waves roll around him. Two of the hydra's heads rested above the water on either side of him.

The sound of flesh hitting flesh followed by Cian's pained groan shoved aside the guilt I'd been drowning in, and my rage erupted like a bonfire. My magic remained out of my reach, but that was fine. Using my devourer flames on them would have been too easy. I'd rather tear them apart with my claws. They didn't deserve easy deaths.

Ares dragged Cian around us and tossed him at Artemis' feet. He was roughed up with a split lip, and the way he was holding his ribs suggested something might be broken, but considering he'd been fighting the god of war a second ago, he didn't look too bad.

"I think he might be a bit damaged from his time with the vampires," Ares said in a cruel voice. "He kept talking to himself, and then he just cried over Hades before kissing him. I watched for as long as I could before the threat of vomiting became too much." He flipped a sword in his hands. Our mother's sword. "Nice blade though."

"You arrived just in time." Hermes grinned at his brother as he pulled a short, curved dagger from his belt. "I was just about to pluck out this one's eyes."

"While you all have your fun, I'm going to relax." Poseidon turned back towards the palace and said over his shoulder, "Artemis, awaken some of the servants so they can bring me wine. Also, the hydra is hungry and needs something more substantial than eyes. Maybe the one with wings. It always amuses me to feed fliers to something of the sea."

The Olympians on the shore laughed, but my eyes were trained on Poseidon, who had suddenly stopped moving. Then he backed up a step. Then another.

All nine heads of the hydra twisted to look behind it, and low hissing sounds erupted from each of them as the water started to ripple. The Hydra stretched further upward, curving all of its necks as it prepared to strike.

Artemis sensed where my attention was and twisted to face the water. "What? What is—"

A tentacle rose out of the depths behind the hydra and slammed into Poseidon, sending him flying towards the beach. The hydra's heads snapped back around, so they missed the other tentacles rising from the water. The serpentine monster's instincts must have warned it of the danger though, because it whipped around to face the new threat, but it was too late. The kraken's tentacles lunged forward and wrapped around three of the heads, yanking the beast under water.

"Who needs dragons when you have the kraken?" A raspy laugh spilled from my lips. The Olympians stared at the churning water where the two monsters were duking it out beneath the surface. Closer to the shore, the water split, and three people walked out.

Hecate, Ashling, and Connor.

I hadn't expected them to come, but I was grateful all the same. My laughing grew deeper, and Artemis slowly turned her head to look at me, her eyes full of wrath.

"Looks like the playing field just evened out." I grinned. "And I think Hecate is going to want a word with you."

Artemis took a step back as Hecate strolled towards her. My eyes dropped to the sand, and I saw large paw prints on either side of her. The tracks shifted until there were multiple, making it impossible to tell where exactly the hounds were as they guarded and guided the ancient goddess.

The Mother of Witches dipped her fingers into a pouch at her side and threw petals into the air. They swirled around her, multiplying until she flung her hand out to the side and the petals dove for it, centering around her palm before stretching out in a straight line in both directions.

A word snapped from Hecate, and the petals solidified into a scythe. Artemis sank down to the sand, clutching the grains between her fingers as magic spilled from her lips. She rose, pulling a spear from the earth, and twirled it as easily as if it were an extension of her. Magic grew thick in the air.

"You sure you want to do this?" Artemis eyed Hecate. "We've left you alone all this time. You can walk away right now and go on living your boring life."

The sand at Artemis' feet writhed and formed into long, slender bodies. Half a dozen snakes struck at the goddess' feet before she dispersed them with a slash of her spear, but several of them had landed bites, and blood dripped from the wounds as the veins around them darkened.

"You harmed my friend." Hecate bared her teeth.

Artemis pointed her spear towards the water where Levi fought the hydra out of sight. "As soon as I deal with you, I'm going to carve him apart and dump the pieces back into that lake. The magic from his corpse will last at least a century."

I didn't hear Hecate's response because the water ropes

around my neck and wrists suddenly tightened painfully for a few seconds before exploding outward. For a brief moment, the droplets just hovered in the air around us before falling to the sand.

Three things happened next.

Poseidon struck out with a whip made of water at both Connor and Ashling, Cian tackled Hermes to the ground and the two of them fought for control of the dagger the god still wielded, and Hecate and Artemis clashed with both magic and weapons.

I only had a second to take all this in before Ares swung my mother's sword straight at my head.

Chapter Twenty-Four

Despite the short amount of time I'd had my new swords, it was already instinct to call them to me. With half a thought, I summoned the one that had been discarded on the ground. Sand launched into the air as my sword flew to my hand so I could block Ares' strike. Or try to. The god of war was far from a lightweight, and even with every ounce of my strength, all I managed to do was divert his blow away from my head and directly into my shoulder.

I screamed as Ares pushed down, my mother's sword digging in deeper, his dark eyes alight with glee. "Killed with your brother's sword. How embarrassing."

"It belonged to our mother," I ground out. "And I'm going to shove it up your ass once he's through with you."

"Wh—" Ares choked on his own words as a blade burst through his chest. I gripped his wrist and twisted, ripping my mother's sword from his hand and spinning away. Mikhail had pierced him through the heart, but Ares was a god; that wound was nothing.

Magos surged to his feet, his eyes cutting to me and then to where Hecate and Artemis were battling in the shallow waves.

"Go!" I yelled and yanked the sword free from my shoulder. Blood soaked my clothes, but my flesh was already knitting itself back together. "We've got this!"

He took off running across the sands. Niall was halfway to my brother and Hermes when a shadow passed overhead. Before I could shout a warning, the fae warrior leapt forward, twisting midair so his back was to the ground as his wings snapped wide. The spear was soaring from his hand a second later, straight through the chest of a monstrous creature with a twisted, humanoid face and a winged body. The oversized talons raked Niall's chest before the creature beat its dark, feathered wings and rose out of his reach.

Blood leaked from its chest where the spear had punched through. The creature reached up with one long leg, and its talons wrapped around the spear and started to pull it free.

"Harpy! Their heart is on the left side of their body!" Before the last word was out of my mouth, Niall had already thrown another dagger. The silver spun through the air before sinking six inches to the left of his spear. The beast let out a high-pitched scream before plummeting to the earth, and a dozen more dove from the clouds. Niall stalked to the downed harpy and pulled his spear and dagger free. "Keep them off us, Niall!"

"With pleasure." The sciatháin shot into the sky with a wicked grin.

Ares coughed, choking on blood as Mikhail ripped his sword free and vanished into mist only to reappear at my side. The coughs gave way to a cruel laugh as Ares stood up straight and looked each of us over. Then he reached over his shoulder and pulled free a double-edged sword. It had to be almost four feet long, which was just ridiculous. At that size, it should have been heavy and cumbersome. If it'd been anyone else wielding it, I would have laughed.

But it wasn't just anyone. It was an ancient god of war who

had run around for thousands of years slaughtering people and fighting in wars simply because he craved bloodshed. I glanced down at my swords and grimaced. My mother's had more reach, but I wasn't used to fighting with it.

To our left, Cian and Hermes broke apart. The god held the dagger in his hand and grinned at my brother, who was now weaponless.

"Cian!" I tossed our mother's sword to him, and he snatched it just as Hermes struck. The god leapt back and pulled a hoplite sword from the sheath at his hip. I had to trust my brother to take care of himself because Ares was on me in a flash. This time, I didn't even try to block his strike. I'd barely managed to keep him from cutting me in half before when he'd only been wielding my mother's totally reasonable sword. I was done if I took a direct hit from the one he had now.

I leaned back, my back parallel to the ground, and let the blade pass over me. The sword was still moving away from me when I twisted back and struck at his exposed side. Steel bounced off black armor. Damn it.

Ares' fist shot out, and the impact fractured my jaw and sent me spinning. Ares started after me only to be cut off by Mikhail. Blinding pain stabbed at my brain as I moved my jaw to better align it for healing. My vision darkened for a split second, but when things came back into focus, I saw I had landed only a few feet away from my poisoned blade.

I snatched it up and stalked towards Ares, who was still trading blows with Mikhail. The god sensed my approach and angled his body to keep us both in sight.

"Good of you to join us again." A cruel smile stretched across his lips. "I was just telling your lover all the things I was going to do to you next to his bloody corpse."

Mikhail struck, aiming for the god's right side, but Ares' sword slammed against Mikhail's, knocking it to the side. Then he twisted his body, intending to ram it into the vampire's smaller frame and knock him off his feet, but Mikhail and I had sparred with Magos almost every day and Sigrun frequently. We were both quite familiar with fighting a larger opponent who could easily outmuscle us.

And more importantly, more often than not in those sparring sessions, Mikhail and I fought as a team.

So when Ares tried to ram his shoulder into Mikhail, he found nothing but swirling mist. I darted in, quick as an adder, and sliced my dagger across Ares' neck before leaping back out of range. Ares let out a hiss of pain, and the cut across his neck darkened. The poison on the blade wouldn't do any serious damage, but it would hurt.

It'd likely been a long time since the god of war had felt pain.

I pointed my sword at him, displaying my fangs in a feral smile as Mikhail appeared at my side. "We're going to cut you apart, limb by limb, and then fuck in your blood."

The god of war blinked.

Mikhail sent me a heated look. "It's like you were made for me, shifter."

Ares recovered from his shock and sneered at us before he charged across the beach, sending sand flying in his wake. Mikhail vanished once again, and I met Ares head-on, dodging every one of his strikes, sliding out of the way with feline agility. Mikhail reappeared, and we moved in perfect step with each other.

Strike for strike. Dodge for dodge.

I may not have been able to dance in a fancy dress on a ballroom floor, but this dance... this I could do all day as long as Mikhail was my partner.

Soon, Ares was bleeding from dozens of cuts on his neck, face, and hands. I sliced with the poisoned dagger at every inch of exposed skin. We'd also been hammering at the armor on his lower back, and I was confident that, with a few more strikes, a piece of it would break off.

A scream diverted my attention for a split second, and Ares seized the opportunity. He spun after striking at Mikhail and slammed the thick pommel of his sword into my chest. Something cracked as air violently whooshed out of my lungs and I flew backwards, crashing onto the sandy ground and gasping for breath.

Mikhail misted to my side and helped me up. Ares halted his march towards us as he watched Poseidon grip the trident he'd skewered Ashling with and lift her into the air. Connor lay several feet away, his blood soaking the sand beneath him. For a second, I thought he was dead, but then I saw his chest fight to rise for a breath. Still alive. Barely.

The Merfolk Queen gripped the trident where it had pierced her stomach, a fierce snarl on her face. She was too far away for us to help, and Ares would have been on us before we could have reached her anyway.

"You thought you could come here and challenge me?" Poseidon mocked. "I'm the king of the seas."

"You're not a king," she spat. "You're just an asshole with a crown."

Two black-and-white sea kraits slid out of Ashling's long, blood-soaked sleeves and struck at Poseidon's face. The god bellowed as he dropped the trident, flinging the venomous snakes away from him. A dark green substance oozed out of the bite marks, and the left side of his face seemed frozen in place.

"I earned my crown," Ashling said between pained breaths before ripping the trident from her body and staggering to her feet. *Bow to your queen, god.*

She thrust Poseidon's own trident at him just as two streams of water whipped out from the ocean and wrapped around the god's arms. He screamed as the prongs of the trident went all the way through his body and out his back. Everyone stared in stunned silence for a moment as the nearly seven-foot-tall ancient god dropped to his knees in front of the small queen.

Ares bellowed in rage and had started towards them when another whip of water shot out and sliced through Poseidon's neck. For a second, the god knelt there with a shocked look on his face before his head slid off his body and rolled across the sand.

"Damn it," Mikhail swore, his dark eyes glittering. "This means she's ahead of us in our game."

"It's fine, love." I threw the dagger, and it slammed into the base of Ares' neck, making him stumble and spin back towards us. He hurled the dagger back at me, but I slapped it away with my sword and grinned at him just to piss him off a little more. "Double points for whoever takes *him* out."

"No fair," Ashling mumbled as she sank to her knees before passing out. She'd heal from the stomach wound, probably, but not from having her head hacked off. We needed to keep Ares and the other gods away from her and Connor and get the fuck out of here before a very pissed-off Poseidon regenerated.

Hecate and Artemis were still battling with magic while Magos struck strategically any time the goddess of the hunt was distracted. The three of them seemed to be locked in a stalemate, but at least my friends were holding their own.

Cian wasn't faring well, but I couldn't help him until we took out Ares. An idea formed as I watched Mikhail barely slide out of the way as Ares slammed his sword straight down with both hands. If Mikhail hadn't moved, he would have been cleaved in half. Two-handed strikes like that were powerful but slow. We needed to create an opportunity.

I leapt forward and sliced at the weak spot on Ares' armor, and the black-scaled material cracked a little more. So close.

"Neither of you are walking away today," Ares snarled.

"I'm going to impale your corpses and let them rot in front of Hades until he wakes up."

"Mikhail, remember how I told you about that time I took Magos to the ground while we were sparring?" I leaned back as Ares' sword passed an inch away from my nose.

"What about it?" Mikhail hammered a fist to the side of Ares' head. The god's head snapped to the side, but he flung his arm back, his gauntleted fist slamming into Mikhail's face. My vampire lover vanished into mist, reappearing at my side, his nose bloody and broken. I grinned at him, and he shook his head. "No. *Absolutely not.*"

"Too late."

Mikhail swore as I ran straight towards Ares. The god let out a bellow of rage and met my charge, his sword raised and angled at my chest. Clearly, he planned to either skewer me or simply knock me down with his bulky body.

Just before his sword pierced my chest, I ducked, dropping mine and throwing myself forward, directly at his knees. I'd pulled this exact move on Magos years ago and had taken his ass down on the mat. It was the first and only time I'd accomplished such a thing. Of course, three seconds later, he'd had me pinned with a baston at my throat.

Ares had excellent reaction time, but with his forward momentum and my speed, there was nothing he could do as I crashed into his knees. It felt like I'd slammed into a brick wall, but he still flew over me and went down hard. On my own, this would have been a suicide move. Ares wouldn't be shoving a wooden practice weapon under my throat, he'd be shoving his sword straight through it.

But I wasn't alone.

The impact had halted my motion abruptly, and I'd crashed to my side, so I had a perfect view of Ares slamming face-first into the sand with his back exposed. Even as he landed, he was already recovering. He was fast, but not faster than a vampire.

In a whirl of mist, Mikhail appeared and rammed his sword straight down through the cracked armor and into the god of war's spine.

The pained scream that tore out of Ares' throat would be something I'd cherish for the rest of my life. I got to my feet, wincing slightly. One of his knees had hit my ribs and definitely cracked a few of them. Ares' body twitched, and he let out another scream when Mikhail jerked the sword back and forth before sinking it deeper. I half walked, half limped over and stomped a foot on the hand still wrapped around the long sword as I crouched down. Ares' head was twisted to the side, and those dark eyes looked at me with such hatred, I couldn't help but smile.

"You foolish, arrogant mongrel," he ground out. "I am *immortal*. There is nowhere you can go that I will not find you. You will know pain like you've never known before."

I raised my sword over his head. "Promises, promises." Ares' eyes didn't close even as my blade cut through tissue and bone, severing his head.

Two down. Two to go.

Hecate had summoned some type of seaweed from the water and had wrapped it around Artemis like a rope. The goddess was fighting for all she was worth, but she was mere feet from the water's edge. Words poured out of her, and Hecate's head snapped to the side like she'd been punched before she fell to one knee. The tension in the seaweed ropes slackened. Artemis started to chant again but was cut off when Magos seized her distraction and planted a roundhouse kick straight to her chest.

She flew across the water, only to be snatched by Hecate's seaweed ropes that cocooned around her immediately and glowed with a faint purple sheen. Magos helped Hecate to her feet, and I ran to where my brother was still squaring off against Hermes, Mikhail at my side.

Every part of my body hurt. The serious wounds had healed, but it'd been taxing on my magic, so all the aches and pains were still present, and I felt like I'd gone through a meat grinder. I probably wouldn't be able to move tomorrow. Assuming there would be a tomorrow. We weren't entirely out of the woods yet.

Hermes was a skilled fighter. He didn't have Ares' over-bearing strength and aggressiveness, but he was lithe and cunning in his movements. My heart raced as Hermes took a step back and staggered slightly, his sword hand trembling before he jerked the hoplite up a little higher.

Despite this, his weight was still perfectly balanced, and his breathing was steady. It was a trap, and Cian fell for it.

"Stop!" I screamed as Cian darted forward, his sword already arching for a diagonal cut across the blond god's chest. Hermes grinned viciously as his blade snapped up, blocking Cian's strike and catching my brother's sword with his before rotating the hoplite down in a smooth, practiced move. Cian stumbled forward off balance before freezing as the god's blade cut into his throat.

Mikhail and I both stopped in our tracks. Hermes moved to stand behind my brother, who still had our mother's sword in his hand, but it was lowered towards the sand. The god maneuvered the hoplite against Cian's throat, one hand on the hilt, the other gripping the blade on the other side of Cian's head. All he had to do was jerk both his hands back and he'd decapitate my brother.

Feline shifters could heal from a lot of things; decapitation wasn't one of them.

My heart was beating frantically, and I knew if I listened, Mikhail's would be doing the same. Ten feet separated us from Cian. We were fast, but not that fast. Even if Mikhail misted, it would take less than a second for Hermes to pull that sword through my brother's neck.

"How the fuck did you think this was going to end?" Hermes taunted. "I'll admit I didn't expect the two of you to bring down Ares. That will be something I'll enjoy reminding him of for at least a few centuries, but you haven't won anything. In a matter of minutes, they'll all be back."

"Then we'll cut them down again," I rasped.

His blue eyes lazily took in the sight of my and Mikhail's bloodied bodies. "No. I don't think you will. Those pathetic merfolk haven't moved since being gutted, and Hecate's magic is running on empty. That winged fae bastard is probably harpy food by now; the flock here is quite large." His gaze drifted over to Magos. "I look forward to keeping you as a pet. Watching you sink into madness and despair might very well be the highlight of my existence for the foreseeable future."

Cian looked at me, his jaw set in that stubborn way of his, which meant he was planning something guaranteed to piss me off. "Promise me you'll save him."

"We both know I'll choose you over him." I shook my head. Hades mattered to me because he'd helped me once and he was important to Cian, but I'd still choose my brother first, which was what Hades would want me to do anyway.

"Nemai—" Cian started, only to be cut off when Hermes dug the sword in a little deeper. Blood wasn't just dripping now, it was rushing out. An artery had been cut, and the blade was keeping it open.

"There's no saving Hades." Hermes laughed. "It's adorable you thought you could wake him with a kiss, but you're not a charming prince, and this isn't a fairy tale."

My heart raced faster as Cian paled, his eyelids starting to flutter. Too much blood loss. I took a step forward, and Hermes pulled the sword deeper, causing Cian to jerk in his grasp.

Pleading for mercy would do me no good. The Olympians had none. It would just give Hermes something to enjoy before killing Cian. Every possible option flew through my mind, but nothing would work. The distance between us was too great, and Cian's position was too precarious.

"Okay... sis." His eyes closed for a long second before opening and latching on to mine. "It's okay."

"The fuck it is," I snarled. Cian's eyes started to close again, and I readied myself to lunge forward. I'd just have to be fast enough to grab that damn sword and trust Mikhail to go for Hermes. A split second before I put my desperate plan into action, the god stiffened and let out a gasp. Some invisible force pulled the sword free with such power, Mikhail and I had to leap as it flew between us.

Something yanked Cian away from Hermes, and I darted forward to grab my brother as his legs gave out. I laid him down on the sand before taking a step forward, placing myself between him and the god with Mikhail at my back.

The air rippled where Hermes still stood rigidly, like something had gripped his heart and squeezed. Cold and glittering darkness shone as Hades materialized, twisting a black ring on his finger.

"Maybe this isn't a fairy tale," the god of death said in a low tone dripping with menace, "but he's still *my prince*. My beautiful, cunning prince who kissed me while slipping an enchanted ring onto my finger. Right under the nose of an arrogant god."

"Hades," Hermes wheezed, "let's talk... about this... "

"Let's not." Hades held up his right hand and clenched it into a fist, and Hermes' whimpering sounds immediately ended as he dropped like a puppet that'd had its strings cut. Then a silvery white wisp streamed out of him and straight into Hades' chest.

Muscles flexed across Hades' broad back as he devoured

336

the soul. Icy magic flowed wildly from him, and I gritted my teeth, but it flowed harmlessly past me. Finally, his shoulders sagged, and Hades turned to face us. His black T-shirt was torn to shreds, and I could see raised, ropey scars through the fabric. Clearly, they'd tried several different tactics to wake him up.

"Jinx?" I breathed out.

"He's sleeping in the chamber," Hades said as he strode straight towards Cian. I stepped to the side, letting him pass, and watched as he fell to his knees in front of my brother, who was out cold, his body shutting down to focus on healing the worst of the injuries.

Relief trembled through my bones.

Hades gently stroked the hair away from Cian's face before carefully collecting him in his arms and rising. The cut across Cian's throat still bled, but it was more of a slight trickle now.

"The ring contained enough of my magic to crack through Artemis' spell, but I needed life to get the rest of the way out. Jinx remained hidden from sight until Ares left, and then I started drawing life from him. I had to go slow so I didn't take too much."

"Thank you," my voice cracked. He could have taken all of Jinx's life and restored himself immediately, but he knew the grimalkin not only mattered to me but to Cian too.

Hades nodded deeply, Cian's head snug against his shoulder. "Thank you for saving Cian… and me."

He walked towards where Hecate stood in the shallow part of the water. Two of the hydra's heads were lying close to her, torn flesh and tissue bleeding into the water, and several of the kraken's tentacles hovered around the ancient witch goddess like a dog begging for praise. I had no idea where the rest of the hydra was, but Levi clearly wasn't worried, so that was good enough for me.

Magos was hovering near Ashling, who was doing her best

to stand on her own… a new, shiny trident in her grip. Blood soaked the front of Connor's chest, but he was also on his feet. I let out a sigh of relief. The merman and I would likely never be friends, but he was Kaysea's brother, and he'd come here to help. Granted, he'd only come because Ashling had basically ordered him to, but still. He'd shown up, and that meant I owed him.

Connor's pale green eyes met mine, and I saw the knowing look in them. Ugh. He'd definitely be calling in a favor at some point, and whatever it was, I wouldn't like it. His lips curved into a faint smile.

Yep. I definitely wouldn't like it.

I glanced up at the skies but saw no sign of Niall. We'd have to search for him after this. I refused to believe the sciatháin had fallen.

Mikhail waited for me while I went into the tomb. It was a simple, square room with stone walls and a raised, obsidian platform at its center. Jinx was tucked up against the side of the platform on the floor, hidden from sight unless you walked around the table. Even knowing he was alive, my tension didn't fully fade until I saw his chest rise and fall.

"Hey, buddy," I said softly. Not even an ear twitch.

I leaned down and tried to pick him up, but he was a hundred pounds of floppy dead weight. Mikhail finally helped me wrestle him into my arms, Jinx's forearms and head drooping over my shoulder.

"You sure you don't want me to carry him?"

"Maybe later." I hugged my arms around the grimalkin a little tighter.

We had stepped out of the tomb and taken a few steps towards the others when two loud pops sounded. Suddenly, Ares and Poisedon were standing only a few feet in front of us.

The others were too far away to do anything, and I had Jinx in my arms. Everything happened so fast. Mikhail stepped in front of me as Ares raised his sword, and Poseidon just smiled, ready to take in the carnage.

Several dark shadows passed over us, and then a flaming blue sword carved Ares in half, the two halves of his body sliding apart before he could even react.

Poseidon's eyes widened as impossibly dark tendrils that seemed to swallow the light wrapped around his limbs and pulled the Olympian apart.

My jaw was hanging open as I took in a blood-soaked Nemesis standing just behind where Ares had stood a second ago, my sword in her hand.

"I find this Slaughter Party disappointing." Nemesis prodded the two halves of Ares' corpse with her boot. The rest of the mageía stood behind her, their features hidden behind masks or hoods. One of them had shadows sliding across their robes, and I guessed that was Nyx.

"Umm… sorry?" I offered, for once not sure what to say.

Niall landed in front of me, almost as blood-soaked as Nemesis but alive and well. Relief flooded me at seeing he'd made it through.

"This lot came across me fighting those harpies and decided to help out." He pulled a few feathers off the dried blood on his arms. "I mean, I would have been fine without them, but it was still polite of them to offer." He frowned as he took in Jinx in my arms. "Furball okay?"

"He'll be fine." I hefted him a little higher on my shoulder. "He has a thing about sand."

"Thank you for the use of your weapon." Nemesis nodded deeply at me before offering the sword to me, hilt first.

I accepted it from her before passing it to Mikhail, who slid it into the harness on my back for me so I could go back to supporting Jinx with both hands. "I'm glad it served you well, and we thank you for your assistance with Ares and Poseidon.

We were just about to speak with Hecate about what we should do next."

Nemesis' head snapped towards the sea at Hecate's name, and she stalked off in that direction, the mageía trailing after her. Mikhail, Niall, and I traded looks before hurrying after her.

"*Rhamnusia*, what are you doing here?" Hecate's eyes widened as she took in Nemesis and the others. Philo and Zephyr, once again visible, raised their hackles and displayed their fangs but obediently sat when Hecate ordered them to. The hounds didn't take their eyes off the mageía.

"You tell me you did not know?" Nemesis' brown wings shuffled. "We've been enslaved here for centuries."

"I… " Hecate squeezed her eyes shut. "I'm sorry, my friend. For too long, I've cut myself off from the world. I just… I was so tired. Too much had been lost."

Niall's eyes darkened in understanding, but Nemesis remained unmoved as her gaze weighed heavily on Hecate before moving to Hades. "Both of you have hidden away from the world. From your pasts. You both swore once to be the balance to their horrors. You have failed in your duty."

Mikhail's hand drifted towards one of his daggers as tension filled the air between the two remaining gods and the mageía.

"We will make amends," Hades declared evenly. "I've already released all the souls trapped here back to the Asphodel Fields."

"I will make sure that any other prisoners here are freed and looked after," Hecate said. "It's time to decide their fates."

Artemis writhed from where she was still wrapped in Hecate's magicked seaweed ropes. The vines that were wrapped around her mouth loosened, allowing her to speak. I felt magic stir from her, but it quickly faded. She was clearly tapped out from her fight with Hecate.

"Dead," she spat. "You're all fucking dead."

"I could take their souls." Hades' eyes glowed white.

"No." Hecate shook her head. "That is a last resort. Artemis is strong, and her will is iron. I have faith in you, Hades, but she has the best chance out of all of them to take over your body if you try, and I'd rather not learn what her twisted soul could do with the power of death at her fingertips."

Artemis bared her teeth. "Go ahead and try, Uncle."

Hades' lip curled, but he kept his magic to himself. I let out a sigh of relief. Magos was still cursed, and we needed to figure out how to break it.

I stepped forward. "Tell me how to break the curse on Magos, and I'll do my best to keep your sorry ass alive and mostly unharmed."

Cold menace radiated from Hades, and I could feel his pissed-off stare on me, but I ignored him. I wouldn't leave Magos to suffer just so Hades could get his vengeance.

Artemis laughed. "My dear child, there is no taking it back."

"Bullshit," I growled. "You made the curse, you can break it."

"I can't." She laughed some more. "Like a cruel word spoken, my curses linger forever, burrowing deep into one's soul. Death is the only way out, and even then, sometimes they'll follow."

She smiled triumphantly at me, and I looked to Hecate, begging her with every inch of my blackened soul to disagree, but the ancient witch just looked at me with sad eyes and shook her head.

Bullshit. I gritted my teeth. There was a way, and I would fucking find it. Still, I couldn't bring myself to look to where Magos stood with Ashling and Connor.

"The gods will remain here," Nemesis decreed, apparently

341

unconcerned with the talk of curses and damned souls. She looked pointedly at Hecate and Hades. "The two of you shall ensure this pocket realm stays secure, and we will be their guardians."

"You're no match for us." Artemis sneered. "As soon as Ares and Poseidon come back, the three of us will tear you to shreds."

For the first time since arriving, Nemesis smiled. I took two steps away from her, and Mikhail rolled his eyes but also took a few steps away.

As one, the mageía stepped forward and pulled objects from their robes, holding them out in front of them. The charred remains of apples.

"You have no magic left, and neither will the other two upon awakening."

Artemis said nothing, but I saw the flash of fear and uncertainty cross her face. Nemesis slowly reached into a satchel on her hip and pulled out one perfectly golden apple, and Artemis' eyes shone with hunger.

"Name your price," the goddess of the hunt said sharply. "I'll remain here willingly. You can have whatever else you want in the name of vengeance. Just let me have the apple."

Nemesis held the goddess' gaze for a long moment before throwing the apple into the air. Sunlight glinted off its golden surface before it started to fall back towards the turquoise sea. Faster than lightning, chaotic darkness struck the falling apple before it burst into thousands of blackened pieces that the tide carried away.

"No!" Artemis screamed.

"I do not seek vengeance." Nemesis pulled the hood of her cowl up once more, her face vanishing into darkness, and faced Artemis. "*I seek retribution.*"

Chapter Twenty-Five

I BARELY REMEMBERED GETTING BACK to our apartment. Hades and Hecate had hashed out a plan with Nemesis and the mageía. Then we'd all had to trek back to the doorway to the death realms so I could open a gateway to get us home from there. Hecate had stayed behind with Ashling to get the kraken to one of the fae realms after I'd opened a gateway to the underground lake again. I hadn't asked for details. Ashling had taken down Poseidon on her own and had been the one to get the kraken into Therrea in the first place. If she said she could get the kraken home, I believed her.

Also, I'd been dead on my feet from carrying Jinx the entire way. As soon as I'd set foot inside the apartment, I'd settled Jinx on my bed and curled myself around him. Mikhail had thrown a blanket over us both and settled onto his little sliver of the bed.

Twelve hours later, I awoke to two sleeping grimalkins and no vampire.

Jinx was in his smaller, glamoured form. I glanced at Luna, and she raised her head, blinking sleepy, lavender eyes at me.

He woke up a little over an hour ago, she said. *As soon as he saw that you were okay, he went back to sleep.*

I let out a deep, shuddering breath and stroked a hand down his silky fur. His body vibrated as he purred, and I smiled softly. "Sleep tight, my little menace."

Luna lowered her head and went back to sleep as I got up and dressed. Someone, I'm assuming Mikhail, had washed me off and changed me. I'd slept through the entire thing. Despite all that sleep, I still felt drained. My body was stiff and sore, and my soul was… weary. We'd been in some major fights over the last few years, and we'd always emerged victorious.

We may have walked away from this one, but we'd still lost.

Lir clearly had set his sights on making me suffer. I'd had to make a deal with my parents' murderer, a faction of the Vampire Council was gunning for us, the family I'd built a life around in Emerald Bay was fractured, possibly beyond repair, and Magos was still cursed.

I quietly left the bedroom, leaving the two sleeping grimalkins in the sunshine beaming through the window. The scent of coffee drifted to me, but it wasn't Magos in the kitchen. Mikhail wordlessly handed me a cup, and I took it from him only to set it onto the counter and wrap my arms around his waist. He hugged me back, pulling me close.

"He's in his bedroom. Only came out to shower, and then he returned to his room and shut the door." I rested my head in the crook of Mikhail's neck and breathed in his scent. "His wounds are healing… slowly. He needs blood."

"But he won't drink it," I said tonelessly.

"We have to figure something out." Mikhail gripped me harder. "I can't lose him."

"You won't." I pulled back enough to look him in the eyes. "I saved him once, I'll do it again, and I have you to help me this time."

Mikhail leaned his forehead against mine. I eyed the buttons of his black Henley shirt. He didn't move as I opened a few more of them and then tugged the opening of the shirt to the side, displaying the skin directly over his heart where Myrna had rested her hand.

A flower tattoo stretched across the skin, identical to the one on my back except for the coloring. While the petals of my flower were an electric blue, his were a mix of dark blue and purple like his eyes. A thorny vine wrapped around the stem and part of the petals. It was a blessing from Myrna, and a warning.

Her threat in the death realm hadn't been an empty one.

"Trust me," Mikhail said dryly, "I understand the meaning."

Of course he knew exactly what I was thinking. I opened my mouth to tease him about it when a loud crash sounded from downstairs, and I felt a wave of powerful magic. Finn.

Mikhail and I both took off towards the door. I was dimly aware of Magos' door opening and footsteps falling after us. I raced past the second-floor apartment where Cian was standing in the doorway, yanking on a shirt as Hades hurriedly dressed behind him.

"What was that?" Cian yelled.

"Finn!" I took the stairs two at a time. "That was Finn!"

Seconds later, I burst through the first-floor apartment door, Mikhail and Magos at my back. Finn stood in front of the hallway that led to the bedrooms. Isabeau was nowhere in sight, but Damon and Misha were both on the ground, thrashing as their bodies jerked in painful contractions.

Magos started forward, but I flung out an arm, stopping him. "Get out," I said evenly. "Just give me a minute with him."

"One. Minute," Mikhail growled before slowly backing out

of the apartment and taking Magos with him. I heard them talking in quiet tones to Hades and Cian. My gaze went to where Niall was crouched next to a makeshift cot on the other side of the apartment. His eyes were locked on Finn, and I was surprised to not see fear in them. Just sadness, and what was probably a healthy amount of wariness.

I took a deep breath and let my magic out. Blue flames rippled across my skin and clothing like armor as I walked towards Finn at a slow, steady pace.

The gold ring of his eyes burned bright at my approach, and I felt his magic hit me like a sledgehammer. I grunted at the impact, but it ricocheted off my flames. His magic was mostly fae in nature, but the taint of devourer ran through it, which meant he couldn't wield it against my flames. Devourer magic always canceled each other out. As long as I kept my fire burning, Finn couldn't hurt me.

I hoped.

"What's going on, kid?" I waved a hand at where Misha and Damon were still convulsing, keeping my face carefully blank. I had no idea what he was doing to them.

"They hurt her," Finn said flatly, his two-toned eyes drifting back to watch the young vampires twitch on the floor. "Made her cry."

Isabeau. Of course. But they would never harm her. No matter what happened between me and the boys, Misha and Damon would *never* purposely hurt Isabeau. They loved her unconditionally. I looked around the room and spotted two duffel bags by the door.

"You're leaving," I said softly.

"They think you're a monster. That I'm a monster." Finn's voice wavered for a moment before something dark passed through his eyes. "They think she's a monster because of what she did. *She saved them.* And they fear her for it."

No, Damon pushed out. *Never. Her.*

I stepped between Finn and the vampires, forcing him to look at me. "Let them go, Finn." He raised his chin defiantly, and more pained cries came from behind me. "Isabeau loves them. They're her brothers. By harming them, you're hurting her."

The magic abruptly cut off as Finn turned around and stalked off down the hallway towards his room. I let out a breath before spinning around to face Misha and Damon, who were sprawled on the floor, breathing hard.

"Where?" I asked curtly.

"Intira and Gensai's," Misha groaned. Niall walked over and helped both boys to their feet. "We already asked them."

"I see." Something inside me broke, and I tried to keep it off my face but failed.

"We just need time, Nemain," Damon explained with a pained expression. "It's not that we don't... appreciate all that you've done for us, but we went straight from the Vampire Council to you. We have no frame of references outside of that. We... we need to learn more so we can decide where to be."

"And you can't do that here or"—I cleared my throat when my voice wavered—"Or at Pele's? She'd give you a room."

Silence.

"Oh." I nodded in understanding. "She's a monster too?"

Misha's jaw tightened. "Are you going to let us leave?"

Did he really think I would hold them here against their will? "Whatever you think of me, I'll always do what's best for you. There is a gateway to the dojo waiting for you outside. Go."

"We just have to say goodbye to Isabeau." Misha turned towards the hallway.

"No." The word cracked like a whip between us.

347

"No?" Misha whirled back to glare at me. "You can't keep us from her. She's our little sister!"

I stalked across the room and jerked the door open. Mikhail and everyone else leaned against the stairwell, no doubt having heard every word.

"Isabeau is upset, which means Finn is upset. You go near her, and he'll rip you to shreds and cry about it later."

"You're punishing us." Misha narrowed his eyes at me.

"I'm keeping you alive," I snapped. "You may not like how I do it, but I don't give a shit. If Isabeau wanted to see you, she'd be out here. When she calms down and is ready to talk, we'll let you know. Until then, respect her fucking wishes."

Damon and Misha snatched their bags and left without another word, and the crack in my soul widened.

———

An hour later, I trudged back upstairs. It'd taken that long to calm Finn and a sobbing Isabeau down. Now they were both curled up on the couch watching a movie. Jinx and Luna went down to keep them company, and Elisa and Bryn would be home soon. They'd stepped out to get everyone pizza, and Elisa had been irate when she'd returned to find the boys gone.

Apparently, they hadn't told their older sister about their plan to leave. After a few minutes of flexing her fingers as if they had claws, she'd calmly asked me to open a gateway to Intira and Gensai's so she could speak to her brothers. Bryn went with her to oversee the meeting. Clearly, the valkyrie didn't trust Elisa's calm demeanor any more than I did.

I'd sent Niall back to the loving arms of Sigrun, and Hades had whisked a completely healed Cian off to their home to finish whatever they'd started in the second-floor apartment. Magos had left quietly at some point; I assumed he'd retreated to his room. I had no idea what to say to him. Everything I came up with felt like empty promises.

Mikhail wrapped an arm around my waist when I stumbled on a stair. He'd waited patiently on the couch while I'd sorted out the kids and then sent everyone on their way. As soon as I was done, he'd guided me out the door and up the stairs.

Bed was calling to me. Even though I'd done almost nothing but sleep since getting back, I just wanted to curl up under the covers with Mikhail wrapped around me. I couldn't deal with anything else right now. All the problems would just have to wait until tomorrow.

I swung the door to our apartment open and took two steps inside before freezing. Kalen and Badb waited in the center of the living space. Kalen's black eyes searched every inch of me, looking for any lingering injuries, and I felt the brush of his magic against mine as if he was checking that too.

After almost a minute, his magic pulled back. I shifted back and forth on my feet like I was a child waiting to get the scolding of a lifetime. Kalen strode out of the apartment without a word. A second later, I heard the building door open and slam shut.

"Is he really giving me the silent treatment?" I raised both brows at Badb.

She sauntered towards me like a predator who had sighted its prey, and I backed up a step into Mikhail, who steadied me before stepping several feet to the side, out of Badb's warpath. Coward. He'd stand with me against a god but not my own damn mother.

"That's how he expresses his rage." Badb shrugged. I relaxed a little at the casualness of her tone and posture. Then, I opened my mouth to say something only to bend over a second later as I alternated between gasping for breath and feeling like I was going to vomit everywhere. Badb slowly pulled her fist away from where she'd viciously sank it into my gut and shook her hand loose. "And *that* is how I express mine." Then she leaned down to whisper in my ear. "Never attempt to keep us out of a fight again, daughter mine."

She didn't bother closing the door on her way out.

Mikhail swept me up into his arms and carried me over to the couch. "This doesn't make me forgive you for abandoning me like that." I sniffed. "Besides, I was planning on going to bed and not leaving it for at least twenty-four hours."

"I know." He settled me into the cushions before grabbing a throw blanket and sitting next to me. I scowled at him but then nestled into his side anyway. He threw the blanket around us and flipped on the TV. "If we go to bed now, you're just going to spin, lost in your own thoughts. Let's do a movie night instead." I glanced out the window at the sun. "Let's do a movie afternoon instead," he corrected.

"Okay," I agreed quietly. Both of us fought hard not to look down the hallway where Magos' bedroom door was closed. We settled in to watch the movie, but it wasn't the same. Usually, we did this in the first-floor apartment with all the vampire brats present. Damon and Misha would talk over each other, cracking jokes, Isabeau would try to over explain everything that was going on to Finn, and Elisa and Bryn would quietly flirt with each other.

Heat built between my eyes, but I blinked it away. I was fine. Everything was fine.

The floorboards of the stairs creaked, and the scent of popcorn drifted into the room. Isabeau appeared a moment later with a large, silver bowl in her hands, and Finn walked in behind her, holding a plate covered in tinfoil. Mikhail and I watched in silence as they put the food down on the coffee table.

Jinx and Luna trotted in after and leapt onto their favorite chair while the kids disappeared down the hallway. Then they reappeared a minute later with Magos in tow. My heart clenched at how dim his copper eyes were and the ugly cut across his neck that should have been healed by now. Would have been healed if he'd drank blood.

I reached out and found Mikhail's hand under the blanket and squeezed. He squeezed back.

Isabeau led Magos over to his chair, which was to the left of the couch and directly opposite the one Jinx had claimed as his. She passed him a blanket, which he blankly stared at for a few seconds before draping it over his lap.

Finn unwrapped the tinfoil from the plate and pulled out what smelled like a peanut butter chocolate chip cookie. He handed the cookie to Magos, who accepted it but didn't eat.

"It helps." Finn gestured at the cookie. "I promise."

"We're also going to kill whoever hurt you." Isabeau nodded quickly, sending her brunette curls bouncing. "Finn and I already discussed it."

"Fuck me." I thumped my head against the back of the couch.

"Language." The smallest hint of a smile graced Magos' lips.

"Elisa and Bryn will be up in a few minutes—they're reheating the pizza," Isabeau continued like she hadn't just casually talked about killing people.

"Not pineapple," Finn said flatly.

"Aaaannnd," Isabeau drew out, ignoring Finn's commentary, "Kaysea is on her way over. She promised to bring snacks. Zareen promised to bring whiskey. Apparently they have gossip to tell you about Connor and someone named Ashling."

"That sounds perfect." I leaned forward and snagged a cookie off the plate. "So what are we going to watch?" I passed the remote to the girl, and she quickly brought up one of the streaming apps. An image of Godzilla shooting a stream of blue fire into the air filled the screen.

Finn settled in next to me on the couch and Isabeau next to Mikhail, who dragged another blanket down for her. The vampire girl grinned, her small fangs flashing. "We're gonna watch a movie where the monster wins."

I smiled broadly at the girl before resting my head against Mikhail's chest and listening to his heart beat in unison with mine.

Epilogue

SHE LEANED back against the desk and studied her handiwork. Almost every inch of the small room's back wall was covered in paper. Maps of different places in the fae realms, newspaper clippings from the human realm, and letters she'd snagged en route or from the trash. A few had been chucked into the fire, but whoever had tried to destroy the evidence hadn't been careful to make sure they'd burned completely.

Amateurs.

Everything in front of her represented her life's work. Well, that and the silver crown she'd haphazardly tossed onto the desk when she'd walked in.

Her eyes darted to where the crown rested. It was heavier than she'd thought it would be. From the day she'd been born, her parents had told her that one day, she would wear it. After generations of planning, it all ended with her.

"You will become the Merfolk Queen, Ashling, and you will avenge our line."

Most children were read sweet bedtime stories, but she was told the history of her family. About how they were once the most powerful seers to walk the fae realms, and how the fae queens had betrayed them by killing almost every last one of the Corcáin bloodline.

Her mother's voice whispered through her mind, *"You are the first Corcáin to have visions in four generations. You are who we have been waiting for, Ashling. The fae queens must die."*

Brigit had died decades ago. She hadn't seen her daughter ascend to the Tír fo Thuinn throne. Probably for the best, since Ashling had no interest in killing the fae queens.

Considering how ruthless her mother had been, Brigit probably would have killed her for disappointing the bloodline or some nonsense and tried again.

Dearest mum had been practical like that.

Which was something Ashling could appreciate, but now, it was her time, and she had her own plans.

The surviving Corcáins had become obsessed with getting revenge against the fae queens, and maybe Ashling would have felt similarly if she hadn't been having the same vision since she was five years old.

Of everyone who opposed Balor's return failing. Of the exiled fae king breaking free. Of death and destruction across all the realms.

It had been a bit much for a five year old to take in.

What made the Corcáin bloodline special wasn't that they were able to see visions—plenty of others could do that. What made her family unique was that they could see the web those visions sat in and all the possibilities.

Cut the right thread, and you could change the future. For better or worse.

A light awareness brushed against her mind. Someone had just crossed her ward. Only one person could do such a thing. She glanced at the antique grandfather clock she'd spent the better part of a month fixing a few years ago. Exactly six o'clock.

Ashling left the office and had just reached the living room of her hideaway cottage when a steady knock sounded on the front door.

"I've told you a dozen times already,"—she pulled the door open and met Connor's cool gaze—"you can just come in."

The muscles along his square jawline tensed before he strode inside. "And walk in on you naked again? No, thanks."

Ashling rolled her eyes as she closed the door. "There are so many ways for me to respond to that, but I'm too tired to bother."

"Good." He crossed his arms where he stood in the center of the living room, and she quickly looked him over. Barely a week ago, the two of them had been bleeding out on the sand after going up against Poseidon. Connor had taken a blow that had been meant for Ashling and, in all likelihood, would have killed her.

Whenever she closed her eyes, she still pictured him lying there in a pool of blood, struggling to breathe. They'd both recovered quickly, but that hadn't stopped Ashling from coming up with excuses to see him in the days after the attack. Just to reassure herself he was okay.

She told herself it was because she needed him for her plans, and she almost believed her own lie.

"Next time, I'll just answer the door naked."

"Ashling." Connor's eyes flashed in warning.

She let out a low laugh. He was so easy to rile up.

"Oh? Now it's Ashling? Not 'my queen?'" She placed a hand over her heart. "Or my personal favorite, '*Your Highness?*'"

He let out a long-suffering sigh and sank into her sofa. It was supposed to fit three people, but his stupidly broad build took up almost half of the damn thing.

Green eyes that were so light they almost appeared white looked at her in annoyance. "Did you have a reason for summoning me other than needling away at my patience?"

"I'm calling in the debt you owe me."

They stared at each other for a long moment before he jerked his head in a nod. "Fine. What do you need?"

A cunning smile spilled across her lips. "Some of the Tuatha Dé Danann are secretly plotting to return Balor to the throne. We're going to kill them all."

Want to Read More?

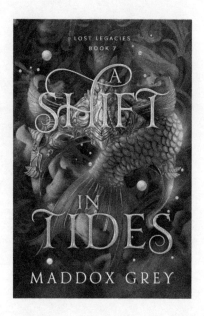

The next book in the series, A Shift in Tides comes out in February 2024! Signed paperbacks with character artwork are available on the Greymalkin Press Shop at www.greymalkinpress.com.

Want to Read a Free Short Story?

Curious about how Nemain and Kaysea met? Want to read other short stories set within the Lost Legacies world? Sign-up for the newsletter at maddoxgreyauthor.com to get free short stories and stay informed of upcoming releases and events!

Acknowledgments

Thank you so much for reading A Shift in Death!

Sorry for hurting Magos but it had to be done. He's going to have a rough go of things for a while but it's going to make the events of his book (Lost Legacies Book 11) that much sweeter. And emotionally devastating. Can't have one without the other.

<Laughs in evil author voice>

Fun fact about me, I'm a history major and originally focused on early civilizations, then got hot and heavy with Ancient Egypt. I know a lot of folks love Greek mythology... but I always kind of hated it, lol. Don't get me wrong, the stories are entertaining and I understand why people enjoy retellings. But the Greek gods were bullies.

I don't like bullies.

So obviously I was going to have Nemain and her merry band of misfits beat the shit out of them.

There are always some scenes that just live rent free in my head. Nemain getting reunited with Myrna has been there since the first book. I cried a lot while writing that one.

And then I giggled manically when the kraken rose up to fight the hydra. This book was an emotional rollercoaster to write and I want to thank my amazing editing team for coming on the ride with me! PollyAné and Rachel for being two of the best editors on the planet and and always leaving incredibly amusing comments while you fix my many, many misplaced commas.

Seriously, commas are a mystery and I don't like them.

Honestly, I'm like 50/50 on whether I used them correctly in this paragraph.

Also thank you to my amazing beta readers Lisa and Fiona! I don't know if an author could ask for better beta readers and I'm so lucky to have found the two of you!

As always, it would be incredibly appreciated if you could leave an honest review on Goodreads or whichever platform you prefer. Reviews are super important for authors and we really appreciate it when y'all take the time to leave one! Plus, it helps other readers find us :)

Lost Legacies Guide

<u>CHARACTERS:</u>

Bryn - newbie valkyrie; her soul is bonded with Finn's and she is his guardian

Cerridwn - dragon, sweetheart of Eddie; daughter of the dragon who rules their realm

Cian - feline shifter with necromantic magic; twin brother of Nemain; has a strained relationship with her but still loves her fiercely

Damon - teenage vampire on the run from the Vampire Council

Dante - necromancer, incredibly powerful and in a long-term relationship with Nemain's brother Cian

Eddie - a dragon who owns and runs a shop of magical oddities and supplies

Elisa - oldest of the teenage vampire runaways

Emir - leader of the Warlock Circle

Finn - fae child of the exiled fae king Balor; a prophecy about him says he will bring about the end of the realms

Isabeau - child vampire that the teenage vampires take care of and treat as a younger sister

Jinx - a fae cat known as a grimalkin, him and Nemain have been together since she was born; he's grumpy and has the ability to inflict bad luck on others

Kaysea - mermaid princess and bestie of Nemain; Myrna was her twin sister; older brother Connor is very protective of her

Lir - fae devourer hybrid, serves as the right-hand of the exiled fae king, Balor

Luna - another grimalkin (because the only thing better than one cat is two cats); unlike Jinx she is sweet and cuddly

Magos - old vampire warrior, his past is a bit of a mystery but he's loyal to Nemain and their relationship is similar to that of a an uncle/niece despite not being related

Mikhail - former vampire assassin of the Vampire Council; nephew of Magos

Misha - part of the teenage vampire group, looks very similar to Elisa but they don't know for sure if they're actually related, either way they consider each other brother & sister

Nemain - feline shifter and fae hybrid with devourer magic; all around freak of nature; raised by Macha and Nevin who she only learned recently were actually her aunt and uncle; biological parents are Badb and Kalen

Niall - fae devourer hybrid who fought Nemain and lost, but she chose to spare his life

Pele - daemon who runs the local tavern, The Inferno; close friends with Nemain who she has been in an ongoing casual poly relationship with for centuries

Sigrun - valkyrie, exiled from her people after the events of Ragnarok; has a wolf companion named Gunnar and a magical cat named Viggo

REALMS:

*Note, this is not an extensive list of all the realms because there are many. Only those relevant to the story are mentioned.

Human Realm - the modern world that humans are familiar with; most humans are completely unaware that their realm is one of many or that magical beings walk amongst them

Meenri - the main realm controlled by the daemons after they fled their original home realm

Acleonia - the new realm for the dragons after the events of A Shift in Ashes

Fae Realms

Mag Ildathach - belongs to the Seelie Court; name means multi-colored plains

Mag Mell - belongs to neither the Seelie or the Unseelie; like all death realms it is difficult to fully comprehend or travel in without necromantic magic; currently where Dante & Cian call home

Tír fo Thuinn - despite being referred to as a realm, this is actually a territory that stretches across all the fae realms, it is the dominion of the sea fae, all the oceans and seas belong to them

Tír na mBeo - only realm shared by the Unseelie & Seelie Queens

Fallen Realms

Kanima - former realm of the feline shifters; this is where Nemain's parents were born; it fell to devourers and the survivors fled to the human realm

Cerulle - former realm of Magos and Mikhail; also fell to devourers; survivors fled to the human realm and were later killed during the vampire and werewolf war

About the Author

After earning a degree in history and political science, Maddox was pulled kicking and screaming from the world of academia and thrust into the tech industry. Because they had bills to pay and nerd muscles to flex.

Whenever possible, they leave reality behind to build fantasy worlds filled with snarky morally grey characters and hot but devious love interests. Maddox currently resides in the northeast, but they'll always consider themselves Californian at heart. They live with their partner and faithful, but often stinky, furry companions.

To get regular email updates about new releases and other announcements, be sure to sign up for the newsletter on maddoxgreyauthor.com

facebook.com/maddoxgrey.author

instagram.com/maddoxgrey.author

tiktok.com/@greymalkinpress

Printed in the USA
CPSIA information can be obtained
at www.ICGtesting.com
CBHW030733060824
12642CB00004B/17